# TimeRipper

---

D E McCluskey

*I hope you have a rip roaring time reading this...*

D E McCluskey

TimeRipper
Copyright © 2020 by D E McCluskey

The moral right of the author has been asserted.
*All characters and events in this publication,*
*other than those clearly in the public domain,*
*are fictitious, and any resemblance to real persons,*
*living or dead, is purely coincidental*

All rights are reserved

No part of this publication may be reproduced,
stored in a retrieval system, or transmitted in any form
by any means, without the prior permission, in writing, of
the publisher, nor be otherwise circulated in any form of binding or
cover other than that of which it was
published and without a similar condition including this
condition being imposed on the subsequent purchaser.

ISBN 9798635987674

Cover art design by:
Forsaken Folklore
*Instagram*
@forsakenfolklore

TimeRipper

D E McCluskey

**For Lauren…**
I'm sorry I dragged you through all those
Ripper Tours, pulling you into
my gruesome obsession!
You are a true hero!

# TimeRipper

## **PROLOGUE**

FIVE HUNDRED THOUSAND pods were deployed; placed in strategic locations around the globe. Containers, filled with death, hidden within plain sight. Each pod was specifically designed to hold the purple mist that resided within them. Every one of them programmed to open at a designated time, to release their deadly cargo. A mist that had been cultivated, meticulously, for at least three years.

Europe, America, South America, Asia, the Middle East, Australasia. Each location carefully chosen for maximum impact.

Death and destruction would be prevalent in its wake. It would tear away the fabric of natural life, replacing it with basic and generic elements. A rolling death would stalk the land, devouring everything in its path. The mist could be contained, but once released, it could not be stopped. Everything it touched would be gone.

When the time came, the five hundred thousand pods would beep. A red light on the casing of each pod would flash five times before turning green. The green light would be accompanied by a hiss. An ugly white noise would precede the release of the purple death.

Once free of the container, it would fuse with the releases of the other containers and encompass a large percentage of all habitats on the planet. The death toll would be catastrophic. The destruction of the Earth's resources would be calamitous.

This was all by design.

It was a terrorist attack. The most successful and evil terrorist attack in Earth's chequered history; all done by design.

There would be no warning. No time to run, nowhere to hide. The attack was inevitable, imminent; the attack to end all attacks.

D E McCluskey

The year was twenty-two-eighty-eight, and nothing was ever going to be the same again.

## PART 1

### 1.

Oklahoma, USA. 2288

JEB OAKENHALL OPENED the front door of his ranch and looked into the dark Tulsa sky. He drew in a deep breath and held it for a moment. His eyes savouring the clouds that were reflecting the light of the waning harvest moon. Where the clouds were absent, an array of stars twinkled their own illumination upon him and his fields.

He never tired of seeing that particular display.

It had just gone four-thirty a.m., and the cold air of the night was battling the warmth that would soon overtake it as the sun rose on another glorious day; Jeb's favourite day of the year.

Today was the start of the harvest.

He was an early riser; always had been. Ever since he was old enough, he had been working this ranch. That was at least forty-eight of his fifty-six trips around the sun. He'd begun by helping his grandfather. After gramps passed, ownership fell to his father, before eventually becoming his. It was damned hard work, but he loved it. Plus, as always, he had the help of his boys.

The harvest was an annual event. It was the one time of the year where job, family, and life commitments, were put aside and everyone came home to the ranch for three days of hard labour.

In truth, he didn't need his boys anymore. Not with the technological advancements there had been over the years. This was twenty-two-eighty-eight; but it was a tradition, and a great time for all the family. This year, his grandson had come to help. At eight years old, everyone had thought it was time he learned the ropes.

Jeb, closely followed by his sons and his grandson, stepped off the porch. They all made their way, in time-honoured tradition, to the combined harvesters that were waiting for them on the edge of the field. With a deep sense of pride and accomplishment, he climbed, with practiced ease, up the chassis and into the cabin of the hulking machine. He tasted another lung full of the morning air. The smell of the wheat lingering on the breeze brought back so many fond memories.

He was a boy again, back in the day, back to his first harvest. He remembered how his heart had pounded in the excitement of climbing into the behemoth that would do his bidding for the first time ever.

With a wistful smile, he started the electric engine, imagining what it must have felt like to fire up a real old-fashioned diesel engine, like the one gramps had used in the olden days. He activated his personal input screen, bringing the overhead illuminations of the field to life. The dark of the morning blinked into daylight over the whole of his sixty-acre estate.

~~~~

His memories transported him back forty-eight years, where, as an eight-year-old kid, he had turned the keys on his very first harvest. He smiled as he recalled it hadn't been a very successful debut.

Eight-year-old Jeb had been practicing all year on the virtual platform that his father installed for him, and the excitement of sitting in the creaking, torn leather seat, taking hold of the controls, real ones, for the very first time, made his stomach swirl. He didn't know if he needed to go to the bathroom or if he wanted to vomit up the grits he had eaten for breakfast. But he did know that he wanted to kick-start this huge machine and go out and cut some wheat.

He knew the drill, he knew how to combat the pitch, he knew how to navigate the three dimensions that this machine utilised hovering over the crops. He even knew the angles that he had to fly to allow for optimal use.

Ten minutes into his first cut and things were going swimmingly. One thing the virtual platform had failed to inform him of was the sweet smell of the moist, fresh cut wheat. He looked around and saw his two older brothers' harvesters droning around the field. His cousins, and the extended family, were running around, playing, enjoying the party atmosphere. He nodded, *I could get used to this*, he thought and sat back, a grin encompassing his whole face.

That was when it happened.

Another variable that the virtual platform hadn't taught him, or readied him for, was barn owls. Huge birds with two-metre wing spans.

From out of nowhere, there was a crash, and the windshield of his harvester spiderwebbed. He looked up, snapping out of his daydream as the shattering of the protective glass made him jump. The huge, white bird, with a dead rat still in its talons, bounced off the glass, falling dead onto the hood of the harvester. As he jolted, he knocked the controls, sending the whole machine into a spiral of uncontrolled madness. Luckily, he was buckled into his seat by a heavyset harness, otherwise he would have been thrown clear of the windshield and into the path of the out-of-control shears.

As the behemoth hit the ground with a thud, there came the squealing of metal grinding on metal. The turbulent sound jolted every bone in Jeb's body. He grasped at the gearshifts, trying in vain to control the monster beneath him.

He failed miserably.

The vehicle hit the wheat field and began to churn huge mounds of earth all around him. It was only then that he remembered the first rule of harvesting. He reached up and slammed the palm of his hand into the emergency shut-down button just above his head.

With another unearthly squeal and another bone shattering jolt, the huge blades beneath the harvester ground to a grudging halt.

He had a horrible feeling that the metallic grinding he heard had been the gears sheering. As the harvester shuddered to a halt, Jeb checked himself. He could still feel his legs and was amazed they were still there. Thankfully, his torso and head were still attached. Despite a few scratches and scrapes, he'd come out of the accident unscathed. Unfortunately, the same thing could not be said for his mighty harvester.

He looked at the devastation around him. Not only had he destroyed one of his father's harvesters, putting it out of commission for at least the rest of the year, but he had churned up a good portion of his area of the field, wrecking the soil and the natural balance of the crop. As he unbuckled his harness, he was dreading what his father and brothers were going to say.

'Jeb... Jeb, are you OK?' The nervous shout of his father came from somewhere outside the hole he had found himself in. 'Jeb, speak to me, son. Are you OK?'

He could feel tears welling up in his eyes, and even though he didn't want his father, or brothers, to see him crying, he couldn't help but blub. 'I don't know what happened,' he sobbed. 'I think it was an owl. It came from nowhere. I'm so sorry, daddy, I'm so sorry!'

His father's face appeared in the shattered windscreen. Jeb was expecting a stern look and an angry voice but was surprised—not to mention relieved—to see the man smiling. 'Quit your babbling, son,' he said, laughing. 'Welcome to the harvest, boy!'

~~~~

Jeb smiled as he sat in his own cockpit, admiring his own sons' expertise at manoeuvring their vehicles around the illuminated fields with the support drones buzzing after them, collecting the harvester's bundles. He remembered an old saying that his father had been fond of. 'A man could die happy bailing hay with his sons in tow!'

He really did believe this.

## 2.

<u>Paris, France. 2288</u>

THE POWERFUL ILLUMINATION of the overhead lights from the Slipstream track masked the fact that it was twelve-thirty in the afternoon. Alphonse knew that at this time of the day, the Slipstream system would be packed to capacity with tourists and commuters. *I'm glad all I have to do is walk the boulevards,* he thought grinning. He turned away from, what he thought of as a technological horror, looming over him, and put his attention back to the street. The Rue de Vichy was rammed. It was crowded both ways, a mixture of people, some of them powerwalking and looking pissed off while others ambled along perusing shop windows and taking in the sites of the famously ancient street.

He knew this many people on the boulevard could only mean one thing; the Slipstream system had ground to a halt again.

*There must have been another accident. Fucking automated cars*, he thought as he stopped and looked upwards. 'Bring back the old manual drive, that's what I say,' he shouted to no one in particular. He watched as a rescue transport manoeuvred itself into position above a small section of the track. A blue magnetic field began to glow from underneath it. The stricken transport, that was blocking the system, was plucked up in the hope that maybe, just maybe, the system would begin to flow again.

Alphonse chuckled. 'Maybe we could do with one of them down here,' he yelled again. No one on the boulevard took any notice of him. Why would they? He was an 'unlisted person.' 'And proud of it,' he'd shout in defiance if anyone asked. Being unlisted meant that he was off the grid, he didn't have to answer to anyone. He didn't have to go through the rigmarole of clocking on, or clocking off, for a mindless, meaningless job that he hated. He could go anywhere he wanted whenever he wanted. Basically, being an unlisted person meant he was homeless, a vagrant; the great ignored. These were some of the names the do-gooders would call his people. He was happy, though. He scoffed at the thought of having to sit in a Slipstream queue for hours on end, only to get to a job that was killing you, to earn just enough money to pay for your house and your kids to go to school in order for them to repeat the whole cycle over and over again!

He was happy!

A rumble in the air caught his attention. He cocked his head as the magnetic field from the hovering rescue transport took hold of another stricken vehicle and began to lift it off the track. 'Go on, throw that motherfucker away. Do him a favour. You're all better off dead anyway! Or maybe you already are! Look at you, walking around like the fucking zombies you are…'

Alphonse liked to shout things like this to tourists and commuters; it relieved the boredom of his days.

A gendarme appeared out of nowhere, like they normally did when the unlisted were making a nuisance of themselves in public. The large, uniformed man took him by the arm, making him jump. 'You! Shut your mouth and move along,' he snarled, dragging him away towards a side street.

He didn't offer much—or any—resistance. There was no reason to. He knew he was in the wrong, but he couldn't help himself. It was all part of his 'freedom.'

The gendarme released him with a look that said, 'get out of here and don't let me catch you bothering these good people again!' when the ground beneath them began to shake. It wasn't the normal tremor he identified with the Slipstream; this had an intensity to it that it knocked the gendarme off balance, sending him tumbling against the red-bricked building beside him.

Alphonse was waving his hands in the air. This time he wasn't shouting at the tourists, he was having trouble keeping on his feet. With a furled brow, he looked upwards, past the Slipstream system, attempting to locate the source of the tremor.

## 3.

<u>Tehran City, Iran. 2288</u>

YOUSSEF HASEEM LOCKED his front door using the remote control and started the electric motor on his vehicle using the same device. It was two p.m., and the Slipstream system to Tehran City Centre should be empty. When the system was working to its full capability, he knew he could make it into the city and back to the office before anyone would even notice he was gone. But, these days, the system was very seldom working to its full capacity.

He'd forgotten Helen's birthday, again! To make matters worse, he'd also forgotten to bring his financial chip to work with him, so he couldn't just jump out at lunchtime and get something for her. *Nope, nothing that simple for Youssef,* he thought. He had to go all the way home, then out to the shopping district, then all the way back to work, in one afternoon. The round trip, including the shopping, was going take him at least two hours. He cursed himself for not getting something online for her in advance—all he'd have needed to do was to have it delivered to her work and that would have been that.

He cursed himself again for his forgetfulness.

He tuned into the broadcasts, hoping to sooth his journey with some ambiance, but as the unit came to life, all he received for his troubles was a burst of horrible white static. It blared out of the auditory devices hidden within the transport's infrastructure at such a force, it caused him to flinch. He oversteered, and his transport swerved off the Slipstream track. The warning sensors began to scream, adding to the cacophony of ugly noise within the cabin. As the transport bashed into the invisible wall off the side of the track, the dulled chrome of the bumper fatigued as the magnetic field bulged, keeping the transport safe, stopping it from falling the hundred or so metres to the ground below.

Youssef cursed as he, eventually, came to a screeching halt. His ears were ringing with the screaming of the buckling chrome, the collision alarm, and the white noise from the speakers. Suddenly, they all, mercifully, stopped at the same time. The sudden silence was deafening. He sat in the cabin for a moment, collecting his thoughts, attempting to calm himself. Opening his eyes, he checked himself to see if he was bleeding. He wasn't. He believed this was due to the deployment of the foam cushions on the impact.

Still catching his breath, he peered out of the window. The front of the transport had dipped over the side of the track and was being held on the system by the magnetic safety field. He had complete faith that the magnetic field would hold, mainly because it was his department that had been responsible for the development of the same system, but still, he was still shook up. He sat back in his seat, breathing deeply through his nose and out through his mouth, attempting to control the racing of his heart.

*Can today get any worse?* he thought.

This question was answered immediately.

A rattle rippled through the Slipstream track, and with it came a deep rumble. The whole track began to shake. He grabbed at the door handle, gripping it with all his strength. He cursed his arrogance of confidence in his technology as he felt the magnetic safety field failing around him. He closed his eyes, mouthing a quick prayer to Allah, as he braced himself for the one-hundred-foot fall, and the inevitable death that would come at the end of it.

The fall never happened. All that changed was the deep-set rumbling got louder, and the vibrations became heavier. *That's not coming from the tracks,* he thought opening an eye to see what was happening. His nose tickled as something trickled from it. He wiped at it, alarmed to find blood on the side of his hand. It wasn't a lot, but he knew by the tingle that the flow was getting heavier.

He looked out of the window, hoping to see what was happening outside. He knew the shaking of the Slipstream had nothing to do with his accident, it was designed better than that. The sky had darkened, considerably. It was an odd kind of darkness; there was a purple hue to the ominous clouds, and the forks of lightning flashing within them burned so brightly they blocked out the midday sun.

Each fork was accompanied by a tremendous crack of thunder that sounded more like an explosion.

It took a few moments for him to realise that the thunder didn't just *sound* like explosions... they *were* explosions. 'Shit!' he whispered, uttering a rare expletive. He watched, his bloody nose forgotten, as a huge ball of rolling purple smoke filled the sky. He needed to get out of his transport. He didn't know where he was going to go, but he knew he had to go somewhere.

His hands, slick with blood, grasped at the door handles. It took a while—in reality, it was nowhere near as long as it felt—before he gained purchase and was able to flick the switch, freeing himself from the vehicle. The odd sensation of being suspended in mid-air by a magnetic field was stomach churning, but it paled I comparison with the backdrop of the terrifying mass of purple turmoil that was rolling towards him.

He made the short jump from the hanging transport onto the system track and turned to witness Armageddon.

## 4.

<u>Oklahoma, USA. 2288</u>

THE FIRST INKLING of the coming end of the world that Jeb received was the total blackout of his harvester's controls. Expertly, his eyes navigated the dials and readouts of the cockpit, he pressed buttons and pulled on levers. Nothing was responding. He had another flashback to his failed outing when he was a child, but as there was no time for nostalgia now, he shut those thoughts away, and continued his battle for control of his vehicle.

The harvester lurched, and he felt himself pitch forwards.

As the ground rushed towards him, his brain searched for the great white owl, the one with the rat still in its talons, but it was nowhere to be seen. *Of course, it's nowhere to be seen,* he thought. *That was over forty years ago.*

He managed to guide the vehicle to as soft a landing as he could. The screaming of the gears and the blades played an ugly cacophony in his head. It reminded him of the fanfare of the four horsemen of the apocalypse from a film he had seen many years earlier.

Although he didn't know it, that thought was rather prophetic.

With a struggle, unbuckled himself and climbed out of the cockpit, onto the disturbed soil of his field. His hands were everywhere checking himself for wounds. He was more than surprised to find that there were none. The harvester, however, was a different story. That would be out of commission for at least the rest of the season. He turned, expecting to see his son's harvesters bearing down on his position, coming to his aid, but they were still over the other side of the field, working their own patch of the wheat.

That was when he felt the world around him vibrate. His head snapped towards the downed vehicle, expecting see flames.

There were none.

He began to run. He knew that he needed to get as far away from the stricken vehicle as he could. It didn't matter what direction he just wanted to get a fair distance from the disturbing vibrations. It didn't seem to matter which way he ran, no matter how far he got away from the harvester, the vibrations were the same.

Realising that the danger was not coming from the vehicle, he stopped. Bent over, his hands on his knees, panting, he looked up towards the sky. Despite the illumination of the lights over his field, he should have been able to get a glimpse of the sun making its first appearance of the day. Instead, all he could see was an odd, purple glow.

It was then that the end of the world truly began for Jeb. It happened relatively slowly, beginning with an explosion.

The field around him lit up, briefly, as one of the harvesters working on the other side of the field burst into flames. He shielded his eyes from the brightness before the realisation of what had just happened descended upon him. 'Christopher...' he yelled! He began to run towards the inferno that, only moments before, had been his youngest son's harvester. He had to stop and throw himself to the ground as debris, and shrapnel, from the explosion began to pelt him and the ground around him. Eventually the bombardment stopped, but he noted that the deep vibrations in the ground were getting worse. He lifted his head from the mud, and his grief filled eyes took in the devastation around him.

Then a second explosion rocked his world.

He watched as another harvester exploded. It became a floating ball of flame hovering in the air. The wheat directly below it was burning. He couldn't believe what he was seeing.

'Michael,' he sobbed and dropped his face, back into the wet ground.

He didn't want to believe what was occurring, what he had just witnessed. Five minutes ago, he had been looking forward to the best day of the year, enjoying both of his sons being home for the harvest; but now they were gone, both of them, in a matter of seconds.

He lifted his filthy face from the, still vibrating, ground and looked up at the sky. Slowly, he picked himself up from the littered ground.

That was when the lights above the field blinked out. As the flickering, amber and orange, illumination of the two destroyed harvesters bathed him in heat, a strange feeling washed over him. Every hair on his body stood on end. He felt his skin beginning to fizzle and crack. There was a sickening buzz of electricity in the air. Within the turbulent, purple sky above him, forks of bright purple lightning flashed across his vision, punching through the rolling clouds. This was like nothing he had ever seen before, as the flashed became even more frequent.

All he could do was watch, motionless, as the huge, rolling, purple cloud billowed slowly towards him.

The wrist device he was wearing began to scream. It dragged his attention away from the mesmerising cloud. He looked at it. The display was blinking, displaying an error message. He never had the time to process what could have been causing the error before the device exploded. The blast tore away half of his hand, ripping three fingers clean off. The pain, and the shock, didn't even register as the hypnotising effect of the cloud took back his full attention. Even as the robotic help—some in the sky, some not—began to explode, he couldn't pull his gaze away from the rolling clouds.

Eventually, it hit him.

The awesome power of the storm engulfed him, stripping the clothes from his back, stripping the skin from his body, eating through his organs, and finally, disintegrated his bones.

As the purple cloud passed it left no sign of life, or debris. Only a scorched, barren Earth in its wake.

# TimeRipper

## 5.

<u>Paris, France. 2288</u>

ALPHONSE LOOKED SKYWARD as the vibrations rocked the boulevard. Of the thousands of fellow pedestrians using the Rue de Vichy, only about a third of them had registered that something was wrong. His gaze passed the small, and seemingly inconsequential, drama of the removal of the stricken transport from the Slipstream track and looked at the sky above it.

He honestly couldn't remember when he had last looked at the sky, but what he could remembered was that it was supposed to be either blue or grey, depending on the weather, but he had never, ever, seen it purple. He was also certain that forks of lightning were supposed to be white, not the multitude of colours that were illuminating the murky clouds above him.

Before he had further time to muse on this, the Slipstream track above him exploded.

The removal transport exploded first, and in doing so caused a chain reaction that gave the illusion the whole Slipstream track had gone up. The vehicle it was lifting from the track exploded next. It showered the other vehicles, that had been caught in the jam, with melted plastics and glowing, red hot shrapnel. This fireball caused the other transports to explode, one by one. The debris and shrapnel from these explosions began to shower the people on the boulevard below.

Panic ensued as thousands of pedestrians began screaming and running in a myriad of different directions.

Chaos took the city hostage.

Alphonse had nowhere to run to. He watched as the gendarme who had accosted him was hit in the face by a large piece of glowing, twisted metal. The missile ripped the top of the man's head clean off, Set his hat alight, and spraying Alphonse with the unfortunate man's blood. As he crumpled, screaming in death throws, Alphonse took the opportunity to take refuge in the corner of the shelter, the one he had called his bed the night before. From his vantage point, he watched as panicked people ran this way and that, knocking over others and trampling them in their rush to save their small, unremarkable lives.

There were more explosions, and despite the heat blasts and the brief illuminations, he noticed the day had become markedly darker. He decided to brave a quick peek out of the shelter to see if he could witness what was happening above him.

His timing was perfect.

The moment he braved his head out of his shelter, a massive globule of melted plastic dripped from one of the burning transports above. It landed squarely on Alphonse's upturned face. The searing heat of the molten liquid sculpted itself into every crease, every orifice, of his face, mercifully killing the vagrant instantly.

He joined the ranks of the hundreds, maybe thousands, already lying dead in the street, ignored by others who were still panicking, attempting to save themselves.

As it turned out, they were all useless gestures.

The large purple cloud rolling its way towards them would bring instant death; instant destruction to each and every person, every object it came into contact with. It would eat them like it melted the bricks and mortar of the buildings, like it burnt, twisted, disintegrated the landing struts of the overhead Slipstream, collapsing lampposts, evaporating vehicles, annihilating any, and every, form of life.

As the cloud passed, it left in its wake, utter, and devastating, serenity.

Paris was gone, devoid of life. All that was left of the ancient, and historic city was dust and emptiness.

## 6.

Tehran City, Iran. 2288

THE PURPLE CLOUD rolled towards Youssef's location at an unprecedented velocity. Inside it, he could see flashes of bright purple lightning. The windshield of his vehicle exploded, and he knew if he didn't get out of here soon, the whole vehicle would blow, or the support struts of the Slipstream would buckle, and he would fall to his death.

For a moment, all he could do was stand and stare into the cloud. Like a man staring into an abyss, it was beautiful, mesmerising, it called to him. A million different shades of purple rolled over and into each other, enfolding the last in the embrace of the next, as it continued its destructive journey, ever nearer.

His nosebleed had stopped—he had not registered this, but it had. He lifted up his hand and looked at the smart wrist device he was wearing. The readout was flashing and looked like it was about to malfunction, but he was relieved that it was still working, although for how long, he couldn't be sure.

'This is Youssef Haseem, code EA, R and D, 5250798. I'm requesting teleportation from my current location. Send me to Orbital Platform One. Please, locate my wife and child and transport them too. Thank you, out.' As he spoke into his wrist, his eyes locked on what was coming for him, not quite believing what he was seeing.

*It can't be...* was his last thought as another shudder tore through the platform, pushing him towards the rail.

His form began to flicker, and without any further warning, he blinked into non-existence.

The cloud rolled ever forward. It engulfed the Slipstream, and his vehicle, maybe twenty seconds later. Everything in the path of the greedy, all-consuming cloud, was gone.

## PART 2

### 1.

YOUSSEF HASEEM MATERIALISED into a cold, clinical room. The dull greys, and the chrome of the walls and floors gave it a functional appearance, and the multiple high-tech displays with various readouts and views of the planet they were orbiting complimented this look.

This was Orbital Platform One, sixty miles above the Earth's atmosphere.

He had materialised into chaos.

The moment he appeared, a man and a woman were at his side, their faces ashen, scared, and serious. 'Youssef, what the Hell is going on down there? Do we have any updated information?'

'I can't update you on anything at this point,' he panted, slightly out of breath, as he stepped off the platform into the busy room. 'I haven't got a clue what's happening myself. Were my wife and daughter found?'

'I, erm... I don't know, sir,' the girl replied.

Everyone in the large room, except for him, was dressed in a militaristic, blue uniform. All that set the uniforms apart were name badges worn above the left breast and lines of rank on the cuffs of the sleeves.

Since Earth had put aside its racial differences and religious intolerances, all the countries and cultures had seen that there was more to be done, more to be achieved, by working together rather than against each other. The Earth Alliance Treaty had been formed. This harmony led to fantastical breakthroughs in science and technology. Hunger and poverty had been all but eradicated, and Earth was now very nearly the Utopia many had dreamed about for centuries. Technology and progress had long since become the main priority of the Alliance.

'Can you please find out? I'm going out of my mind with worry about them.' His voice was hushed, and he was smiling politely.

'Yes, sir, right away,' she replied, walking off into another melee of gibbering people.

'I'm going to need to bring the council together for an emergency session, can you arrange for France, Germany, Uganda, USA, and Brazil to be patched through to my personal room?' Youssef asked the man who was following him as he made his way out of the busy control room, removing his jacket.

'I'll do my best, sir, but there's crazy congestion at the moment. Too many reports from too many locations,' his colleague explained.

'OK, well, do what you can, just put someone through to me as soon as possible. We need as much information as we can gather on this,' he replied

'Yes, sir,' the man snapped prior to speeding off in the same direction as his female colleague.

'Mr Haseem, your wife and child have been tagged at platform twelve, sir,' his female colleague gasped as she rushed back into the room.

'Oh, thank the lord Allah,' he said and crossed his lips and forehead. As he entered his office, he put his coat over the chair behind his desk and slipped on his uniform jacket. 'Do we have any idea what's going on, or how bad it is?'

'Not yet, sir! The congestion seems to be halving our communication abilities.' She stopped and looked at him, her face falling into a sombre expression. 'We do know that it's big, sir. And it looks bad.'

Youssef sighed, resting his hand on the girl's shoulder. 'Understood,' he nodded solemnly. 'Get as many of the council members patched through to my office as possible, please.'

The young officer offered him a resigned smile and turned away.

'Amanda, as soon as you can, please,' he added in a soothing, but authoritative, voice before she left.

## 2.

<u>Inverness, Scotland. 2288</u>

THE DRIVING RAIN was assaulting the ancient bricks of the building. The sky was dark, brooding, and turbulent.

This was nothing new for Inverness.

The heritage that was the castle, built in 1836 on the banks of the River Ness, was illuminated from the darkness that the current storm had brought. Huge, upwards facing lights, well hidden in the moat, illuminated the great castle, offering a grandiose look, emphasising its many beautiful, original, features.

A crowd of cold, wet, and scared people had gathered in the grounds, occasionally sending small, petrified, glances skywards, as if expecting sudden death to fall on them.

The large screens dotted around the town were playing, non-stop footage, of the events that had been reported via satellite from various locations around the globe. Each of them depicted footage of a rolling, purple, cloud making its way across the various locations. The footage highlighted the complete, and utter, devastation left in its wake.

The people were scared, but they were sure of one thing: the group, the custodians of this historic castle, would be able to give them succour, support, and possibly even safety.

~~~~

In contrast to the ancient external veneer of the castle, the interior was a marvel of technology and industry. The outside had not changed much in the four hundred years since it had been built. The original brickwork and battlements were still in place, as was the drawbridge that opened over the, now drained and illuminated, moat.

The current interior, however, would have been incomprehensible to the original architects. The courtyards had been built over, and most of the walls and rooms had been knocked through. In place of the maze of musty old corridors, and banquet rooms, there was now a single expansive, open-plan room, illuminated by a bright blue light.

Inside, the enormous room was a hive of activity and technology.

Hundreds of people were bustling about, most of them working between different stations dotted here and there. Large screens were located on the walls, streaming footage of different locations around the globe. Others were displaying images and schematics of the twenty-five Orbital Platforms stationed above the planet.

Suspended from the ceiling was an impressive hologram depicting an orange circle intersected with small, jagged, lines of purple.

This was the logo of The Quest.

The Quest was a pseudo-religious organisation of like-minded people who derived their doctrine from their quest to investigate and expose what was fake in a world dominated by the Earth Alliance. They worshipped freedom above all else. Freedom to exert their own control over their own people. They knew that was essentially a paradox, but they revelled in it.

Over the course of twenty years, their movement had expanded from six founder members, a splinter group from the Earth Alliance, to almost six million. Despite this fact, they still considered themselves as an underground movement. At their root, they were anarchists, but the worst kind of anarchists. Organised, well equipped, and with nothing to lose.

In the centre of the room stood one of the few remaining original features of the castle: a stone staircase that spiralled downwards into the dark depths of the original foundations. Its dungeons.

A magnetically sealed entry point barred access to these lower regions from all but a few privileged members.

Six females were lined up by the barrier, each waiting patiently as the computer checked their credentials before allowing access to the mysterious depths, below.

3.

Orbital Platform One

YOUSSEF WAS SITTING at his desk in his personal room, surrounded by ten large screens. Each represented an Earth Alliance main region: London, England; Paris, France; New York, USA; Kampala, Uganda; Rio, Brazil; Berlin, Germany; Sydney, Australia; Moscow, Russia; Toronto, Canada; Tehran, Iran.

He was alone, with the doors closed. The anguish within him lay so heavy that he was certain he could feel the physical weight of it crushing him, dragging him down below the surface of reality, of normalcy. He was staring with wide, vacant eyes, shaking his head. Each screen displayed fifty inches of static. His anguish derived from the fact that these were supposed to be 'never fail' screens, meaning they should supply, around-the-clock, twenty-four-hour, seven-days-a-week, three-hundred-and-sixty-five-days-a-year, connectivity. They should never display pure static, not with the fail-safes and redundancies in place to keep them live.

Fighting off the cold sweat he could feel creeping over his entire body, he leaned forward and pressed a button on his desk. The image of the woman, the same one who had greeted him on his arrival at the platform, appeared on a small screen. She was smiling. He knew it was a false smile, he could see the same anxiety that he was feeling within her expression. 'Amanda, I'm going to need someone to find out what is happening at our main offices. I'm getting static on every channel. Surely this can't be right!'

'I'm on that right now. We're not getting anything back from any communication relays so far.'

'Have we managed to get any channels open between the other Orbital Platforms yet?' he asked, the waver in his voice giving volume to the levels of despair he was feeling.

'Only sketchy information is coming through, but we've had confirmation that at least seven of them are still functioning, up to now.' She paused for a few moments, swallowing hard before continuing. 'Sir, I'm still getting nothing from Earth Alliance headquarters.'

He bowed his head for a moment. He had an inkling about what had happened below but didn't want to give it a voice, just yet. 'Have we got any satellite coverage?'

'Again, sketchy sir,' Amanda replied. 'I'll pass over what we have onto your screen, hang on one moment.'

'Thank you, Amanda,' he whispered. Before long, an image winked to life on one of the large screens, thankfully replacing the static of what should have been Berlin with something more pleasant.

The image was of a city. The caption over the top of the picture identified it as Orleans, France. Nothing looked out of place. The populace was moving freely. The Slipstream was fluid, and there were vehicles in the air. Suddenly, the image began to glitch. It became fuzzy, as if the recording equipment was malfunctioning.

It soon became apparent that it wasn't the equipment that was to blame for the picture quality.

The image began to shake, and Youssef watched, with interest, as the sky began to darken. Dirty, heavy, purple clouds rolled into view, undulating rapidly into the shot. Vicious thunderbolts began to form within the turbulent mass. Within seconds, the thunderbolts escaped the vicinity of the cloud and cascaded downwards, striking the city below. Explosions rocked the picture, and it looked like the power grid of the city had gone offline. The camera compensated for the loss of light by automatically brightening, thus allowing him to see what he needed to see.

He watched as the cloud fell from the sky, enveloping the city below.

It was difficult not to turn away as the cloud continued to roll. *If this wasn't so horrific, it would almost be funny*, he thought. The cloud trundled across the city, leaving nothing in its wake. It was the only phrase he could think of to describe what he was witnessing. *Nothing in its wake!*

Nothing, except dust, sand, and desolation.

Something caught his eye. Quickly he pressed a button on his console and the video stream reversed. He watched again as the thunderbolts struck the ground, causing the explosions. In his head, he relived the moment on the Slipstream track when the explosions hit, the precursor of the purple cloud. He walked over to the screen just as the cloud dropped. He paused the playback. Holding his breath, he raised a hand to touch the image. 'I know what it is…' he whispered. His voice wavered as he spoke. He looked at his hand touching the screen and saw that it was shaking, violently. 'They're insane,' he mumbled. 'I don't… I can't believe what they've done!'

He turned on his heels and exited the room, disturbing Amanda, who was busy at her desk outside his office. He took a moment to notice her, to notice the level of concentration on her face: it was the same look everyone on the station had. It was the not knowing, the uncertainty for loved ones, and the life that may, or may not, have been taken away. He needed to help these people, but right now, he didn't know how.

'I need to brief everyone as soon as possible. Get whoever you can into the main conference room ASAP. This meeting is mandatory. I'm going to need feeds to any Orbital Platforms that we know are functioning, and any locations below we've managed to contact.'

'I'm on it now, sir' she replied, looking back at her display unit. 'Sir,' she continued, a ghost of a smile on her face, Youssef thought it looked proud. 'I just wanted to inform you that we've been in touch with London. It looks like they've come through unscathed.'

He raised his head to the ceiling of the room and kissed his hands. 'Thank Allah for that,' he whispered before turning back. 'Now get me that room.'

~~~~

Twenty minutes later, the main conference room was full to capacity. Earth Alliance personnel and the few civilians on board were filling every inch of space. The murmur of quietened voices was weighing heavy as everyone hoped for news from Earth, preferably regarding loved ones.

# TimeRipper

There were several screens on the walls displaying live linkups with the other twelve Orbital Platforms and one that was linked-up with London. These connections were grainy at best, and almost non-existent at their worst; but everyone agreed, they were better than nothing.

Youssef was standing at the front of the room, cutting a lonely figure with his hands behind his back and his head bent low. His eyes were distant, dark, and lost. He was biting at the insides of his cheek as he ran through the news he was about to impart, in his head. He wanted to doubt the news himself, and he worried how these, good, and scared, people were going to take it.

Before him was a portable holographic device.

'Ladies and gentlemen,' he spoke. The room immediately quietened at the sound of his voice. 'Thank you for attending this presentation with so little notice. I'm a man of few words, as most of you know, so I'll cut straight to the chase.'

He pressed a button on his wrist and the holographic device flickered into life. It displayed the scene of Orleans that he had been watching earlier.

'I won't apologise for the content of this video, but I'll tell you that it's not easy viewing. This is the only footage we currently have of the…' he paused for a moment, thinking about what to call the devastation, wondering if he could even conjure up a name for something so hideous. '…event, below.'

Even though most of the people in attendance had seen it before, a shocked reverence took over the room.

Once the video had played it course, he turned it off. The silence lay heavy in the room, like a physical presence. He regarded everyone before him, including the video screens of the other platforms, and the glitching picture of London. He swallowed and bit the inside of his cheek again, before exhaling deeply. 'Without going *too* deep into the physics, or the history, of this; around two-hundred and fifty years ago, a discovery was made. This discovery became known as the Higgs-Boson Particle. It was more commonly referred to, in the day, as The God Particle. It was widely regarded that this particle was, theoretically, responsible for the Big Bang that created the universe. At the time it caused quite a stir as scientists around the globe debated whether they could, or indeed, should, attempt to re-create one of these particles in a Hadron Collider. The scientific community was concerned that it could cause localised black holes and bring about the end of all life on the planet as we know it. Needless to say, it didn't... until now!'

After the silence that had befallen the hall, the murmur that was now rippling through the auditorium felt deafening.

'Please, please, ladies and gentlemen, I do not... sorry, *we* do not have time to debate any of this. I need to tell you what I know now, before anything else comes to light.'

Youssef stared hard at his audience. His palms were sweating, and there was a queasy feeling deep in his stomach, but he knew he had to continue.

The story must be told.

'Twenty years ago, when I was a much younger man with ideals about how to change the world, I started work, straight from university, in the laboratories of the Earth Alliance...'

## 4.

<u>Earth. Twenty years earlier.</u>

'DO YOU THINK these fields will hold? I'm not so sure,' Youssef whispered to his colleague as he bent over the long trench of the Hadron Collider they were working on. He was holding a glowing rod in his hand that was hooked to a lead tank behind them.

'I hope so,' his female colleague replied with a smile on her face. 'Otherwise, because of the amount of radiation coming from that tank, we can kiss goodbye to any chances of future Youssefs or Carries, that's for sure,' she laughed.

He didn't see the funny side of the joke, and he gave the tank behind them another worried glance. He looked behind the lead structure, towards the large group of people who were standing behind the glass screens, observing them. He gestured towards them with a flick of his chin. 'They're not stupid, are they? Stood out there, getting us to do all the dangerous stuff.'

Carrie Millwood looked towards the glass and smiled again. 'They've done their stint in here. It's time for us to get our hands dirty,' she said, shaking her head.

'I just don't trust this stuff, that's all.'

'You trust the force field, don't you?'

He couldn't reply to that question. The force field she was referring to, the one that was emanating from a small box attached at both of their hips, covering their bodies in a light-yellow glow, had been his invention. It was what had gotten him his position in the Earth Alliance laboratories, straight from the University of Tehran, in the first place. It was a feat that had been relatively unheard of. Under normal circumstances, students were required to sit a two-year entrance course before they were accepted, but Youssef, as such a promising student, hadn't needed to.

The laboratory they were working in was vast. In it, there were another three Hadron Colliders, with two students manning each machine. The Colliders themselves were constructed of long trenches that looped around in a rectangle with rounded corners. They were encased in thick glass, and at each end were computers and monitors displaying and analysing exactly what was happening during their use. In the trenches, various atoms and particles would race around the loop while other materials were introduced at various locations along the way. The idea behind it was to see how different materials reacted as they smashed into each other at different velocities. It was this precise operation that had led to the discovery of the God Particle in the first place, all those years ago.

Youssef and his team were experimenting on a recent breakthrough they had recorded involving the Higgs-Boson particle. Their job today was to test and refine the outcome of the experiments.

The theory was, that if you accelerated the particle to just under the speed of sound—roughly three-hundred-and-forty meters per second—before injecting a wall of modified hydrogen for it to collide through, the hydrogen molecules would begin to act erratically. By erratically, it meant that some of the molecules disappeared while others were displaced. The displaced molecules had a habit of turning up, almost instantaneously, inside one of the other Colliders on the other side of the lab.

It was all very exciting!

No one could explain this phenomenon, but it interested the hierarchy enough to engage a large percentage of their best students to analyse it. Their best guess was that the Higgs-Boson particle had created an unexplained, and unexpected, vortex that *teleported* the molecules from one location to another.

What had excited them, even more than the teleportation, was when the first experiment was completed and the apparatus cleaned, they came back the next day and could not explain the presence of hydrogen molecules already in the Collider. This phenomenon continued to occur after each experiment. It thrilled the scientists so much that the strangest properties regarding these displaced molecules was very nearly overlooked. The molecular structure had been altered; they were older than any of the molecules that had been prepared, ready to be used in the next experiment.

This discovery gave light to another theory, one that had been previously thought impossible. Before anyone could get overly excited and announce this theory, or even give it a name, more investigation was warranted.

For the next experiment, they tagged the molecules with magnetic signatures and replicate the experiment.

As was hoped, but not entirely expected, the molecules began to act erratically. They confirmed that the ones that turned up in the other colliders were indeed the same tagged molecules.

It seemed like teleportation had indeed been discovered; but something even more significant was recorded. The set of molecules found prior to the next experiment were analysed and found to have the same magnetic tagging signatures attached to them, but the date stamp on the tag related to four days in the future. This caused untold confusion, not to mention excitement, within the community.

It was widely regarded that time travel could never be achieved due to the paradox theory. The theory stated that if it was to be invented then we would already know about it; but with this discovery, it seemed that paradox was about to be blown out of the water.

~~~

Only the most promising students had been recruited to work on, and hopefully expand, both discoveries. Teleportation had been chosen to be the main, and public, area of research, while time travel, although deemed to be *the* discovery of the last five hundred years, was given a more discreet classification.

Youssef had been recruited directly from the University of Tehran, and his counterpart Carrie Millwood had been recruited from Cambridge University. Both were leading prospects in their fields of Quantum Physics, and they had been selected to support the fledgling research team into both phenomena. The initial work was coming along nicely. They had stabilised the teleportation. All tests had been, at least, partially positive, and they had successfully teleported various multi-cellular objects over various distances. Plans were now in place to experiment on organic tissue.

The time travel aspect was proving more difficult. The first obstacle they hit was a quantum one. They kept finding results of experiments in the lab that they hadn't done yet. This had proven to be mind-blowing; but the second and more pressing issue were the aftereffects of these experiments.

At first, they had been working on a molecular level so small that the by-product of the experiments had not even registered, but as the experiments became larger, so did the by-product.

This became a problem.

As a particle passed through the time barrier, there was a reaction. An extremely violent and unpredictable reaction. The mass of the by-product was directly dictated by how big the particle was and by how far back in time the particle was sent.

Carrie Millwood had become obsessed with this.

They called it the Higgs Storm, as it resembled rolling, stormy thunderclouds, complete with lighting. It never survived long, but it left behind it complete devastation. A void of life! Nothing could survive its brief, but destructive, power. Many pieces of expensive equipment and apparatus had been lost during the experiments.

Then, almost inevitably, there was an accident.

~~~~

'I just don't trust this stuff, that's all,' Youssef whispered to Carrie as he injected the modified hydrogen into the receptor on the Hadron Collider.

Carrie turned to look at him, her eyes were wide behind her mask. 'But you do trust the force field, don't you?'

'Yeah, of course I do. I developed it. It's just the Higgs-Boson particle, the radiation it emits is off the scale.'

Today, their team was working on time travel. It was a top-secret project, and as far as he was concerned, hugely dangerous. Using his magnetic field theorem, they had developed a containment field for the destructive by-product. It worked like surface tension within the air. It created what they had dubbed a Storm Bubble. This bubble could be maintained for up to an hour, so there was plenty of redundancy in case of an emergency. There was also a redundant containment field that could detect a weakness in the first and envelop them both. They had discovered that the environment was still inhospitable for up to half an hour after the storm dissipated, so the bubble needed to contain this toxic atmosphere too.

'I'm just glad that I'm not this onion,' she scoffed from behind her mask, holding out the unpeeled stem before her.

He raised his eyebrows, enjoying the brief levity of the situation. 'Me too,' he replied. 'You best put it down or it'll have me crying,' he quipped. Inside he cringed at his stupid joke.

The onion was the case in point. No one had consciously intended to attempt time travel with an onion, but a magnetically tagged onion had turned up in the lab two mornings ago. It was presumed that it had been sent back, by themselves, a few days in the future. So, in order not to unbalance that future, or the past, they decided to continue their experiment with a large Spanish onion.

As he injected the purple gas into the collider, Carrie made the calculations at her console to differentiate between time travel and teleportation. They both watched as the gas leaked into the Collider like oil into water. Its tendrils reaching out as if searching for something to engulf. Eventually, they found the onion and wrapped themselves around it, swallowing it within the billowing, purple mass. There was a bright white light, and the onion was gone.

It was always a marvellous thing to witness.

Normal protocol stated that during a Higgs Storm event, all personnel were to evacuate the vicinity immediately.

As the onion disappeared, it was replaced by the by-product, the Higgs Storm. Alarms sounded, and the doors to the laboratory unlocked, allowing everyone inside to leave. The alarms continued blaring around the room as the destructive Higgs Storm began to manifest itself from where the onion had been. There were eight students working on the four Colliders; all of them stopped what they were doing and exited the lab in a hurried, but organised, manner. Several anxious eyes watched the growing, turbulent storm when a whoosh drowned out the alarm as the primary containment field deployed. The storm floated around the lab, contained within the shimmering, yellow, sphere.

One of the women working on the team, the last one in line to exit, realised at the last minute that she had left her personal pad over on the table next to her station. She turned back and ran across the room to retrieve it. As she did, she tripped over a chair that had been left half sticking out from underneath a table. By the time anyone noticed she was not out of the room, it was too late, the timer on the doors had activated.

She was locked inside.

Carrie was the first to notice. She tore the mask from her face and grabbed at the door handle. 'Gloria's still in there, Gloria…' She was shouting as she pulled on the handle. It was a futile gesture as the magnetic lock was protected by another of Youssef's fields, a third failsafe in case of containment degradation. 'We have to get her out of there,' Carrie screamed, all the colour had drained from her face, making her lips look almost blue.

'Relax,' Youssef said, putting a hand on her shoulder. Carrie dropped her shoulder, attempting to shrug him off in her desperation to open the door. 'All she has to do is sit tight for an hour. There're double redundancies in place against the storm. She's as safe in there as we are out here.'

Ignoring him, she looked back through the window.

Gloria was inside, her back was to the door, looking out at them through the glass walls.

Youssef watched her. He didn't think he had ever seen anyone look so terrified in his entire life. He activated his communication device, linking it with hers. 'Gloria, listen to me.' He paused as the fear in her face piqued. He knew he needed to continue but was worried that the rest of what he had to say would cause her to panic and become irrational. 'Listen to me. There's nothing we can do right now. The doors are magnetically sealed. They will automatically reopen once the Higgs Storm has dissipated, and the magnetic field has uncoupled. One hour at most. Please, stay calm, breathe, and wait for the thirty-minute alarm.' He looked at his wrist device, and then back to her. 'It's already been three minutes, only twenty-seven left.' He smiled through his lame joke and was relieved when she smiled back, relaxing her grip on the door handle.

He sensed that the smile relaxed Carrie too, but she still had her hands up to the glass, showing Gloria support. Gloria mimicked the gesture, putting her hands to the glass too.

Everyone in the anteroom, except for Carrie, began to remove their protective clothing, knowing that when the storm had passed there would be no need for protection from the radiation.

The minutes passed slower than an electron at drift velocity in a copper wire!

Then something terrible and unprecedented happened.

A second alarm began to blare through the complex. This was the only time, ever, that this alarm had sounded. It signalled that the primary containment field was failing. Everyone in the room switched their gazes from Gloria towards the purple bubble. Unbelievably, to everyone, but especially Youssef, it was deflating. The billowing, purple storm was seeping from the bubble. It was leaking in-between the areas of the magnetic field that were beginning to decay. A light flashed on a control board, and he sprinted over to the station where it was located. The secondary containment field was attempting to deploy, but due to the spread of the leakage, it couldn't lock onto one location. For this reason, it too was failing.

Gloria had been in the room for twelve minutes. She needed to stay away from the storm for another eighteen minutes, at least. Youssef, and everyone else, knew that was a big ask.

Gloria knew it to, as she began to panic.

Her screaming, piping in through the speakers, filled the room as she clawed at her mask and began to attack the small box on her hip. She was trying to turn off the magnetic shield around her body.

'Gloria, what are you doing?' Carrie shouted, her breath against the glass causing a fog. Her voice had risen more than a couple of octaves. 'Gloria, listen to me, put your mask back on and re—'

She never finished her sentence.

Gloria began to scream at the top of her lungs. For some reason, instead of staying as far away from the gas as she could, she ran *towards* it at full speed. As she did, she must have realised what she was doing, and where she was going, and attempted to change direction. By then it was too late. She tried to stop but her momentum carried her on, into the cloud. She tried to dodge it, but it was no use.

As she bent to escape the purple mass, her face skimmed the edge of it.

Unfortunately for everyone behind the glass, and for Gloria, the rest of her body completed the turn, and she ended up facing the window.

The result was hideous.

As a reflex action, everyone stepped backwards, and a collective gasp filled the room. Nobody had the foresight to turn off the speakers, so the blood-curdling screams continued to squeal through them, filling the shocked silence of the anteroom. The scientists who hadn't been mesmerised by Gloria's half face held their hands to their ears, attempting to block out the noise. The others were rewarded with the worst thing they would ever see in their lives.

The cut across the woman's face was smooth; but bloody. Thick, pink liquid dripped from where her temple and right eye had been. The grey-white matter of her lacerated brain had mixed with her blood, her melted skin, and her liquified bone.

The cloud had, in simple terms, erased half of her head.

Staggering like a drunken sailor in a children's song, she lurched towards the wall of glass. Her nervous system had not had time to realise that half of its messaging system had ceased to exist, and she must have seen the glass as a means to escape the lab, and the horrors within it. She hit the glass at full speed. The contents of her exposed head lurched forwards, with force, leaving an ugly, smeared, pink smudge across the once clear surface.

Everyone had no option other than to gawp as her body ceased functioning. She looked like she was deflating. Blood was flowing freely from her nose and mouth; the dark red mixing with the viscous, ugly pink, as her body shrunk.

Carrie was the only one left at the window, and she still had her hand up, offering it to her friend. But, by the look on her face, Youssef guessed that she was repulsed too by what was happening and must have known Gloria was already dead. His heart went out to the brave woman. She had decided that showing her stricken friend she was with her right until the very end was the best course of action.

He hadn't been anywhere near as brave as Carrie. He'd *had* to turn away, mostly to stop himself from vomiting, but part of him knew it was also to stop himself from seeing anything more. He didn't want to remember anything more, he needed to prevent this... what? This hideousness, from reoccurring in his dreams. He swallowed the saliva that had built up in his mouth, a precursor to vomit, and braved a glance over towards Carrie. There was a distant, vacant, look on her face. It was as if she were watching what was happening on a view screen rather than in real life. The only telling sign it was real in her world was the slow shaking of her head and the slight tremor in her hand, the one still on the window.

Gloria's body took at least another minute to realise it was dead. Once his nausea passed, Youssef marvelled how someone, with only half a brain, could last so long.

Gloria Hartigan died at the exact same time as the Higgs Storm began to dissipate.

He pondered on how much one onion could shape a person's fate.

~~~

From that day, Carrie Millwood changed. She became different, mostly in relation to her work, but her personal habits and sense of humour changed too. Prior to the accident, she had always been open and social, always the first to volunteer for a night out; but after those events, a different Carrie emerged. Theis one was serious, brooding, studious, singular, these were just some of the words her peers began using to describe her. She became blinkered in her experiments, preoccupied with the Higgs Storm almost to the point of obsession. She spent every free moment studying anything she could find regarding the phenomenon. How it was created, better ways to contain it, what happened in its aftermath. She had a strange theory that it could be harvested, its life prolonged. She asked to be removed from the initial time-travel and teleportation project to be allowed to head up a team solely set-up to study the Storm.

This request was denied.

Her attitude changed again.

She began coming in later each day, she stopped wearing the authorised uniform, and her reports of the experiments she was tasked with became shoddy and brief. All she would talk about was the Higgs Storm, and every time she did, it was in reverence.

She related to it as if she was a high priestess to its deity.

She also began to influence other members of the team. They would hold secretive meetings during lunch breaks and spend time with each other during the weekends. Carrie had attempted to coerce Youssef into her passion, but he had not wanted anything to do with it, thinking it was folly, especially when there was so much else to be learned from the particles themselves, not the by-products.

One thing he had to concede was that the unauthorised research the team conducted was fantastic. Every day and every night, they were gathering more information regarding the phenomenon. He managed a brief look at a document they had produced relating to how the Storm could be utilised, used as a Genesis particle to reset land back to a baser form; basically, starting again.

It was chilling reading, but he was secure enough in the fact that it was only theoretical.

Finally, and almost inevitably, the day came when Carrie walked into the laboratory headquarters and handed her notice in to the lead scientists. She walked out the very same day. Another five members of the team, all of them women, did the same.

Youssef heard on the gossip train that they had managed to secure funding from somewhere to set up their very own lab where they could spend their days worshipping the Higgs Storm.

Once again, on the gossip train, he heard that they had created their very own 'pseudo-religion' and were now calling themselves The Quest.

~~~~

For a few years, that was all anyone ever heard of them, except for the odd scientific papers they produced regarding their findings.

Then, almost from out of nowhere, The Quest became big news. They emerged as the only group ever to challenge the Earth Alliance on a serious level. Over the course of a few years, they had grown from the initial six women who walked out of the Earth Alliance to a count of almost six million in their ranks.

They began to publicly challenge almost every viewpoint that the Earth Alliance held. Freedom of religion: they wanted religion banned and for science to be revered. They wanted freedom of rule, they wanted one central government, i.e. them, to control all the governments of all the countries on Earth. They thought they had the 'new way,' and they wanted to enforce it on everyone.

Carrie Millwood and her cohorts became the darlings of the news. There were always bulletins regarding them doing this or attending that, but they never once gave personal interviews.

They saw themselves as a democratic unit, there was no one ruler.

In reality, everyone knew that it was Carrie who was in charge, everyone else was in her thrall.

They built a lot of credibility with their initial mandate, but as their demands began to become more erratic, the public started to see them as a joke.

That was when the violence started.

There were a few attacks at EA facilities around the globe. No deaths were ever reported, just chaos and mayhem. They were seen as coincidental accidents at first; before they began to turn nasty. Specific EA facilities were their targets, and during this campaign, there *were* deaths, many deaths. Next were the science and research facilities, and once again, death followed them.

The Quest became a constant, and legitimate, thorn in the side of the EA.

They had also become a public nuisance.

All public events were now heavily guarded, and security doubled, tripled in some cases, and once or twice, even quadrupled. Intercontinental transport security was reinforced too. Instead of influencing the public and winning hearts, they were beginning to irritate. A few times they threatened a 'major' incident, but nothing ever materialised.

Then, with no warning, they disappeared. Nothing was heard of them, and it had been assumed they had given up their 'Quest.'

That was until now...

## 5.

### Orbital Platform One: 2288

YOUSSEF WAS STANDING before the gathered crowd and the display units. The room was silent. Everyone present, including the other Orbital Platforms and London, had absorbed every word of the tale he had just relayed.

'The last I heard of Carrie; she was continuing her research into the Higgs Storm.' He paused for a moment, collecting his thoughts, before looking up into the eyes of everyone, looking back at him. 'I want to show you some footage of the phenomenon caught in the primary containment field.'

The holographic device blinked again. It displayed an image of a Hadron Collider laboratory. The image zoomed in on an object that was sat on a plinth in the middle of what looked like a miniature racetrack.

'What we're seeing here is a typically small object that we are about to send back in time.' There was a mumbling from the audience as they digested the information he had just divulged. He ignored their initial shock; he'd deal with questions later; this information was more important. 'First, the object, in this case an apple, is magnetically tagged.'

The scene changed to show a syringe being inserted into the skin of the apple, the pinprick glowed purple for a moment.

'Then the collider is started. It takes roughly five minutes for it to get up to speed. For the interests of brevity, I've moved it forward a little.'

Another syringe is seen inserting what looked like nothing into a tube.

'This is the hydrogen being added into the mix.' Another solution is added, this one is purple. 'Next, the serum is prepared. This is genetically altered hydrogen… it was actually found by accident. Now watch this…'

The visual panned back out to show the apple sitting on the plinth suspended above the Collider. The long turrets of the track began to glow. 'The glowing is normal, we're speeding the hydrogen around the track to almost the speed of light,' Youssef explained. 'Then the apple is lowered onto the track.' He could feel the anticipation in the room, almost as if it were a physical thing.

Nothing happened.

The track continued to glow.

'We then add the modified hydrogen particles into the mix.'

Suddenly, the apple disappeared in a bright flash. In its place was a large purple cloud, expanding into a bubble. Inside the bubble, a violent magnetic storm was raging.

The silence in the auditorium was complete.

Youssef's voice broke it after a few, long seconds. 'This storm, ladies and gentlemen, is currently the most destructive force known to man. It eradicates all life; it leaves behind it total and utter devastation.'

An excited mumble rippled through the audience.

'Unfortunately, I believe that this is what has happened on the planet below us. At present, I don't have any evidence that The Quest are behind these attacks, but all indications are steering me towards that conclusion.' He stepped away from the microphone for a moment, mopped his brow, and took a couple of deep breaths. 'Does anyone have any questions?' he asked eventually.

The room was silent for a long time, before one person from the back spoke in hushed tones. 'Excuse me, Youssef, but… is this the end now? I mean of life on Earth. Has the whole planet been attacked?'

He swallowed and exhaled a long sigh. 'The short answer is we don't know. We do know that London is still functioning, and from some sketchy reports, it looks like most of the British mainland has been untouched. As for anywhere else, at this moment in time, we can only hope.'

'What about the future?' someone else asked.

'Well, our early research, and some of the research we managed to glean from The Quest, suggested that the storm doesn't completely kill the nutrients in the ground. It looks like it, kind of…' Youssef paused, searching for the correct analogy. '…resets it,' he finished. 'Almost like a reboot. We think, hope, and believe that life can, and will, eventually resume in the affected areas.'

His audience became uneasy at this news. All he could do was attempt to placate them. *I can't and won't lie to them*, he thought as he stepped down from the podium.

## 6.

THE SPIRAL STAIRCASE in the castle was dark and moody. It was in sharp contrast to the bright technological marvel that was the ground floor, but The Quest leaders had wanted to keep at least some of the original features when they remodelled. The underground room was vast. It had previously been a banquet suite. Apparently, through history, some of the previous owners had been paranoid enough to create a whole subterranean working castle built into the hill of Inverness that would allow them to live a semblance of normal existence while under siege from above.

It had suited The Quest's needs perfectly.

Six women, the unofficial hierarchy of The Quest, were seated around a long, oval, mahogany table. Six visual display monitors represented the only technology in the room.

There was very little cheer.

'We need to release a statement, and it needs to be done soon,' one of the women along the table shouted.

'Agreed, but how do we announce it? Do we call it a victory? A triumph?' another woman answered.

'No!' came a definitive answer from the tall, thin woman who was standing in the shadows. She moved into the light of one of the monitors, and the glow from the screen partly illuminated her face. 'We simply announce it as a matter of fact!'

Carrie Millwood looked around at the other women in the room, taking every one of them in with her gaze. 'It's not a triumph, or a victory. Far too many innocent people have died today. This is a stance for what we believe in. The Earth Alliance has denied us for too long. Soon, they'll no longer exist. We are the government of this planet now. We *will* put out a statement. We *will* lay claim to this event. But there will be no celebration. How can we celebrate the death of so many of the Earth's population?'

The silence from the room was complete.

'The EA will be scraping together anything they can to offer succour to the survivors of The Event, and they will fail, miserably. We, on the other hand, have built our reserves. We knew that this apocalypse was coming. We will offer help, food, and shelter to the populous, but most of all, we'll offer hope. Hope in a new dawn, in a new regime, in a new way.'

The silence prevailed. The other five women looked at her. There was reverence within their gazes, and there was awe. All six of them had planned this event, down to the very minutest detail. Ever since they walked out of that lab, almost twenty years ago, they had dreamt of this moment. The moment they took control.

'When do we announce ourselves as the new power to the people?' one of the women, asked.

Carrie smiled; it was a rare occurrence these days. 'As soon as the Earth Alliance admit their inadequacies in dealing with this global catastrophe. It shouldn't be too long.'

Everyone in the room smiled, none more so than Carrie herself. She had handpicked this team, groomed them, recruited them from the Earth Alliance herself.

She had chosen wisely.

## 7.

'YOUSSEF, WE'VE MADE contact with New Mexico. It looks like they haven't been affected by The Event, but their communications array has been down under the pressure of so much traffic passing through it,' Amanda reported as he walked into the control room.

'Excellent, how many is that now?' he asked. His spirits were rising, only a little, but every person found alive was something to celebrate.

'Twenty-five cities in total, and all but one of the orbital platforms,' she replied. 'Up to now, it constitutes maybe thirty percent of Earth's inhabited regions.'

Youssef sighed. 'Well, it's a start. Have we had any reply from the teams we put in place to contact these cities?'

'We've had communication from some of our teams in Mexico, and some in Eastern Europe. They're reporting mass rioting, looting. Murder and suicides are on the increase. The situation is dire, sir. It seems that the areas attacked were targeted for good reason. They were mostly areas of high production of either food or other essential products. Analysis points to them hitting these locations to create scarcity.'

'This hasn't been a random terrorist strike,' he mumbled, more to himself than to Amanda. 'It's been well planned, probably for years. It's my bet that they've been stockpiling supplies to hand out to the stricken populous in return for their loyalty. How have we not seen something like this coming?'

'Sir, a communication's coming in,' Amanda interrupted. 'It's using almost every frequency, even the emergency ones. I'm patching it into our system now.'

A holographic device blinked into life. A symbol of a rotating Q appeared. Inside it was a small purple globe. Underneath it, in purple upper-case lettering, were the words, THE QUEST.

Eventually, the symbol faded away and was replaced by the image of a woman. She was tall and elegant. Her face, like her attire, was serious.

'Carrie Millwood,' Youssef whispered.

She looked old, and tired, nothing like his vibrant former colleague from the lab twenty years ago.

The holographic Carrie raised her arms and spoke, and as she did, her voice came from everywhere. 'Citizens of the planet Earth. If you are listening to this broadcast, then you are the lucky ones. You have been chosen, and you have been spared.'

A shout of anger flared up in the room. Youssef tried his best to silence it, he needed to hear every word of this message.

'You may not understand this now,' she continued, 'but in the future, you will know the benefits of what has transpired here. We are not celebrating a triumph. We take no joy in what we have done, but please know that what has passed *has* been done for the benefit of this planet and the future of everyone left upon it.'

Another burst of anger filled the room.

'We have lived in the shadow of a fascist regime for far too long. The Earth Alliance tell us how to think, they tell us how to live; but no more. Their time is over. The Quest will now be your government. We will allow the Earth Alliance one calendar year to relinquish all control over to us. We are the ones with the resources now. You'll find that the major production plants and food processing plants, that you have relied on for too long, are now gone. You have little to no resources left. We, on the other hand, have an almost limitless supply. To show our benevolence, we will offer you, the people, unlimited access to these supplies on one condition. The condition is that you renounce the Earth Alliance, you join with us in The Quest. Our quest is not only for a brighter future for you, but a better future for all. Representatives will be communicating with the leadership of the Earth Alliance to work out the transition process. We want this to pass as smoothly, and as peacefully, as it can. *We* now own the immediate issue of feeding the remaining population. This is our highest priority, and all petty squabbles *will* be overlooked.'

There was no sign off. Carrie's holograph simply blinked into non-existence, and the symbol of The Quest reappeared.

Youssef stared at the spinning symbol. *Why would Carrie be sending representatives to speak to our authorities? Why not come herself?* he thought.

He took this thought with him as he re-entered his office. Once the door was closed, the rest of the people in the control room went back to their duties, shooting sparing glances towards his office, mumbling to each other in hushed tones.

~~~

Over the next few days, the situation on Earth worsened. The Quest's broadcast had been shown in what was left of every country on the planet and had been broadcast in every language. In a number of these countries, the Earth Alliance headquarters had been overrun and the personnel forced to leave, to be re-housed on orbital platforms, for their own safety. Youssef had been watching events unfold from his safe haven above the troubles.

This disturbed him more than anything.

He was in his personal quarters with his wife; his daughter was playing with some old-fashioned cars on the floor, at their heels. They were trying to eat a family meal, but he couldn't focus.

'I don't understand why they would do such a thing.' A statement he had made repeatedly over the last few days. 'They're holding the planet to blackmail; and worst of all, they're winning.'

'Youssef, you need to relax,' Helen, soothed. 'I swear your hair is already going grey.' This was her attempt to lighten the mood a little, a hard task considering the recent activities.

'What's getting to me, though…' he continued, ignoring Helen's last comment, '…is why she said they'd be sending representatives to talk to EA. We have history, she knows my position. Why not come herself?'

'That's probably why she won't come herself. You do realise that you're now the highest-ranking officer in the EA, don't you? It would have to be you she dealt with.'

He stared at his wife. His face was a blank canvas, but his eyes were working. He hadn't thought about that; he *was* the ranking officer in the EA. It was up to him to sort out this mess. 'Well, Allah be praised,' he mumbled. 'The buck stops with me.'

There was not a lot of humour in his voice.

Helen looked at him, an enigmatic smile on her lips.

He hated that the precious time they had together had to be tainted with work. They hadn't seen much of each other in the last few days as he'd been putting out metaphorical fires left, right, and centre. He knew that Melissa, their daughter, had missed him terribly. She was not taking to life in the sky too easily. He had explained to her, and Helen, that this was really the only safe place left to them since The Event. But he knew that it wasn't ideal.

Her smile grew in confidence as she took his hand in hers, locking their eyes. 'Youssef, you need to start delegating some of this work you're doing. You can't do everything yourself. I understand that the EA needs you, and the survivors on the surface need you, but do you know what? We need you too, Melissa and me. I won't ever stand in the way of your work, I know how important it is to you, but please think of what you are putting yourself through.' As she spoke, her eyes locked on their daughter who was looking up at them both.

He closed his eyes, took in a deep breath, held it for a moment, and exhaled as he bent down to pick her up. She flung her arms around him, planting a wet kiss on his lips. He smiled, laughed a little even, and for a moment, things felt like they could be heading in the right direction.

His personal intercom chirped, and Amanda's voice brought it all back. He rolled his eyes towards his wife, who rolled hers back, as he handed Melissa to her.

'I'm sorry to trouble you on your personal time, but we've just had a communiqué from Orbital Platform Three. They've made contact with Antarctica. The operations team stationed there are alive and active. They're teleporting in as we speak.'

'Fantastic news,' he replied. This time there was genuine happiness in his voice.

'Sir, Kevin Farley is with them, and he's asking to talk to you right away.'

'Kevin? That's great news.' He turned to his wife, and there was genuine cheer in his features.

'It looks like you might have gotten what you wished for,' he whispered to her. 'My workload has just halved.'

Helen pulled an exaggerated smile.

'He's requesting to talk to you right now. He's on line twelve in your office.'

He gave his wife a pleading look, coupled with a shrug.

'Go on!' she hissed, ushering him away. 'You can't leave the world waiting for Kevin Farley.'

He offered her another apologetic smile, kissed Melissa on the forehead, then leaned in and kissed his wife on her lips. 'I won't be long, I promise.'

Helen nodded. 'I'll see you tomorrow sometime then,' she replied with just the right touch of sarcastic frost in her voice. She watched as he jumped out of his seat and left the room.

~~~~

'Kevin… Praise to Allah, you're a sight for sore eyes!' Youssef shouted as the image of a cold and dishevelled Kevin Farley flickered onto the monitor.

'Jesus, man, I'm gone for less than a month and literally the whole world goes to shit!' His smile faded, and Youssef could see desperation in his cold eyes. 'How are you, man? It's good to see your face again, even if it is the ugly one that I know and love.' Kevin would always squeeze a joke into any situation. If he wasn't joking, then you knew you were in trouble. 'In all seriousness though, what's the damage?'

Youssef's face fell from the smile he'd been wearing into the deep-set frown it was accustomed to these days. Kevin also had the ability to do that to a person. 'As an estimation, from a potential ten billion people on Earth, we think we've lost somewhere between forty and sixty percent. We can't get precise records yet because everything is crazy.'

A moment of silence passed between the two men. It was Kevin who broke it. 'Jesus. Four billion people, gone, just like that?'

'It looks that way. We've no way of knowing for sure. Communications are still sketchy, even in the areas we know haven't been affected.'

'Word on the street is that it was The Quest that did it,' Kevin stated. Even though he already knew it was, Youssef knew that he needed to hear it from the one man he could believe it from.

He dropped his head and averted his eyes before he could answer. 'Yeah. It was them.'

'Have they been in contact yet? You know, regarding a meeting?'

'Only to say that they want one. To tell you the truth, when Amanda told me we had a communiqué, I was hoping it was them.'

'Well, I'm sorry to disappoint you with, you know… just being alive,' he joked, breaking another pained smile. 'Is there any way of us getting hold of *them*? Don't they hole themselves up in a castle in Bonnie Scotland somewhere?'

'Yeah,' Youssef replied. 'But our resources are so dilapidated, we've got no way of tracing them back to their origin.'

'Youssef, I'm on my way up. We need to get together on this. Between us, I don't think I would be wrong in saying that we're the highest-ranking officers in the Alliance, God help us.' He shook his head, the smile on his face remaining steadfast. 'I'll be there in ten minutes.' Kevin looked like he was about to get up when an arm appeared on the monitor and rested on his shoulder. Youssef heard a voice talking off camera.

'You need to rest, you have hypothermia, and you also have malnutrition.' The disembodied Germanic voice off the monitor spoke softly, but assuredly.

He watched as Kevin, ever the hothead, grabbed the arm and held it. 'I'm required on OP One, Doc. I'm going whether you like it or not.'

As the doctor held his ground, Youssef smiled to himself. *That sounds like Hausen! This is going to be one hell of a stand-off.*

'I'm fully aware of who you are and what rank you have, but I'm your doctor, and I have the authority to override any order, or command, that you make if I feel there is a legitimate medical reason to do so. I will not hesitate to exercise this.'

Youssef watched as his friend staggered to his feet; his face like thunder. 'Look, doctor, this is a matter of global security, and I…'

'I don't care about global security, sir, I care about my patients getting the correct…'

'Guys, guys. Stop,' Youssef shouted into the screen. 'Listen, Kevin, Doctor Hausen is right. You get some rest, there's nothing we can do until they contact us anyway. I promise I'll let you know if anything happens. You're no good to anyone dead.'

Kevin's face was a picture. He had climbed up the ladder in the Earth Alliance to Director of Operations solely because he hated being told what to do.

'You get twelve hours of uninterrupted sleep, some food and liquids, and I'll call you later,' he commanded. 'Oh, and just one more thing before you go. What's the state of your team there?'

'Full compliment. Why?'

'Just in case we need some operational personnel.'

Kevin smiled into the monitor and winked. 'They're standing ready and waiting orders.'

As the screen went blank, Youssef saw it as an opportunity to go back and spend the rest of the evening with his family. He checked in with Amanda first to see if The Quest had been in touch. She informed him that there had been no further communications. Thankful for that news, he went home.

## 8.

CARRIE MILLWOOD WAS alone in her office in the lower chambers. She was reviewing the footage of what everyone had come to call 'The Event.' The smile she was wearing was cold as the room was, and sad. She knew that the others would be there soon. It was almost time to finish what they had started. The task they had been working on for nearly twenty years. The ultimate sacrifice to true science. They were about to risk everything for the Higgs Storm.

When Carrie left the Earth Alliance, taking the others with her, she had an idea. The idea had taken root after she'd watched Gloria die. She did not crave power, nor did she have radical idealism, she was a pure scientist.

Her idea had been to start again. To reboot.

She'd known back then that it would involve sacrifice, both personal and public, but the science of it was far too alluring for her to let it go. She had begun small. She started stealing equipment from the lab. Little by little, she accrued the raw materials to build her own rough Hadron Collider. It was then that she began to recruit other, like-minded, scientists in her team to her own way of thinking. The one scientist she had really wanted, even needed, had resisted her; he had outright refused to join her.

Youssef Haseem.

Without him, it had been slow going. He had an almost unnatural ability to traverse problematic situations and come to logical conclusions that had been overlooked.

Unperturbed, they persisted without him, eventually coming to fantastical conclusions on their own. The best conclusion was the invention of a containment field that could not only harness the power of the Higgs Storm, but could also preserve it.

Primarily, they were looking to use it as an alternative fuel source, but after several costly failures, this idea was disregarded.

Then, unexpectedly, something occurred, something wonderful. A by-product of the by-product was revealed. They knew that the Higgs Storm was a devastating force that destroyed everything in its path, eradicating all life except. However, the scientists were dumbfounded when they discovered that, post exposure to the Storm, a secondary, and prolonged, exposure to the cultivated storm matter allowed life to grow, and at an expediential rate.

Theoretically, this would allow them to reboot the planet. To terraform Earth from scratch; to start again. Adam and Eve style.

Life that would normally take generations to evolve was emerging again in a matter of hours. Within a day, the cellar area of the mansion they had been squatting in, performing their experiments, was a veritable jungle. All it was waiting for was animal life to be introduced.

Carrie and her second in command, the brilliant Mary Kelly, released the funds they had embezzled from the EA and purchased Inverness Castle. They changed their organisation's name to The Quest, emphasizing their quest towards a utopian society, under one rule... theirs.

They then began to recruit.

It was easier than they thought it would be. A few promises of a better life here, a glimpse of a utopian Earth there, and the public were all but ready to throw funds and resources at them. Their numbers swelled, they redesigned the castle as a technological fortress, and they devised their plans. It was Mary's idea to explore beneath the castle, and they were glad they did. It was a labyrinth of caves down there. Some with vast openings, some with freshwater lakes. The only thing that was missing was a natural light source, but they didn't need it. The Higgs Storm produced all the power they required to build their farm.

They began to harvest and store every seed they could find from across the globe before they released the Storm within the confines of their newly built laboratory. It did exactly what it was supposed to do. They then exposed the area to the secondary storm particles, and life occurred. Before long, another world, a better world, was emerging. New, fresh, and healthy within their subterranean compound.

When it was safe, they planted their seeds, and the produce grew.

They were now self-contained.

As it turned out, they were more than self-contained.

Within a year, they had more produce and resource beneath the castle than they knew what to do with. All the cards were in place for their master plan. The only thing they required was enough Higgs Storm to complete their reboot.

This had proven a slow process, involving sending thousands, possibly millions, of objects back in time and harvesting the Storm on every occasion. Their new containment process allowed them to store it cumulatively, and experiment after experiment was performed. Inadvertently, they discovered another piece of this never-ending jigsaw. The larger the object they sent back; the more Higgs Storm was produced. Not only that, but the further back they sent something increased the amount of Higgs Storm exponentially.

After nearly twenty years of hard work and sacrifice, they were finally seeing the fruits of their labours.

The Event.

Now, post Event, everything was within their grasp. Everything they had ever desired. All they needed was but one year away.

Mary Kelly entered the office. 'Carrie are you ready?' she asked.

Carrie turned to witness her best friend's entrance into the darkened room. Mary was stunning. She stood a little over five-foot and had raven hair that spilled just passed her shoulders. She also had a brilliant mind. She smiled at the newcomer. Before answering she spared a glance towards the monitor readouts on her desk. 'I am! Are you prepared for your meeting with the EA?'

'I am,' Mary mimicked. 'I've already been magnetically tagged, so straight after my meeting, I'll rendezvous with you. The next time we see each other, we'll be in another time.' She held her arms out.

The women embraced.

'Are the others ready?' Carrie asked, fighting back tears.

'Yes. Everything's set. They're just awaiting instruction.'

'You know what you're going to say to the EA don't you? One year is all they have. You can even let them know the overall plan, there's nothing they can do to prevent it anyway.'

'I will,' Mary smiled.

'Good. Then I'll see you back there. Godspeed, Mary.'

## 9.

YOUSSEF'S ALARM WAS screaming in the darkness of the room. It was a loud, static noise, specifically designed to alert you as soon as it went off and not allow you to go back to sleep.

'Can you turn that thing off?' Helen complained from her side of the bed.

He was awake now, fully alert, as his legs swung out of the bed. 'You know I can't. I'm in charge, remember,' he mumbled as he reached an arm over to turn the screaming off. He stretched and yawned, wrapping a housecoat around him, and made his way out of the bedroom. He closed the door, wanting his wife to catch a few more hours of sleep and not be disturbed by his business, and sat on the chair before a large monitor that was flashing red. He paused for a moment, collecting his thoughts, before clicking the button. His own image flashed up on the screen, scaring him a little. He hadn't noticed that he was looking so rough. There hadn't been much time to groom himself over the last few days. Shaking his head, he clicked an icon, and a young man's image appeared. 'Thomas, you sent an alarm. What's happening?' he asked, stifling a yawn.

The man's face was pale. 'Sir, The Quest have been in touch. They're going to visit us at ten GMT. Today!'

'What? Today? Shit!' Youssef blushed slightly at his cuss. He disliked swearing, especially in front of his subordinates, but on reflection, he thought that this news warranted a good curse.

'What was the message? Did it give any details?'

'No, sir,' Thomas replied. 'All it said was *Prepare to accept a visit from Mary Kelly, ten a.m. GMT, to Orbital Platform One. She will teleport on and teleport off when she is done.* That's the sum total of the message, sir.'

'OK! Listen, Thomas, while I'm preparing for this meeting, I need you to get in touch with Kevin Farley. I know he isn't in good shape at the moment, but I'm going to need him here for this. If

Doctor Hausen gives you any grief, tell him to speak to me. Have you got that?'

'Yes, sir, speak to you. Got it.'

'If he keeps on shouting, tell him that he can come too if he wants. Thank you, Thomas.' He clicked the monitor off and sighed. There would be no going back to sleep now.

Helen walked into the room. 'Youssef, it's three in the morning. What's so important?' she asked.

He closed his eyes and said a small prayer under his breath. 'They're dictating the terms of our meeting to us now,' he replied, shaking his head and looking up at the ceiling. 'I really don't know how much more of this I can take. I don't have time to go back to sleep now.'

His wife allowed the blanket she was covering herself with to slip, surprising him with her nakedness. 'In that case, let's see if there's anything I can do to take your mind off it for a while. You never know, it might make you sleepy too,' she whispered.

For the first time in, he didn't know how long, his grin was one-hundred-percent genuine.

## 10.

THE WOMEN WERE gathered in one of the subterranean rooms beneath Inverness Castle. They were all dressed in shabby clothing, attire that wouldn't have looked out of place in the poorer, lower class Victorian areas.

'Today is a historic day in many ways,' Carrie addressed the nine women gathered before her. 'Today, we embark on the final stage of our plans. Today go back in time. We will be gone for exactly twelve months. It will not be a comfortable year by any stretch of the imagination. We have chosen somewhere where ten women can easily slip into society, and slip out again, without causing many, if any, questions. For this reason, we have chosen to travel back four hundred years, to Victorian England. London to be exact. We will live the lives of poor women, doing manual labours to earn our crust.'

Everyone in the room shuffled a little, none of them comfortable with this news.

'For our ultimate goal to reach fruition, we computed that ten of us, going back four hundred years, will produce the right amount of Higgs Storm that will be required to follow through our plans. We will each be tracked by magnetic tagging. This tag will emit quantum signals, allowing our colleagues, in this time, to follow our movements. It will be this device that will enable them to recall us at the allotted time.'

There was a look of relief on the women's faces.

'Ladies, I will see you in London, at the rendezvous.'

A cheer rose from everyone present, including the support team who would be manning the Hadron Collider that was pivotal to their plan.

Mary Kelly was present to see them off. With a smile on her face, she addressed the man working the collider. 'Brian would it be OK if I activated the Collider?' she asked.

He nodded and stepped away from the control panel.

Carrie saw what was happening and smiled.

'OK,' Mary shouted over the room. 'Who's first?'

The six leaders of The Quest had been natural choices to go, the other four had been selected for security purposes. They were women trained as able bodyguards; they knew it was going to be tough in, the male dominated, Victorian London, but they were up for the fight.

Martha Tabram stepped forward. She was a well-built woman with a stern nature. She had volunteered to go first to secure the rendezvous location. To make sure there were no witnesses to the event of their arrival, or at least no surviving witnesses. As she climbed onto the track of the Collider, Mary gave her a hug. 'Good luck, Martha,' she whispered before stepping back to the control panel. A glass shield lowered over the woman, and a mechanical syringe implanted a very small chip into her stomach. She flinched a little as it pierced her skin. Everyone present smiled at this, Martha was supposed to be the tough one.

Mary smiled again as the syringe left the collider before activating the quantum transcoder. Once the transcoder was live, the chip would enter the carriers blood stream. She thought this was a genius invention, mostly because it was hers. It was designed to hide within the body, avoiding any form of detection, but it would also allow the controllers, in the present, to locate the carrier with ease.

She pressed the *engage* button and pushed the lever to release the regular hydrogen, and the Higgs-Boson modified hydrogen. As she did, there was a roar that filled the room. The collider began to spin.

All eyes were on Martha as her hair began to blow in the wind within the chamber.

With the exception of the collider, the room was otherwise silent, as Martha became bathed in a purple glow. She opened her mouth, and a small, muffled scream, or prayer, was heard before she disappeared in a bright purple flash. The light then drew back into a single, brilliant pinprick of purple.

The expected cloud appeared within the chamber. A flickering yellow film enveloped it, encasing the purple smoke within its bubble. The sound of a vacuum became prevalent as the magnetic field holding the storm was sucked into the specially designed storage containers.

# TimeRipper

The calculations had been made, checked, and then checked again. Ten women, sent back four hundred years, for a one year duration, and then returned, would generate enough Higgs Storm to complete their plan. The rebooting of the remaining sixty percent of the Earth's surface.

No one moved, no one even dared to breathe. The wait for the confirmation felt like an eternity.

'I have it,' Mary shouted, suddenly. 'I've got the signal, it's her. She's arrived safely in eighteen eighty-eight!'

The room erupted into cheers and applause.

'OK, who's next?' Mary shouted above the cacophony.

## **PART 3**

### 1.

<u>London, 1888</u>

IT WAS THREE o'clock in the morning, and it was raining. Spitalfields, for once, was quiet, mostly because it was cold and wet. The few bodies lying in the grounds of Christ Church were huddled together. Poor souls trying to locate the illusive warmth and safety that maybe, just maybe get them through the night. Many of them, children included, were drunk. They were so drunk that nothing in this world could have woken them. It was a means to an end. The large corner windows of The Ten Bells pub were dark, but that didn't mean nobody was inside. Even though it was a damp, cold, Wednesday morning, there would still be stragglers and revellers who refused to give up the ghost of the last weekend, or who were starting early for the next one; or even those who would just never stop the party. Either way, when the strange wind came and the eerie purple light illuminated the dirty street, there were few witnesses to the event.

In fact, there were only three.

Under a bench on the opposite side of the road to the pub lay the first witness. He might have been a young man, or a middle-aged man, he may even have been an old man. No one, not even those who might have taking the time to notice him, would have been able to tell. His filthy, multilayers of clothing, and the long scruffy hair hanging over his bearded face, gave him an ageless appearance. He could have been anything from seventeen to seventy. He had been hanging around this area for the last two weeks. During the day, the more respectable residents, of which there were few, had in passing been complaining about his smell and the rude behaviour towards anyone who accosted him. As this was Whitechapel, that didn't cause much controversy, in fact, he was part of the majority in this multi-national, but impoverished, area of the city.

Tonight, due to the inclement weather and the fact that three out of the five streetlamps were out of commission, he had chosen to lie in the shadows, hidden beneath the bench, out of the view of any passers-by.

Just the way he wanted it.

The second witness was a man who was pretending to be a drunken reveller from The Ten Bells pub. He was smartly dressed, not expensively, but smartly. He had the look of a man who worked with his hands. There was dirt on his face and in his moustache, and a smell of oil, sweat, and booze about him. He was drinking with a gang of local workers who had just been paid off on a job they had completed, and had decided that, rather than go home to their families, they should spend a little of their surprise bonus in The Bells. This man had been quietly switching most of his beverages, so he hadn't been supping half of what his colleagues had.

He was a reporter; he was hoping to get a scoop on the unethical practices of a local firm of engineers. The very engineers he was drinking with now. For the moment, he'd had enough of the smoky, sweaty, atmosphere inside the pub and had stepped outside to get some fresh air. In reality, he had wanted to make notes on some of his overheard conversations.

The third and final witness was also in hiding; purposefully keeping out of the way of any prying eyes. He was a large man with a thick, black handlebar moustache. There was an eastern European look about him; his dark eyes were smouldering, and his pallid complexion was suited to the shadows. In one of his hands was a cutthroat razor, a sharp one. As a barber, it was a tool of his trade, and he had always prided himself on the quality of his blades. The knuckles of the hand that held it were swollen and bloody. He had recently been dealing his woman some home correction, perhaps with a little too much vigour. His entire body, from his feet to his teeth, was trembling, but his bright, piercing, eyes never once wavered from the doors of The Ten Bells pub.

All three of these men witnessed something strange that night in eighteen-eighty-eight, something that only two of them would survive.

## D E McCluskey

~~~~

A strong wind whipped from out of nowhere. It blew the driving rain into the doorway of The Ten Bells pub, soaking Michael Stratton, the undercover reporter for The Star newspaper, to the skin in an instant. In the shock of his soaking, he dropped the notepad he had been writing on into a muddy puddle. He cursed as he bent to pick it up. As he shook the dirty water off his expensive paper, he noticed something rather odd in the centre of the deserted road. It was a light, an unnatural, purple glow beneath one of the streetlamps, one of the ones not working. The very air around him began to pulse, he could feel it in his chest, and his throat, as the purple phenomenon began to expand.

The glow also bathed the man beneath the bench in its strange light, giving up his location to anyone with a mind to look. Although, given what was happening in the middle of the road, there wouldn't have been anyone watching *him* anyway. He covered his eyes as the glare from the light concentrated. He then covered his ears as the pulse intensified.

The third man dropped his razorblade, the swollen wounds of his hand forgotten, as he gawped at the growing light. He looked like he wanted to bolt, to run from the strangeness of what was happening, but for some reason, he didn't. His body swayed, but his feet remained rooted to the spot. His jaw mimicked his eyes, as if in competition to see which could open wider.

The light continued to grow, and the wind intensified as it whipped and whirled into a localised mini tornado, right there, in the centre of London.

A purple flash, at least ten times brighter than any of the dull and dirty streetlamps, took all three men by surprise. It burned for a brief moment before it began to ebb, taking the wind and the rain with it. All three men removed their protective hands from their faces and stared in wonder as they witnessed the bizarre sight.

There was a woman standing in the middle of the road.

All three of them would have sworn oaths, there and then, that the woman had *not* been there prior to the flash.

Of this fact, Michael Stratton was certain. The newcomer was standing in the centre of the road where there was no shelter from the brief storm, but she was dry. He noted that she was dressed in the style of the day, but there was something strange about her attire. To him, it looked like she was trying to fit in, like the style was somehow forced. There was also a bewildered look about her. She staggered a little, looking around the street as if it was the first time she had ever seen the city.

Slowly, he edged out of the doorway, unsure whether to approach her or not.

The man under the bench was attempting to free himself, also to investigate the apparition.

The man hiding in the shadows slid further back into the darkness, allowing it to envelope him. He attempted to become one with the dirty wall he was leaning against, to become an unseen shadow, an unknown witness to these strange events.

'Hello!' Michael shouted towards the confused woman. 'Hello there. Are you OK?' He held out his hands to her as he made his way into the centre of the road. The woman looked at him as if it had been him who'd appeared from nowhere.

'Do you know where you are?' There was a slight Irish lilt to his voice. 'Have you been drinking, sweetheart?'

The woman continued to look around her, as if she was looking for someone or something. 'What year is this?' she asked, slowly.

Michael cocked his head and offered her a crooked grin. 'Darlin', you must have had a skin full tonight. Here, let me help you. It's not safe for a lady to be out in these streets on her own. Not at this time of night, anyway.'

He held out his hands again. The two other witnesses watched the encounter with suspicion. The woman tentatively accepted Michael's offered gesture. As they touched, a small, purple electric arc pass from her hand to his. Unperturbed, he gripped her hand and gently brought her towards him.

'What year is this?' the woman asked again.

Michael flashed her a reassuring smile. 'It eighteen eighty-eight, darlin'. July twenty-first, eighteen eighty-eight.'

Her face lightened at this news, and a smile took over her features. 'Good,' she said. Then, from within the folds of her dress, she produced a small metal device. She pressed a button on it that unleashed a thin metal blade. Before he knew what was happening, Michael was clutching his throat. Ironically, he was still smiling as he pulled his hand away and the hot, thick, claret poured from the deep gash across his neck. He looked at his hands. His wide eyes were confused at the blood that covered them. His gaze then shifted towards the woman moments before he fell, hard, onto the cobbles in the road.

The man under the bench watched as the reporter fell. He was now struggling to get up again.

The man in the shadows held his breath and stayed where he was, as still as a statue.

As Michael Stratton died, the woman swooped him up and carried his lifeless corpse over her back, making her way up Spitalfields with the cadaver dripping in the receding rain.

She was long gone before the man could free himself from beneath the bench, and before the man in the shadows slinked off into the dark, wet July night.

19.

<u>Inverness Castle. 2288</u>

EVERYONE WAS SPURRED on by Martha's success. Mary Kelly smiled as she shouted, 'Who's next?'

A tall, thin woman stepped up. 'I'm next,' she said.

'Liz,' she smiled. 'Step right in.'

The woman did as instructed, and the process began again.

When all nine of them had been sent back to July, eighteen-eighty-eight, Mary stepped away from the console. She turned to Brian who was standing off to one side. 'Are you ready to send me to OP One?' she asked.

He smiled and nodded back at her. 'Co-ordinates have been entered. Are you ready now?'

She walked over to the teleportation pod in the corner of the room and climbed in. 'No time like the present, is there?' she laughed at her own joke. 'The sooner I get this done, the sooner I can get to London. Do it,' she commanded.

Brian pressed the buttons and pushed the lever. Instantaneously, Mary dissolved into a purple flash before his eyes.

~~~~

Teleportation did not leave any residue, no one knew why.

~~~~

At nine-fifty-five a.m. on Orbital Platform One, Youssef was pacing the floor in the teleportation room. He checked his wrist device almost every fifteen seconds. Kevin Farley and Dr Hausen had arrived half an hour earlier and had been briefed on the recent events. They agreed that they would allow whoever it was coming to do the majority of the talking. They would then re-group after the meeting to talk strategy.

At the stroke of ten, an alarm cried out, informing them of an impending teleportation.

*This is it,* he thought as the EA personnel manning the teleporter boosted the containment field around the pod.

'Sir, you do know that we could contain her almost indefinitely within this containment field,' the officer advised him.

'I know, but what would they do if we took one of them prisoner? We have to remember that we're the ones on the back foot here. Right now, they hold all the cards.'

Reluctantly, the operator nodded and watched as the diminutive figure of Mary Kelly appeared within the teleportation pod.

Youssef recognised her immediately. She was the once shy, but absolutely brilliant, research assistant who had worked the lab with Carrie Millwood.

It was obvious that she didn't recognise him.

As she stepped out of the pod, a decontamination wave passed over her, blowing her hair and her clothes in its strong wake. Although she did not recognise Youssef personally, she did recognise his authority within the room. She walked over to him and offered her hand. 'Hello, my name is Mary Kelly. I'm a representative for The Quest. May we go somewhere private to chat?'

'Of course,' he replied shaking her hand. 'My name is Youssef Haseem. I believe we've met before. We worked together in an Earth Alliance lab many years ago.'

She showed no interest in renewing old acquaintances.

'I've taken the liberty of booking a meeting room for us to chat in. I have also invited my colleagues, Kevin Farley and Doctor Hausen, I feel they should be included in what we will be discussing.'

'I've no problem with that,' she shrugged. 'If we may convene then, Mr Haseem.'

As they entered the meeting room, Kevin and Dr Hausen stood to greet their guest. Youssef watched Kevin's eyes follow her around the table. He couldn't disguise the look of disgust on his face as Youssef introduced her. Dr Hausen curtly nodded to their guest before sitting down.

Mary sat facing the three men. The room had been designed to intimidate her, psychologically, to make her feel like she was under scrutiny.

It didn't work.

The moment she sat; she took control of the meeting.

'Mr Haseem, I'm here to expedite the standing down of the Earth Alliance, and to begin the transfer of power, and resources over to The Quest. You have no leverage here, you have no counter offers, you simply have no option.'

Kevin's face went red. 'Excuse me young lady…' The irony on the word 'lady' wasn't missed on anyone present. 'Do not forget that you're stood on our Orbital Platform. You're here alone. I feel that it's you who has no leverage.'

She turned to face him, cocking her head, and smiling. It was a patronising smile, in ever Youssef had seen one. 'If anything were to happen to me while I'm here, there would be dire consequences to the food store that we have. The same one that the remaining population currently rely on.' As she spoke, she offered another condescending smile towards Kevin. Youssef didn't believe it was possible, but he watched his colleague's face grow redder.

'Listen, no one is threatening anyone here,' Youssef interrupted, trying to placate both parties. 'What we want is to come to an arrangement.'

'I'll stop you there, if I may,' Mary said shaking her head, her attention back on Youssef. 'There's no arrangement to be made. I'm here to inform you that you have exactly one year, to the day, to have abandoned these orbital platforms. You will hand over all scientific licence, all research licences, and all physical assets that Earth Alliance currently hold to The Quest. None of this is negotiable.'

'Now hold on a minute,' Kevin shouted again. 'You expect us to just get up and…'

'*And* to have informed the rest of the population of Earth that you plan to disband as an organisation and will join The Quest in making this planet a better place to live on,' she continued, as if Kevin had not even spoken.

He jumped out of his seat and made a grab at her. Youssef jumped too, matching his colleague's speed. He just about managed to grab Kevin's arm, stopping him from striking their guest.

'The threat of physical violence does not scare me, gentlemen. I can teleport out of this room at any given time, but I'm not finished here. You need to listen to this last part, very carefully.'

Both men sat back down. Dr Hausen listened raptly in the corner of the room.

'When we get back in one year, we will point our Higgs Storm turrets towards these platforms. They will all be destroyed. If you haven't complied with our orders, and deserted them, then you will be destroyed with them. We will then disable a further twenty percent of the Earth's surface, and another ten percent one month later.'

The three men were silent.

'You must believe that this is not a bluff. We've already destroyed forty percent …' she cocked her head towards the three men, '…on a whim! So please, believe me that we will do it. You *will* step down.'

'What's to stop you crazy bastards from doing it anyway, even if we do step down?' Kevin asked, incensed again at how this meeting was shaping.

Their guest turned calmly and shook her head. 'We have given you no reassurances, Mr Farley. If we do decide to do it, then please believe me, we *will* do it. There'll be nothing that you, or any other power on this planet, can do to stop us.'

'If you wanted to do it, then why didn't you just do it on the first strike?' Youssef asked.

Mary Kelly blushed, only slightly, but undeniably, and she looked at him. *Your first tell*, he thought. *You were not ready for that question. There's something you're not telling us here.*

Youssef stood and offered his hand. 'Ms Kelly, thank you for your time. We'll be having considerable talks between our heads of departments, and I'm sure we'll be liaising with you quite a bit. Do we have any way of contacting you directly?'

She blushed again; however, it was more fleeting than the first one. This time he was watching for it.

She smiled; he noted that it looked forced. 'My representatives will be in touch with you, Mr Haseem. This will be the last time we communicate personally.' She shook his hand and gave curt nods to the other two men. Kevin ignored her but Dr Hausen stood and offered his hand. She took it, then pressed a series of buttons on a control on her inside wrist and promptly disappeared.

Kevin was on his feet within seconds of her departure. 'I can't believe you showed that bitch courtesy,' he snapped. 'We should have taken her the moment she stepped outside the pod.'

'Please, Kevin. Calm down. She was hiding something, and something big.'

Dr Hausen was smiling. 'You saw it too, didn't you? The twitches and shuffling. Her small tells. She was good, but she would never make a poker player.'

Kevin was looking at the two men as if they were mad. 'What are you talking about?' he asked.

'There's something else going on here. Ms Kelly made three big mistakes this morning, and I'm ready to find out what they are.' Youssef moved away from the table. 'Gentlemen, follow me.' He walked out of the office with a little smile on his face; Dr Hausen did the same.

Kevin followed, shaking his head.

## 20.

MARY MATERIALISED IN the laboratory beneath Inverness castle. Brian was waiting for her. 'Thank you, Brian. Can you now make the calculations to send me to my sisters? I just need to get changed.'

He smiled at her. 'Yes, ma'am, the calculations are ready and stored into the collider. I'm just waiting on you.'

She smiled back and slipped out the door. Ten minutes later, she emerged wearing her Victorian garb and stepped into the collider. Brian manipulated the controls and the protective shield was deployed. He then activated the Higgs-Boson particle accelerator, and Mary disappeared, four hundred years into the past.

Brian was left alone in the large subterranean laboratory. He sat for a while listening to the extractor fans do their work. When their work was done, and they shut down. Whistling, he powered down the Hadron Collider and left the room. As he flipped the large power switch, all the terminals in the room went dark. On closing the door, he produced a light lock from his pocket, pointed it at the entrance, and keyed in a code on the device.

The room was now light-locked for exactly one year.

## 21.

THE THREE SENIOR EA members hurried into the main control room of OP One. 'Amanda, give me some good news, please.' Youssef quirked as they ushered past her station, heading towards his meeting room.

Amanda spun on her chair to face them; she was wearing a neural interface adaptor and was reading data while talking to them. 'I don't know about any good news, sir, but we've gleaned *some* information from her visit. First, she was magnetically tagged, we got that reading as soon as she exited the pod. Unfortunately, the magnetic tagging stopped us from tracing her signal back to the source; without the correct encryption key that's difficult to do. But what has given her away, to a degree, is that she was flashing some kind of quantum signal. It didn't seem to be active within her, like what we would have expected. It was akin to her having been spending quite a bit of time around quantum flares.'

'So, she'd been tagged to allow them to be able to locate her physically, and she has been tinkering with quantum tags.' Youssef wrapped his arms around himself and put a finger over his mouth. 'Correct me if I'm wrong, but aren't they used for locating objects in time?'

'Yes, sir. Theoretically only. The time-travel experiments were closed after the accident with the Higgs Storm, so no more research was done on quantum tagging.'

'Do we have any knowledge of how they would deploy a quantum tag? Within the body, I mean.' Dr Hausen asked.

Youssef shook his head. 'Not off hand, doctor, but I'm sure if we did some digging in the data files, we could find something.'

'Do it,' Kevin ordered and then dragged the two men into Youssef's waiting room, slamming the door behind him. 'OK, you two, no more holding back. What's going on here, and why am I the only one who doesn't seem to know anything about it?'

'When we knew there was a representative of The Quest coming, we decided to scan her on entry, and on exit. We found it difficult due to the magnetic tagging she had, probably injected under the skin.' Dr Hausen explained. 'This means that someone wanted to be able to verify her location.'

'OK, so she was tagged, so what?' Kevin asked, sitting down and listening intently. 'We do that all the time.'

'Well, she also had a lot of quantum signal residue about her,' Youssef continued, 'Much like what we did with the apples and onions back in the day. This is another clue to what they're doing. Quantum signals are used to locate items in time, not space.'

'So, do you think they are planning on going back in time?'

Hausen shrugged. 'Maybe. At least some of them. She made her first mistake by telling us 'when they get back'. I think the leaders are going into hiding. Maybe somewhere in time.'

'Are they going to try to change the future? To wipe out the EA before they're even formed?' Kevin asked, the worry in his voice palpable.

Doctor Hausen shook his head. 'You have been watching too many old films,' he laughed. 'That's impossible. If I remember from the quantum lectures, back when we were studying time travel as a legitimate science, nature has its own paradoxical law. It will fight, tooth and nail, to keep the timeline correct. You're simply not allowed to change it.'

'So why go back then? There must be a reason. There're plenty of places to hide on our planet.'

'I'm wondering why they have the need to give us one year to stand down. A year is a long time, a lot can happen. It feels like they have no choice but to give us a year,' Youssef mused. 'There has to be a reason for it, and if there is, it'll probably be something, a hole that we can exploit.'

'Now you're talking my language. Exploitation is what I do best,' Kevin added, glad to be back in the conversation.

## 22.

<u>London: 1888</u>

LIFE IN THE PAST was hard, harder than any of them had envisioned. It had rained constantly since they'd arrived, and the streets of London were muddy, filthy and dank.

As were the people.

Carrie Millwood had gathered all ten of them together in a lodging she had taken, and paid, much to the astonishment of the landlord, in advance for a few months. She had made provisions for a limited amount of funds to be brought back with them, but it had proven difficult to obtain legitimate currency in twenty-two-eighty-eight that could be used in eighteen-eighty-eight. They had been careful not to obtain anything that would disturb nature's paradoxical laws and cause issue for their stay.

All ten of them had made the transition with ease. Only Martha had any issue on arrival, but it had been swiftly dealt with, as was her mission brief.

For the last fifteen days, they had lived a free and unmolested life.

'I've gathered you here today, as we now have to begin to integrate ourselves into this society. The start-up funding that we brought with us is almost depleted, most of it on lodgings and such. We must now insert ourselves as if we're natives. Each of you have been given back stories, where you have come from, distant family etc, and I hope that you've memorised these tales. It'll help you in getting jobs, making friends, and blending in.'

'Has anyone noticed anything strange while we've been here?' Mary Kelly asked.

'Apart from the fact that we're four hundred years out of time you mean?' Catherine Eddowes asked. A petite woman in her mid-thirties, she and Kelly had been the pioneers of the quantum tagging.

Everyone in the room laughed.

Mary smiled. 'No, I meant anything that may look out of the ordinary? Martha had to kill the man who witnessed her arrival. We need to be careful about killing people in this time, as we don't want to fall foul of the paradoxical laws. I wondered if there was anything happening in relation to this. She says that she didn't see any other witnesses.'

'I noticed a lot of the people just seem to be hanging around, not really doing much,' Mary Nichols spoke up. For some reason the women all called her Polly. 'They just seem to, I don't know, watch us. Mostly the men.'

'They'll be thinking we're prostitutes,' Mary replied. 'There's little employment for women in these times, and women on their own will almost always have to resort to selling themselves in some fashion. These men will be thinking that's what we are. We should, in no way, discourage this. It'll be a big part of our blending in.'

'We can't all stay in these lodgings together for much longer than we already have,' Carrie Millwood added, taking the meeting back. 'The landlord is already suspicious of ten women lodging together. He's insinuating that he's not running a brothel, and if he is, then he wants his cut.' The girls laughed at this little joke, even if there was more than a little nervousness about it. 'If Mary's theory regarding the paradoxical laws are correct, and we have no reason to believe any different, then no one from this time can kill us, but that doesn't mean that they cannot harm us. They can beat, rape, and dismember. I understand that I'm being a little theatrical, but I want to hit home that this is a dangerous time to be a woman. We need to keep on our toes.'

'If no one here can kill us…' A small voice arose from the back of the room, Rose Mylett stood forth. 'If no one from *this time* can kill us, then how did Martha go about killing the man who witnessed her arrival? Is it one rule for us and another one for them?'

Carrie didn't have an answer for this. 'I think we should get Liz to answer that one.' She gestured towards Elizabeth Stride to stand and address the meeting.

Liz was a tall woman, striking in appearance with her short cut blonde hair and piercing blue eyes. She stood before the meeting with confidence. 'Ladies,' she addressed them. 'All of this is theoretical.

But we believe that nature could not allow us to pass backwards in time if we could do anything to alter the timeline. It's that simple. We cannot kill our own great, great, great, grandmothers. It's my theory that Martha was able to kill the witness because nature had already earmarked him to die. That neither he, nor any lineage that he may have produced, had any bearing on the future. So, it's my understanding that if we keep our noses clean and we stay out of trouble for one year, then our colleagues, four hundred years in the future, will be able to get us back to where we belong.'

A murmur of consolidation passed among the women. The meeting had calmed a lot of nerves.

'So...' Carrie brought the focus back to her again, '...to reiterate why we're meeting here tonight. We have a long year ahead of us, but with a fantastic pay off at the end of it. You all know why we're doing this, and we all know what we must do. Starting tomorrow, we become fine upstanding members of this community. The Quest shall be fruitful, and The Quest shall be successful.'

There were cheers and claps as she stood down from her makeshift plinth.

~~~

The next day, the owner of the rented accommodation was watching as the ten women left their lodgings in Spitalfields Chambers, Whites Row, London, to look for work within the community. He had taken a special interest in these ladies, and to why there were ten of them living in the same room. At first, it titillated him to think of what they were up to in there, cooped up together for all hours of the day. It intrigued him so much that he took to spying on them for his own voyeuristic intentions.

The night before he had listened in to their strange conversation. *Para-what's-ical laws? Four hundred years in the future? That all sounds queer to me,* he thought watching them leave. It had confused, and worried, him all day, so he thought he'd let one of his drinking friends in on this little secret. Although he'd have to wait until he saw him again in the pub, enjoying one of those real ales he loved so much. He'd been missing for a few weeks, someone said they had seen him sleeping under a bench outside The Ten Bells pub, but he didn't think that Inspector Frank Abberline, of Scotland Yard, would be doing that. He'd be back supping ales soon, and he'd tell his story to him then.

Instead, John Downing went out that night and decided—mainly due to the strange nature of the conversation he'd overheard, and also due to the fact that the Millwood woman had paid him a few months rent in advance—that he was going to go out and get smashed. *You never know*, he thought, *I just might get lucky with a woman, or ten!* If his wife knew he was thinking something like that, she'd have made mincemeat out of him.

So, it was in this frame of mind that John Downing found himself in the Princess Alice pub in Whitechapel. He was a man well known for his loose tongue, with a reputation of spinning a yarn or two. Most of the time, his drinking companions took what he was telling them with a large pinch of salt.

'I'm telling you,' he shouted at the top of his drunken voice to anyone who was listening, which was quite a few. 'I've got my pick of *ten* of them, ten, I tell ya. All of them handsome women, and no mistake. I don't much care for their talk about coming from the future, or about para-bloody-oxicals or wot-not.' He paused then, thinking about what else he overheard. 'Or that thing they said about killing a bloke. He was from our time, they said. He just happened to witness one of them arriving, they said. I'll tell you, though, I'm going back to have my wicked way with at least two of them tonight. Yes, you heard me, *at least*, two of them,' he bragged.

A man was sitting in the corner of the room nursing a small tankard of ale, and occasionally blowing on the bruised and swollen knuckles of his hand. He listened, raptly, to every word John Downing was bragging. His brooding, dark face was known to the locals, although most people knew to leave him well alone. He was notorious for having a sharp tongue, and an even sharper temper.

Something about what Downing was saying struck a chord with him, something that had been bothering him for the last two weeks. A man killed by a woman who had arrived from somewhere strange.

Aaron Kosminski was going to have to have a talk with John Downing.

Kosminski waited until the bar was almost empty. He'd had to order another few drinks in order for the landlord not to throw him out, but eventually his patience paid off and he got what he wanted. 'Well that's me done. I'm off back to my harem,' the fool boasted to the mostly empty pub. Kosminski doubted the man even knew what a harem was. 'To take my pick of the ten,' the drunkard continued.

He watched as the man struggled to put his coat on without falling over. *He'll be lucky to make it home, never mind having his pick of ten women,* he thought. Downing put his hat on and staggered to the door. Kosminski finished his drink and stood up from his table. He shrugged on his coat and busied himself in his pockets, watching as Downing staggered to the doors and out into the dark street beyond. He followed him all the way home, keeping to the many shadows of the dimly lit streets. He didn't want to be seen, at least not until he needed to be.

John, it seemed, was very drunk, and Kosminski thought, a couple of times, that the man didn't know his way home. It took him almost twenty minutes to get to an address that was no more than a five-minute stroll from where they'd been.

Kosminski had an axe to grind; he had recently beaten his wife so bad that she had to be taken to hospital, when he found out that she had been having *liaisons* with an engineer who drank in The Ten Bells pub. He had gone there that night to confront him regarding these dalliances. He'd watched as the man had left the pub to have a smoke, and for some reason scribble some notes onto a pad of paper. He'd been ready to make his move then, when he witnessed the strange event of that night. The woman, or whatever it was, appearing from the purple glow. He watched as she'd killed his intended victim before disappearing, with his body, into the night.

Since then, he had been plagued with bad dreams.

There had been a recurring one where he watched while women were mutilated, ripped apart. A dark, mysterious figure was always lurking in the shadows. He'd seen each woman's face, and knew that the woman, the one who had appeared from nowhere that night, had been one of them.

He had obsessed over who, or what, it was that had appeared in the purple flashes, ever since. He had attempted to follow her that night, but if he was honest with himself, he'd been too scared, and had allowed himself to lose her in the dimly lit streets. Now, it appeared, he had another chance to find out where she was. All the talk he'd overheard about 'four hundred years in the future' had excited him. It was all beginning to make sense.

'If you open your mind to new experiences, then even the most improbable situations can be explained.' This was his own saying, he knew he was not ever going to win any awards for it, but he liked it.

As he watched John Downing let himself into a dark house in Spitalfields, a strange feeling overwhelmed him. He was scared, that much he had already admitted, but he was excited too. He could also feel rage building up inside him. A rage that was fuelled by embarrassment that he could allow dreams, and dreams of women of all creatures, frighten him. He checked his jacket pockets and felt the reassuring weight of his razorblade nestled inside.

He watched as a light in one of the rooms flickered to life, and waited until the noises, the bangs of John obviously falling over inside the house, receded, and all was quiet again.

He then made his move.

He crept his way to the house, wincing a little as the fingers of his injured hand wrapped around the handle of his blade. 'Someone is going to pay for making me feel like this,' he whispered. A drool of saliva dripped, unnoticed, from his mouth, dribbling over the front of his dark coat. *The back door will be the best way in,* he thought logically, before entering the dark alleyway that ran the length of the side of the house. There was a light on the first floor, and from the half open window he could hear talking.

The voices were, unmistakably, female.

He needed to get closer.

There was a shaky metal staircase leading to a wooden door where the talking, and now laughing, was coming from. Slowly, careful to make as little noise as he could, he climbed up the ladder and peered through the dirty window. From his vantage point, he could see a gathering of women inside. Thankfully, due to the room being lit, he knew that none of them would be able to see him.

Suddenly his breath caught in his chest.

She was there! The woman who had appeared from nowhere and killed the man he was supposed to kill. The woman who had mocked him in his dreams, and the one he had marked for death.

*No, not a woman*, he thought. *A witch!*

Kosminski licked his lips. His newfound hatred of women since his wife's infidelity filled him with homicidal rage. He enjoyed the pain that screamed from his fingers as he wrapped them tightly around the handle of the shaving instrument in his pocket. He attempted to extract the weapon, but it got stuck in the fabric of his overcoat. He tutted in frustration as he tugged, attempting to free it. Sweat was building on his brow as he looked into the room. They were *all* there, every woman he'd dreamed about for the last few nights, they were all sat in this room, mere feet away from him, and his blade.

*Am I the killer from my dream?* he thought, dribbling again. *Am I going to rip each of these women?* His breathing became rapid, and he smiled at the delightful tingle that was tickling his crotch.

'You there!' The shout came from nowhere. Or maybe it was everywhere. 'What are you doing up there, man? Get down at once.'

It was strange to feel the the blood drain from his face, and he was disappointed as the tingle in his crotch disappeared.

'You do know it's wrong to spy on people in their own homes, don't you?' the disembodied voice shouted again.

Kosminski scanned the darkness, searching for the source of the voice. He could just about make out the silhouette of someone approaching from the alleyway he'd used just moments ago. He could tell that the man was wearing a dark uniform. *A policeman*, he spat in his head. Panic rose in his stomach, as he looked for an escape route. He jumped down the other side of the staircase and ran along the other side of the alley in the opposite direction of the approaching lawman.

~~~~

The policeman's official report stated a man, sporting a thick moustache and a cape with a red trim, jumped with 'supernatural agility' to evade capture.

23.

Orbital Platform One. 2088

TWO WEEKS HAD passed, and Earth had descended into chaos. Massive movements of migrants, survivors from the less habitable areas, had begun to move into the habitable areas. Borders between countries no longer existed. No one knew who, if anyone, was in charge. Large swathes of the populace were actively refusing help and guidance from the remnants of the EA. Others were embracing them as if they were the only ones who could help them to stave off further attacks from The Quest.

The EA had been trying incessantly to contact The Quest. They still needed answers as to their reasons why they had done what they did, and why they wanted the world to start again. All efforts had failed. Every known member of the organisation had gone dark. The only reminder to the populace of their demands was a replay of their transmission on all communication channels, twice a day, every day.

Youssef had resumed full control of the remaining EA personnel and was acting as commander in chief. He did this with the support of Kevin Farley and Dr Hausen. He busied himself putting forth plans to attempt unification of the remaining countries. It was consuming most of his time. *Too much of my time,* he thought.

Kevin had been working with the scientific departments. He knew he was out of his depth, he was no scientist, but he was an excellent motivator, and was helping them devise an understanding as to how The Quest had disappeared into the past, and where they could have gone.

Dr Hausen was spending most of his time on the planet, co-ordinating rescue aid missions with the migrant populace.

The thought had occurred to Youssef that this might have been what The Quest wanted. To use divide and conquer tactics. But what they could not have taken into account was the organisational skills of him and his teams. Things were happening, and for the first time in what felt like a long time, they required very little of his time. This gave him space to devote himself to his family, and the scientific element that he was so good at.

'Cut off the head and the body withers,' was the only advice he could offer to the table, of the best scientists the EA had left to offer, in a meeting room on Orbital Platform One. 'We need to focus all of our efforts towards blocking the return of the leaders from wherever, and whenever, they are,' he offered. 'So, we need ideas on how we can do this.'

Everyone around the table was quiet.

'What?' he asked, sensing something was afoot with this normally unruly bunch.

'Well,' one of the scientists replied. 'We think we might have an idea why they have gone back in time. Now, it's only a theory, and it doesn't get us much closer to where, or when, they are, but it seems like a start.' The scientist was young, but already she was renowned within the EA for her wild theories, theories that were, usually, not far off the mark.

'OK, Jacqueline, please give me your theory. At this moment, I'll take anything I can get.'

The young Hispanic woman stood up. She was in her early thirties but looked younger than her years. She fixed her uniform, pushed her long, dark hair behind her ear before clearing her throat. 'Thank you, sir.' She spoke with the confidence of someone who wasn't as nervous as she looked. 'Well, I haven't had time to prepare a full presentation, and I haven't done a full research document to allow you to see my work yet, but here goes.'

Youssef was impressed with her assurance.

'We, that is my team and I, were thinking about the theory behind the Higgs Storm, the element that we know was responsible for the recent atrocities. We were thinking about how long they must have been storing the Storm to be able to render forty percent of the Earth's surface uninhabitable. We did a few small experiments of our own, after blowing the dust off the time travel research.'

This caught his attention straight away.

'We thought of measuring the amount of Higgs Storm that was produced when sending an apple back fifteen minutes, then an hour, then a day, then a month. We found that the bi-product increased the further back in time it went.'

Youssef was silent as he listened to what Jacqueline had to say.

'We sent a marrow back ten minutes, then an hour and then a day. We had marrows lying around all over the place. Anyway, we found that the larger the mass, and the further back it went, the more Storm was produced.'

'That's important work,' he interrupted. 'So, if a one-hundred-and fifty-pound woman went back, say one-hundred years? Then...'

'We did the calculation, sir.' It was her turn to interrupt. 'Ten of them would have had to go back nearly eight-hundred years to create enough Storm to devastate the remainder of the Earth's surface.'

He nodded, making the mental calculations himself.

'This is all theoretical anyway. We have no idea about containment fields, storage facilities, or how they can stop the decay in the Storm. There's still a million questions unanswered,' she replied.

Youssef was not enamoured with this. 'Life would be considerably intolerable for someone of our time to go back that far. Even the hardiest of person,' he mused.

'Any earlier and they would only have enough Storm to destroy maybe twenty percent. That's a long way off from their threat of the full sixty,' another of the scientists in the room offered.

'Maybe it's a bluff! Maybe they think that the *threat* of the full sixty percent is enough,' another scientist at the table put forward.

Youssef pulled a face. 'I don't know. I got the impression from Kelly that they were not messing about. If they had the potential to do that amount of damage right now, then why would they go back in time for a year?'

The room went silent.

The same scientist who put forward the question about the bluff asked another. 'Did you report that they threatened to turn their Higgs Storm turrets towards these Orbital Platforms on their return?'

'Yes,' Youssef answered, almost snapping at the scientist. 'We have to stay focused here team, we can't be going over old ground.'

'Well then, the only question that is left to be answered is: how are they planning on returning?'

He regarded the man asking the question. His face was blank, devoid of any emotion. Then slowly it changed into a mask of wonder. 'The quantum residue,' he whispered. 'Why else would they need a quantum signal? They would need to track their movements if they were going to attempt to bring them back?'

'That's so simple. If the event of pulling something, or someone back to the future, so to speak, caused the same amount of Higgs Storm then they'd have doubled their stores.' Jacqueline was speaking aloud, but it was obvious to everyone in the room that she was really speaking to herself. 'And if they went back for a prolonged amount of time, for example, one year, then that would add to their tally also.'

'That has to be what they're doing,' Youssef said, standing up. 'We need to get some research into bringing objects back from time. We'll need magnetic tagging, and quantum tagging too. Let's get onto this, people! Time, as they say, is of the essence.'

As the other scientists hurried out of the meeting room, buzzing with excitement and mumbling to each other, Youssef pressed a button on the desk. 'Amanda, I'm going to need to talk to Farley and Hausen, immediately.'

## 24.

London: 1888

*Jesus, this place is nothing to write home about*, Martha Tabram thought as she ambled along the dark, dirty streets of Whitechapel. She'd been out all day looking for gainful employment, but opportunities for a single woman were scarce. She'd approached most of the barrow men in Spitalfields market and been systematically knocked back by every one of them.

'Sorry, darlin', but if I wanted a bit of skirt, I'd go to The Ten Bells,' was just one of the rebuffs she had gotten. *How things have changed*, she thought as she trudged back to the shared lodgings.

Lost in her own misery, she was surprised when she was accosted by a man. He looked like he had not seen land for a few months, and it also looked like he had not seen a bath for most of that time too. His sailor's uniform was filthy, he stunk of cheap ale, and there was a stupid grin plastered across his face.

'Ello luv,' he slurred. 'Do you wanna earn yourself a crust? Do ya, eh?'

Martha pushed past him and continued towards her lodgings.

'Your loss, sweetheart, would have been the easiest groat you'd ever made, slag.'

*A groat*, Martha thought. *That's the price of a room for a night?* She turned back towards the sailor, who was staggering down the street propositioning other women. *If I could get the likes of him to pay up front, I could make a fortune in one night without actually having to do anything.* This thought brought the smile back to her face.

'OK then, you're on,' she shouted back down the street after the dirty sailor. 'But I wanna see the colour of your brass first.'

The sailor turned back to her, and his stupid, drunken smile widened. He reached into his pocket and produced a small bag of coins. There was enough in there to earn ten times what he'd offered.

'Come on then, you smelly bastard. Up this alleyway.' She pointed towards a small entry between two houses and disappeared in a flash. 'Come on, sailor,' she taunted. 'If you're not too scared of a real woman, that is. But I want your money first. I've been had by the likes of you before.'

Grinning, the sailor entered the alleyway. 'I bet you've been 'ad thousands of times,' he laughed as he held out his bag of money in one hand while undoing his trousers with the other. Before the drunkard knew what was happening, she grabbed him around the neck. She pressed, applying just the right amount of pressure, in the right places, to render him unconscious. It wasn't difficult, and the drink helped. As the grubby sailor went limp in her embrace, she let go of him, swiped his bag of money, and waltzed back out of the alley, taking the long way back to her lodgings.

~~~

In an alleyway across the road, lurking in the shadows, unbeknown to Martha, was Aaron Kosminski. He had been following her obsessively since he laid his dark eyes on the women sharing the lodgings. He watched as she propositioned the sailor, and as he showed her his money. His interest grew as the drunken man followed her down the alley, only for her to emerge alone, with his bag of money in tow, barely two minutes later.

He waited until she was away, down the street, he knew where she was going and knew where he could find her if, and when, he needed to. He crossed the road and entered the alleyway, looking both ways for any witnesses. It pleased him that there were none. It took a few moments before he noticed the sailor lying on the floor. The man was obviously dead.

Every instinct screamed for him to run, to flee the scene, but he knew the image of a grown man running through the streets of Whitechapel would cause suspicions. He gathered all his mental strength and walked, calmly, out of the alley. He scanned the roads, searching the faces of pedestrians, looking for the witch. Eventually, he found her heading towards Shoreditch. *That evil bitch has turned her last trick,* he thought as blood pumped through his ears, causing them to thud! *Today is going to be the day that she gets her just desserts.*

He knew where she lived, and he knew that for her to get to her room, she would have to cross the yard at the back of the lodging. That was where he would spring his trap, in the gloom of the alleyway. *My razorblade will make easy work of her throat*, he thought, grinding his teeth together. *A quick, easy slice, and the world will be a better place, without that* cunt *in it.*

He hurried through the streets, circling around to get ahead of her before making his way down an adjacent alleyway that would allow him access into her yard. He could feel his heart pounding in his neck.

Once inside the yard, he crouched into a shaded corner and waited.

He heard the gate spring close behind her. He gripped his hand tighter around the hilt of his razor, noting, with a smile, for the first time in a while his knuckles no longer screamed at him. He tightened his grip, poised to jump.

That was when a voice shouted down from above him. 'Martha, where've you been? You've had the girls worried sick. You know Carrie doesn't want anyone out late after dark.'

'I know,' she laughed, it was a harsh sound. 'But I turned a trick tonight and made us a small fortune.' She wiggled the bag before her, showing it off to whoever was in the window looking down at her. 'I think there's enough to pay for new lodgings for at least a week, maybe two.'

She passed by him, so close, he could smell her.

Another voice joined the conversation. 'Martha, please tell me you never sold yourself to get that money?'

'Oh, behave, Rose. Do you think I'm going to do anything like that?'

The other woman laughed. 'Well, you always were a dirty old witch.'

Aaron's eyes widened in the dark. That confirmed it; they *were* witches, and therefore they *all* needed to die. His dreams were indeed showing him glimpses of his destiny.

After she entered the lodgings, he made his way back to the alleyway where the attack had happened. He thought about reporting the murder to the police. This would give him a local hero alibi when the time came for him to do his dirty deeds.

He had expected a crowd to be gathered around the dead body, maybe a few policemen controlling the nosey onlookers, but to his surprise, the scene was empty. There was no crowd, and most peculiar of all, there was no dead body. *Witchcraft indeed,* he thought, crossing himself, religiously. He made his way back to the street and into the Princess Alice pub, where he drank, brooding on his missed opportunity, all night.

## 25.

<u>Orbital Platform One. 2288</u>

'KEVIN, I THINK we're onto something here. If they've gone back in time and are due to return in a year, then they must know something about time travel that we've missed. It's my guess that whatever it is, it's linked to the production of Higgs Storm,'

'I hear what you are saying, Youssef, but what does it have to do with the ops team?'

'I think we're going to need a mission,' Youssef began. 'We need to know where they intend to come back to; we need to be ready and waiting for them. It pains me to say it, because of all the violence and death that's already occurred, but I think we need to take these women out of the picture.'

'You want them eradicated?'

'As much as it goes against my religion, and my personal ethics, yes. We're going to need them gone.'

Kevin raised his eyebrows and breathed out a long sigh. 'Well, OK. I'll get a team together. We'll start at the most obvious location, the castle in Inverness.'

Youssef nodded as Kevin stood from the table and left the room.

'This is a big undertaking, Youssef,' Dr Hausen warned in his thick Germanic accent. 'Will you be able to live with yourself after making this decision?'

Youssef put his head in his hands. 'I don't know, Sven. I've been making too many decisions lately. Isn't this just another one?'

Dr Hausen sat his considerable frame down into the seat next to his friend and leaned forward on the table, joining his hands. 'There comes a point when there are things you just have to do, whether you want to or not. I think, personally, that this is a good decision. But I do worry about the effects it will have on you when you see the bodies that you have ordered. I'm not trying to make you second guess yourself, but just warning you about the crash that will inevitably happen. Make sure that Helen and Melissa, when she is old enough, know and understand the anguish this decision put you through.'

'I will and thank you for your kind words my friend.'

'That's what I'm here for, Youssef. Remember that you still have friends, and they are ready, willing, and able to help you whenever you need them.'

He reached out and took the big man's hand in his, as he did, they both smiled.

## 26.

THE SCIENTISTS IN the labs were working around the clock. They were so busy that they had to draft in other scientist from other fields, as this was now the highest priority for global security.

The experiments had not been going well. The information they had on Quantum signals, and tagging, were old and sketchy at best. There had been some success with the magnetic tagging and the relocation of objects in time. It meant that they could now pre-programme wherever they wanted to send an object to, but they had very little evidence to support that they had gotten it right.

One of the scientists had the idea of attempting to hack into The Quest's databases to extract their information regarding quantum tagging. The initial problem with this plan was that it was proving difficult to locate any known key-personnel since the group leader's disappearance. Searching for any information relating to a network or a database containing quantum information was proving tricky.

That was until last week.

Andrew Byrne was the EA's leading networks expert. He had been placed in charge of the search for anything even remotely relating to The Quest on the Rapidnet. His quest had been fruitless for over a week, that was until he discovered a single, almost obscure reference to Mary Kelly and her work in the theory of quantum signals in time.

He expanded his search, utilising everything he could find on the name and the locations. Very soon, he hit the jackpot. Mary had posted an innocuous report regarding the effects on live organic matter and time travel. To his amazement, he discovered that she had posted it from her own private portal. He could now trace her back across the Rapidnet and isolate the original report, the original portal, and hence any network she had ever hooked into. All the information on quantum signals and tagging, that they needed to begin testing on bringing time and spatially displaced objects back from the past, was now at their fingertips.

He passed the information to Youssef's team, and they poured themselves over it. Within the week, they were ready to begin experimenting. They had built a test quantum transponder and inserted it into an apple. They then magnetically tagged the apple and sent it back in time, one week, to a location other than where they were working. It had created the expected amount of Higgs Storm as it disappeared, and the containment field did its work.

Then came the tense waiting. The transponder decoder was on and open for a signal.

There was nothing.

They waited an anxious ten minutes but still there was nothing. Disappointment tore through the lab. No one had expected it to work on the first-time round, but still, failure hurt.

Just as Jacqueline gave the order to pack up and to build a new quantum transcoder for another test, there was a faint bleep. It would have gone unnoticed if it hadn't been followed by another, and then another.

Everyone stopped what they were doing and stared at the screen. 'I don't believe it.' Jacqueline shouted though the lab. 'Monitor that signal, make sure it's the correct one.'

'It is! It's the signal. The one with the correct transponder code. We're communicating with the past!' one of the scientists shouted, and a cheer ripped through the lab.

'Can someone let Youssef know that we've been successful in the first part? I want to stay here and do a number of other tests.' One of the junior scientists nodded and left the room. 'Right,' she addressed the room, her voice a couple of pitches higher than normal, 'let's try this on something bigger!'

~~~~

The young scientist burst into Youssef's office without knocking. 'Mr Haseem, it works. We've got the quantum transponder working!' She paused then, to catch her breath. 'We can track the apple back in time.'

Youssef stood up and looked at the scientist. 'Working? Already?' He ran out of the room, leaving his portal in mid-report.

As they raced to the lab, he was full of questions. 'Was the signal strong? Did it do anything to the Higgs Storm? How big was the apple? How far back did they send it?'

'Sir, Doctor Escobia will be able to answer your questions when we get there. She has a better understanding of the whole procedure than I do.'

As he entered the lab, he had to take a moment to understand what was happening. There were people running every which way, shouting, waving papers, pointing at screens. 'OK, can someone please let me know what's going on?' he shouted. The bustle didn't stop; however, a few people did look over to see who was shouting.

'Dr Escobia, Youssef is here,' came a shout from behind the Hadron Collider.

'Good, it's about time,' came her reply.

Youssef turned to see her standing behind him with a smile plastered across her face. 'We've tagged the apple with a message; the message says *send me to another Orbital Platform*. The apple has now moved from Orbital Platform Four to Six. We can now track the things we send back, using an amalgamation of quantum and magnetic tagging.'

His face beamed. 'Jacqueline, I could kiss you right now.' Immediately, he realised what he had just said and his face bloomed maroon. He cleared his throat and turned towards the Collider. 'Show me how it works.'

She was laughing as she took another apple and ran a handheld scanner over it. 'This is the bog-standard magnetic tagging. It allows us to tag objects with dates and locations, and other stuff.'

'Stuff?' Youssef laughed; his embarrassment passed.

She smiled back. 'Yeah, stuff,' she laughed, picking up a long device from the worktable next to her. It had a shaft with a diamond head on the end. The head began to glow yellow when she pressed a button with her thumb. 'This is our quantum signal generator. We hold this device to the skin of the fruit. At present, we can only quantum tag organic objects. Plastics and metals don't work. So, we place this against the skin and depress the trigger. The diamond flashes yellow as it painlessly cuts the skin and deposits a small, what we have christened 'slug', into the dermal layer. This slug then finds its way into the core and begins to emit a quantum pulse. If used on a human or animal, the slug would find its way into the blood stream and work from there. The pulse it emits can't be read within the same timeframe as the quantum receiver, that allows us to filter out any other transmissions that might be coming from our time. When it receives the quantum code, the transponder collates the information into an accurate time frame.'

Youssef was nodding his head as he followed Jacqueline's explanations. 'So, how do we follow them physically?' he asked.

'The magnetic and quantum tags bash against each other as they pulse. They piggyback onto each other's signals, so we receive a quantum signal with a magnetic signal embedded into it.'

'Accident or design?' he asked shaking his head slowly in awe of the science. 'Come on, doctor, you can tell me,' he chided.

She looked at him with pretend puppy dog eyes.

'Come on, it'll be our little secret.'

Her eyes shifted from one side to the other, 'Accident.' she confided. 'But it happens every time, almost as if they're attracted to each other. Quantum does time, magnetic does space, it's a perfect cocktail.'

'This is outstanding. It truly is. So, now all we have to do is work on how we bring them back.'

'Well, we've already started on that. It may be a little trickier than we thought,' she winced as she confessed this. 'We've only gone through it theoretically, but it seems that the hardest part of getting them back is the fact that we have to boost our quantum signal, on this end, to allow their transponder to see our code. We're also dealing with signal degradation. There's an added complication that when the quantum slug enters the body, it disguises itself, so the cells don't reject it. That part is actually very clever. Because of this, to pick up the return signal, the return code has to be localised to the slug. We need to saturate the entire body with the code serum in order to catch it. We've left instructions with our counterparts on the other Platforms on how to inject the code serum. If and when we do use an agent, that agent will have to take the serum with him. We think this is how The Quest have done it.'

Youssef was still shaking his head as he digested the information. 'I tell you what, it's a good job Farley isn't here as he would have started a fight by now,' he laughed.

'We don't know what, if any, reaction all this quantum signal will cause on return…' she paused and smiled, 'but we're dying to try.'

He stopped shaking his head and began nodding instead. 'Let's do it then.'

## 27.

<u>London. 1888</u>

OVER THE NEXT few days, Aaron Kosminski watched the comings and goings of *his girls*, as he had come to think of them, closely. What little relationship he still had with his wife had deteriorated, broken down completely, but he was beginning to see that as a blessing.

He had a new vocation; one he couldn't afford any distractions from.

In a private room above his barber's shop, he kept an in-depth dossier regarding the girls. He had worked out most of their names from conversations overheard while walking behind them in the streets, at the marketplace, or in the various bars of Whitechapel. He had also produced a diary of his dreams and how they featured in his plans. He'd realised that if he could embrace these dreams, their actions and locations, then they may be able to help him fulfil, what he thought of now, as his destiny.

He paid special attention to his favourite. The large woman they called Martha. He felt like she had a power over the other girls. He knew she wasn't their leader, that seemed to be a woman named Carrie. She was a handsome woman if ever he had seen one, but Martha, she was feminine, yet could fight like a man. He'd watched her on many occasions. She would seduce a mark, get him to show her his money, take him down an alleyway, attack him, and take his money. She would take the men in a strange hold, trapping them until they stopped fighting, before dropping them to the floor and leaving them to die.

Each time he had gone back to investigate the body, it was gone.

More proof that she and her friends were witches.

~~~~

'I have a moral obligation to rid this place of their vile filth,' he mumbled to himself while following Martha down towards the bottom of Shoreditch High Street. The sun was dipping behind the large buildings on either side of the road, casting long shadows in the twilight of the day. He watched as she met with a small, blonde woman, who he recognised as Rose. He had seen Rose fight too. The way she looked after herself brought to mind images of men fighting in wars. The two women exchanged pleasantries, no more than a few words, before parting and continuing their separate ways.

A strange feeling on the back of his neck, like the hairs rising, alerted him to the presence of someone else watching his girls.

He looked around, not knowing what he was searching for, but confident he would know it when he saw it.

There was a man over the other side of the market square. The way he was idling in the street, it looked to Aaron like he was trying his best not to be noticed. He didn't look like a trader, and he didn't seem the type who would be looking for *business* with the ladies of the evening who frequented the market after the stalls were gone. No, this man seemed to be rather *too* interested in his ladies. Aaron could see something in his hands, from this distance, and in the failing light, he couldn't make out what it was. He was covertly pointing it at the women and then looking at it afterwards, as if reading something on it.

This odd activity unnerved Kosminski, but he pushed it to one side, *a musing for another time,* he thought, as he noted Martha's movements in his notepad before going home.

~~~~

That night, alone in his bed, as his wife had taken to sleeping in the other room with the children, the murder dream came again; but this time it was different. This time he welcomed the chaos, he embraced the mutilation and the gore.

The next morning, he woke extra early. He felt refreshed from the relaxing night of sleep. His thoughts wandered to the man on the street, the one who had been watching his girls. There was something about him that he didn't like.

He arrived at the women's address in Whites Row and took up residence in his usual spot. He was just in time to witness an exodus from the lodgings. Eight of the women left the house carrying bags that looked like they were packed to leave. *Are they all fleeing the nest?* he thought, as the dilemma of which ones he should follow sunk in. He hadn't thought this far in advance. Deep down though, he knew that Martha deserved to be his first victim.

Luckily for him, his two favourites were heading off in the same direction. Martha Tabram and Annie Chapman paired off and made their way towards the High Street.

He decided to follow them.

The sun was not long up, and it was already warm. It looked like London was going to get a little bit of summer after all. It didn't matter much to him. In East London, no matter where you were, rain or shine, day or night, there were always shadows to hide in.

As he stalked the two women, the strange feeling that he'd had the day before was back; a feeling that he was not alone. He scanned the already bustling street but, to his relief, he couldn't see anyone following him.

There was no sign of the man from last night.

He continued walking, but the feeling persisted. He kept stopping and searching, but still, there was no one there. That was until a small flash of red caught his eye. The colour screamed out to him in the drabness of the dirty, grey street. It looked like the lining of an expensive cape.

His heart began to pound as he recognised the wearer of the cape as the man from last night and realised that he *was* stalking his girls.

This infuriated, and scared him, in equal measure. Irrationally, he wanted to cross the street to confront him. He wanted to find out what he was playing at. The irony of the situation almost forced his dour face to break into a smile.

The man was holding something in his hands again.

This time Aaron could see it, due to the light of the day. It was a small device of some kind; he had never seen the likes of it before. From time to time, he would point it towards the two women strolling before him. Every now and then he would touch it and read from it.

It confused him. He hated the feeling of not being in control and thought that he should try and find out more about this stranger and his odd device. A thought occurred that he might be an agent of the police. Maybe they were investigating the murder outside the pub on the night Martha, the witch, arrived?

*Probably best if I keep my distance for now,* he thought.

He didn't like the police, they unnerved him. He tried his best to push all thoughts of them aside as he fed his obsession with the women. 'Police don't investigate witches,' he mumbled. 'That's down to the likes of me!'

*Police, or no police,* he thought. *Tonight, I will rid this world of their evil.*

He entered the shadows of a nearby building and watched as the women entered one of the lodging houses in George Yard Buildings on George Street. He smiled as he recognised the address from his dreams. Martha stood in conversation with a small man who had opened the door, then handed him something—he assumed it was money. All three of them then entered the building.

'Time to get organised,' he told himself. 'There's no doubt she'll be out looking for more victims tonight. That's when she'll find her last one.' He smiled as he gripped the razorblade in the pocket of his overcoat. 'Me!' he snarled.

With that, he left the scene and walked back across the East End, towards his home.

There was no sign of the other stalker anywhere.

## 29.

Orbital Platform One. 2288

THERE WERE SIXTEEN scientists on hand to witness the return of the apple. Youssef and Jacqueline were included. He was excited for the return, but he was also reticent. He knew how much was at stake if this was a failure.

'OK, reverse the collider and prepare the Higgs-Boson hydrogen mix. Let's bring Granny Smith back from the past,' Jacqueline shouted.

Everyone put on their goggles to protect their eyes from the reported bright flashes that would come with the reversal. The lights dimmed as the whooshing of the Hadron Collider filled the air and the racetrack began to glow.

It was the only sound in the lab.

Jacqueline was monitoring the hydrogen acceleration from her console. She gave the order to inject the mix when she saw the optimum conditions flash. The recall signal to the quantum slug, buried deep inside the subject, was sent.

As the mix entered the stream, another lab scientist entered the instructions on a portal next to the device. After a few moments, there was a bright flash of purple and alarms began to blare as the magnetic containment fields deployed around the Collider's racetrack to contain the Higgs Storm that would be produced by the recall.

The flash was sustained, and Youssef turned to face Jacqueline. Her eyes were hidden by the darkened goggles she was wearing, but she couldn't hide the grin on her face. The light began to oscillate. It flashed faster and faster as the alarms continued to blare louder and louder.

Suddenly, the flashing and the alarms stopped. The silence in the room was pronounced as every noise ceased at once.

No one breathed. No one even moved as the smoke inside the glass room began to dissipate.

It took a while to see, but there, dead centre of the racetrack, was an apple. It looked as fresh as it did when it had been sent. There was no visible damage to its dermal layer.

In the jubilation, and the celebration of the returned apple, no one noticed one faint alarm still ringing in the background. In the midst of the shouting, cheering, and hand slapping, it went unnoticed.

'We did it!' Youssef shouted, shaking his head, holding his hands in the air. Several of the other scientists had been hugging him, and he even acknowledged a few kisses. 'I don't quite believe we did this.'

'Well, believe it, sir.' Another scientist who was stood at a monitor next to him was beaming as she ran scans on the returned apple. 'That's the exact same apple we sent back.'

He grasped at the handle of the glass door; eager to see if there was any damage to the fruit that they couldn't see. The door was still magnetically sealed. 'Why is the door still locked?' he asked the scientist at the console.

She shook her head in response. 'It shouldn't...' her fingers began to tap at her console faster. 'Sir...' her voice had lost all its former joviality; she was now all business. 'Sir, it seems that there's an anomaly. An inordinate amount of Higgs Strom is swelling within the containment field.'

'Is it holding?'

'Erm, negative, sir. It's more than we were expecting, and its expanding.'

The containment field had been programmed with the correct power to contain more than double the amount of Higgs Storm produced as the apple left. They had not considered that the recall would produce so much more. The field was straining like an over blown balloon.

'Everybody, out of the lab, NOW!' Youssef shouted as he grabbed the scientists, pushing them towards the door. The celebrating had stopped as everyone watched what was occurring.

'GET OUT NOW, ALL OF YOU.'

Youssef was manually throwing people towards the exits. None of them had ever even heard him so much as raise his voice before, so the physical acts of violence that he was bestowing upon them now were a cause for alarm.

Jacqueline was about to protest the manhandling of her staff when she saw what was happening. The containment field was too swollen. It was straining; like it was about to pop at any given moment.

The Storm's growth was relentless.

'DO AS HE SAYS! DO AS HE SAYS!' she shouted, as the containment field continued to swell, out of all control.

'ITS GOING TO BLOW! GET OUT, ALL OF YOU… NOW!' Youssef yelled, grabbing the nearest scientist and jumping towards the exit, pulling the scared, and confused man, though the door with him by the collars of his white coat. Most of the others were already behind the door as the two of them fell through. 'LOCK IT DOWN!' he screamed, as the door hissed closed behind them.

There were four scientists still trapped in the room.

He got up from the floor and looked through the window. He watched and whispered a small prayer. 'Allah, have mercy on their souls.' He closed his eyes in a futile attempt to block out what he knew was coming. Gloria Hartigan's face—or what was left of it—came forth like a ghost in the darkness. He could feel a scream rising in his chest. It took most of his will to beat it down.

Eerily similar to the events of twenty years prior, no one could look away from what was happening in the lab.

Jacqueline took it the worst. 'We have to get in there and help them. They need our help!' There was no conviction in her voice; Youssef knew, deep down, that *she* knew the four poor souls inside were lost. She looked to her boss and mentor. She needed guidance; guidance he knew he couldn't offer. Everyone else was motionless, all of them silent, dumbfounded, helpless.

Finally, the Higgs Storm breached the containment field, and the lethal purple gas spewed forth towards the petrified scientists inside.

One, obviously resigned to what was about to happen, ran towards the cloud and allowed herself to be immersed within its destructive embrace. Her scream was mercifully muffled as a wave of blood spilled out before being greedily sucked back in again by the purple mass. The other three scientists were screaming, banging on the glass doors, trying to get out, to get away from the path of the rolling, purple death.

Youssef opened his eyes. A reality had just occurred to him, it was a terrifying reality. He sat up and cast his panicked gaze back into the room.

The single glance confirmed his fears.

As the remaining three colleagues within the room succumbed to the creeping cloud, his fears were founded.

The Higgs Storm was *still* expanding.

'Fuck!' he uttered. Jacqueline looked at him. She had never heard him swear before now. 'We're going to have to evacuate the OP! We have to go, NOW!' He pushed away from the door and ran from the lab in the direction of the bridge. 'Everyone, follow me,' he screamed.

None of them needed to be told twice.

As he ran, he tapped a small device on his wrist. 'Amanda, order a widespread evacuation of OP One, immediately. No time to explain. Do it right now!' The thing he liked most about Amanda was that she never second guessed his orders, any of them. Five seconds after their conversation, the OP's lights dimmed, and the emergency evacuation klaxon sounded.

Amanda's tinny voice spoke through his wrist device. 'Sir, emergency evacuation of OP One, to the nearest functioning base, that's… erm, Liverpool, England, happening in five… four… three… two…'

The world began to dissolve around him, and he felt the familiar, but never comfortable, sensation of falling. The next instant, he was on the ground in one of the functioning EA's headquarters. He had materialised into a huge warehouse. 'Amanda, get me the readout and make sure everyone is out. Also, find out who's in charge of this station.'

As he looked up, he saw Amanda in the crowd of people materialising around him, she was using a tablet portal that was interfacing with her headset. 'Sir, everyone accounted for, with the exception of…'

'I know who the exceptions are, Amanda,' he snapped. He knew there would be a time to grieve their lost colleagues, but that time was not now.

'The officer in charge of this station is…' he watched as she tapped furiously on the tablet, 'Commander Lisa McFadden! I'm patching you through to her now.'

'Amanda, you're a star!'

'I know, sir,' she replied.

'Dr Haseem, this is Commander McFadden. Welcome to Liverpool, England,' the comforting voice spoke through his device.

'Thank you, Commander. Sorry to have to jump right into business, but has OP One exploded?'

'No, sir. We're monitoring the situation right now. It seems that most of the systems are functioning correctly. If it wasn't for the fact that you have a hole stretching from decks four through to twelve, I'd think that you were here for a holiday. What could have caused that kind of damage? Are we under attack again?'

'No, Commander,' Youssef spoke into his com patch. 'It was an experiment that we completely underrated. Although it has answered a good few questions.'

'Do you need anything from me, sir?' McFadden asked.

'Can you deploy a containment field around the stricken area? Also, I'm going to need another Hadron Collider in lab, erm, let me think…' He rolled his eyes as he mapped out the labs in his head. 'In lab eight. It's more or less the right size, and I need to get back up there asap. Are there any casualties, apart from the obvious?'

'No further injuries or fatalities recorded sir,' Amanda spoke from the crowd of displaced scientists.

'Fantastic! Well, Commander, thank you for your hospitality. I'm sorry that it was only a fleeting visit, but could you send us back up please?'

'Doing it right now, sir. I hope the experiment is a success.'

'It may not look that way, Commander, but I think it has been.'

He felt himself falling and dissolving again, before reappearing, to his relief, in a corridor outside the containment field of OP One.

The massive breach was like a mouth to Hell; the clear space beyond was like staring into the Abyss. From where he stood, he had an unhindered view of the night sky above them, with a view of Earth below. It was beautiful, mesmerising, and dangerous.

As he regarded the damage, he did some quick calculations in his head. He estimated that the Higgs Storm had magnified by, at least, twenty times. 'All this from one apple sent back one hour, for five minutes. Imagine what ten one-hundred-and-twenty-five-pound women, sent back a few hundred years, for one year could produce.'

He shuddered at the thought.

He watched as the others began to reappear around him. 'Jacqueline,' he shouted as his colleague appeared next to the shimmering hole in the bulkhead. She jumped back, startled at the gaping maw before her. 'That's how they're getting the extra Storm they need. They're going to bring the women back, and a huge amount of Higgs Storm will follow. I need you and the rest of the team in my personal room, immediately.'

'Sir,' Amanda cut in. 'Your personal room no longer exists.'

'Oh, right, erm, are there any conference rooms still existing?'

Amanda replied with a small smile. 'Yes, sir, room two on the second floor.'

Youssef nodded. 'Room two it is. Amanda, send a crew to Lab eight to install the equipment that is being teleported there by McFadden. Get hold of Farley too. I'm going to need his skills with the plan I'm formulating.'

## 30.

<u>London. 1888</u>

AARON KOSMINSKI WAS home, but he couldn't settle. He had absolutely no intention of cutting anyone's hair today. There were bigger issues rushing through his head, and the concentration needed to style a gentleman's hair wasn't flowing for him. So, he closed the barber's shop and went out. He was dressed for a warm August afternoon and ready for some revelling on this bank holiday evening.

Even though it was still early, the people in and around the pubs of Spitalfields were already drunk, and most of them were either looking for a fight, another drink, or someone to engage in lewd sexual practices with. Most people that was, except him. He was not looking for any of these things.

He was looking for murder!

All he wanted was to rid his beloved city of the ten witches that had infested it. He fancied he might start his business this very evening. He knew that for most of the day, Martha would be in the company of men. Businessmen, soldiers, sailors, policemen; but very soon she would be in the company of him, and he would be the last of them... forever.

He hoped tonight that he might get a chance to use his, specially purchased, new toy. He had seen it in a window of the curiosity shop opposite his barber's, and it had called to him. It was an obsidian cane with a silver handle. When the handle was tugged, it produced a long, sharp rapier blade. The instant he saw it, he knew that he had to have it, to use on the witches, along with his trusted razorblade.

As darkness drew across the city, feeling like a real dandy with his cane, he'd followed Martha into a bar called The White Swan in Aldgate. All day there had been men passing through the pub, making suggestions towards the women, Martha included. Most of them she laughed off, others she took advantage of. Right now, she was in the company of another woman. This one he didn't recognise. He guessed that she might just be another guttersnipe, another product of this godforsaken city, but not a witch. They were whispering to each other conspiratorially, and their interests lay in two soldiers who were drunk at the bar.

He watched as the soldiers made their way over to the women, who marvelled as they flashed their cash to them. It was obvious they were all thinking there would be more to this dalliance. Sipping at his brew, he pretended to be drunk, like the other foolish revellers in this den of iniquity, but all the while his dark eyes never left Martha and her flirting and seducing.

After maybe an hour of this horseplay, *or should that be whore's play,* he thought with a humourless chuff, all four members of the party left together, and less than two minutes later, he followed, ignoring the salacious, glowering looks of other women in the bar.

One grabbed him as he left. 'Ello, love,' she drooled. 'You wantin' some company to warm your cold bed, eh?'

Without even looking at her, he flicked her off her arm and stormed past.

'Alright, you old wanker, spit on yer then!' she shouted, hocking up a mouthful of phlegm and spitting it in his direction. She missed but laughed anyway. Tomorrow she would be telling tales of the strange man with the expensive cape and odd walking stick.

Out on the street, he cursed the old wretch who had grabbed him, as the slight delay had lost him his mark. The street was almost as busy as the pub had been. There must have been some ships in the docks, as it was littered with sailors, all of them out for a good time and to spend their bounty on whatever they could get. He liked this fact, as when they found Martha's body tomorrow morning, no doubt one of them would get the blame for it, and he would be free to move on to his next victim.

With his fists clenching in his thin leather gloves, he turned the corner onto Commercial Street, leading towards the marketplace. That was when he saw them. The small group had stopped and were talking. He stopped himself, pretended to show interest in a shop window while glancing secretive looks over at them. After a short exchange, they paired off and split up. Martha disappeared up an alleyway that led to George's Yard, where she had been living. The other two, the woman he didn't recognise as one of the ten, went in the opposite direction, passing him by, but ignoring him completely.

This was his chance. Fate had brought her to him, and now he would take her.

He followed Martha and the soldier up the alley, listening to them giggle and laugh, before stopping in the shadows of the yard. He watched as the soldier showed her a purse and jingled it, then begin to kiss and grab at her.

With a deft flick of her arms, she was behind him. The drunken soldier didn't have a clue what was happening. Her arms wrapped around his neck, and Kosminski watched as the poor, unsuspecting man silently began to thrash, and kick, before falling limp to the wet cobblestone street. A dazed look of desperation haunted his face.

After a few moments, he fell still.

She released him, and his dead body crumpled to the floor. With a deft look around her, she bent down and retrieved his full purse.

Kosminski saw this as his window of opportunity. He unsheathed the rapier blade concealed within his new cane and readied himself for the attack. A euphoria was coursing through him, and his senses felt hyper aware. Blood was pumping, and his stomach was churning, in a delightful way. He felt like he could do anything.

He felt God-like!

He moved forwards out from the shadows; the handle of his blade gripped tight in his leather gloved hand. That was when he saw something, something that caused him to halt his activity.

There was someone at the other end of the alleyway.

Martha had noticed him too.

'Who's there?' she asked, there was real alarm in her voice. 'What do you mean by lurking in the shadows back there?'

'I've come to stop you, Tabram,' the figure whispered.

Kosminski slunk back into the shadows and watched as, whoever it was produced something out of the folds of his cloak. From his distance, and in the shadows, the object looked like a ball with a short nozzle and a glowing blue light at the end of it. As he revealed it to Martha, the light it produced illuminated the man's face, and for the first time, Kosminski saw his likeness.

He had thick black hair and a heavy moustache. There was something about him that looked odd, like he shouldn't be here; like he was a man out of place in this world.

There was also a familiarity about him, and it took a few moments for Kosminski to recognise what it was. *He's one of them*, he thought. The horror of the situation dawned on him. *A male version, and that device he's holding must be an instrument of his witchcraft.*

He flattened himself against the wall that was shading him and re-sheathed his weapon. He watched the proceedings with interest. As the man advanced on Martha, he assumed she would run away, back down the alley towards him, shouting and screaming. But she didn't. She surprised him by standing her ground, staring the man down. He noticed that she wasn't just looking at *him*, she seemed focused on the sphere he was holding too.

As Kosminski watched, his curiosity piqued when he realised that she was not standing still. Her body was twitching, as if something—some unseen force—was stopping her from moving.

As the mystery man scrutinised the yard for witnesses, Kosminski pressed himself deeper into the shadows to avoid detection. It was a successful manoeuvre, the man obviously didn't see him, as he began to advance upon the stricken woman. He pressed something on the sphere, and there was an audible whirring sound. The light on the end of the nozzle turned green, and a strange illumination issued from it. He pointed the light at Martha, and her body was instantly bathed in the eerie green light.

Within the light, he saw a bright purple blip that appeared to be moving around her body. The only part of her that was free to move was her head. As she looked down towards her own body, she said something Kosminski couldn't hear, then the mystery man delved his free hand into the folds of his cloak and produced another strange object. Again, it was a small hand-held device, and although he had never seen one in real life, Kosminski thought it looked like a gun. Only it wasn't realistic, it looked like a child's toy.

It was cumbersome in his hands, and it was glowing red at the end of its double barrels. There were two levers at the top that the man activated with his thumbs, and Kosminski was able to see, due mainly to the glow of the strange lights, that it was trigger activated.

# TimeRipper

The mystery man's face showed little emotion as he pointed the weapon. A red light beamed from it into the green glow, where it began to pursue the purple dot around Martha's body. It was a cat and mouse chase for a few moments until a pinging noise broke the silence of the scene. The red beam had locked onto the purple blip. The man pressed another trigger, and the beam flashed thicker for a moment.

Kosminski couldn't believe what he was watching as the light tore through Martha's flesh, like a hot knife through butter.

Her face screamed. Her mouth was open wide, as were her eyes, but no noise came forth.

The blip had not, as he had first thought, been caught in the intense beam, it was still moving. The man shot another ray from the gun, then another, and another. The beams were literarily ripping the woman apart. But still the purple signal avoided them. As the light tore the woman's flesh, her eyes rolled back into her head, and Kosminski could tell she was close to losing consciousness. He couldn't understand how she was still on her feet, as the beams continued to cut deeper and deeper into her body.

The attack continued with a frenzy of deep cuts for a short while, he guessed that it couldn't have been more than a few minutes, but watching, it felt longer, almost like a lifetime. His hand covered his mouth, he wasn't sure if it was to stop him from screaming or from vomiting, or maybe both, as he witnessed Martha's body torn to shreds before his very eyes.

Finally, the red beam caught its purple prey.

He was transfixed now as the blip grew brighter and brighter. His eyes widened in horror, and more than a little perverse voyeurism, as a small glowing ball was removed from Martha's abdomen and allowed to hover in the air before her, still held in the infernal red beam. As the green light faded, the man reached out and grabbed the floating ball. Martha's eyes focused on it briefly before her head dropped. Kosminski would have sworn an oath, there and then, that he saw a smile twitch over her mouth before the small spark of life that was left in her eyes slipped away.

Once the glowing ball was in his hand, the sphere opened, and he placed it inside. The green light encasing Martha blinked once, before dissipating, and her body fell to the floor.

She was dead!

Her mutilated corpse lay unmoving on the cold, dark ground, next to the forgotten body of her soldier friend.

The man put both devices away within the folds of his cape. He looked down, once, at the body, before disappearing down the other end of the alley to the yard.

Kosminski couldn't believe what he had just witnessed. He waited a moment, bathed in the beautiful shadows, before delicately making his way to Martha's corpse. He gave her leaking body a small nudge with his foot. She was unresponsive.

The depth of mutilation to her flesh sickened him. He raised his hand to his mouth again, this time in an attempt to quell the hot bile he could feel rising in his stomach, then he turned on his heels, and ran.

Even though his mission had been successful—the death of Martha Tabram was confirmed—he felt cheated that it hadn't been him who had killed her. Also, the violence that had ravaged her body until she died unnerved him.

He was scared, but deeply incensed at the same time.

## 31.

EARLY THE NEXT morning, Inspector Frank Abberline entered Scotland Yard police station to an excited buzz. He smiled as he watched the confusion, even though deep down he was dreading whatever it was that could cause such a fuss. He made his way through the melee and into his office without asking, and he sighed deeply as he pulled his chair into his desk. He always liked to get his paperwork done early and out of the way of any business that would, inevitably, fall into his lap.

This morning he was not even going to be allowed to load his typewriter.

'Inspector, oh thank the lord you're in,' puffed an out of breath, uniformed officer who had seen him enter. 'There's been a murder, murder I tell you. It's a mess, sir, a bad one, and no mistake.'

Abberline looked up, rolling his eyes. 'Nothing like a good murder in the morning to make your day that little bit more exciting, eh?' he asked the officer. 'So, there's murder afoot you say! Pray, tell me where and who?'

'Well, she ain't got no name yet, sir. We're getting a sketch done as we speak, but that takes time now, don't it? We do have one of them photograph thingies sir,' he said dropping a black and white picture of the victim on his desk. 'It looks like she was done for up there in Spitalfields. In George's Yard to be specific. That's your old stomping ground, off Whitechapel, isn't it, sir?'

'Thank you, officer,' Abberline interjected. 'I'll take it from here.'

The relieved looking officer backed out of the office, offering a small salute.

Abberline picked up the photograph and looked at it, making note of the wounds that the woman had sustained. Multiple lacerations and some mutilation. 'Nasty,' he hissed as he breathed in through his teeth. He then allowed his eyes to wander up to the woman's face.

It was the face of a woman he would not forget in a hurry.

He held the photograph out before him and sat down. His thoughts travelled back to his stakeout beneath the bench outside The Ten Bells pub. His mind's eye cast back to the purple lights, then the murder of the reporter.

'Officer Bellis,' he shouted. 'Could you come back in here, please?' The same officer who handed him the photograph popped his head around the door.

'Sir?'

'Fetch me my hat and my investigating satchel. We're off to Whitechapel to unravel an enigma.'

'Sir?' Officer Bellis stared at him, there was a vacant expression on his face.

'Get my bag, I'm going out,' he ordered the uniformed officer, shaking his head.

## 32.

<u>Orbital Platform One. 2288</u>

'DID WE MANAGE to scan the apple before the Higgs Storm destroyed everything?' Youssef asked while sat at a large table in conference room twelve.

'We did. The scan was set to run automatically when the apple returned, and all information recorded is stored directly to the cloud. I should be able to punch it up here.' Jacqueline was using her portable portal. She sent the report up to the big screen at the end of the room.

All essential personnel were present. Everyone was still shocked by what had happened in the lab, but Youssef had told them that there would be time enough to grieve for their fallen comrades when the task at hand was complete.

This seemed to focus them.

The screen showed the molecular structure of the apple, with the quantum slug still in situ. 'We can see that there was no discernible damage to the apple in its journey to the past and back again; but one thing we can tell is that it has aged. It would seem that time passes the same back there as it does here, if that makes any sense to anyone.'

Youssef was nodding.

She gave him a quick glance, as if requesting his permission to continue. 'So, we know that if these women survived their journey into the past, then they're living a life there within a similar time structure to us here,' she concluded.

Youssef had his hand over his mouth. He nodded. 'In The Quest's research documents, were there any records regarding trials with living organisms? I'm assuming there were, as ten of their best operatives are not just going to jump into a collider and hope for the best,' he asked.

'We haven't gotten that far into their experiments yet, sir. We were looking for pure theory to move this forward. I can get a team of research assistants onto that as soon as this meeting is over.'

'If you could, that would be fantastic,' Youssef replied standing up. 'Right, everyone let's get back to work. I need the new Hadron Collider installed and working as soon as possible. I also need another containment unit, one large enough to contain the amounts of Higgs Storm we saw today, maybe even larger. I'm not losing anymore personnel.'

The group stood and began making their way out of the room, chatting excitedly about their next challenge.

'Jacqueline, can you stay behind? I want your input in this next meeting I have.'

'Sure, I'll just set my team their objectives and be right back.'

'Appreciate it,' he replied, tipping her a wink.

He sat in the room and sighed. *There's already been too many deaths, and now this plan might have to go into action,* he thought as Kevin blustered into the room. He looked like he hadn't slept for two days, or even bathed for that matter, but he looked happier than Youssef had seen him since The Event.

'Wow, you stink!' Youssef informed him, holding his nose. 'Where've you been?'

Kevin smiled. 'Manoeuvres,' he replied, offering nothing more.

'Well, we've answered a question, a big one, and I've formulated a plan. I'll be counting on you for your help on this.'

Kevin cocked his head. 'You know you can always count on me. What is it?'

'I'm waiting on Jacqueline to get back, then I'll outline it to you both. It'll be a dangerous mission.'

'You know the ops team. Danger is what we do,' he replied with a smile.

With that, Jacqueline re-entered the room looking at both men. 'Sorry, I was just giving the team a brief. So, what's this all about then?' she asked, offering a nod towards Kevin as she sat.

'Would you say that our experiments into the time travel realm have been successful?'

'Moderately, yes. If you remove today's unfortunate incident, then I would have to say yes.'

Kevin was looking confused. 'Sorry, I've been away for a few days, can you fill me in? What unfortunate incident?'

'We successfully sent an apple back in time and brought it back again.'

'You what?' he asked ruffling his brow.

Youssef was smiling. 'You heard correctly. We sent an apple back in time and brought it back again.'

Kevin shook his head. 'So, what was the accident?'

Jacqueline looked at him for a moment, shaking her head. 'Did you not notice the huge hole in the centre of OP One?'

He shrugged his shoulders and pouted. 'I was teleported into T-Six, normally it would be T-One, I didn't think anything of it. So, what happened?'

She relayed the incident. When she was finished, he looked at Youssef. 'This is their plan then?'

'I think so,' he replied. 'I've got mathematicians working now to estimate how far they would need to go back in order to create enough Higgs Storm on their return to carry out their threat.'

'I have people working on trying to locate the transponder signal from their quantum slugs, it will help us locate them in time and space,' Jacqueline added.

'So, what's the big plan then?' Kevin sat back into his seat, as did Jacqueline, both wanting to know what was brewing in the boss's head.

'There is a natural paradoxical law, am I right?'

'Theoretically, yes,' Jacqueline replied.

'So that means that no one from the time they are in now will be able to kill them, so we can guarantee, that barring accidents, they *will* be coming back. We now have an almost certainty that they'll carry out their plans on their return. We have to stop them, and I think that we'll have to do it in the past.'

Kevin's smile was spreading across his lips. 'Are you thinking of sending someone back in time to get them? You are, aren't you?'

Youssef bowed his head and looked at the table. 'Yes, I am.'

He sat back and pushed out a sharp sigh. Jacqueline sat silently; her eyes were wide open.

Youssef regarded them both, looking them in the eyes. 'I need the best you can think of for this job. Someone who is a tracker, physically fit, and doesn't have a problem with the...' he paused again, '...grittier sides of a mission.'

'Clarence,' he replied without hesitation. 'Vincent Clarence is the man you're looking for. He's young, and brilliant. He reminds me of a younger me. He's capable, and willing, to do whatever it takes to get the mission done.'

'He'll need to know the dangers and the pitfalls of an operation like this. And the obvious involvement in taking out ten marks,' Youssef spoke slowly, his disdain of sending someone on a mission like this was obvious.

Kevin sat back and put his hands to the back of his head. 'None of that will be a problem to this one. I'll get him to report to you straight away.'

'Just hold out on that for the time being. Jacqueline, this is where you come in. Do you know if there is any way of getting communications to and from the past?'

'Sir, I've only just found out this morning that an apple can travel through time, I haven't got a clue about comms.'

'Can you get a team to work on it? If we go ahead with this mission, I don't want whoever goes in to be in the dark. I want to be able to get updates and give orders.'

'I'll get onto it right away, sir,' Jacqueline said easing out of her seat.

'Err, Jacqueline, I haven't quite finished with you yet.'

Looking confused, she sat back down.

'I'm going to need you to work closely with this Clarence.'

'Me?' she asked alarmed. 'I'm a scientist, not a field agent. I couldn't possibly...'

'If this mission is to be a success, I'm going to need someone I can trust supporting the front line. I want that person to be you. I need someone with a level head who is able to fix things on the fly if anything goes wrong. Someone who can think outside the box. We don't know what we'll encounter back there. I'd like to think I can trust you to do this job. You have one of the best analytical minds I've ever come across, and if I'm correct, you have completed extensive military training.'

'Yes, sir, I have.' Her brow furrowed as she asked the next question. 'Will this mean time travel for myself?'

'We'll cross that bridge when, and if, we come to it. We're going to have to hit the ground running, and I want to deploy as soon as we know it's safe to do so.'

She swallowed hard before answering. 'Yes, sir.'

'Good. I'm going to need you to get Vincent ready for time travel, meaning, we need to make sure it's safe. We're going to need to know that our technology will still work when he gets there.'

'Agreed, but the first thing I need to work on, I think, is the communications. How are we going to communicate with him while he is in the past?' Jacqueline asked, more to herself than to the other two men.

'He could leave us as series of messages,' laughed Youssef. 'We could find them from four hundred years in the past. I think I saw that in an old film.'

'A film?' she laughed. 'It's a little impracticable, don't you think?'

He smiled. 'You're right, though, we can't send him into the field incommunicado. So, you work on that and get into Vincent's head. We need him in tip top condition.'

## 33.

<u>London. 1888</u>

CARRIE MILLWOOD WAS worried. So worried that she had called all the girls together to her lodgings for a meeting. Back and forth she traipsed, biting at her fingernails and mumbling to herself as she waited for them to file in. She felt as though she was wearing a tread into the bare floorboards of her room. Everyone was present, with one glaring exception. 'Has anyone seen Martha at all in the last week?' she asked, looking at Annie Chapman in particular.

Annie shook her head. 'She hasn't been back to the lodgings since the Bank Holiday. She went out with another woman from the house. One of the prostitutes, I think. She said she needed to get a payday and said that night would be her best chance to make enough money to pay for the lodgings for at least the next two months.'

Carrie pulled a disapproving face. 'Please tell me she's not turning tricks for money.'

Annie smiled and shook her head. There was no humour in the smile at all. 'No, not Martha. She was leading them on. She'd take them into the back alleys, making them think they were on for a bit. Then she'd knock them out using a strangle hold. It is how she's made her money ever since we got here.'

'Do you think someone might have gotten onto this and, I don't know, arrested her, or kidnapped her, or something?' Mary Kelly asked nervously, she didn't like the idea of one of them being missing.

'There was a murder on the night of the Bank Holiday in the alleyway that leads to our lodge,' Annie added. 'It was a woman, apparently. But I can't see Martha allowing any of her tricks to get the better of her.'

Mary turned on her with intensity in her wide eyes. 'A murder by your lodgings on the night she disappeared? And you didn't think to let anyone in on this?' she snapped.

Annie dropped her head. 'It was all over the news. I didn't say anything because of the paradoxical law. No one can kill us in this timeline, remember.'

'Unless it was one of us!' came an ominous voice from the back of the room. Rose Mylett was one of the security details who had volunteered to come back with them. 'If it was one of us, then murder wouldn't be a problem. We can't be killed by anyone from this time, but it wouldn't be a problem if the murderer was *from* our time! Is it possible we have a traitor in our midst?' she asked, stalking around the room with a suspicious gait.

'Enough talk about traitors!' Carrie shouted. 'None of us are traitors to this cause. We've all proved our worth to The Event, and no one here would give up on our plans now.' She addressed the whole group, but Rose in particular. 'We'll need to investigate if she's been taken prisoner or something. Annie, I'll need you to find out anything, and everything, you can about the murder. It'll do us no harm to have information regarding it, especially with it being so close. Do we know how this poor woman was killed?'

'The gossip around the lodge is that she was ripped apart. Nearly forty stab wounds. Nobody has come forward to say they saw anything, and the police haven't released the victim's name yet,' Annie reported.

'Well, let's keep double vigilant for if, and when, she turns up, and let's all be more careful about our comings and goings.' Carrie dismissed the meeting. 'But also remember, without sounding callous about the situation, Martha was a good source of funding. We're going to need to find another one.'

Everyone left the room except for Carrie and Mary Kelly.

'You look tired,' Carrie spoke softly, fixing a lock of Mary's auburn hair back behind her ear. 'You don't think anything could have happened to her, do you?'

'Not unless the theories of nature's paradoxical laws are wrong. If they are, then we could all be in peril, and we'd have to lookout for each other.' She paused, but Carrie knew that she had something more to say.

'Or?' Carrie asked, not willing to wait on a cliff-hanger.

'Abandon the mission.'

The tall woman recoiled as if slapped. 'The paradoxical laws are true. If someone from this time tried to kill us, nature couldn't allow it to happen. Something would step in to stop the death. It would affect nature's timeline too much. Martha can't be dead; someone must be holding her somewhere.'

'Agreed,' Mary replied nodding her head. 'But who, and why?'

~~~~

Aaron Kosminski was watching everything from his usual spot outside the window of Carrie's room in White's Row. By now, he knew all the women. He knew their faces, he knew them intimately in his dreams, and he knew their secret. He also knew something else that they didn't know. Their friend Martha was lying dead on a slab in the mortuary, the victim of a savage attack by an unknown assailant.

*She should have been my victim,* he thought.

As the women left, he focused his attentions to the next on his list. Polly, they called her, although he had a feeling that it wasn't her real name. She was a tall woman, and she looked the oldest of the lot, but that did not mean she *was* old, quite the contrary. She was striking, with handsome features, and a voluptuous figure.

Of all the women he was following, she was the only one he found physically attractive. *That's just her sending out her witchy allure, covering herself in the bitch smell so I can't help but lust after her,* he thought. This had become his mantra, he told himself it again and again, attempting to wipe any of the irregular thoughts running through his head.

He had watched Polly for a while now. She, too, was using a trick to solicit money. Wherever there was a game of cards, or a game of chance, you would find Polly. He thought her name was rather apt, as she would sit at the shoulders of her marks, whispering into their ears what they should do next. This whisper meant the man invariably won, and then Polly would take a cut of the winnings.

He had watched her take a pretty penny over the last few nights.

Since the death of Martha, there had been no sightings of the mysterious stranger, he had been looking for his odd, false face in every crowd. Tonight, he was not going to be disturbed. Tonight, was his night. He was going to murder pretty Polly, and there would be no one to stop him this time.

He followed his potential victim as she journeyed from pub to pub all through the West End. He watched as she drank and gambled until late into the night. She left the Frying Pan public house and staggered out into the street, drunk as anything, carrying a large amount of money.

His blood was tingling in his veins, and his heart was pounding within his chest, like it was attempting to free itself from the prison of his ribcage. A quick scan of the street told him there was no stranger around to take this one from him. His dreams about this woman had been intense. Horrific, but intense. Each time they came he woke up with a strong, throbbing erection. The only way he could rid himself of it was to take matters into his own hands. As he had been brought up Catholic, he had been taught that this kind of thing was forbidden, a sin. But he had to admit that he enjoyed it.

He stood in the corner of the crowded room and curled his hand tight around the handle of the small, but dangerous, razorblade in his coat pocket. It was one of a fine set he had purchased from a barber in Fleet Street. He had used it once or twice on a gentleman's chin, giving him the finest shave that he had ever had, so he knew this instrument would be ideal for the new job it had to undertake.

He gave the woman two minutes before following her out of the pub.

The moment he stepped onto the street; he saw him.

The mystery man who had killed Martha was back. He was walking slowly, careful to stay in the shadows, and was wearing the same cape and sporting the same cane as he had the other night. There was no mistaking that it was him.

In normal circumstances, a man walking these streets wearing the attire he was, would have caused him to stand out in the crowds of scruffy revellers, making himself a mark for the street gangs and muggers, but this man didn't. It was as if the shadows suited him, like they shielded him from the depravity all around him, allowing him to stalk his prey unmolested.

Kosminski cursed under his breath as he kept his distance. He didn't want to be in the company, or indeed the sights, of this strange man with his even stranger devices. *If he's stalking her too, then I must be onto something about them being witches*, he thought.

As if reading his mind, the man turned towards him as he stalked the stalker. In a flash, Kosminski dipped into the shadows of the wall, flattening himself in the gloom, trying his best to disappear.

Unperturbed, the stranger continued into the night, following the hapless witch.

When he was sure it was safe, he followed them both as they made their way towards Polly's lodgings on Thrawl Street. He didn't know who he was trailing now, the mysterious man, or the witch. Either way, it no longer mattered to him. One of them was going to get what was coming to them tonight; and get it good, of that much he was certain. He reached into his pocket again and caressed the handle of the sharp blade. It reassured him; calmed him. The chance to use it last time on what would have been his first victim had been denied to him, but he was damned sure he wouldn't let this stranger block what he saw as his destiny again.

With his heart pounding and his stomach churning, filling with butterflies, he watched as Polly turned into a dark yard. With escalating anger, he saw the mysterious man enter behind her.

He ran, as quick as he could without making any noise, to the entrance, he needed to see what was happening inside.

What he saw surprised him.

Polly was bending over, like she had dropped something on the ground and was trying to retrieve it. In the meantime, the stranger was behind her, holding the glowing sphere again. He was pointing it towards her, but the eerie beam had missed. He retracted the device and looked at it intently, pressing buttons, or something of that nature, frantically. With his attention distracted from the woman, Polly noticed her assailant and ran from the yard, towards where Kosminski was hiding.

With a frustrated growl, the man dropped his device as he noticed his prey escaping. He darted after her and tackled her, wrapping his legs around her waist. They were both on the floor instantly, the stranger having the advantage.

Polly was not as agile as Martha, and her attacker had the better of her in no time.

'Mary Nichols...' he growled, '...you're going to pay for what you've done. Did you think travelling back this far would help evade capture?' he snarled, as his hands wrapped around her throat.

'It doesn't matter if you kill me,' she croaked. 'They'll still bring my body back to complete the mission.'

'Not if I have your slug,' he replied, producing the device he had used in his last attack.

Kosminski was close enough to see her eyes, which, although in pain from the chokehold he had her in, shifted to look at the device. He noted them changing, recognition widening them, before fear took over. It was almost as if this situation she found herself in meant a whole lot more to her.

Suddenly there was a movement from behind the mysterious man, and he turned to see what the noise was. As he did, another woman flew at him from out of the shadows; her feet connected with his jaw, and again he dropped his device. His hold on Polly weakened as he crumpled to the floor.

Try as he might, Kosminski could not make out who the other woman was, so he pressed himself further into the shadows as the newcomer knelt by the side of the mysterious man's head. She took him in the same embrace Martha had used on the sailors. After a moment or two, the mysterious man stopped moving and flopped to the floor. Kosminski assumed he was dead. The newcomer stood up, and wiping her hands on her dress, she admired her work. That was when he recognised her as the one they called Emily. She was in the same vein as Martha, strong, fit, and seemingly well trained.

She knelt, helping Polly up off the floor and supported her towards the house.

Kosminski was dumbfounded at what he had just witnessed, he was also curious, *and* intrigued; but mostly he was scared. 'Not tonight, old man,' he told himself. 'But soon, very soon.' As he slunk back into the street, he offered one more gaze towards the yard. He thought he saw some movement, but dismissed it as his shocked brain playing tricks. *Tonight*, he thought, *is not going to be a night of my dreams.*

## 34.

EMILY CALLAGHAN LAID the shocked and shaking body of Polly on a mattress in the poorly furnished lodging they had paid for. Dark bruises were already showing on her neck from the attack. Her face had drained of colour, and she was shaking violently.

'Will you be OK there for one minute? I knocked the bastard out. I'll have to go and finish it.'

Polly nodded as she looked up at her.

Emily paused on her way out of the room. 'Did he have what I think he had in his hands?'

She sat up, touching her neck as she tried to speak. 'H- he was talking ab- out the slu- slug.' She swallowed hard, looking pained as she did. 'He knew everything, Em. Everything.'

'Shit! OK, I'm going back out there. I think he dropped something in the yard when I hit him. I need to see what it is. You stay here, I promise, I'll be back.'

Polly nodded and lay down on the bed, touching her neck.

Emily ventured out into the dark yard. She cursed the lack of technology in this age and went back into the larger, downstairs room, that was used as a communal sleeping room. The smell was rank as she manoeuvred around several sleeping bodies leaning on a rope that had been crudely hung the length of the room. The smell of cheap alcohol, vomit, faeces, and sweat should have been overpowering, but she was becoming used to it these days. She found a flint lucifer and used it to light a small candle. A few of the sleeping bodies murmured, in protest at the light, but she knew none of them would wake from their stupors and challenge her. Eventually, she made it back to the yard, where she gratefully took in a deep breath of the semi-fresh night air. She then set about doing what she had come out to do. To kill the man she had just incapacitated.

She shone the light around the yard, but to her amazement, the body was gone. As were his tools.

Every instinct in her military training was now on high alert. *How the Hell did he get up from that? I knocked the bastard out cold. He should be out for at least an hour!* Slowly, she retreated into a corner of the yard, deeming it as the best location to defend herself from any surprise attack.

A noise on the other side of the yard caught her attention. Something, or someone, was there. *He's heading for Mary's room*, she thought and left the protection of her corner, heading towards the direction of the noise.

None of her training could have helped her in what happened next.

The world went darker than it already was as she felt something strong wrap around her head. Her hands and legs went stiff, and the next thing she knew, she was lying on the cement floor, face to face with the body of the man she had knocked out earlier. She felt her hands being tied behind her back but was unable to do anything about it. Something was pushed beneath her. There was a quiet beep, and she felt herself floating. As the ground got further away, she tried her best to scream, but no sound escaped her. A brief glimpse of a black trouser leg and a strange kind of cane came into her limited line of sight, then disappeared as she floated off down the deserted street.

A few minutes later, again from her limited viewpoint, she saw that they were entering an old building. Whoever it was controlling the platform activated something and the door dissolved into light particles. It was something she had seen a million times before, but it scared her more than anything else. It meant that whoever this was, was definitely from her time. It meant that right now, she and all the others, were in real danger. This person could kill her without disrupting the paradoxical laws of nature.

The platform landed, and someone stood over her. Then her vision went fuzzy and the world turned black.

~~~~

Polly was in the room, lying on her mattress, shivering. She couldn't believe what had just happened to her. *Who could it have been?* She'd had her doubts about the paradoxical laws, and those doubts were running through her mind now. Slowly, she lifted herself off the filthy mattress, the one they had paid far too much money for and swung her legs onto the floor. Her throat was tight; it felt swollen. *Maybe he can't kill me, but he can have a bloody good go at it.* She attempted to smile, but it hurt so much, she gave up.

'Where is she?' she mumbled, getting up to look out of the window where the body of her assailant should have been. By what little light there was down in the yard, she could see that the body was gone. *Has she moved it by herself?* She knew that Emily had been in the military and was stronger than she looked, which was the main reason she'd been chosen for this mission, but moving a grown man, that quickly?

A noise from outside the room alerted her. 'Emily? Is that you?' she croaked. It could have been anyone from the multiple rooms in the lodging house, but there was something about the noise that put her on the alert; it sounded... stealthy. With her heartbeat thrashing in her sore throat, she made it to the door and looked outside.

'No... it's not Emily,' the voice from the other side announced. 'It's me!'

As the door burst open, she backed away, losing her balance as her feet hit the mattress. She only just managed to dodge the dark figure as he poured into the room. Luckily for her, he stumbled too, lost his balance, and fell. This brief reprieve gave her a chance to get off the mattress and out of the room; she took full advantage of it.

She raced along the landing, and down the stairs. As she reached the ground floor, she risked a glance back towards her assailant who was still on the stairs. It was a man. He had longish dark hair and a thick black moustache, fashionable in this time by the gentry. As his cape flowed in his pursuit, she noticed there were several devices tucked into his belt, devices that were, by no means, of this time and age.

Putting this information to the back of her mind, she focused all her attention on her escape route.

The mystery man was out of the house and after her faster than she had bargained for. The slight advantage she had, was now lost by her dithering, and she no longer had much of a head start on him. She burst out of the yard, running blindly through the streets of London, trying to find her way back to White's Row. She needed to alert Carrie and Mary. In her panic, she took a wrong turn onto Brick

Lane. She thought she was heading for Fashion Street, which would lead onto White's Row, instead she had turned left and found herself on Old Montague Street, the opposite direction, heading towards Kempton Court.

Disorientated and terrified, she turned many times to see if her attacker was still in pursuit, mentally giving thanks to Mary Kelly who had motivated them into maintain the best physical shape they could.

The adrenaline in her system was burning low now, and she found herself slowing down. She had run full pelt for almost a mile, and a stich was burning a small inferno in her stomach.

A man was walking along the street, he was about a hundred yards before her. Without any thought, other than to get away from her pursuer, she ran towards him. Somewhere, deep down, she knew that a man walking the streets alone at this time of night was probably not going to want to offer her help, but considering the alternative, she felt she had nothing to lose.

'Sir, sir, please help me! I'm being chased by a stranger. I think he's done one of my friends in, maybe even two,' she panted, clearly out of breath. 'I think he's wanting to do me in too,' she pleaded to her potential saviour.

She could smell the alcohol on him before she got within five steps of him. As she grabbed at the lapels of his jacket, his eyes widened, as if the idea of a woman accosting him in the street was totally out of the realms of reality.

'You!' he growled at her. 'You filthy, unholy witch! Unhand me, you whore. I thought you'd been done in for sure by now!' His face became a fierce snarl beneath his moustache. 'But no,' he spat. 'You and your like, it's my reckoning that you probably have nine lives like a filthy cat. I watched as one of your coven killed that man, and I saw…'

Polly gave up on this man protecting her and wasn't even listening to his drunken ramblings anymore; she realised she was on her own and had now lost valuable time pleading with a drunkard. The assassin following her had now turned the corner and was making his way towards her. She thought that she might have out run him, as there had been a few twists and turns through the dark side streets, but nevertheless, he was still in hot pursuit.

The drunkard was still rambling and cursing at her as she left him behind, turning into Bucks Row, a gloomy, dimly lit street. There, she found a small hiding spot inside a dark gateway that lead to a stable. She pressed herself into the gateway, turning this way and that, taking stock of the street—there was a single streetlamp and a few lodgings a little further up. *These stables will have to do*, she thought as she fought to catch her breath.

She pulled on the gate, but it was locked. She looked up, looking for a foothold, or anything that would allow her to climb over it, but there was nothing.

Exhausted, she dropped down into the dark corner, cowering in the shadows, attempting to make herself as small and she could and, hopefully, invisible.

~~~

Kosminski had been drinking heavily when the witch had accosted him. He couldn't believe his luck. He leaned back against the wall and watched as she moved away from him and continued, heading towards Bucks Row.

Maybe he'd get another crack at her after all. After what he'd witnessed in the yard, he thought it had been his lot for the night. But it seemed fate had other ideas for him. A tight smile took over his lips. *Maybe there'll be murder after all.* This thought pleased him, at least until he saw the mystery man skulking in the shadows.

*Now's my time,* he thought, making his way over towards where the shadow was lurking.

'Excuse me, sir?' a deep voice from behind shocked him.

He jumped a little as he turned, on his guard, wondering if there really had been two shadows, ready to wreak revenge on him for watching the other witch attack him, and not helping.

To his relief, and also his chagrin, there was a policeman standing behind him.

'Can I ask what you're doing walking alone at this time of night, sir?'

'Oh, Officer,' he slurred. 'I'm just out trying to walk off the legion of ales I supped tonight in the Frying Pan. The missus'll have my guts for garters if I get in stinking of booze and tarts again, and no mistake.'

The policeman's eyes narrowed as he looked at him. 'Where do you live, sir?' he asked with authority.

'Wodeham Gardens, just around the corner, actually.' Kosminski spoke this address with authority too, knowing that the policeman would discontinue his line of inquiry if he knew he lived in Wodeham Gardens. It was as nice an area as the East End could offer.

'Well, just see that you get back there, sir, and soon. It's not safe for a gentleman to be walking alone at this hour of the morning.'

'Very well, officer, and thank you,' he replied and turned as if heading towards his stated destination. He watched as the policeman walked off, heading towards Whitechapel.

He cursed the policeman under his breath. He'd lost sight of his little witch now. He felt in his pocket and was relieved to feel the cool handle of his razor. He was ready, and set, to continue his wrath against these unholy women. He scanned the road, searching for any evidence of the shadow he'd seen before the policeman poked his nose into his business. He knew there wouldn't be any. He was beginning to think that this mystery man might be some kind of supernatural being. He had witnessed his death earlier and then seen him again only moments ago. *Normal men don't get up so soon after having their necks broken,* he thought, causing a chill to run down his spine. There was no sign of him now, and that suited him fine. The witches were *his* prey, and he was more eager than ever to get to them now.

~~~~

From her sanctuary in the shadows, Polly witnessed the drunken man talk to a policeman, and a sense of relief descended over her. She was just about to stand and call out for help when something in her peripheral vision stopped her. It was a swish of red on black, like the inside of a gentleman's cape, the same cape of the man who had been pursuing her. It disappeared behind a wall at the entrance to the row. She turned back towards where the drunken man and the policeman had been talking, and to her horror, she saw that they were now both gone.

She was alone!

Only not quite as alone as she hoped to be.

'Mary Ann Nichols…' The whisper came from behind her, and instantly she felt goose-bumps raise over her entire body.

The mystery man was standing next to her.

He reached out and grabbed at her.

She managed to dodge this advance and escape from the shadows, running in the direction of the small row of houses by the streetlamp. Panic had taken over, and in her confusion, and disorientation, she readied herself to scream. She was just about to release it and raise hell, waking every single occupant of Buck's Row from their slumber to get them to come to her aide; but no sound escaped her.

A strange sensation enveloped her. She tried to move, she needed to get away, as far away from this man as she could, but no matter how hard she tried, her limbs refused to comply; only her head had any freedom. She looked down at her body and was surprised to see it bathed in a green light. She looked towards her attacker. He was holding a small sphere in his hands, it had a nozzle on the end, and it was glowing green.

*Killed by my own invention*, she thought. *This man* is *from our time!*

She looked back down at her body and saw the tell-tale purple signal flashing within the green.

It was her slug.

The man produced a laser scalpel, and she watched, with dawning horror, as he activated the switch at the side and the red cutting beam blinked into life.

~~~~

Kosminski was once again relegated to the role of voyeur. He couldn't believe what he was seeing. The assassin was indeed back from the dead. He shook, uncontrollably, as he witnessed the drama before him. The ghost ignited the same red candle from his gun and pointed it towards the glowing purple thing that was flashing inside the green light, covering the witch's body.

He knew what was going to happen.

The purple blip began to move. It looked like a game, like the blip was playfully attempting to evade the red beam. As it made its way up to her neck, the red light followed it. In death, he didn't seem to be as experienced a user as he had been in life, and he made two clumsy passes attempting to catch the purple within the red. Where the beam touched her, it bit into her flesh and Kosminski was forced to watch as her face contorted and writhed in agony. Dark, fresh, blood began to flow from the cuts produced by the light, it steamed as the warm liquid met the cold air of the night.

Alas, for Polly, the purple light was not to be caught so easily, and it changed direction again, darting down her body towards her abdomen.

The beam cut through Polly like a surgical knife, ripping into the soft flesh of her belly. It chased the elusive blip, travelling down towards her crotch. The shadow's hand wavered a number of times in the pursuit, causing untold carnage to her body wherever the light touched her.

Polly's eyes were rolling to the back of her head; the pupil-less whites glowing with the reflection of the green mist holding her.

He watched, in rapture, as saliva drooled from the witch's mouth as it hung wide and helpless. It looked to him as if she were attempting to vocalise her torment for the world to hear, to scream blue murder, to cry for help, but it was all to no avail; the night, and this murderous assault, were both as silent as the grave.

Eventually, the red beam caught the purple flashing light, and Kosminski watched its illumination bloom as it was torn from the pouring wound in the woman's stomach. As it hit the air, the light dimmed before eventually dying out completely. The man reached out and snatched the gore-soaked object. He held it up towards the single light in the street and admired it, just for a moment, then the top of the sphere he was holding opened and he deposited it inside. The object gave a small, clink as it landed inside.

The husk that used to be Mary Ann 'Polly' Nichols fell to the floor, into a pool of her own blood.

He didn't need to investigate this body; he could already tell that she was dead. The mystery he had wrapped himself up in, had just deepened. What he didn't know was what he could do next. He was stuck in the gateway of the yard—if he moved now, the assassin would no doubt see him, and he didn't fancy his chances against him and whatever his lethal devices were. All he could do was slide further back into the shadows, waiting for the silhouette to make his exit. To his surprise, the stranger sat down next to Polly's body, his back against the wall of the nearby house. Kosminski couldn't tell for sure, but he thought he could hear mournful sobs in the still of the night.

He watched with interest as the ghostly assassin lifted his sleeve and adjusted something on his arm. He put his wrist towards his mouth and talk into it. Kosminski strained to hear what was being said but could only make out the odd snippets of words.

'...come in, Jack... ripped her... dead, yes I think it... Nichols... secured... my best from now... my own, understood. Jack... out.'

The conversation didn't make any sense to him, but one phrase did stand out. 'Jack, ripped her.' Or was it: 'Ripper'? *Is that his name? Jack Ripper?*

Eventually, the stranger stood, put his devices back into the folds of his cape, and sloped off into the night, his black cloak once again blending with the darkness. Kosminski didn't have the energy to follow him, not tonight, not after what he had just witnessed, and not after all the ale he had drunk earlier. Once again, he set off home; disappointed, angry, and scared.

## 35.

<u>Orbital Platform One. 2288</u>

'COMMUNICATIONS ARE WORKING, sir,' Jacqueline bragged, puffing her chest out, her smile almost splitting her face in two. 'It's a simple matter of piggybacking them onto the quantum signal. There's a small delay, but we contacted Chris Webb, our first human trial. We sent him back ten years for ten minutes. He knew the risks and was more than willing to do the trial for the good of humanity. While he was there, he reported, and I quote, 'It's cold and wet.' Considering that we sent him to Birmingham in England, I would say it was success.'

Youssef was delighted; everything was slotting into place. The organic trials had gone without a hitch, the human trials, which he had been loathed to do but knew the urgency of the situation warranted them, were successful too. Now, the communications were working.

Ever the pessimist, he was starting to think that things were going a little *too* well.

He looked around the table. Dr Hausen was absent as he was coordinating the aid workers who were busy attempting to bring order to some of the worst hit locations on the planet. It was a job hampered by the majority of the citizens being too scared, of ramifications from The Quest, to accept help from the EA. Youssef, as ranking member of the EA, had built a team to deal with this situation. Hausen had been the obvious choice to head it up. He had carte blanche to make any decisions he thought correct; he had Youssef's trust.

Kevin was present in the room, as was Vincent and Jacqueline.

'I only want the people in this room, with the exception of Dr Hausen, to know what we propose to do here. You'll be aware that, over the last few weeks, we've been working to understand the fundamentals to create a secure transportation back in time, to send an operative...' he looked at Vincent, but never mentioned him by name, '...back to the same era as The Quest. Jacqueline, I'm handing this meeting over to you.'

'Thanks, Youssef,' she said, standing to address the table. 'We've been working with the data we archived from The Quest's network regarding quantum tagging and magnetic tagging, and we have successfully sent a human test subject back in time. We tracked their movements, communicated with them, and recalled them back to our time. We now think it's operationally feasible to go forth with this mission.' She took a moment to take in what she had just said and couldn't help but smile. She cleared her throat, getting herself back into the professional attitude needed to deliver this address. 'We've also been working on the Higgs Storm issue too. Now, this has fundamentally been an equation. We measured the quantities of Storm that was produced when we sent the apple back, and also our human test subject. This information, coupled with what we know about the size and weights of the women, gave us the sum, approximately, as to how much Storm would be required for them to destroy the remainder of the Earth's habitable surface. We now have an estimate of when they are! We've narrowed it down to summertime eighteen-eighty-eight! July, to be exact.'

Kevin's face dropped as he shook his head. 'How did you narrow that down?'

'If you have a baseline to work with, it just becomes a pure maths problem,' Jacqueline answered. 'But we do still have one issue to iron out. In theory, we know when they are, but we have no way of telling where they are. As the Higgs-Boson is mixed with hydrogen, we know that the atoms can be sent basically anywhere in the world. Even if we can receive the quantum signals from the women that tells us when they are, we still need the transponder codes to track them. These will be masking the magnetic signals. It's my thinking that the codes are only held by the personnel who are tracking them. That's how I would do it, anyway.'

Kevin smiled a little at this information. 'I can smell an operation coming on. You're going to need a team to infiltrate their base and steal the transponder codes, then we can find them and bring them home.'

Youssef smiled back. 'We've already sent a cyber tracker into their portals to find this information electronically, but to no avail. So, it's over to you, my friend. We need this information before we can send Vincent back in time. He'll be aided in the present by Jacqueline. She'll monitor everything he does. If we get all the codes, then we can zap them all back, straight to jail. If we can get just one code, then we'll at least know where they are, and we can physically go back and bring them to justice. We'll need to be ready for the massive amounts of Higgs Storm, though.'

'My team can be ready in an hour. I'm assuming that we're going to Inverness?' Kevin asked standing up.

Youssef nodded. 'For this mission, your team will consist of you and Vincent. We need to minimise our liability. The EA is growing more unpopular every day. I wouldn't be surprised if The Quest hasn't already infiltrated our ranks. My present thought is that everyone in this room, and Dr Hausen, are the only personnel I'm willing to outright trust. We're going to be working on this premise for the time being. The people are scared, there's a threat of mass violence and death if we don't stand down, and as we have no plans to do that, then it's just us, my friends. I need you two to be ready within the next hour. Failure is not an option. We need those codes.'

Kevin looked at Vincent, winked, and then turned his attentions back to Youssef. 'You know you can count on us.'

## 36.

VINCENT CLARENCE AND Kevin Farley were standing inside the Hadron Collider pods, awaiting teleportation to Inverness. Both were dressed, head to toe, in black.

'You do know it's cold up there this time of the year?' Kevin said to Vincent.

'I've heard its cold up there every time of the year,' Vincent replied with a smile. They were both in their individual pods, checking their equipment, weapons, illuminations, emergency tele-packs, and handheld portals.

Youssef was operating the collider. 'Jacqueline and I will monitor you every step of the way. You'll minimise any contact with the enemy. We don't want a fire fight down there. If you're compromised, use your tele-packs and get yourselves back as soon as possible. Do you understand?'

Kevin slipped a look that Youssef knew only too well. It said 'Whatever', but his mouth said; 'You know me, Youssef, I always err of the side of caution.'

Vincent scoffed as Youssef shook his head. 'Are we ready, Jacqueline?' he asked.

'Just adding the coordinates now,' she replied, typing into a glass panel. 'Right outside the castle; sorry, boys, I can't get you inside,' she said shrugging her shoulders.

'It's OK, I forgot my tie anyway. It looks like we'll have to crash this party,' Vincent wisecracked.

'May Allah be with you,' he blessed them both.

Kevin pulled a mock angry face. 'Who's this Allah guy? You told us we were the only ones to know about this mission…'

Youssef shook his head at the terrible joke as he watched the duo disappear into a purple light. 'What are they getting themselves into down there?' he asked Jacqueline as she meddled with the monitor.

She shook her head, looking more than a little confused. 'I don't know. I'm not picking up any heat signatures, I don't think there's anyone down there.'

~~~~

The two soldiers materialised in a secluded section in the grounds, behind a large wall in a garaged area. 'Good move getting us into a garage, no one will have seen us arrive,' Kevin spoke into his wrist.

'I'm a professional, you know. I have looks, brains, and the moves to back them up.'

Vincent smiled. 'Well that's good to know…'

'Cut the chatter, Clarence, you have a job to do,' was her curt reply.

Vincent poked his head out of the garage as Kevin readied his weapon. 'You're clear for the next hundred metres,' Jacqueline reported through their earpieces. 'We have reason to believe that the subterranean compound, the original castle, is where the strongest quantum signals are coming from. It could be a laboratory.'

'OK, we're going to radio silence until we're inside. Only contact us if we are in imminent danger,' Kevin commanded into his wrist.

'Will do, out,' she replied, and the com went dead.

'How do you want to do this, sir?' Vincent asked.

'I always think the direct approach is usually the best, don't you, soldier?'

'That's a positive, sir. The front door it is then.'

Kevin took out his handheld portal. The full known schematics of the castle had been preloaded onto their devices. They knew that once inside they would have precious little cover if their presence was known; but they also knew that these were acceptable risks.

In stealth, they made their way to the front of the castle. The dark and damp conditions gave them the exact cover they needed to go undetected. Vincent took the lead to the main gate, where they were both surprised to find it unguarded. There was evidence of a large gathering here not too long ago, but it seemed everyone were long gone now.

He gave Vincent the signal to move forward with caution.

As they entered the main gate and into the single chamber inside, the size of the place hit them. All the rooms and floors had indeed been gutted and replaced with computer terminals and technology, but the place was deserted. Every portal was dead and there was not a soul to be seen anywhere.

'Don't get me wrong,' Vincent whispered. 'I'm glad there's no one here, but it's creeping me out a bit.'

Kevin replied with the signal for him to shut up before walking towards the large spiral staircase in the centre of the room. He lowered his weapon.

Vincent did another sweep around the room before deciding it was safe to do the same. 'Maybe there's nothing here worth protecting,' Vincent offered.

'Or maybe that's what they want us to think,' he replied. 'Watch your step, there could be booby traps anywhere.'

He looked at the readout on his handheld portal. 'I'm reading our target location is down these stairs. There's an underground complex.'

'Me too, let's go.'

Kevin grabbed him and pulled him back. 'Easy now, lad, don't go rushing in until all exits have been identified and all threats have been neutralised. Now we need to circumvent this stairwell and check out any sensors or monitors.'

Vincent nodded, a little abashed for his excitement. 'OK, sir, understood.'

'Don't apologise, just learn from it. Remember, when you get back there, you'll be on your own. Your only ally will be Jacqueline on the radio.'

Silently, they made their way around the staircase, identifying and easily neutralising a number of potential threats; cameras, scanners and the like. When they assessed it was safe, they made their way down the spiral staircase.

'We've entered the stairwell and heading towards the source of the quantum signals,' Kevin reported.

'Received. You'll need to go down... three levels. There's an open area that we can't scan. It might be light locked. If it is, we'll have to interface to get through it,' Jacqueline replied.

'I had a feeling it would be. It's not the lock themselves that's usually the problem, it's what's hidden inside them.' He signalled to Vincent to continue down. 'I don't think there's any personnel here, but it looks like we'll have a light lock situation when we get to our destination.'

'Understood.'

~~~

A small light flickered on Jacqueline's console. As she looked at it a frown grew on her face. She had no idea what it was. She was just about to report it to the operatives when a message flashed up on her screen. It opened of its own accord.

It was an image of a woman.

'We have received notification of an unauthorised entry into Inverness Castle. The DNA has been scanned and found to originate from your operative database. Please be informed that we have antipersonnel systems in place, your operatives...' there was a slight pause, '...Kevin Farley and Vincent Clarence, will very soon be neutralised. Please use this as a deterrent from trespassing on The Quest's property in the future.'

The image of the woman disappeared. Jacqueline punched up a screen showing representations of the two soldiers making their way into the chamber beneath the castle.

Her face was white.

'Kevin, Vincent, you'll have to get out of there NOW, you've been compromised. Antipersonnel systems are in place to stop your progress.'

'That's a negative. We've come here to get something and we're going to get it. Over and out.'

She pressed another button on the console. 'Youssef, you'd better get up here, we have a situation.'

'On my way,' came the electronic reply.

'Can you give me a status update?' she asked into the console, her mouth was completely dry, and she was finding it hard to speak.

'We've reached the root of the quantum signals. It seems to be an entrance to a lab of some sorts, and indeed it is light locked.'

'I'm monitoring your situation from every conceivable angle, physical threats, electronic threats, environmental threats. I'm not picking up anything, as of yet, to say you're in danger, but I'd feel better if you abandoned the mission. I'll continue to monitor if that's how you want to play it.' She began to press buttons on her console frantically now, attempting to assess every angle of the team. 'Vincent are you OK?' she asked. Sweat was now beading on her forehead, and she could feel it trickling down her back. 'I'm reading elevated stress levels in your stats.'

'I'm fine, it's just a little adrenalin kicking in, that's all.' Vincent turned towards Kevin and whispered. 'Are we going to do this or just talk about it all day?'

Kevin smiled. 'Let's do it.' He reached around his belt for his handheld portal.

'Jacqueline, interface with my portal, the address is KF Zero-Zero-Nine Hash Seven. You got that?'

A clicking sound came through his earpiece, and a second later, Jacqueline's voice broke through. 'I'm in. Point it towards the light lock.'

Kevin did as was requested, and a slight rumble passed from the portal to his hands. 'Shield your eyes,' he commanded.

Vincent obeyed as a bright flash issued from the doorway, and the doors opened, slightly.

As soon as the flash was gone, a series of clunks and clicks began to echo from the walls around them.

'Guys, it looks like every exit to the castle has just been hermetically sealed. I'm reading an energy field that has generated around your perimeter. Jesus, that's hermetically sealed too. You guys have about five minutes of air, total. I'm pulling you out, now,' Jacqueline shouted from her position in the control room.

'Stand down!' Kevin shouted. 'We have a job to do here, and we're going to do it. You work on getting us an exit, or just lock onto our signals and be ready to pull us out on my order.' He turned to Vincent. 'Get your ass over to the nearest console or portal you can log into and start to upload everything you can from the database.'

'I'm on it, sir.' He ran into the room straight to the nearest portal.

'Jacqueline, can you read my portal? The address is VC Two-Two-Eight Hash Nine-Eight.'

'I'm in. Just interface with the console, and I'll do the rest. I need to let you know that I'm having trouble locking onto your signals. The energy field seems to be scrambling them. I'm also failing to find an exit.'

'How long do we have?' Vincent asked.

'A little over three minutes. The problem is that to get the database successfully uploaded, it is going to take...' she paused as she looked at her screen. 'Roughly six.'

Kevin cut into the conversation. 'The database takes priority. Concentrate all your efforts onto retrieving that.'

'Sir, if it's all the same to you, I'll continue to do both.'

He looked at Vincent. A surge of pride swelled through him as he noticed that the young man was not showing any signs of stress, even in the face of death. 'You OK, son?' he asked, tipping the younger man a wink.

'I think I just might survive *you*, sir!' he smirked. 'In fact, I think we should have a bet to see who survives the longest.'

Kevin laughed.

It was at this point Youssef walked into the operations room and put his hand on Jacqueline's shoulder. 'What's the situation?'

'They're trapped, sir. We've interfaced with the database, but the upload is going to take another five minutes. They have just a little over two minutes of air left in the room. They're sealed in. I can't lock onto them.' She relayed all this information while simultaneously monitoring the database, looking for an exit or a weakness in the force fields and trying to lock onto their signals.

Youssef leaned in to see what was happening on the monitor. 'Kevin, how are you two holding up?' he asked.

This seemed to brighten him up. 'We're holding up fine, my friend. Will you still be able to upload the database after we're gone?'

Jacqueline answered that one. 'That won't be a problem, sir. The interface is now nothing to do with any physical connection. We've got all the addresses we require to analyse it from here, we just need the portal device to be there until the upload is complete. I am so sorry, guys, I just can't find a way out of that force field.'

Vincent looked at Kevin. 'How long?' he asked.

'Less than a minute, you're going to start to lose your breath pretty quickly in there.'

'Can you just talk to us, as we go? You've got such a nice voice,' Vincent said.

'Sure, I can,' Youssef replied.

This cracked Vincent up, and he began to laugh. 'Yeah, you have too, sir. Kevin, Youssef, and you, Jacqueline. I just want to let you all know that it's been an honour working with you and—'

'GOT IT! I'VE FUCKING GOT YOU!' Jacqueline shouted suddenly.

She pressed a few keys on her console, and Kevin and Vincent disappeared in a purple flash.

~~~

Two figures appeared within the racetrack of the Hadron Collider. They were both crouched, and both were coughing as they fully re-emerged. Jacqueline ran to them and flung open the glass doors. Both men spilled out onto the floor.

'You did it!' Vincent spluttered. 'You didn't give up!'

'That wasn't an option, soldier,' she replied curtly.

'Did you get the whole database?' Kevin asked staggering towards the console, doubled over and coughing

'It is just finishing now, sir.'

He unstrapped a small device from his pack and put it down on the table next to Jacqueline's console. He then turned and patted Youssef on the back. 'Well, Youssef,' he said stretching. 'It looks like we have a couple of fine recruits here for this mission.'

'These are two disciplined kids alright,' he agreed.

Vincent and Jacqueline looked at the two men with distrust.

They both returned their look.

'The situation was real,' Youssef explained. 'We knew about the antipersonnel systems from the database we got last time, but we couldn't get any transponder info, so we had the ideal opportunity to run a real mission, and in the meantime, we got to monitor your reactions to real-life stress tests. I'm pleased to inform you that you passed, both of you. With flying colours.'

'You pair of bastards! That was the worst five minutes of my life,' Jacqueline stuttered, trying not to smile.

'It was supposed to be. You may well encounter worse than that on the real mission. It was good to see that you both kept working until the very end. I'm proud of you, and very pleased to be working with you.' Kevin extended his hand towards them both.

Vincent knocked it away and grabbed him in a huge bear hug. 'You bastards,' he said, his voice muffled from his face being buried in Kevin's shoulders.

## 37.

<u>London. 1888</u>

'ANOTHER ONE, SIR. Mutilated just like the last. It looks like it could be the same weapon, and the same modus operandi,' the tall policeman reported as he stood to attention, almost regimentally, in Inspector Abberline's office.

'Do we know what type of weapon it was?' Abberline asked the officer.

'Not as yet, sir. Whatever it was, it was sharp. It cut the woman open like a hot potato, sir.'

Abberline sat back in his chair and sighed. He held his fingers to his mouth in a peak as he looked wistfully past the tall man before him. 'Were there other mutilations? Was anything removed, like in the other murder?'

The officer removed his hands from behind his back and regarded the notepad he was holding. 'Yes, sir, it looks like there was something removed from the body, although the morgue doesn't know what it was yet. I heard on the grapevine that it was…' he looked at his notepad. 'organs, sir. Something called the 'vital' organ.'

Abberline looked at the officer and shook his head, he sighed as the man put his notepad back in his top pocket. He looked at the inspector with a smug grin, as if he had just broken the case himself.

'OK. Thanks for that, Bellis. I'm going to speak to my superiors. I need to get myself back to Whitechapel. I want in on this case.'

'Why, sir? It's a routine murder. You know what the natives are like after a skin full of ale. They'd chop up their own mothers for another drink and a whiff of quim.'

'I beg to differ on this one, officer. It's nothing I can share with you right now, but I've got a hunch about it. Even if it means taking a demotion back to my old desk in Whitechapel, I have a feeling this will not be the last body we see passing through the precinct. Is there any evidence of a connection between the two cases?' Abberline asked.

'A bit of a tenuous connection, it seems. They shared some lodgings a few weeks back, but then, those lodgings were shared by eight other women too, all randoms apparently. Same old leaky records from the landlord. Cash was swapped, so precious few questions were asked.'

'My hunch tells me that there's a stronger connection than that. I wonder if the murderer was familiar with the victims or had at least singled them out for some nefarious purpose.'

Bellis had only understood half of that conversation and didn't know how to respond. He didn't even know if Abberline was still talking to him, or if he was talking to himself.

The detective picked up the case file that Bellis had put on his desk and looked at it. Bellis remained in the office, watching as Abberline put the file next to the one he already had on Martha Tabram. In Fred Abberline's world, the officer no longer existed as he immersed himself into the file.

After a few moments of being ignored, Bellis saluted, turned, and left the room, closing the door behind him.

## 38.

'IT'S BEEN CONFIRMED that the body found in George's Yard was Martha,' Mary Kelly reported with her head bowed low. 'They say that she was cut up so badly, it's taken them this long to get a handle on her identity. There was a rumour in The Ten Bells that her body was half eaten, although I think that was just drunk talk. There was a doctor who would tell anyone who'd buy him a drink that there were parts of her missing, or at least something had been cut out of her.' She paused for a moment in reflection of their fallen comrade. 'It's amazing what people will talk about if they don't think anyone of note is listening.'

Carrie was looking away, staring out of the small, grubby window onto the street below. It was busy out there, filled with hawkers, street gangs, and prostitutes. Every one of them now a potential threat to them and their mission. 'This is worrying. Martha being dead means that there is either someone from the future, here, to try to stop us from getting back. That means that the EA have discovered what we've done. Or, the paradoxical laws, as we thought we understood them, are wrong and we're as vulnerable as everyone else. Now, with Polly and Emily missing too, I'm afraid things have gotten rather serious.'

Carrie's emotionless face was alarming Mary. 'Do you think whoever killed Martha killed Polly and Emily too?' she asked.

'We can't rule it out. We need all the information we can get on this situation. Emily is not the type to just go missing and not inform us where, or why, she was going.'

'She can handle herself; we know that. She was a personal security specialist before joining our cause,' Mary offered.

'None of that will mean a thing if whoever this is gets a jump on her with a binding field. Have any of the women mentioned anything peculiar? People hanging around, or being stalked, anything like that?' Carrie asked, turning away from the street scene below her.

'I spoke to them yesterday after Polly and Emily never checked in. But Carrie, this is the East End of London, eighteen-eighty-eight. Have you seen the quality of the locals around here? The only people who stick out here are the normal people!'

'What did you say?' Carrie snapped her head back towards her friend, her brow ruffled.

'I said the only people who stick out are the—'

'Normal people,' Carrie finished for her. 'Exactly!' She walked away, holding her hands to her face in contemplation.

'Exactly what?' Mary asked.

'Who are the only 'normal' people around here who you know?'

She thought about this for a while. 'Probably only us…' she paused, taking in what she had just said. 'Oh my God, do you think we're being targeted because we stand out from the crowd?'

'It's a distinct possibility. Do we have anyone working in a pub?' Carrie asked.

Mary thought about this question for a moment. 'Annie Chapman is in The Ten Bells.'

'Excellent,' Carrie replied. 'Get her to keep her eyes open for anything strange, and I'll have a word with the others too. Is she working tonight?'

'Yes. She's taken on extra shifts as the landlord in her lodgings is pressing her for more money.'

'Keep her on the shifts, the more eyes we have out there, the better.'

Mary nodded. 'OK, in that case, I'll have to get going, because she's on at ten this evening, and I'll need to speak to her beforehand. I'll pop in and see you tomorrow, give you a report of the night's activities.'

'Thank you, Mary,' Carrie said softly as the other woman began making her way to the door. 'Be careful, won't you?'

She nodded as she closed the door behind her.

## 39.

EMILY CALLAGHAN WAS immobilised in a chair. There was a hood over her head and something in her ears was playing white noise. The combination of the hiss and the dark gave her complete sensory deprivation. She couldn't smell anything other than the overpowering stink of rotting leather from the mask over her face.

She couldn't feel any ropes around her wrists or feet, or anything holding her to the chair, but still she couldn't move. *It's a binding beam,* she thought, a difficult thing to do through the white noise. *This has to be someone from our time.* She had trained as a personal protection agent while in the EA, and she had a very tactical, analytical mind.

Even though she had no perception of time, she guessed she'd been sat here for two days. There had been no contact with anyone in all that time. She was hungry and uncomfortable. She had been forced to do her ablutions while sat on the chair, and even after all the years of tough, intense training, that was still one of the hardest things to do.

Ignoring the discomfort, she tried her best to assess the situation. *If the binding beam has been on me for two days, then I'm guessing that the battery is going to need to be charged sometime soon. Unless it is a nuclear battery, then I'm out of luck, them bastards will run and run and run.* She mused; she had a lot of time to muse. *But, if I remember right, you can't travel time with nuclear devices, or at least you can't travel time accurately with a nuclear device. So, it must be cell based, therefore it should be due to run out soon.* She hoped she was correct, as she needed to make sure Polly was OK.

The white noise in her ears suddenly stopped, and it took a moment for her brain to register that it was no longer there. The sudden silence snapped her out of her thoughts.

'Hello?' she shouted, not entirely in control of her voice levels. 'Is anyone there? If so, can we try and sort this out as sensible, civilised human beings?'

'Civilised? You?' the voice sneered. 'After what you've done to the planet, to your own people? You have the audacity to talk about being civilised?'

'I'm just a soldier,' she replied.

'Oh, and I suppose you were just doing your duty, eh? Obeying orders? Hasn't that been the excuse for atrocities performed for thousands of years?' the voice sneered again.

Emily thought there was something funny about the voice, something she couldn't put her finger on.

'If any of you sheep stopped to question your orders from time to time, then we would be in a whole new world.'

'They weren't orders, they were suggestions. Suggestions that were voted on, democratically, among the group.'

The voice laughed. It was a strange sound, devoid of all humour. 'Democratically? How can you begin to call the decision to genocide the human race democratic? Did you cast a vote between the four billion victims? I think not.'

Emily smiled underneath her leather mask. 'Are we here to talk about the ethics of what The Quest did? Because if we are, I'm afraid that I have other things to do.'

She heard the stranger move around the room; the voice got nearer. 'No, Emily, we're not here to talk about ethics, because I'd win that conversation hands down. We're here to talk about how much you want to save the rest of your group.'

Emily remained silent.

The voice laughed; it was mostly a chuff. 'I admire your silence, I really do, but if you want to save your friend's lives, then I'd give me what I'm politely asking for.'

'And what's that?' Emily asked.

'I want your transponder codes.'

She couldn't help but laugh. 'You want our transponder codes. You travelled all the way back from twenty-two-eighty-eight to Ye Olde London, and you don't even have a plan.'

'Oh, I have a plan all right. This binding beam I've got you in, well it's also monitoring your quantum slug. I can actually see it right now; it's currently residing in your shoulder. Now if I was to set this quantum tracker to search for nearby slugs, I have no doubt that it would find yours. Your slug would know that it was being tracked, and it would hide. My beam would chase it, and it would eventually win. I would then be able to retrieve your slug and deactivate it. Then no one from the future would be able to locate you and bring you back, and therefore, no Higgs Storm. Oh, and there would be no chance of you surviving the extraction either…' the voice paused for a moment, allowing the drama of the speech to lie heavy in the air. 'Or at least, there wasn't for the last two I got. Martha and Polly.'

On hearing the names, Emily began to struggle against her chair. 'You bastard, you killed them, didn't you? You bastard,' she began to shout, her voice muffled beneath the heavy leather hood.

She heard the voice tut. 'Yes, I killed them. I didn't particularly take any pleasure from it, as I'm not murdering scum like you, but I'll do it again. If it means stopping you from completing your sick mission, I'll do it again, with… aplomb.'

Emily began to calm down, she knew that there was no point struggling with the binding beam, she would just have to bide her time until it depleted. She didn't think that there would be anything to power something like it in this time. 'I'll never tell you the codes.'

'In that case, you've condemned yourself, and all your colleagues, to death.' Due to the white noise she had been listening to, she couldn't differentiate anything from the voice, neither gender nor an accent. To her, it sounded purely neutral. It paused for a short while. 'I'll give you another few days to think about it. I think this binding beam will last longer than you will, it is nuclear after all. We'll see how you feel tomorrow when I bring you news.'

~~~~

Annie Chapman was behind the bar in The Ten Bells. Normally she worked as a cleaner, rinsing the vomit and the blood from the floors, collecting tankards, and wiping them into a passable form of cleanliness to be reused. Tonight, however, one of the regular girls had let the landlord down at the last minute, and he had asked Annie to step in to cover the shift.

'You're a cheery sort, and not all that bad to look at,' the fat landlord spat, looming over her as she scrubbed the floor under the bar area. He down out and grabbed at one of her breasts. 'You'll do all right behind the bar tonight. Bring a few of the fellas in, you will. An extra two shillings do ya?' he asked as she brushed his molesting hands away from her. He harrumphed as he turned away. 'Well it'll 'aft to anyways, coz that all ya getting. It's more than the others, mind, so don't you go blabbing ya mouth off or ya won't get it again, d'y'hear me?'

Two shillings was not to be sniffed at; it would pay for at least another two nights in her lodgings, all for a six-hour shift. She was more than happy to accept it. 'I'll do it,' she answered.

'Good,' the landlord grunted, pushing past her.

She felt his fat, grubby hand cup her backside as he went. She turned to face him, ready to give him a piece of her mind, but she saw that he was still facing her, one of his hands down his trousers, grinning as he winked at her. She decided it would be best just to give him the widest berth she could tonight, *and every night,* she thought.

It was a Friday in the East End. The weather had been warmer than usual, and the revellers were out in force. She knew she would have a busy night ahead of her. She thought that this would also be a good opportunity to keep her ear to the ground regarding any 'queer activity,' as the locals would put it. Maybe get some of that information that Mary wanted her to report.

The night did indeed prove to be eventful. There were four fights, three of which were serious, involving either knives or the pewter tankards used as blunt weapons to the head. There were several people caught fornicating in the latrines around the back who had been forcibly removed, only to return again an hour or so later. Two gypsies had been caught lifting wallets and purses; a few curses were uttered while they were ejected. But all of this was just another weekend in The Ten Bells.

It was around midnight, the room was at its fullest, and Annie was avoiding another groping by the, now fully inebriated, landlord. She was also doing her best to avoid the advances of an older gentleman, who too was in a state of advanced drunkenness, and obviously out for a 'bit of rough.' She had been considering allowing him some of the advances in order for her to attempt to lift his wallet, as he looked like he was good for a few bob.

'You! Wench! A pint of ale, warm!' came a shout from the other end of the bar. There stood a well-built man with a fine example of a moustache. *He also looks like he's not short of some coinage, maybe more than the old codger over there*, she thought. She looked him up and down and thought that she might actually let this one do what he wanted. *It's been a while*, she smiled at the thought.

'Hey, slag! I'm telling you to get me a pint of ale,' he shouted again.

All romantic notions she had of him being a knight in shining armour were flushed away like twenty-minute-old vomit. She sighed as she sauntered towards him, flashing a forced smile. *Oh, you don't know what you've just lost, mate*, she thought. As she poured him the pint of ale, slipping in a large deposit from the frothing drip tray, she studied his features. He was tallish, well-built, and had a foreign look about him. Mediterranean maybe. He wasn't a bad looking type, until she got to his eyes. *Wow! His eyes*, she thought, scaring herself a little. They were large and dark, much darker than was the norm around here. The sparse whites were intertwined with bloodshot tendrils, giving him a slightly vampire-ish look.

As she handed over the drink, he dropped some coins into her other hand, and as he took the handle of the tankard, their hands touched. It was only a small, light brush, but it was enough to shock both into silence.

He snapped his hand away in a flash. His wide eyes looked at his flexing fingers, then slowly up at her. There was a moment of clarity between them; it hung there, still and timeless, until he lunged over the bar and grabbed her.

Their eyes stared into each other's for mere seconds, but it felt like an eternity. Images of the next four hundred years pass between them. Electricity, light bulbs in every home, cars, world wars, aeroplanes, television, computers, handheld computers, networks, portals, Slipstreams, Higgs Storm, and then right back into this pub. They both flinched, as if they had been hit, before Kosminski pushed her away. He reeled back from the bar with a wild, untamed look in his eyes.

He seemed to sober up, instantly.

Annie fell back against the bar, causing some of the tankards to fall off the shelf and bounce onto the floor, and a small clatter ensued as recognition descended upon her. She didn't know how, but she knew that there was a connection between them. *Could we be related?* she thought, but the coincidence would have been too much for her to even consider.

~~~~

When the world stopped spinning, and the thoughts in his head were not so… *so what?* he thought. *Fantastical? Is that even a word?* Kosminski regarded the woman before him. He recognised this foe for who she was, and what she was; one of the witches, a*nd obviously a powerful one too judging by what she has just done to me.* He backed away from her and away from the bar, staring in awe and disbelief, and yes, fear!

No one else in the bar existed in that moment. A mist was settling over his eyes, it felt red. He didn't know what colours felt like, but it felt red to him. He pulled the handle from his cane to release the long, deadly blade hidden inside. He dropped the sheath onto the floor and raised the sword. Before anyone knew what was happening, he yelled and dived at the witch. He swung the weapon with wild abandon aiming for the wicked female before him.

Annie's reflexes were quick, and all Kosminski hacked away at was air where a mere millisecond before, she was stood.

The punters stopped their merriment, turning to see what this crazed lunatic was doing. If there was entertainment tonight, they all wanted a bit of it.

~~~~

The landlord, seeing what was happening to one of his girls, ran to the front of the room just in time to see Annie cowering beneath the bar. She was crouched in a puddle of spilled ale while an ape of a man was attempting to jump over the bar and hack her to bits with what looked to him like a sword. He didn't know what angered him more, that this lunatic would see fit to do this in his pub, or the pools of spilled ale. His profits would be down at this rate. A fight was normally good for business, a murder however, was not. It was not going to happen on his watch, and not to the wench that he had is greedy little eyes on either.

With an effort, he hefted his bulk up to the bar and grabbed the attacker underneath his arms, pulling him away. Aaron Kosminski was not, by any stretch of the imagination, a small man, but the sheer size of the landlord almost dwarfed him. He was screaming and thrashing like a mad man, but the landlord subdued him easily. 'Whoa there, guvnor, what's all this about then?' he asked in a tone that he used when he wanted to talk down a punter.

'She's a witch,' he spat, pointing behind the bar where Annie was still cowering. 'She deserves nothing better than to die, just like the others. The ones that I witnessed.'

'Sir, I don't know what you're referring to, but make no mistake, I'll make short work of your fucking arms if you do not cease threatening the wenches in my establishment. Do we understand each other? Do we have an agreement?'

Kosminski calmed down as he looked at the size of his adversary, and at the excited, angry, faces of the pub's clientele. Reluctantly, he nodded his head. The landlord released him from his grip, and he straightened his cape and the jacket beneath. He picked up the sheath from his cane, slid the blade back inside, and looked around the bar. Everyone was looking at him as if they were seeing a crazed madman.

*They don't realise that they have a witch in their presence*, he thought.

Slowly, and with a look of terror still etched on her face, Annie stood up from behind the bar. He looked at her, and she looked back at him. He saw the fear in her face, it was etched onto her lips, and in the wrinkles on her forehead. He smirked before turning towards the exit.

'Please feel free to give this establishment a wide berth from here on in, your ugly mug is persona-non-grata.' The landlord waved his flabby arms around his head, indicating the bar around him. 'OK, OK, the show's over now, you wallops,' he was now addressing the rest of his punters. 'You can all get back to quaffing and wenching,' he shouted with the smile back on his jowly face.

A loud cheer went up around the bar at this announcement.

He turned back to face the pale and shaking Annie Chapman. 'What did you do to bring about his wrath?'

Annie shook her head. 'I didn't do anything, sir. I poured him his ale and gave him his change. Then, the next thing I knew he was on the bar, as lively as you like. Calling me a witch, he was, saying I was going to die like the others. What do you think he meant?'

The landlord shook his head. 'I don't know, but there's been tell of murder around these streets the last month or so. Two birds have bitten it, and no mistake. In grizzly fashion too. I warrant it was him that did it. You best watch yourself girlie.' He licked his lips and then held his gaze towards her low-cut dress and ample cleavage. 'You might want to think about getting someplace near to stay tonight, with someone who could, maybe, keep you safe.'

Annie noticed his gaze on her breasts and she quickly folded her arms across them. 'I think I'll be fine. I'll find myself a nice soldier to keep me safe on my walk home.'

The landlord pulled a disgruntled face before grunting and stomping back into the room behind the bar. 'Get back to serving, wench! You've got another hour to cover,' he yelled.

## 40.

IT WAS PAST one-thirty in the morning, and Annie was exhausted, and hungry. The shock of the earlier altercation had not been lost on her, and the wariness of pulling pints all night, coupled with constantly being groped, had taken its toll on her weary bones.

With trepidation, she left The Ten Bells pub and started her short walk home through the night air of Spitalfields. She made a point of not walking down any dark alleyways and keeping to the streetlamps and within the more densely populated areas of the streets.

She passed by a young boy of about fifteen years of age. He was stood next to a fire he had constructed within a wheelbarrow. He was roasting and selling hot potatoes. She purchased one and continued on her way.

The day had been warm, but the night was now cloudless and cold. She revelled in the warmth provided by the potato inside her overcoat. She arrived home without incident, looking forward to tucking into her warm meal.

There was a man on her step.

She could just make out his silhouette in the shadows. Stopping suddenly, she felt her heart thudding in her chest. He stood up as she neared, and Annie was ready to throw her potato at him and run.

'You owe me money, Chapman,' the man said in a menacing voice. 'You're behind on your rent, and I overheard that you got yourself some extra work. So, how's about paying your poor, starving landlord, eh?'

The relief that it was only John Evans acting on behalf of Tim Donovan, her landlord, washed over her, and she visibly relaxed. She knew she could wrap John around her little finger with a wink, and maybe flash of her cleavage. 'John,' she said saucily undoing the buttons of her overcoat. 'Can't we come to an arrangement here? You know I'm good for it.' She took his hand and put it over one of her breasts. She could feel it trembling in her embrace. He licked his lips, his eyes flicking, greedily down her top. She smiled as his hand cupped her. 'Can you feel my heart beating, John? It's fast because I've been pulling pints all night, and my little legs are dead tired.' She lifted her skirts to flash a little ankle and calf his way.

With a nervous jolt, he pulled his hand away as fast as he could, 'I'm sorry, Annie, but Tim says I can have a percentage of what I get from you. Now, I'm not really sure what that means, but it has to be a good thing. My kids are starving these days too, so I got to bring home the bacon, don't I? I 'ave to get the money from you. He said eight-D should cover it.'

'That lousy bastard,' she cursed, and reached inside her dress pocket for her purse.

It wasn't there.

'Oh, fuck,' she cursed. 'I've left my purse on my hook in the Bells, it's got all my wages in it, tell Tim…'

'I'll tell Tim nothing, except that I got his money, Annie. You're not getting in here tonight unless you got your lodging. I'm sorry, love,' he shook his head slowly as he barred her way towards the front door of the scruffy house. His face looked pained but determined.

'Prick!' she spat before storming off, out to the street, back towards the pub.

John watched her go, scratching his head. 'What's a prick?' he asked himself before shrugging and sitting back on the stoop.

~~~~

Annie was fuming with herself. She hoped that the pub was still open, so she wouldn't have to knock the greasy landlord up from his bed. He would have his mind dead set on other, more salacious, things. She was also hoping that no one else had seen her purse and taken a liking to either it, or its contents.

She was in luck. There was a light coming from the inside. She could see it through a small chink in the curtains. She slipped around the back and let herself in the tradesman's entrance.

'Hello, Annie.' A voice from behind startled her into spinning around, her hand automatically covering her chest in surprise. She stumbled over a step and fell into the arms of a stranger who had been lurking in the shadows; a man she'd never seen before in her life.

'I'm sorry, but you're not allowed back here, sir,' she said, breathlessly. 'This is for staff only. I'll have to ask you to make your entrance round the front of the pub,' she said struggling to catch her breath.

'I'm not here for drinks, Annie, I've got something for you.' He lifted his hands, and in them, he had a black bonnet.

'What is it?' she asked casting a worried glance down at the gift. *It looks like Polly's bonnet, the one she'd bought the day she disappeared.* This thought offered her no comfort.

'Polly wanted me to give this to you. She wanted to let you know that she died needlessly,' the stranger whispered.

'What?' Annie hissed.

'I said, she died needlessly. All I want from you are your transponder codes. Once I have them, I'll take you, and all your friends, safely back to twenty-two-eighty-eight. There, you'll stand trial for your crimes, but you'll live. How does that sound?'

There was something about this man's voice that didn't sound right, but she put it to the back of her mind, there were more important things to think about.

'What's going on back here?' a booming voice came from just inside the back door of the pub. 'If anyone's out here fucking again, I'll do you both in with my bare hands.'

Annie reluctantly drew her eyes away from the stranger and turned towards the door. Half an hour ago, she wouldn't have believed that she could have been thankful to hear the landlord's voice. With a smile on her face, she turned back towards the mystery man, but the smile didn't last long.

The man was gone!

'Well, hello, love,' the landlord crooned when he saw that Annie had returned. 'I knew you'd be back. Come for a little of the old slap and tickle, eh?'

'Something like that,' she replied with a forced smile, trying her best to control the shake in her voice.

'You look freezing, girl,' he said, looking her up and down, licking his lips. She cringed at this scrutiny, but it was better than the chilling alternative waiting for her outside. 'Come inside, child, I'll keep you warm,' he said with a silky salaciousness that made her stomach churn. She decided that inside the pub was much the better option. He held the door open, and as she passed, he pushed himself forwards so her breasts pushed along his arm. This coupled with his filthy stench made her skin crawl.

'Maybe you want to earn yourself an extra shilling, maybe even two if you're lucky,' he said as she slipped inside the back room to the pub. She spied her purse containing her wages and hurried over to it, grabbing it and stuffing it, and its thankfully full contents into her pocket. As she did, the landlord eased his bulk into the room. She smelt him before she could see him.

'So, Annie, tell me how you want to earn your extra shillings? We'll have to be sharpish though, as the missus is still upstairs counting the takings. I've kept a little aside for you though.' Unbuckling his trousers, he advanced on her.

There was very little time to waste; she needed to act quickly. Cornered in the small room by this mammoth of a man, she felt she had two choices: either stay here and be molested by this disgusting creature or take her chances outside with the mysterious man from the future.

Looking at the grin on the big man's face, she decided that she would be better off taking her chances.

The landlord's trousers were down by his ankles now, displaying a filthy pair of yellow and grey, stained undergarments. They looked like they hadn't been washed, or even changed, for weeks. As he attempted to slip his leg out of his trousers, she noticed he was slightly unbalanced. She lashed out an almighty kick, connecting with him right between his legs. The howl of agony was ear-shattering as she darted past him and out into the crowded bar. Even through the hubbub of the bar, she could still hear him screaming in agony as she slipped out of the front door, and onto Commercial Street.

*Say goodbye to that job, Annie,* she laughed as the cold night hit her again.

The street was now almost deserted, and there was no sign of the mystery man anywhere. With furtive glances up and down the thoroughfare, she embarked on the five-minute walk back to her lodgings.

She walked swiftly and soon found herself on Princelet Street. At this hour of the morning, it was all but deserted too, just a few drunken stragglers staggering towards The Ten Bells for a late drink that they couldn't get anywhere else. She gave the revellers a wide berth as she turned onto Spelman Street. Another cursory glance back the way she had come satisfied her that there was no one following. She breathed a sigh of relief as she saw the gate to her lodgings; they were open, and there was no one between herself and home. She'd made it! She needed to sleep for a while before reporting back what she had seen and heard to Mary, or Carrie, first thing in the morning.

As she reached the gate, she stopped, looking behind her.

A shiver ran through her as she entered darkness that swamped the yard. The hackles on the back of her neck were standing on edge. She has a feeling that she wasn't alone. She wanted to put it down to the odd experience she'd had in the bar, with the strange man, but this felt like something else. She turned around, hoping to see John Evans demanding his money, when someone grabbed her from behind and threw her, roughly onto the floor.

A leather clad hand was over her mouth, stifling her scream. There was a noise from the yard next door, someone was using the outside privy. The wooden door banged closed, and whoever it was trudged back towards the lodgings. She wanted to cry out, to scream for help, but the hold over her mouth wouldn't allow any noise to escape.

Whoever it was walked off, back towards the house. A sinking feeling overcame her as she realised that there was no help coming. She lay on the cold, stone floor looking up at a clear night sky. Her eyes shifted slightly to the left, and she saw her assailant crouching over her. He was holding something in his hand, something spherical, something that she recognised but knew had no business being here in eighteen-eighty-eight.

He removed his gloved hand from her face to adjust something on the sphere, and she had time to utter one, small word, before the green beam from the sphere enveloped her, rendering her immobile.

'No!'

The man, or woman, from the next-door yard stopped their advance on the house. They must have heard her and were looking around for whoever it was in trouble. With the bang that accompanied the door to the house shutting, the slim hope of rescue died with the sliding of a lock.

~~~

Annie felt the cold of the stone floor biting into her as she looked up at her attacker. He had a slight frame and a thick, fashionable moustache that was curled out towards the sides of his face. It was waxed to perfection. She could just about make out his eyes, as the dim light of the nearby streetlamp cast most of its illumination over next door's yard. They were wide, and focused, but they didn't look crazed, like she would have expected. She thought there was a distinct look of fear in them, as if they had seen, and done, more than they had wanted to. She thought it maybe a weakness to exploit, if she ever got the chance.

'It doesn't have to end this way,' he hissed. 'Just give me what I need.'

She looked at him; she couldn't speak, so she was trying to communicate with her eyes. She widened them as if to say she was open to listen to what he wanted.

'All I want are the transponder codes. Once I have them, I'll take you all back to our time. There, you'll stand trial for your crimes. You and your friends can either spend your life in prison, or you can die here tonight, on this filthy stone floor. It's your choice,' he whispered from his close vicinity.

Annie blinked her eyes, twice.

He moved his face closer to her. 'You'll give me the codes?'

She blinked twice again.

He pointed the spherical device, and she felt blood rush back into her hands, her feet, then her throat. Even though she could now move, she stayed motionless as the man leaned into her. 'Do you have the codes for me, Annie? Will you give them to me now?'

She nodded and closed her eyes. The man was so close that she could smell him. It was a familiar smell; there was something about it, but once again, she couldn't put her finger on what it was.

As he leaned in, Annie opened her eyes and lunged at him.

163

Although surprised by the attack, he was agile enough to dodge it. For maybe five seconds, Annie had an advantage, as he stumbled backwards.

It was an advantage she didn't take, therefore sealing her doom.

Instead of attacking him, and attempting to disarm him, she struggled to her feet, turned on her heels, ready to run out of the yard. Opening her mouth ready to let out a blood curdling yell, she was suddenly shrouded in the green light again.

*Shit* was her only thought, as she felt the pain of something cold, sharp, and terrible rip into her flesh.

The agony was immeasurable.

She couldn't move.

All she could see was the red glow of the light beam. Her immobility, unfortunately, didn't numb her senses, and she could feel every moment of searing torture as the beam bit into her stomach, cutting away swathe after swathe of flesh. In her mind's eye, she could see the vivid images of the light cutting with precision through her skin. She opened her mouth, she needed to scream, but there was only silence. Her eyes rolled in her head as the agony doubled, and her vision blurred as the beam continued to chase the purple blip that was rushing through her stomach. Intense, white pain made her eyes bulge, they felt like they were ballooning, swelling, too large for their sockets, as the heat of her innards, her brain told her they were probably her intestines, spilled forth. She could smell her own filth; the stench overwhelmed everything, the grime of the back yard, the constant stink in the air that hung over Whitechapel, the smell of her attacker. She wanted to move her head, to look up at the man preforming these atrocities upon her but couldn't.

A gagging noise, it was coming from him, it told her that he was taking no pleasure from the activities he was performing.

Finally, she reached the point of intense agony where her body's defences took over, and mercifully, thankfully, she went numb from her abdomen down. Unfortunately, it didn't steal her lucidity from her, and she was forced to continue to be a witness to her own demise. Her eyes stung as they filled with bloody tears, which dribbled down her cheeks, leaving pink traces in their wake. The cold stone beneath her was warmer now as her life blood ebbed from the open, and the steaming, wounds to her stomach. She was slipping away. She thought that, in the end, after the initial pain and shock had subsided, it wasn't as bad as she expected it would be. It was almost peaceful, in complete contrast to the violence that was being inflicted on her body.

From her blurred, peripheral vision, she saw her murderer lean over her. He placed something on her shoulder, something wet and heavy. Then the strange sensation of something inside her stomach moving, cutting, was back.

Through her dying eyes, she could just make out the face of the mystery man. His features caught her attention. *That's why I recognised the smell!* she thought with a sad smile.

This was her dying thought. She watched through dimming eyes as her attacker held up a small, purple, glowing object and looked at it. Blood clung to it as it passed by her face.

It was her own blood.

The world swam in a deep grey before the darkness came. It was blessed, welcomed. With it, came peace.

41.

Orbital Platform One. 2288

'HOW ARE THINGS progressing with those transponder codes?' Youssef asked as he entered the lab. The four portal experts were pouring themselves over transcripts from the information they lifted from Inverness Castle. One of the technicians raised her head in recognition that he was there and then nudged the others. As they all jumped to attention, he marvelled at their ages. None of them could have been any older than twenty-one. *Was I ever that young?* He thought the answer must have been *no*.

'It's OK, you don't have to stand to attention when I come in. I just need to know what progress you're making.'

'Well, sir, we haven't found any transponder codes as such, but the syntax in the blog is a little obscure.'

'In what way?' Youssef cocked his head as he leaned in to look at one of the stations. He had asked Jacqueline to set these interns the job of locating transponder codes, or any reference to transponder codes, within the retrieved data. He had not given them any information about why they were looking for them.

'We've found *reference* to transponder codes, but the codes themselves are encrypted none of us have ever seen the depth of them.'

'Do you think you can break it?' he asked.

'I don't know. We've split into two teams. Two of us are working on the syntax and the others on the encryption, this way we can get the job done faster. We've drawn a blank up to now on the encryption.'

He liked the use of the term 'up to now', it showed that they were willing to keep at it. He marvelled to himself at the tenacity of the EA personnel.

'In the texts, there are a lot of references to London, England,' the technician continued.

'London? Can you be a bit more specific?'

'I can be a lot more specific. It's London, Whitechapel, to be exact. The part that jumps out at us is the historical aspects to the references. It looks like they were mapping out an area of about five square miles in Whitechapel, in eighteen-eighty-eight.'

*Gotcha*! Youssef thought, smiling to himself. 'Fantastic work, guys. Keep it up on the encryption, and I'll be in touch.' He burst out of the lab in a run, and the young portal experts watched him leave before returning to their duties.

He rushed into another room where Jacqueline and Vincent were sat at a table working something out on a portal. Both jumped up as the doors opened. There were guilty looks on their faces.

'Ah, Youssef! We were just, erm…' Jacqueline stuttered.

Youssef didn't care what they were doing, this news was more important than anything else right now. 'We know *when* they are, and I think your kids on the portals know *where* they are,' he announced. 'London, Whitechapel. Eighteen-eighty-eight.'

She sat for a moment taking in this information. 'London, eighteen-eighty-eight? Isn't that a little downbeat for them? Either they're living it up with very little money they took with them, or they're on the poverty line.' She was shaking her head. 'There was no middle class in them days.'

'If I was them, I'd be mixing it up with the lower classes,' Vincent replied. 'Think about it, it's a perfect cover. The lower classes around that time would have been almost transient, coming and going as they pleased. Disease was rife, so there was always a lot of death around, and very few official papers to carry. It's the perfect hiding spot.'

Youssef and Jacqueline were looking at him as if he had two heads.

'Who are you, and what have you done with Vincent?' Jacqueline asked with a playful frown.

Vincent began to laugh. 'I can read a book, can't I? Actually, back in school, I had a real interest in history, that and fighting.'

The two scientists shared a look. 'Soooo,' Youssef drew out. 'It looks like this mission is officially on. I just need to get Kevin up to speed, and then it's onward and backwards, as they say.' He paused for a moment, waiting for them to get onto his small joke. When it became obvious that they weren't going to get it, he continued. 'So, suit up, sir, we have a mission to complete and a world to save.'

## 42.

London. 1888

AARON KOSMINSKI AWOKE on a chair in a small downstairs room behind his barber shop. He was tired, and in a foul mood. The sounds of his wife cleaning up in the rooms above aggravated the pulsing in his head, which in turn pushed his anger further and further to the fore. Since this whole situation had begun, he had not been able to look at her. Every time he did, he saw the face of one of the dead women, or of that witch Annie. It brought his rage back.

He stormed up the stairs, his vision swimming in a pink mist. He paused as he saw her in the bedroom changing the covers on their marital bed, the one that she had been sleeping in alone for the last few months. Breathing rapidly through his nose, he strode purposefully into the room and grabbed her from behind, pulling her hair, which had been tied back while she did her chores. She screamed in surprise, and in pain, at the mauling.

He then proceeded to beat her.

He couldn't help himself.

Mrs Kosminski was no stranger to a beating, not long-ago he'd had to take her to the hospital due to the severity of one of his beatings, but the one he was giving her now, this was the mother of all the beatings he had *ever* administered.

His bloody knuckles were cracking and snapping from how tight he was flexing them as he threw the punches into the poor woman's face. The cartilage in her nose shattered with the ferocity of the blows. Every time he hit her, her face changed, morphing into one of the witches' faces. All of them laughing at him, defying him. It took almost five minutes for her to fall unconscious, and limp, onto the floor, but not before he had damaged her permanently. Her nose was shattered, and at the very least, two teeth were now missing from the front of her swollen, bloodied mouth. The mutilation around the socket of her left eye was so bad that he thought she might never see from it again.

He didn't care about any of this.

As she lay unconscious on the wooden floor, moaning and twitching in a pool of blood, he stormed around the room grabbing her, and their children's things, and stuffing them into a large suitcase they kept underneath the bed. When it was full, he carried it downstairs. He then went back and dragged her body downstairs, dumping her by the door.

He then took their two, small, screaming, children and thrust them out of the door as well. He was done with all of them.

That was when, out of the blue, an idea hit him.

He was going to write a letter.

He considered himself to have a bond with this killer—*or killers,* he thought, thinking back to the night in the yard when he had witnessed one of the women kill the stranger, only for him to return moments later. They were both going in the same direction. He felt like he was obligated to help wherever he could. A little bit of misdirection could go a long way. He wanted the police to stay off the scent of the mission. *If I can't kill them,* he thought, *then someone else might as well!*

He had rather enjoyed the fact that the public had thrown all their suspicions onto the Jewish community, and specifically to a man they were calling 'Leather Apron.' Kosminski thought, with more than a little amusement, that whoever that man was, he was in a world of trouble when they caught him.

He sat down at his desk to begin his letter. Before long, he had written almost sixteen different versions of it, using different inks—blue ink, black ink, and finally deciding on red. The red reflected his mood rather accurately.

Another idea came to him. *Nice and creepy*, he thought. He attempted to harvest his wife's blood from the floor. Unfortunately, it had a habit of drying up on him before he could finish the words, and the rest of it was already thick and gloopy. He managed to write a few words, but when it dried, it turned brown and flaky, mostly useless, so he reverted back to the red ink.

Eventually, from downstairs, he heard his wife pick herself up from the floor. He shouted to her, rather coldly, that her things were packed, and she should leave, and take the infernal children with her. He recalled telling her that it was for her own safety, because he couldn't, and wouldn't guarantee he wouldn't beat her again like he had done today.

She had left willingly, collecting the shaking children from the doorstep, where he had dumped them. Aaron Kosminski never saw her, or his two boys, ever again.

This suited him fine!

Free at last, he opened a bottle of cheap whiskey, and taking a long swig, he stuffed the finished letter into an envelope and sealed it. 'Who should I send it to?' He was giggling like a schoolgirl as he spoke aloud. 'The police? The press? Ah, what about the friends of the victims?' This last thought was particularly gruesome to him, but then he thought that they all deserved what was coming to them.

He wanted to make as big an impression as he could with this letter, so after taking another long swig of his firewater, he made up his mind. 'The press should have something like this, something to prove that we believe in what we're doing and that we mean to carry it on until they're all dead and gone,' he spoke aloud, and alone, in his bedroom. He was holding the lapels of his jacket as if he were addressing a large, formal crowd. He took another swig of his drink and began to laugh again.

He wrote the address on the envelope in the same ink he used for the contents and addressed it to:

*The Boss,*

*Central News Office.*

*London City*

He left his house to purchase a stamp and post it. He was giggling merrily all the way.

D E McCluskey

## 43.

*Dear Boss*

*I keep on hearing the police have caught me but they wont fix me just yet. I have laughed when they look so clever and talk about being on the <u>right</u> track. That joke about Leather Apron gave me real fits. I am down on whores and I shan't quit ripping them till I do get buckled. Grand work the last job was. I gave the lady no time to squeal. How can they catch me now. I love my work and want to start again. You will soon hear of me with my funny little games. I saved some of the proper <u>red</u> stuff in a ginger beer bottle over the last job to write with but it went thick like glue and I cant use it. Red ink is fit enough I hope <u>ha ha.</u> The next job I do I shall clip the lady's ears off and send to the police officers just for jolly wouldn't you. Keep this letter back till I do a bit more work, then give it out straight. My knife's so nice and sharp I want to get to work right away if I get a chance. Good Luck.*

*   Yours truly  Jack the Ripper*

*Don't mind me giving the trade name*

*PS Wasn't good enough to post this before I got all the red ink off my hands curse it No luck yet. They say I'm a doctor now. <u>ha ha</u>*

## 44.

'HE WAS UP on the bar, knocking over drinks and waving a long sword around in the air, shouting *die witch, die*. That's a direct quote from someone actually in the bar?' Abberline asked Bellis.

'Yes, sir. The Ten Bells was busy that night, and there are a lot of witnesses saying almost exactly the same thing.'

'Aaron Kosminski, eh? I think we need to bring this fella in to have a little chat. Do we know where he lives or works?'

'Not far from Spitalfields Market. He owns a barber shop, and get this, sir, the shop is located not one hundred yards from where the Tabram woman was found.'

'Gentlemen,' Inspector Frederick Abberline addressed the room of police officers 'We may have found our first major suspect.'

Abberline had forced his standing, and proven record of accomplishment at this sort of investigation, down his superiors' necks and gotten himself exactly what he wanted: re-assignment to Whitechapel division. He had gained himself a reputation for something he called 'hunches' regarding high profile murders, and he had used his considerable political leverage to manoeuvre himself into positions of advantage for these investigations.

This case intrigued him more than any other, and he had followed it closely from day one, ever since the photograph of the body of the Tabram woman had fallen on his desk. The coincidence of her being the woman he witnessed appearing from out of nowhere, and killing the journalist he was following, was just too much.

'Do you want me to bring this fella in, sir?'

'What?' he asked looking around, realising that the officers were still in his office. 'Oh sorry, I was a million miles away then. Eh, yes, let's bring him in here and see what he has to say for himself.'

'Sir, the Chapman murder, do you think it's the work of the same man?' another officer asked.

'I do,' he replied. 'I think these women have been targeted for a reason, and I want to find out what that could be.'

'Righty-o, very good, sir,' the officer said, turning away from the table, gesturing to the others to do the same. 'We'll leave you to your musings then. I'll start to get a handle on this Kosminski fella.'

Bellis was looking considerably pleased with himself as he left the office.

Abberline wanted to get to the morgue as soon as possible. He wanted to see the bodies for himself, to make his own conclusions regarding the causes of death. Once he'd heard about the Tabram murder, an interest had formed. He took a deeper interest in the next one, Mary Nichols, and had called in a favour from an old acquaintance.

The coroner on these cases was a friend. He'd spent a number of nights with him in the, nicer, taverns of London, supping fine ales and generally having a good time. Unfortunately, or fortunately for Abberline, the coroner was a heavier drinker than he was, and when he was drunk, he liked to use his fists a little. The problem he had was that he wasn't very good with them. Abberline had gotten him out of more than a few scrapes where he had found himself out of his depth. So, when he found out that he was working these cases, he wasted no time in pulling in his favours and persuading him to do a separate investigation into the deaths, more of an unofficial version.

These cases were indeed unusual; after all, people don't just appear out of thin air and then end up dead on a morgue slab within weeks. He reached down into his bottom draw and produced a file. Large red letters emblazoned across the front read: POLICE FILES: FOR INSP. F. ABBERLINE'S EYES ONLY.

He opened the file and re-read the contents. It was the unofficial report on the method of the murders. It differed somewhat from the official one produced for the police. This mentioned facts regarding the wounds that had been omitted from the official investigation. It mentioned that the cuts had been cauterised, most probably at the source, and the wounds were deeper internally than they looked superficially. It was as if the killer had stabbed the victim and then rummaged around inside with whatever weapon he had used. It stated that the cuts had been made randomly, not by someone with a knowledge of surgical techniques and anatomical acquaintance, like the papers were stating, and also by someone with a shaky hand, and not the steady, practiced hand, the press had ventured.

He had been doing his own investigations into the backgrounds of the women and had uncovered something very interesting about them. None of them had any accountable witnesses of any of their historic movements. There were fantastic mosaics painted of who they had been, where they lived, who they were married to, where they worked, there was even mention of family, but there was no one to hand who could corroborate these stories. No living spouses could be identified, no children who would return messages, no friends, or even acquaintances. All this was coupled with the curious fact that at one time or other, these three women had all lived together.

This was also true of the missing woman.

Abberline flicked to the back of the file and read a few lines regarding the woman who had been reported missing the same night Mary Nichols died.

Emily Callaghan. She sold flowers on the stalls in Spitalfields Market. There was no husband and no children. She had moved to London from Grimsby in February, apparently to get away from an abusive father.

He looked up from the file towards the grubby window besides his desk and scratched the stubble underneath his chin. He stood, put his hat and coat on, and made his way out of his office.

He crossed the street from the police station to the small morgue opposite. Inside, he gave the attendant a shilling to make himself scarce, which was received without any questions regarding why he was here. Once satisfied that he was alone, he unveiled the body of Annie Chapman. She had been sewn up but was still gruesome to behold.

Abberline leaned into the body and examined the linings of the wounds. They had only been roughly sewn together and still revealed all the intricacies of the attack. He ran his fingers along the ridges and looked at the residue. It had scabbed, but not because it was congealed, it had scabbed due to cauterisation. It confirmed what he had read in his private report: something hot had caused these wounds.

He looked around the room, making sure there was no one observing him. When he was satisfied, he reached inside his pocket and produced a small device.

The sphere glowed green while it was in his hands. He cast the glow over the full length of the cadaver. It uncovered an internal view of her insides. The edges of the wounds shone red beneath the glow. Abberline, satisfied with his findings, turned the device off and concealed it back into the inside pocket of his jacket before leaving the room.

## 45.

<u>Orbital Platform One. 2288</u>

VINCENT AND JACQUELINE were in bed in Vincent's room. She was lying on her side with his arms wrapped around her. Both had a sheen of sweat over their skin and were slightly out of breath as they stared up towards the ceiling. 'Are you nervous?' she asked, burying her head into his chest.

He thought for a moment before answering. 'Yes, and no. Yes, because I'm going back in time, four hundred years into the centre of the unknown. God only knows what that's going to be like.'

'What about the no, then?'

'Well, I've been training for this mission all my life. In the EA, we get the best physical and tactical training, but because the whole of the planet comes under the one umbrella, we get very little action.'

'So, you'd say you're ready, then? Psychologically, I mean.'

He smiled as he removed his arm from underneath her and flexed his hands, ridding himself of the pins and needles that had built up. He sat up and turned towards her. 'Jacq, the only things I actually think too deeply about are dinner, and just lately, you.'

She blushed a little. *Why am I blushing at what he has just said after what we have just been doing?* she thought. *Come on, he's a grunt, don't go falling for him.* She already knew that thought was a lost cause.

'Anyway,' he continued as he got out of the bed. She couldn't help marvelling at his well-muscled physique, and she was already eager for more of what they had recently taking to doing at any given chance. 'I'll know that I'll have you looking out for me, keeping me safe.'

'Yeah, four hundred years in the future.'

'Still on the end of a communications line.'

Jacqueline sighed. 'I don't want you to read too much into this, but I really don't want you to go. I think I've finally found someone I can connect with, and now you have to go the furthest anyone could ever go away from me.'

Vincent laughed as he slipped on his exercise trousers. 'I'll only be in London, we orbit London every day,' he teased.

'You know what I mean,' she laughed, sitting up, giving him something to look at.

'Look,' he said sitting down on the bed. 'I'm not going for a while yet. I've got to do that week of training, and you guys still need time to sort the Higgs Storm containers out for when I return, and for when I bring the prisoners back. So, let's make the most of it. I want to be here with you, you want to be here with me. I say c'est la vie.'

Jacqueline looked at him, a sly smile creeping across her face. 'I love it when you talk French,' she joked as she dragged him back underneath the bed covers.

'Moi?' he asked with an expression of injured innocence.

## 46.

London. 1888

THE LETTER DROPPED on Abberline's desk. He took one look at it and knew what it was. *Oh, fantastic*, he thought with a small shake of his head. *A letter, possibly from the murderer, and it will have passed through the hands of every officer in Whitechapel before it's gotten here.*

'I think you'd better have a gander at what has just come through form the newspaper today, Inspector. We think it's from the murderer.' Officer Bellis announced proudly.

'It says it is, look...' added another, pointing at the envelope. 'Right there, in the words.'

'It's written in blood, sir,' a third proud-looking idiot chirped in. 'The bastard has written it in the victim's blood.'

The officers were looking towards the stated letter as if it were a stray dog that just might bite them at any moment. Abberline could see the crowd gathering outside his office. They were all vying for a look at the famous artefact. He shooed everyone out of his office, leaving only Bellis, his second in command. He picked up the envelope, turning it in his hands, examining it from every angle.

*The Boss*, it stated on the front.

'If this was written in blood, then the wording would be brown by now. Blood only stays red while it's warm and free flowing. As it dries, it turns brown.'

Officer Bellis dropped his head and his face began to turn crimson.

'It's a common mistake, Officer, don't beat yourself up over it. Go out there and tell them that we've both realised that it's red ink instead of blood.' This cheered the officer up, and Abberline watched as he made his way outside to address the crowd. 'Close the door would you, Bellis, there's a good fellow,' he shouted to the officer, who turned and closed the door with the trace of a smile on his face.

As soon as he was alone, he drew the curtains he had installed when he took over the office. Satisfied that no one would be able to observe him, he returned to his desk and the envelope. He opened a drawer and retrieved a pair of silver tweezers. He removed the contents of the envelope. Careful not to miss anything inside, he turned it upside down, and tapped it. When nothing else fell out, he was satisfied that all it contained was the paper lying on his desk. It was two pages of unremarkable text, some terrible spelling, and the worst punctuation he had ever read in his life. All of this coupled with a few vague threats. The part that Abberline liked most was the signature. Jack the Ripper. *Inspired name*, he thought. *Much more inventive than Leather Apron.* He had never liked that name as it wasn't either inspirational or creative, but Jack the Ripper? 'That's a name I can make use of,' he mumbled.

He re-read the letter before removing a device from the locked bottom draw of his desk. He needed to know who wrote it, and the only way he was going to find out was to retrieve DNA from the paper. He set the scanner to filter out any DNA that had been added to the paper in the last two days, thus eliminating any of his policemen, the press, and the postal service.

He watched as holographic images emerged from the device, images of all the people who had handled the paper. It stopped on one. It was a well built, moustached, foreign looking gentleman. His name appeared underneath a grainy image. 'Severin Antoniovich Klosowski, you'll do for me.' He was smiling as he put the scanner away, back into the drawer, and locked it.

'Officer Bellis,' he shouted. *He might as well have a bit of glory too, he isn't a bad sort*, he thought.

'Yes, sir?' Bellis replied, popping his head back into the office.

'When can we be ready to move? I've got an idea on who this murderer might be.'

'Well, erm, just about any time, sir. You really think you know?'

'Let's just say that I have another of my hunches,' he replied.

Bellis smiled as he entered Abberline's office. 'When you get hunches, sir, murders get solved. So, did you get something from the letter then?'

'Yes. There's just something about what this Kosminski man was supposed to have been shouting in The Ten Bells. I get the feeling that it was him who wrote this. The writing has a foreign tint to it. It's my opinion that he thinks he's doing something noble. Something like, killing witches.'

'We can have an arrest squad ready to go in about ten minutes, sir,' Bellis replied, straightening his woollen police tunic.

Abberline took in a deep breath and sucked on his teeth. 'I think I'd rather it was just you and me, if you don't mind.'

Bellis beamed from ear to ear. 'I don't mind at all, Inspector.'

'Good! We should leave right now. Do we have his home address?'

'It's the same as his business address, sir. Cable Street. St George's in the East.' The policeman looked at his wristwatch. 'He should be there now.'

'Fantastic. When we get there, I want to talk to him on my own. I'll take him into the barber shop while you do a thorough search of his residency. Thorough, though, you got that?' Abberline emphasized.

'You can count on me, sir!'

## 47.

EMILY CALLAGHAN WAS cold, hungry, and desperate to go to the toilet again. She had been held captive for at least a week, although this was only guesswork. She'd been fed and had been let out of the chair occasionally, but not for long. Each time she had been let go, her captor had not entirely released her from the holding beam, and therefore, she had no means of escape. He allowed her to stretch her legs and go to the toilet. Painful sores were developing on her behind and the tops of her legs, and she knew that she was weakening.

'Callaghan, I swear if you don't give me those codes today, I won't give you another chance,' her captor spoke from behind her.

'I won't give you any codes,' she croaked. Her voice was dry from lack of any real nourishment. 'I'd rather die than give them to you.'

'Believe me, you'll die if I don't get them. But I'm hoping that you might want to save the lives of your colleagues. I'm giving you fair warning. You have one hour before I start to prepare for retrieving another of your friends' quantum slugs.'

Emily remained silent.

He entered into her field of vision, his face was distorted by the collars of his cape and his moustache. He jangled three small, flat, scraps of metal in her face. 'You know what these are, don't you?' he asked as he threw them onto the floor, one by one. 'These are Martha Tabram, Mary Nichols, or Polly if you want to call her that, and Annie Chapman; or what's left of them anyways. There'll be at least another one of them tomorrow night to keep them company. Is that what you want?'

Emily's sore eyes were regarding the quantum slugs on the floor. She knew that she should be feeling more empathy towards them, as each one was an epitaph for one of her friends, but she was too tired, too exhausted, to elicit much emotion towards them. She tried to avert her gaze, but it kept reverting back to the gruesome sight.

'You know I'm not joking here, don't you? It *will* happen. I'm committed to this mission, and something you may want to know is that I'm holding a large grudge against you, in particular.'

'Why me?' Emily asked.

The man smiled beneath his moustache, but Emily couldn't see any humour in his dark eyes. 'You don't need to know that right now, all you need to know is that if I don't get those codes this afternoon, you'll be condemning another of your colleagues to a slow, painful death. I've been watching the movements of Stride. Tonight, could very well be her last night alive.' He leaned into the emaciated woman. Emily could smell mint on his breath, and something else, something that didn't quite sit right for a man in this time. 'That's up to you,' he concluded.

'And if I give you their codes, then what?' her voice was attempting to be defiant, but the croak, and the weakness, in it, lost its credibility. 'You take us back; we stand trial and get put to death for what we've done. Liz's dead either way.'

'The EA don't put people to death. Unlike The Quest, we don't kill innocent people on an ideal. We don't kill guilty people either; if we don't have to, that is. So, you see, your friends will be able to live long, and if they chose it, productive lives back in twenty-two-eighty-eight, otherwise, it all ends tonight, in the squalor of the east end of London.'

Emily stayed silent, even though a multitude of different thoughts were racing through her head. 'Can I go to the toilet, please?' she asked eventually.

'Of course, you can.'

## 48.

KOSMINSKI WAS BUSY scheming. Since he had rid himself of his wife and children, and delivered the letters, he had become frustrated, bored even. Everything seemed on a low ebb, he needed a way out of his trough. He had expected there to be a lot more excitement regarding the letters, especially due to the name he had given the murderer.

'Jack the Ripper,' he mused. He had gotten the idea for the name from the small snippets of conversation he'd overheard after the Nichols woman was killed. The murderer had spoken into his wrist and said something about 'Jack, ripped her.'

Also, since the witch in the pub had charmed him, and given him a silly, if not petrifying, vision of the future, he had kept his distance from the women. They scared him now more than he'd ever been scared before. He knew that he had an affinity with the killer, but he thought now that the killer was watching him too. After the altercation in the pub, he had gone straight home, but it was all over the city the next day that they'd found another woman, mutilated, slaughtered, like the other two. It hadn't taken him long to find out that it had been Annie Chapman they'd found, *the bitch who put the hex on me.*

'They should have that letter by now,' he mumbled almost incoherently as he paced his bedroom, his wife's bloodstains still drying on the cheap carpet. 'I'll start flooding them with letters. That'll keep them busy while my dark friend continues his work. I wish I could do some of the killing for him,' he mused. 'His methods look fun.'

A sharp rap on the door pulled him from his inane ramblings.

His stomach dropped.

He hurried to the window and peered out of the lace curtains. Two men were looking through the window of his closed barber shop downstairs. One was wearing a policeman's uniform, the other was not, but by his demeanour, he could tell that he was the law.

Today was Saturday. By all rights, the shop should be open as this was traditionally his busiest day, but due to his fragile mental state his mind had wandered during the last few haircuts and he had cut two of his customers and ended up giving them their cuts for free. Other than this, he had no excuse as to why his shop was not open today. But it was his shop, and he could open and close as he saw fit.

'Aaron Kosminski are you in there, sir?' the plain clothed policeman shouted as he banged his fists on the door. 'If you are, I have a few questions I'd like to ask you. I assure you that you're not under suspicion of anything. I just want to ask a few questions regarding a certain letter I've obtained.'

At the mention of the letter, Kosminski flung himself against the wall, trying his best to meld into the shadows of the room, as if they could see him. *How could they have gotten that letter back to me so quickly?* he thought. *I didn't put an address on it. Shit! Shit! Shit!*

There was another loud banging on the door. 'Mr Kosminski, we know you're in there, so please, open up.'

*How am I going to talk my way out of this one?* 'I'm on my way, I'm just finishing lunch,' he shouted out of the window. 'Give me a minute.' He watched the uniformed officer stand back in the street, straining to look into the window from which he had just shouted. There was something odd about the officer in the plain clothes, he had a feeling that they had met before. 'Bastard thoughts,' he whispered, hitting himself on the side of his head with his fists. 'Get out of my head, leave me alone!'

By the time he got downstairs, the uniformed officer had commenced banging impatiently on the window again.

'You took your time, sir. May I inquire why?' the officer asked as he unlatched the door.

'Bellis, stand down, there's a good man.' Abberline put his hand on the officer's shoulder, and he reluctantly backed off.

'What can I do for you gentlemen?' George asked, his eyes switching from man to man. Even though he knew why they were there, he feigned innocence regarding the nature of the call.

'May we step inside, sir? What we have to discuss is probably not something that should be debated in a public thoroughfare. It will also be something you might not want the neighbours to hear.'

Raising his eyebrows, he stepped back, offering the men room to enter. 'You mentioned a letter, sir,' he spoke as the two men looked around the small barber shop. 'Can I ask you to clarify what you mean?'

'Bellis, would you be so kind as to stay down here in the shop and make sure no one enters? Our friend here, and I, are off upstairs for a chat; we shan't be long.'

'Very good, sir. Holler if you need me,' Bellis said, eyeing Kosminski as if to tell him he would not tolerate any funny business.

Abberline smiled a pleasant smile. 'I will indeed. If we may?' He motioned towards the stairs at the back of the shop that led to the living quarters above.

~~~

Kosminski was attempting to light his stove with a long match. His hands were shaking so much that he was making rough work of it. 'How do you take it, sir?' he asked from the small kitchen area, his back to the policeman in his lounge.

'With a small drop of milk, if you have any, otherwise pretty much as it is,' Abberline replied.

Satisfied that the stove was lit correctly, he walked back into his living quarters. He considered himself a lucky man that he hadn't been carrying the cups of tea in with him, as he guessed that he would have dropped them, probably scalding himself in the process, as he gazed, slack-jawed, at what was happening in his room.

The policeman had laid out what looked like a placemat on his table. He had extended it, unfolded it somehow, revealing a shiny surface that had moving pictures, and words, that were scrolling down the sides.

'Don't start playing the fool with me now, Kosminski. I know that you've seen some fantastic sights of late. Strange lights trapping and cutting the women, people appearing from out of nowhere. Do any of these things sound familiar?'

Kosminski was too dumbfounded to speak.

Abberline smiled. 'I thought so. This should be a trifle to your senses now, sir.'

Kosminski dragged his eyes from the flashing placemat to look at the policeman. He shook his head, slowly. 'What are you?' he whispered.

Abberline chuffed. 'Sir, I assure you, I'm quite the same as you. Human, that is. Flesh and blood. But unlike you, I don't belong in this time. That's all you need to know, for now.' Abberline paused, rocking back on his heels. He regarded Kosminski and smiled again. 'Now, may I bring your attention to this?' He pointed at the screen on the table.

The big man sat down and leaned in to get a closer look. 'Is... is that London?' he asked, his wide eyes drinking in the sight, with all the wonder of a child in his voice.

'It is, and these purple dots are technology. Technology that should not exist in this time.' He highlighted with his finger seven points of purple spread out over the map.

'You would think there should be eight points on here, but there's not. This device doesn't show my own tech. The others it does show are related to the recent murders. Murders that you seem to know a thing or two about, Mr Kosminski.'

Aaron looked horrified, 'I, I...' he stuttered.

'Oh, don't worry, I know you didn't do them,' Abberline soothed, with a disarming smile. 'However, there should be a ninth point on this map, that point would correspond to the murderer. But it doesn't, and I don't know why. Now, I've been running a few checks on you, and I've found that you do seem to have a propensity for violence. So, as you may have already fathomed, there *is* something 'different' about these women, and I'm guessing that you've witnessed all three murders, not including the one who is still missing. I need to engage your services.'

'I didn't see the last one, honest,' Kosminski uttered, his eyes shifting from the marvel on his table to the man in his living room— the one with his moving pictures and the talk of time, technology, and murder. 'What, what do you want me to do?'

Abberline smiled, almost as if he had been asked if he wanted tea, not talking about killing witches. 'Nothing too taxing. Your job will be to follow this map. I'll give you times, dates, and locations. You will be my unofficial eyes and ears on the street.'

'You're an inspector in the police, can't you run your own investigation? Run disinformation, or whatever you call it?'

'I can, but I need to continue my official investigations into these events and whatever happens from now on. I can't be seen to be doing both. That is why I need you to keep your eyes open and report everything you witness back to me. You *will* do this, won't you, sir?' There was a threat in Abberline's voice, it was subtle, but it was all too apparent for Kosminski.

He nodded.

'Excellent!' Abberline grinned as he pressed a button on the side of the strange screen. Kosminski was dumbfounded as it disappeared into itself, becoming a box small enough for Abberline to pick up and slip neatly into his inside pocket.

'I'll be in touch, Mr Kosminski.'

'How?' he asked, looking like a child awaiting instructions from a stern adult. Abberline smiled and threw something at him; blessed with good reflexes, he caught it easily.

'Put this on,' he ordered. 'It slides over the wrist. It'll allow us to communicate over distances.'

He rolled the device around his hands, marvelling at what it was.

'So, if we have no more business here today, I don't think I'll bother with that cup of tea, sir. I'll be off. I have a murderer to catch. Good day to you.'

As he walked down the stairs, Bellis was eager to greet him. 'Did he admit it, sir? Is he the murderer?'

Abberline screwed his eyes and frowned. 'I'm not quite sure on this one. Come now, Bellis. I feel we'll be having an eventful few days.'

As both men exited the barber shop, Kosminski watched them, peeking through the nets covering his windows. On his wrist was his brand-new communications device.

## 49.

'THIS IS YOUR last chance, Emily! Give me the transponder codes or Stride dies tonight.' He dangled the small metallic shards before her again, allowing the small metallic slivers to clang together in his hands. 'Time is not on your side, not this time anyway.'

Emily was exhausted. She was covered in her own filth and stank to high heaven. Her hair was dank and lifeless. She wanted to cry, but due to dehydration and hunger, her body wasn't willing to let go of the nutrients required to release tears. 'You know I can't tell you; you know I can't, and won't, give up that information. I'd rather die,' she whispered; her voice had long since given up on her.

'And die you will,' her captor nodded. 'Believe me. But first, I'll cut out your slug, slowly and without anaesthetic. You'll see your own innards steam as the heat of your body escapes into the chill night air. This is something that you can look forward to, I assure you!'

Emily shook her head. Even the smallest of movements made her feel dizzy.

'Do you want that? Then give me the codes. You can save yourself, and your friends.'

'I CAN'T, YOU BASTARD, I CAN'T,' she shouted into his face. The effort of the scream brought fireworks into her vision, and she struggled to keep conscious.

'Can't or won't?' he asked quietly.

Emily's head dropped, and she began to sob. 'Won't...' she whispered.

Her captor leaned in close and whispered into her face. 'Well then, say goodnight to Stride, maybe that Eddowes too. Millwood, Mylet. They could all die tonight.'

Emily lifted her head and spat some much-needed saliva into his face. He stood, wiping the spit away. She noticed something then, something that could be significant.

'Well, it doesn't matter now either way,' he said. 'You've killed your friends when it was in your power to save them.' He removed a handkerchief from his pocket and cleaned the rest of his face. 'I'll let them know as they die, horribly, that you could have saved them the pain of the extraction, but you chose not to.'

Emily was thinking about what she had just seen on the murderer's hands as he put his handkerchief back in his pocket. She pondered on it as he turned and walked out of the dank warehouse, slamming the door behind him.

~~~~

Elizabeth Stride was nervous. She'd been a nervous person all of her life, but since they had come back four hundred years, her nerves were getting the better of her. The only time her confidence had never been a problem was when she had been in the lab. Her knowledge and understanding of the Higgs Storm had been second to none. Ever since the first time she had encountered it back in the EA labs when that poor woman lost her life, she had been fascinated. She wanted, no she needed, to hold it. The feeling of pure, unadulterated power in her hands excited her more than anything else ever could. It had been her and Youssef who had conceived and developed the field for the mass containment.

Right now, all that seemed like another lifetime away. Or several lifetimes away, to be precise. The months she had been here had been the worst she'd ever endured. She couldn't get used to the squalor they had been forced to live in, or the way the men of this age thought they had a God given right to manhandle her at every given opportunity.

During her time here, she had tried her hand at several jobs. She had sold matches and coal in the market, but she had been too shy to shout out her wares, resulting in poor sales. Next, she tried to work behind the bar in a pub, but the men were far too rough for her. She had the disadvantage of standing at nearly five foot nine, tall for a woman in this age, meaning the men of the time felt that she was a challenge and that they could do, and say, what they liked to her. When they saw her crying while pulling pints of ale, it made them worse, they had sensed blood, and doubled their efforts. This job hadn't lasted long. The last job she tried was working in a small solicitor's office as a junior clerk. She got this because of her ability to read and write, skills that were rare in a woman of this time and age. However, she lost this job because she proved herself to be cleverer than her employer; he didn't like being corrected by an 'uppity' woman and promptly fired her.

Eventually, she had resorted to selling her body to the local men. This had made her feel physically sick, not only due to the terrible personal hygiene practiced in this time, but also because she had been a lesbian for all of her sexual life and the thought of a man touching her made her ill. Her one and only outing resulted in her being violently attacked by her punter for not letting him touch her where he wanted. He also took what little money she had managed to scrape together and the whole event had been a disaster.

Out of all the women who had travelled back, Liz thought that she was the least suited for the harshness of these times.

Eventually she found work as a cleaner in an eatery on the corner of Berner Street, just off Commercial Road. The work suited her as she didn't have to talk to anyone, and she enjoyed the fact that she was able to clean, even if it was just a small, tiny section of this squalid world. She took pride that her area would be the cleanest area in at least a square mile. It was hard going as there were no hygiene laws in eighteen-eighty-eight, but she took solace in knowing that she was only going to be here for a year. After that, they all—well nearly all, God rest her friends' souls—would be going back to twenty-two-eighty-eight to take their rightful place as rulers of the new order.

It was dark outside. The eatery stayed open until late, catering for the hungry revellers from the local pubs. Liz was hard at work scrubbing, attempting to get the deep-set grime from the floors. She was alone in the shop; exactly how she preferred it, and the owner was more than happy to allow her to lock up. It gave him more time to drink in the nearby Northumberland Arms, a nasty pub, in a mean side road, that was a popular haunt of their customers. With it being mid-week, the place was quiet, and she could happily scrub away at the grease and the grime with her bucket of warm, soapy water.

As she scrubbed, a strange feeling befell her. She became aware that there was someone else in the shop. She looked up from her work and was shocked to see a man, whom she didn't recognise, standing in the doorway. He wore a large bushy moustache, and she noticed that it looked funny on him, as if it didn't belong. He also wore a hat and a cape and carried a cane. None of this attire was out of place in this eatery. Some of the more affluent gentry would eat here prior to going home for the night or going out wenching for the evening.

He stood and walked towards the counter, careful not to stand in Liz's cleaned area. *Strange*, she thought. *No one usually cares, they usually walk right through.* She averted her eyes as he passed. She didn't care what he looked like, she just wanted to finish her work, go home for the night, and sleep until late tomorrow.

He didn't say anything before selecting a table opposite where she was working. He sat there, as if waiting for her to serve him. Eventually, she built up the nerve to look at him. He caught her eye and smiled. She found herself smiling back. There was something disarming about the smile, something... attractive.

This in itself was strange, as she had never found a man attractive before, especially one who had such a bushy moustache. But there she was, smiling back at him, feeling her heart beat a little faster. He raised his hand as if heralding her, and she felt her face instantly heat up. 'I'll be with you in a moment,' she called. 'But I have to tell you that were nearly closed. There's not much left, I'm afraid.' She then abruptly turned her back on him, picked up her bucket and cloth, and headed towards the back of the shop.

As she emptied her bucket down the drain, she heard the door open and close again, announcing that the man had left. She felt relieved, but also a little sad. *Why do I hope he hasn't left?* she thought, when a gruff voice shouted from the counter.

'Is anyone serving here?' There was something about this voice that she didn't like, and she remembered Carrie's warnings about keeping their eyes peeled for anyone strange.

She thought back to the meeting they had had after Annie Chapman's murder.

~~~~

They had gathered in the small room where Carrie lived with Mary Kelly. Liz had always been a little jealous of this arrangement as she'd always had a bit of a crush on Mary. She thought she was beautiful with her Celtic features, her auburn hair and deep green eyes.

Carrie Millwood was standing at the front of the group, she was crying. Everyone could feel that her sorrow was as deep as it was true. 'We need to keep vigilant,' she said once she had composed herself. 'There's someone in this time who knows who we are. This can be the only explanation. The paradoxical laws simply do not allow for people of this time to harm us, yet someone is. The only clue we have is the information on the streets about the man shouting and screaming at Annie the night of her...' she paused for a moment, dabbing her eyes with a small handkerchief, '...her murder.'

Everyone in the room shifted uneasily.

Carrie was unable to go on, so Mary stood, put her arm around the taller woman, and whispered something in her ear. Carrie nodded and sat down, a little shakily, on the stool behind her. Mary smiled at the group and continued the address.

'The man in The Ten Bells was apparently screaming at her, calling her a witch, shouting that he knew what she was. He's reported to be maybe five foot nine or ten. He has a thick moustache and a foreign look to him. He has a gruff voice and dark eyes. Some say he's a local barber, others say he works in the meat factory. How much of this is true, I don't know. I'm surprised how quickly horror stories pass around these parts, but it's all we have to go on. We know that Martha, Polly, and Annie are dead, and Emily is still missing, presumed dead.'

'Can't we just contact home and get them to bring us back now?' Liz Stride asked, her eyes shifting from woman to woman.

'It's a good idea,' Mary replied. 'But unfortunately, we instructed the team to desert the castle when we left. They were instructed to check on us every three months. Our headquarters were not exactly a secret, and the EA would undoubtedly begin their investigations there. The next contact we have with them will be November thirtieth. Until then, we're on our own. I'll see if it's viable for us to go back on that date, or as near to it as possible. It's becoming dangerous for us to stay here, but it'll mean the terraforming project won't be complete on our return. We're hoping that the EA don't know what our end-game is, so, at least our threat will still be valid.'

Everyone in the room agreed that the bringing forward of their mission was the best, and safest, course of action.

'Can I please reiterate to everyone,' Carrie said, looking more composed. 'We need to be extra vigilant for ourselves and each other. Any suspicious circumstances, and I mean anything, get the hell out of there. We only need to stay alive until the thirtieth of November. It's a little over a month and a half.'

'I think we should adopt a buddy system,' Mary continued. 'If anyone has any long walks, or lonely routes, then they do not do it alone. Has everybody got that?'

Everyone agreed, and the meeting was adjourned.

~~~~

A deep shiver ran through Liz as the gruff voice shouted to her from the counter. She placed the washing bucket on the floor and turned towards the main eatery. To Liz's delight, the gentleman was still there, sitting at the same table. She tried not to look at him for too long as she didn't want to alarm him, but her gaze kept flitting between him, and the rough looking man at the counter. *Does this count as a suspicious circumstance?* she thought.

She entered the room, ignoring the newcomer, and made her way over to the gentleman at the table. 'What can I get you, sir?'

The man looked at her. *His eyes are beautiful,* she thought, and felt the burn of a blush returning over her whole face.

'Just a warm bowl of soup if there's enough left, please.' His voice was so gentle that Liz was confused as to what to do.

Fixing her hair back behind her ear, she struggled to meet his eyes. 'Yes, sir, I think there's enough left for another bowl, or maybe even two.'

As she turned to fetch the order, the rough man grabbed her by the arm, squeezing tightly. 'Aren't you going to serve me?'

She looked up at him, he was also sporting a heavy moustache underneath a large nose and dark, foreign eyes. 'Y- yes, sir. Of course, I was. Let me see to this gentleman first, then I'll see to you.' She shrugged off the grip and disappeared into the back.

As she ladled the last of the soup into a clean bowl, she looked at the small clock on the wall and sighed. It was nearly eleven-thirty.

Catherine wouldn't be meeting her until after one-thirty, when her shift in the bakery ended. Normally she wouldn't have minded waiting around for an hour or so, either inside or outside the shop, for Catherine to meet her, but tonight was different. These men were unnerving her, both for different reasons.

She was rooting in the drawer for a clean spoon when she felt the uneasy presence of somebody standing behind her. In a slight panic, she turned around to face whoever it was.

Thankfully, it was the gentleman and not the rough looking foreigner. 'I'm sorry to scare you, miss, but I was wondering if I could have a cob of bread to go with my soup. I'm really rather hungry tonight.'

Liz's heart was racing now. She was more than a little uncomfortable in the man's presence; there was something... she didn't know what it was about him, he was just distracting. She was attracted to him, that was for sure, and that in itself was unnerving, but there was something else too.

'Erm, you aren't supposed to be around here, sir. If you make your way back to the main room, I'll be happy to bring it out to you.'

The man smiled; it was almost a sweet smile.

*What the Hell is happening here? I don't even like men, but this one is pressing all my buttons*, she thought, blushing again.

'It'll be ha'pence more on your bill, though,' she gushed.

The man winked at her and went back to his table.

She spied at him through the door as he walked back into the room. There was just something about him that she couldn't put her finger on, something... delicious. Shaking her head at her silliness, she grabbed two small cobs of bread and hurried through into the main eating room. As she hurried, she bumped into the other moustachioed stranger—this one she didn't care for in the least.

'Watch yourself, young lady,' he chastised her patronisingly. 'You never know who you're going to bump into. The next one could be Death himself.'

Liz shivered at the words. *Was that a threat?* she thought, feeling the rise of panic in her chest. 'I'm sorry, sir. I'll look where I'm going next time, for sure.'

He grabbed her again and looked deep into her eyes. She watched as his dark pupils expanded. Recognition dawned on his face.

'You're one of them, aren't you?' he whispered. 'One of the witches! Oh, you'll get yours, young lady, you'll get yours, and soon. Mark my words!'

He pushed passed her and made his way towards the back room leading to the yard, where most of the customers went to relieve themselves.

Liz couldn't move. All the colour drained from her face and her bladder was in danger of overflowing. The gentleman had been watching this encounter, and he came over to her. He held her in both of his arms, stopping her from falling over.

'I saw all that. Did that man threaten you, miss?'

'Well, erm, no. Not exactly. But after all those murders recently, I just got a little scared. That's all.'

'Do you want me to wait here for you after you finish? I can walk you home, make sure you get there all right?'

Liz smiled, then shook her head. *Yes please*, she thought. 'There's really no need, sir. I'll be waiting round for my friend who works next door. We walk together since all this murder malarkey began. Don't want to be a victim of old Leather Apron, do I? Safety in numbers, don't you know.'

'That's very wise, very wise indeed. Am I right in thinking that the bakery doesn't close the doors for its staff until at least one-thirty? This eatery closes at, what? Twelve-thirty? What do you do until then miss?'

Liz shrugged, and pushed the imaginary lock of hair behind her ear again. 'Usually I stay around the back, out of sight. Keeping warm and enjoying the smell of the bread.'

The man smiled. 'Well, if you're quite sure you don't need my assistance.'

Liz stared into his eyes. Then she slowly, and reluctantly, shook her head.

He released his gentle hold on her and walked back to his table. He left money on the side and made his way towards the door. As he was just about to leave, the rough man reappeared from the back room, still buttoning his fly. He stopped and watched the gentleman walk out of the door.

'Who was he?' he barked at Liz. She ignored him as she watched the door close.

# TimeRipper

The rough man grabbed her by the wrists and turned her towards him. 'I asked you a question!'

'No one! I've never seen him before,' she whimpered. In the embrace of the gentleman, she had almost forgotten what this one had whispered to her before he left.

'Did he talk to you?' he barked again.

'He beckoned good night as he left,' she lied.

He let her go before storming off in the direction of the door, not bothering to continue ordering his meal.

As it slammed behind him, Liz was relieved when Israel Schwartz, the owner of the eatery, turned up from wherever he'd been.

He looked around, taking in the empty room. 'Stride...' he shouted, a little drunkenly. 'Where've all the customers gone? And, more importantly, where's the payment for the meals?'

Liz gave him a look that was filled with contempt, then walked off into the back room, leaving him scratching his head and looking around.

~~~

Kosminski raced outside into the cool night. He was ready to confront the gentleman who had just left the eatery. There were a few people hanging around outside the bakery next door, either relieving themselves in the street, or lighting up fags, but his mark was not one of them. There was nowhere to hide within one hundred yards of either side of the building. 'Into thin air,' he mumbled to himself as he scanned the street.

He lifted his wrist to his face and pressed a button on the device he was wearing. A small, tinny, voice issued from it. 'This is Abberline, report!'

'I've seen him. He was in Schwartz's eatery on Commercial Road, the one next to the bakery. Long Liz works there.'

'Long Liz?' asked the disembodied voice.

He shook his head. 'That's not her real name, I gave them nicknames. Long Liz because I have heard people call her Liz and she's tall for a woman.'

'That would be Stride. I've got her on my map in the location you've given me. Thank you, Mr Kosminski. Do you have any other business?'

'Yes, the man I told you about was in there, Jack the Ripper. I'm sure he was talking to her, but I never got the gist of what they were saying.'

'Is he still there now?' Abberline's voice sounded interested in the conversation now.

'No, he left. I tried to follow, but he disappeared into thin air. Can you people do that? Disappear as if you were never there?'

'No, sir, we can't. I need you to find this man. I've a feeling he was there for a reason.'

'Yes, sir,' Kosminski replied, gripping the handle of the razorblade he kept concealed in his pocket.

'Oh, and, Kosminski, you are, by no means, to apprehend this man, for reasons that you will not understand. You wouldn't be able to defend yourself against him if he had cause to attack you.'

'Understood. I'll try to find him again.' He felt more than a little silly talking to his wrist, and even sillier that his wrist was talking back to him. Not entirely sure if he was living in a delusional state, or if this was now his new norm, he took solace in the solidity of his blade as he turned into the dark London night to continue his mission.

~~~~

Liz left the eatery at just after twelve thirty. She was glad she had decided to put on her thick cloth coat and wrap up, as a chill had crept into the evening. As she exited the employee's door at the back of the shop onto Dutfield's Yard, it was pitch black. There were no streetlamps in the yard, and the ones in the street didn't have the power to extend over the large brick walls.

She was nervous tonight, more than was usual for her. Normally this area never bothered her, as it was warm and dry. The yard was in use both day and night, but tonight it seemed like the loneliest, darkest, most hostile place she had ever been in her life.

Every movement of the wind was the large man with the thick moustache, every noise from the opposite corner of the yard was a rapist ready to pounce on her and have his wicked way. Every shadow was Leather Apron come to rip her to pieces as had happened to her friends. Madness lurked in every darkened window, and there was murder behind her eyelids every time she blinked.

A shuffle snapped her out of her waking nightmare. It came from her left, by the main gate into the yard. Her heart began to beat double time in her chest as she made out the silhouette of a man advancing towards her in the darkness. She could see that he was wearing a hat and a cape. He was walking with pace and determination in her direction. The gloom of the yard only gave her an outline of him, but she could see that whoever it was had a large build. She ruled out the mystery man from earlier, who she'd had a stupid giggling schoolgirl crush on. The only person it could be was the ruffian from the eatery.

She turned so she could watch him advance but made it so that it looked like she was stood with someone else, in a passionate embrace.

She giggled as the silhouette drew nearer. 'Oh, you cheeky thing!' she exclaimed. 'I will, but not tonight. Some other night maybe,' then she giggled again.

The man continued past her heading towards the Fairclough Street entrance. He gave Liz a cursory glance as he passed by, then strode off into the dark of the night. She noticed a smell as he passed, like he'd been inside the eatery and gotten something to take home with him. *He must be one of Schwarz's friends,* she thought, a little relieved.

Exhaling a deep sigh and rubbing her eyes with her cold hands, she estimated that about ten minutes had passed since she had left work. *I still have ages to wait before Catherine gets out*, she thought with an exasperated breath.

That was when she heard another man walking through the yard. He sounded slower, more purposeful than the last. He was coming from the same direction and she thought about employing the same trick again. This time, however, something about the way he was walking told her the same trick wouldn't work.

The dark shadow came into view. Her eyes had gotten used to the darkness of the yard by now, and what she could see made him look sinister in his cape and hat.

'Long Liz,' the man whispered. 'Long Liz, I know what you are. I have a little friend who has some long-awaited business with you...'

*Who is Long Liz?* she thought. She decided that she didn't really want to know and made a move, darting from the shadows, heading towards the middle of the yard. She just had time to see the man following her.

'Elizabeth! Elizabeth, over here.'

Surprised to hear her name being called from the darkness, she looked up. The gentleman from the eatery was standing in the gateway that led onto Fairclough Street. He was silhouetted against the night, but she could make out his slight frame. His cape was lined with red silk. He held out a hand towards her, and she accepted.

He pulled her into the relative safety of the gateway and put his hand over her mouth to stop her from making any noise. From their hiding place, they watched as the larger man passed by, searching this way and that as he made his way across to the other end of the yard, heading towards Commercial Road. He lifted his hand to his face and looked like he was talking into his wrist.

*Oh shit, it is him*, she thought. *He's talking into a communicator, he's not on his own. How many of them are there?*

She turned towards her saviour to thank him for the rescue.

He shushed her. 'Don't mention it. I'd have done the same for anyone,' he replied.

'If there's anything I can do to thank you, just ask and you shall receive,' she whispered, there was more than a touch of flirtation in her voice. *What am I doing?* she asked herself.

'Well, there's one thing you can do for me,' he replied in an equally flirty voice.

She cocked her head and looked at him. 'Oh yes, and what might that be?' she thought about adding 'kind sir' on the end of the question, but decided that it sounded like something out of a cheap romance novel. *Oh my God, I could lose my straight virginity right here in a gloomy, dirty yard, in the eighteen hundreds!* The thought made her giggle again.

'You could give me the transponder codes for all the women who've come back to this time.'

Elizabeth's blood froze, and she lost all feeling in her legs. They buckled as her head began to swim.

~~~

The man struggled to stop her from falling and clattering into the gate. It would have made a noise, maybe loud enough to attract the attentions of another man who was now crossing the yard.

The newcomer looked over into the shadows to see a man holding a woman. A flash of recognition passed over his face, 'Liz?' he asked, 'Liz, it's Israel, are you OK?'

He began to make his way to where the couple were struggling. As he got closer, he noticed that the woman was looking a little dazed and confused.

'Come on, darling,' the man scolded. 'Is it not enough that you're my wife, that I have to carry you home almost every night? You're a no-good drunkard.'

Israel Schwartz stopped and watched as the man in the shadows helped the woman to her feet. *That can't be Liz*, he thought, *she hasn't been drinking, and she's not married*. He shook his head and smiled as he continued his way out of the yard.

~~~

As Liz came to her senses, she found herself in the yard gateway with her assailant pressed up tight against her. A leather clad hand was over her mouth. She was trying to scream, but the hand was easily muffling it. A driving fist into her stomach pushed all the air out of her, taking the scream with it. Her eyes were filling with tears, obscuring her view of her assailant's face. 'You want what?' she asked breathlessly, feigning innocence.

'Don't act innocent with me, Stride. I know it was you who perfected the method of handling the Higgs Storm, which ultimately led to the mass destruction of nearly half of Earth.'

'What do you want?' she asked again, this time it was in resignation.

'I want your transponder codes. Yours and those of the rest of your friends. If you give them to me now, I'll take the rest of you home to stand trial. If you don't, you'll die, right here, right now. I'll tell you from experience, it won't be the nicest of deaths.'

'You bastard,' she spat. 'You killed my friends.'

'Not quite,' the stranger replied. 'Callaghan is still alive. I've been trying to persuade her to give up the codes, but she won't. Believe me, I don't want to kill you, all I want is to stop what you have planned for Earth when you get back.'

'What we did was necessary,' she hissed, resigned now to her fate. 'There needs to be a new start. Commercialism and personal greed have gone too far. Society is broken and we intend to fix it. Yes, there'll be devastation, but it's a requirement if we want to build a new Eden.' In the dark of the courtyard, she smiled, even managing to laugh a little. 'You can't make an omelette without breaking some eggs.' She had not intended to talk so much, but she was so passionate, and proud, regarding The Event that her mouth ran away with her.

'I can take it then that you won't be giving me access to the codes?' he asked in a soft, almost sad voice.

'I won't,' she replied, defiantly.

'Then you'll die right here, knowing that your mission has failed. The Event has failed. You won't have nearly enough Higgs Storm to bring about the destruction of the rest of the planet.'

'Maybe not, but we've still made our stance against greed and corruption.'

'Greed, corruption, and religious hatred were eliminated years ago. All the ruling countries work together now, for the common good.'

'You missed your own point there though, didn't you? All the *ruling* countries. The people did not have a say. The people didn't get what they wanted.'

'Did you consult the people when you killed almost four billion of them? Did those people want to die? Did they vote for it? No. You took it upon yourselves and grasped that little bit of power that was there for the taking. You're worse than anything that has ever come before you. You're the real terrorists, you're the real scum. You deserve to die like the filth you are!' The gentleman took a moment to step back and look at Liz. He shook his head slowly. 'Of all of them, of all the women who are dead, you're the only one who has made me feel sick. Yet, unlike you, I'm a civilized human being, and I'll give you the chance to live. Will you give me the codes?'

Liz stood her ground, only her eyes gave away the terror that coursed through her as he produced a metallic sphere from inside his cloak. He activated it, and her body was suddenly immersed in a dull green light. Within the green was one small flashing purple spot.

On activation, the purple light darted around her body. Liz wanted to wriggle free, but the binding beam held her tight. She was unable to move anything below her neck. She opened her mouth to scream was rewarded with silence.

The man produced another device and activated a red beam. He touched it to her neck, and instantly an agonising, searing burn took his in its embrace, as it pierced her flesh.

Suddenly, a noise filled the yard as the heavy, wooden gate opposite them began to wobble.

Someone was opening it.

The gentleman whipped his head around just in time to see the latch draw back. 'Fuck...' Liz heard him mumble.

A horse's whinny and a hooved clip-clop on the pavement outside the yard disturbed the proceedings. Liz would have relaxed every muscle in her body if she hadn't been trapped in the binding field. *Oh, reprieve at the last sec...*

She never finished that thought.

~~~~

Liz's assailant angled the red beam and sliced her throat, deeply, from left to right. He stood back and watched as dark blood gushed from her fatal wound. Once satisfied she was dead, he turned off the sphere and the green glow instantly disappeared, dropping her lifeless body onto the cold ground.

As she fell, he noticed something was in her hand, but he didn't have time to see what it might have been. The gate swung open, and he only just made it into the shadows, avoiding detection.

The horse, however, knew that he was there, and it reared up on its hind legs, startled by what was in the shadows.

'Easy there, old girl,' the man walking her in offered, trying to sooth the panicked beast. 'It's OK, there's no one here.' The horse reared again. 'Whoa, Jess, what is it, girl? Are you spooked?'

The killer watched as the nervous beast was placated. Once she was under control, the man looked around the yard. The killer held his breath as the man's eyes came to rest on the body of Elizabeth Stride, lying at his feet. The old man rummaged in his pocket for something, and the assassin took this chance to wriggle a little further into the shadows of the yard. The man struck a match, illuminating the scene. The hidden assassin watched as the man's eyes widened at the sight of the dark pool of blood expanding around the woman's, still warm, body. He dropped the match onto the floor, turned, and ran from the yard towards Commercial Street.

'Murder… Murder, I tell you. Oh, holy murder!' he yelled.

The man in the shadows took his reprieve and slipped out of the yard and into the shadows of Fairclough Street, towards Back Church Lane. From there, he disappeared into the night.

~~~~

Once again, Aaron Kosminski witnessed most of what had happened. It had been him in the yard whispering to Long Liz, but he'd had no intentions of hurting her, not yet anyway. He wanted to play Abberline's game out to the end, so he'd followed the mystery man since leaving the eatery.

He lifted his wrist to his mouth. 'Abberline, are you there?' He had become deft at using this device.

'Yes, I'm here. What do you have to report?'

'He's done it again. I think Long Liz is done for.'

Abberline tutted. 'I'm not at my console, where are you right now?'

'Dutfield's Yard, just off Berner Street. Do you know it?'

'Yes, I know it. Tail the murderer if you can and report his movements back to me. I'll be there shortly.'

He slunk out of the shadows before the man with the horse could return with a crowd. He headed off towards Back Church Lane, following the movements of the killer.

## 50.

Orbital Platform One. 2288

'OK, VINCENT, YOU have the test run tomorrow. You're going back one-hundred years. You're going to watch the Olympics in Cardiff. I had a relative who worked on the Olympic committee on that one, maybe you could look him up.' Youssef looked at Vincent with a lopsided grin. It took about ten seconds before Vincent realised that he was joking. 'You'll have to keep yourself to yourself. You'll be living in the past for one week. You're not to make any friends, just nodding acquaintances to the natives. You are not to stand out in the crowd in any way, do you hear me? This mission is about stealth. Jacqueline will be monitoring you all the way; she'll be relieved by either myself or by Kevin. Under no circumstances are you to take direction from anyone other than us three. Understood?'

'What about Dr Hausen?' Vincent asked.

'He's still in France trying to stop them dismissing the EA in favour of The Quest. If he takes over, you'll be given a special code, it'll be your security code. If you don't receive this code and you hear anyone other than us three, assume the mission is a failure and you are to make a life for yourself in that time. Understood?'

Vincent nodded.

'If that happens, you cannot, under any circumstances, attempt to make a family. The paradoxical laws would probably prevent that anyway, but no relationships.'

Vincent spared a swift glance over to Jacqueline, who blushed as their eyes met.

'Understood, sir. What time do we commence?'

'We'll begin at ten-fifteen. I'll need you kitted up and ready for briefing by eight-thirty. Go and get a good night's sleep, soldier.'

Youssef watched the furtive glances between the pair. 'Jacqueline,' he added almost dismissively. 'I'm going to need you in tip-top condition for tomorrow too. I want you to take the rest of the day. I need complete relaxation. Understood?'

They both snapped to attention. 'Understood, sir,' they replied in unison.

He smiled a sad smile as he watched them both leave the room.

~~~~

'How the hell did this happen?' Jacqueline sighed as she lay back on Vincent's bed, both of them a little out of breath.

'I don't know, but it's always the same. I get nothing for ages, and just before I have to go back a hundred years, I meet someone.' Vincent smiled as he stretched and put his hands under his head.

She smiled too, before wrapping her arms around him and snuggling in closer. 'Do you think anyone knows about us?' she asked.

Vincent snorted a laugh—it made him sound a little like a pig. 'Are you kidding? We've been about as subtle as The Quest!'

She gave him a playful little slap on the arm. 'That's a terrible thing to say. I thought we'd been totally discrete.'

'Well, Youssef knows! I've seen him watching us. I don't think he approves, probably because we're not married, or because of the difficult mission we're about to embark on, but he knows. He hasn't said anything about it yet, and I deploy tomorrow.'

'I wish you weren't going. I've got a bad feeling about the mission.'

'I have a bad feeling about every mission. It's just jitters. Everyone from the beginning of time has had jitters before a mission. You're by no means the first.'

'I know, but what if I mess this up or something? What if I don't see something and you're hurt, or worse, killed?'

'Jacq, you were fantastic when we were in the castle; you've got nothing to worry about. Come here.' He pulled her closer and kissed her mouth. She responded in kind.

## 51.

London. 1888

THE MAN REMAINED in the shadows; it was something he seemed to be very good at. Kosminski had been doing his best to keep up with him, and not be noticed, in the dark of the night. He'd followed him onto Back Church Lane and again onto Hooper Street. There were still a few stragglers hanging about, obviously going from one of the many pubs in that area back to someone's lodgings for a party of sorts. Nothing was further from his mind than following them and joining in. As he watched, the man crossed from Hooper Street onto Prescot Street. He noticed a woman walking alone in the opposite direction to the revellers. He guessed she was scared by the way she dived into the shadows as the mystery man made his way past her.

There was something about her, something he thought he should know, but didn't. This troubled him. He almost forgot about the man he was following in his musings about this woman.

Then the penny dropped.

'Kelly...' he whispered in the dark, 'It's Kelly from the Isle of Man.' His heart began to beat a little harder as he watched her approach. She would pass so close that he would be able to reach out and grab her. He thought that might cause a fuss, so instead, he stepped out of the shadows, revealing his presence to her.

~~~~

Catherine Eddowes reeled as the large man loomed out at her, seemingly from nowhere.

'Hello, Kelly,' he said, 'Fancy meeting you here.'

The woman held her hand up to her chest in shock at the man accosting her. 'I'm sorry, sir, you startled me, and no mistake. I'm thinking you've mistaken me for someone else. My name's not Kelly, that's for certain.'

Kosminski pulled a mock hurt face. 'I'm sorry, love. You just reminded me of someone I used to know, that's all. Sorry to have bothered you.'

Catherine Eddowes was not someone who scared easily. She may have only stood five foot exactly, but most of her frame was muscle. She was one of the lead scientists for The Quest and had been one of the main vocal advocates for The Event. She was also a mean fighter and could look after herself when push came to shove.

After the initial shock, she took a good look at the man. Instantly, she summed him up, and by instinct, she knew what his physical vulnerabilities would be. He was large, but top heavy. She could see a paunch in his stomach beneath his cape. This would mean weak legs. She could see he had thick arms, but they looked slow, and she could smell alcohol on his breath. *If he was to come at me, a swift kick into his kneecaps would topple him over. I'd just need to dodge his slow arms. That cane he's using; it'll probably have a blade in it. I could have that off him before he knew what's happening*, she'd thought all of this within the few seconds of seeing him, even before he'd called her Kelly.

'So, who's this Kelly one you're harping on about?' she asked saucily. 'I could do with a few extra bob tonight, especially after they sent me to work in the other bakery; no tips, you see.' She forgot all about meeting Liz, as she was supposed to do after work.

She disliked Liz.

She scared too easily and jumped at every noise. *Liz'll be fine*, she thought. *I'll go back and get her right after I've rolled this drunken old letch*. She smiled at this thought but passed it off as a smile towards the man.

'So, do you know this Kelly one well?' she asked him salaciously. To Catherine, he looked like he was about to wet his pants, he was that excited.

'Well, a little. I'd like to know you better than I know her,' he replied.

She noticed a small line of drool drip from his mouth as he replied. It turned her stomach, but then, there was no way that she was going to let him anywhere near her anyway. 'Well, let's see how much you really want to get to know me, if you know what I mean.'

'I've got money on me, not much, but I own a barber shop off George Yard, a mere stroll from here. A girl like you could make a good night's wage in my shop, if you know what I mean.' He winked before offering her his arm.

She chuckled. 'I 'ain't going to be taking no arm, now, but I might just venture to this shop of yours.'

'Well, let's go then.'

Kosminski had forgotten all about the man he was chasing for Abberline. Tonight, he wanted to do a little ripping himself.

~~~

Carrie was pacing around her lodgings. She had not slept for several days. She was grieving for the three girls they had lost, most of all Annie. She was glad that Mary, her second in command and the only one she trusted to be able to second guess her actions and orders, was still around. She was worried about Emily. She had been missing now for over two weeks with no sign of her or even a body to say that she had been the fourth victim. She was beginning to think this whole idea had been a bad one. *Maybe we'd been greedy, wanting to finish off the job. But then, if the terraforming of Earth back to its origins is going to work, all of this is necessary.*'

Thoughts like this had been running through her head constantly. For how long? She couldn't remember. She had been attempting to calculate if they had enough displaced mass to create the right amount of Higgs Storm to complete the job on their return. She seriously doubted it, but then she wasn't the mathematician in the group.

Mary was.

She paced back and forth. She knew that she was losing control—of her thoughts, and of the mission. She desperately wanted to get in touch with the castle and get them to recall the rest of the group prematurely. The problem with this was that there was no one monitoring the system except for at nominated times, which would not be for over another month. She could only hope that someone would disobey her direct orders and pick up her message.

She lifted her head towards the dirty white ceiling of her lodgings. The discoloured damp spots up there depressed her just as much as this situation had. 'Oh, Emily,' she sobbed. 'Where are you right now?' she cried. A tear welled in her eye before trickling down her cheek.

She removed a small black box from the chest that she kept beneath her bed and carefully put it down on the desk in the corner of the room. Slowly and cautiously, she opened the lid.

The portal lit up. Flashing red and green lights blinked at her. She smiled a sad smile. *How odd to be nostalgic for the future,* she thought. She typed in a password on the small keyboard, and the portal screen illuminated, bathing her face and reflecting the tears in her eyes.

She selected the application that would send a communication back to the castle in Inverness, piggy backing on the quantum signal from her slug. The message read quite simply:

*Mission compromised. Members expired in unforeseen circumstances.*
*Require emergency recall as soon as possible.*

*Carrie.*


She clicked send.

## 52.

<u>Inverness Castle. 2288</u>

THE LIGHTS ON one of the consoles in the castle began to flash, and an alarmingly loud klaxon broke the silence of the large room. The guards, who had been playing cards, looked at each other before reacting. They didn't know what was happening.

They watched as more consoles began to flash around them. The urgency of what was occurring was not lost on them. As they read the report on the consoles, they looked at each other, smiles emerging on their faces.

'Contact Youssef Haseem on OP-One. Tell him we've received communications from eighteen-eighty-eight. We should now be able to follow those bitch's quantum signals.'

## 53.

London. 1888

KOSMINSKI WAS ATTEMPTING to make small talk with the witch as he led her through the back streets of London towards his shop. He felt more than a little sickened by her saucy talk, but he humoured her with hints of payment for sexual encounters. Once again, he tried to take her arm, but she dodged him.

'I'm sorry, squire, but I'll not link arms with any man, except my husband. You don't want to be my husband, do you?' she laughed as she pushed him away.

'No, not me. I've had enough of being the husband. For now, I want to stay single and fancy free.'

Catherine forced a giggle at this statement as they continued through the deserted back streets of the East End. She was careful to keep him in sight, and at arm's reach. The thought had crossed her mind that he might have been the killer. *If it's him, then it means he must be from the future.* She shook her head as she regarded him. *This is a nineteen-hundreds man if I ever saw one*, she thought.

They turned onto India Street just off The Minories, and he suddenly stopped dead in his tracks. Catherine walked on a few steps before she noticed. He was staring straight ahead of him through wide eyes. The sweat on his forehead was reflecting the dim streetlights.

She looked to see what could have scared him, but nothing obvious was evident. Mentally she readied herself for an attack. Instead, it was her turn to look agog as he lifted his hand to his face and spoke into his wrist. There was a communications band there.

*It is him*, she thought.

'Abberline, it's Kosminski. I'm just off The Minories, can you hear me?'

'Loud and clear my, good man, but why are you telling me this?'

'Because I'm here with Catherine Eddowes, and *he's* here, at the end of the street. I think he's waiting for me.'

'Bugger. I'm about forty minutes' swift walk away, maybe twenty-five if I can summon a carriage. Would you be able to keep them there until I arrive?'

'I'll do my best, sir.'

'Oh, no you won't,' Catherine shouted as she dealt him a terrific blow to the back of his neck. 'You murderous bastard,' she spat.

Before Kosminski blacked out from the second blow, he heard her scream. 'Bastard. I'll kill you, you bastard.'

~~~

Kosminski was flat out on the floor. Catherine thought that she had killed him, and the thought made her smile. She couldn't wait to let Carrie know that she had gotten the bastard. As he lay defenceless, she leaned in and grabbed him by the neck, ready to remove the communication band, and have a word with whoever was on the other end. That was when she noticed a movement in the direction the killer had been staring only moments before. She looked up towards Jewrey Street. She *had* seen someone down there, but whoever it was, they had gone now.

She leaned back Kosminski, ready to give his neck a fatal twist, when something hit her from behind. The last thing she remembered was feeling the cold of the cobbles under her face as her head hit the road.

~~~

She came around a few minutes later to the sensation of movement, her movement. When she opened her eyes, all she could see were cobbles moving before her. She tried to wriggle her hands and feet but couldn't, they were bound by something. The slight green tint to the road beneath her gave it away. *A binding beam*, she thought.

The throb in her head was making her dizzy, coupled with the motion of being carried along at such a rapid pace. She opened her mouth to let her assailant know she was about to be sick, but no sound came forth, only a hot stream of vomit. She felt herself being laid on the floor, and as her assailant cleaned her up, she managed to get a quick look around. She recognised where she was; it was near to Aldgate High Street. This didn't bring her any comfort as she knew this part of London would be mostly deserted at this time of night.

They continued travelling for a minute or two, when she saw they had crossed Aldgate High and were now heading into a small, dark, square that she didn't recognise.

She could just about make out the man's back as he reached into his pocket with his free hand and produced a small keypad. A door to the building before her dissolved into a million light particles, opening into a dark warehouse. She caught part of the sign on the front of the door. It read '...of Mitre Square'.

Once inside, she was unceremoniously dumped onto a cold floor. The first thing she noticed was the stink of sweat, urine, and faeces. *Someone else is here,* she thought. *Emily?*

Using the only muscles that she could control, those of her eyes, she employed them to look up from her prostrate position. A naked and filthy woman was sitting in a chair. Before her was a small spherical device. The glow from it had wrapped her in a green light. In the centre of the green light there was a purple flashing blip.

She recognised it straight away as a quantum slug.

*It is Emily*, she thought. *She's still alive.*

As her captor entered her line of vision, she could only see the bottom of his trousers, his shoes, and the dark, red lining of his cape.

'Catherine Eddowes, you have something I want. You have the chance to give it to me now, of your own accord, or I'll take it by force, and I'll force your friend here...' he gestured towards Emily, '...to watch. Then, just maybe, she'll realise that giving me the codes is the best way forward.'

The sound of his voice roused Emily from her sleep. Her dazed eyes roamed the room before settling on Catherine. They went wide with fear and, Catherine thought, recognition.

She started shouting, but no sound was produced. The man pressed a button on the spherical object and the beam around Emily weakened.

'Catherine? Is that you? Are you OK?' she gasped while trying to take in air.

Catherine couldn't move due to the binding beam that confined her arms and legs; all she could do was turn her head and blink her eyes.

Emily looked over to the man, who had retreated into the shadows of the room. 'Why are you doing this? Why are you taking us one by one? You BASTARD!' she shouted.

Then she screamed and screamed and screamed. The man stood in the corner, allowing her to continue.

When she was done, she flopped back into her seat, exhausted. All the fuss had achieved was to cause Catherine to panic.

The man stepped back out of the shadows. 'You see, Catherine,' he said, stooping down to where she lay on the cold floor to look in her face. 'Your friends don't seem to care if you live or die, and if I don't get the transponder codes right now, you'll die, horribly.'

He took a small device out of his pocket and pressed a few buttons. Catherine felt the release of the beam from around her neck and chest. She gagged, trying to take in as much of the stale air as she could.

'What is it you want?' she croaked, grasping at her neck. 'I've never met this woman in my life,' she gasped, gesturing towards Emily.

The man leant back in and slapped her hard in the face. She felt her lip begin to swell. After the initial flinch, she looked back around at the man and smiled. 'I told you, I don't know anything.'

He hit her again, with equal force. 'Don't insult my intelligence, Eddowes.' The spittle flying from his mouth landed on her face. She blinked as it went into her eyes, stinging them slightly. 'I know exactly who you are. You began your career in the operations division, where you specialised in personal protection. You were once an Earth Alliance scientist, you specialised in molecule transportation, but your real passion lay in the Higgs Storm that was produced after temporal relocation. You left the EA and joined The Quest; where you then became a terrorist. You are jointly responsible for the worst atrocity known to history. Do not try to pull the wool over my eyes. Give me the transponder codes now or I'll remove your slug. You have one minute.'

Catherine looked up at the man, right into his eyes. 'Go fuck yourself,' she said and spat in his face.

His eyes bugged and his brow ruffled. He reached in and tore the shawl she was wearing off her bodice. He wiped the saliva from his face before dropping the rag onto the floor, where it landed in a pool of Emily's blood. Absently, he picked it up and stuffed it into a pocket in his cape.

'So be it,' he said. The quiver in his voice belied his rage. 'This will be the second tonight. Poor, nervous Elizabeth Stride has already felt this cutting beam this night. I wasn't able to retrieve her slug, but… I don't think I'll be needing it now,' he hissed as he grabbed her by her coat and dragged her out of the door.

At the mention of Elizabeth's name, Catherine began to scream.

~~~~

Emily could only watch as her colleague was dragged out of the cold, dark room. 'No!' she whispered into the, now empty, warehouse. The man came back in and removed the spherical object in front of her. The green light blinked off, as did the purple flash.

He then walked back out of the door.

Emily could see the green glow filtering in through the cracks in the door frame, she wanted to close her eyes, to turn away as a red glow joined it, but she couldn't. The sound of the ripping and tearing of flesh caused her empty stomach to churn, as, in her mind's eye, she could see her friend being cut open, torn apart by the beam as it chased her elusive slug. Even through her closed eyes, she could see Catherine's face contort in agony as her steaming innards fell, mutilated, from the fresh wounds in her stomach. She could see her friend choking and gargling on her own, free-flowing, blood.

Then the glow disappeared.

Emily hung her head; she knew that it was over.

After a short while, the door was pushed open and the man re-entered the warehouse.

His cape was covered in blood. A mist was rising from him in the cold of the room.

In his leather gloved hand, he held a small metallic object, which he threw at her feet. It landed on the floor with a muffled chink and, reluctantly, she cast her eyes down towards it.

It was a quantum slug.

# TimeRipper

It was Catherine Eddowes's quantum slug.

As he walked back outside, Emily's tears finally began to fall.

~~~

Kosminski watched as the man in the cape stood up from his work. He was covered in the woman's, *the witch's,* he corrected himself, blood. He then picked up the small object that he had retrieved from the dead bitch.

He scanned the dark square, with an emphasis towards the street at the far end. He was aware there would be a policeman—on his scheduled beat—due at any moment. The killer would not want to give the Bobby any reason to deviate from his beat other than to shine his lamp into the square.

The man made his way through the door back into the warehouse. Kosminski thought it might be the only chance he'll get to inspect the body, to make sure the witch was dead. He felt it was his duty. He rose, ready to make his way over, when the man appeared back in the doorway.

Kosminski ducked back into the safety of the shadows and watched as the killer regarded the mess on the floor. He removed his hat before picking up the body parts he'd removed, obviously to get at the object he'd wanted. With care, he placed them next to the woman's ruined body before folding her intestines, and other parts, over her shoulder.

He took his time over this, almost as if he was trying to keep the scene neat.

He then re-entered the warehouse.

Kosminski's greedy eyes had taken in the whole, gruesome, scene from his vantage point, in the doorway of the warehouse adjacent to the attack. His bruised and bloodied face was shrouded in darkness. He lifted his arm and whispered into the communications device. 'Abberline, I'm now in…' he looked around for anything that would give him an indication of where he was. 'Mitre Square,' he said at last, seeing a sign on one of the walls. 'I think he's done another. It's Kelly, sir, no, sorry, not Kelly, it is, erm…'

'Eddowes?' asked the voice from his wrist.

'Yes, Eddowes. He's ripped this one good and proper by the looks of things. There's bits of her all over the shop.'

'Is he still in the vicinity?'

'Yes, he's in a warehouse on the far side. Do you want me to go in?' He hoped Abberline was going to say yes. He was craving a fight, after his failure with the woman.

'No! I want you to wait for me there. I'm maybe... five minutes out, in a Hansom.'

'What if he leaves?'

'If he does, follow him, but keep in touch with me on this channel.'

'On this what?' he asked sounding confused.

'Never mind. I'll see you in a moment.'

As the communication ended, the killer exited the building.

*He can't be going for another one, could he?* he thought excitedly. Kosminski watched as the man strolled out of the square towards Aldgate High Street. He didn't seem to be in any rush as he strode down the cobbled lane. He turned onto Goulston Street before disappearing from sight.

Kosminski had an idea.

In his letter, which the press had taken into their hearts, he said he would take the ear lobe from his next victim. He decided it would be fun to do that, right now. It would also add some credence to his fabricated words.

He crept, ever so slowly towards the mess on the floor. He looked at the remains of Eddows, not really wanting to see the gruesome mess the killer had left; but needing to at the same time. It was all he could do not to vomit at the atrocities that had been performed on the poor woman's body. *Stop thinking of these as women, they're anything but...* he thought. He had a job to do, and as nasty as it was, he had to do it. He took the razorblade out of his pocket and quickly scalped at the earlobe of her right ear. 'Finally getting a bit of work, eh, boy?' he whispered to the razor. 'Sweeny would be proud!'

The work was tougher than he'd imagined. He didn't know if this was due to the cold, or to the blood coursing through his body, or even due to the beating he had taken a little earlier, but his sharp blade was shaking. By the time he finished, he had mutilated half of her face.

Finally, happy with his work, he put the ear in his pocket and limped off in the direction the mystery man had taken.

He made his way, as fast as he could, given his condition, down Aldgate High Street. He caught sight of his ward just prior to him disappearing into the darkness of another street. As the killer disappeared, Kosminski noticed something fall from the back of his cloak, something that looked a like a handkerchief.

He made his way towards the discarded rag and picked it up. Holding it by the corner with one finger and thumb, he was careful not to get any of the blood that was dripping from it anywhere near him. He studied the piece of cloth.

It was a shawl. It felt like it was made of silk. It was difficult to make out the design through the gore and blood, but it looked like it was printed with a design of Michaelmas daises.

Looking around the street, he was happy to see there was not another soul in sight. Thoughts a plenty were running through his head, none of them good. He had in mind a little bit of mischief. Something that Abberline did not have to know about, something that only he would know about. Something that could throw a spanner into the works of Abberline's strange involvement in these crimes.

Kosminski was truly the kind of man who sought to watch the world burn.

A thought struck him.

It was a damned good one too.

There was already major conflict in Whitechapel due to the rise in numbers of Polish settlers, and already the Jewish population had separated themselves from the rest, causing suspicions and unrest. *This could light a fire underneath all of that, and maybe even flush this bastard killer out into the open.* A small piece of white stone had fallen from the arch of a dark doorway. He picked it up and studied it. *Excellent*, he thought, then scribbled something almost nonsensical onto the wall inside the archway.

Standing back, he admired his handiwork with a child-like grin growing on his face. He then dropped the blood-stained garment onto the floor next to the writing. He limped off in the direction of his home, humming a jaunty tune.

## D E McCluskey

~~~~

Abberline stopped his Hansom Cab about a hundred yards away from the opening to Mitre Square. He thanked the driver, muttered something about policework never being done—he needed an excuse to be here—then payed him and let him go.

He waited for the carriage to disappear down the street before reaching inside his cape and removing his torch. He scanned the square for anything that resembled blood or a body and was rewarded as his beam found what looked like a bundle of clothes nestled in a corner. He stepped closer. He knew it was be a body, his years on the force had taught him that much. He checked behind him for any witnesses, before getting as close as he dared to his find.

He steeled himself for what he was about to see, but it didn't do him any good. What he saw shocked him to the core. He wanted to identify the body, but the blood and her mutilated face made it an impossible job.

Careful not to get the thickening blood on his trousers, he kneeled next to the body and injected the corpse with a syringe and removed a little of her blood. He took a small box from his cape—the same one he had shown Kosminski in his room—and pressed one of the buttons. A compartment opened, and he squirted a little of the blood inside before closing it. He pressed a few more buttons on a readout panel and waited for a few seconds.

A small beep announced that the portal had found a match, and a picture of Catherine Eddowes, wearing an EA uniform, flashed up on the screen.

He then removed a small spherical object from his cloak and activated it. The body was instantly bathed in green light. He frowned as he noticed the absence of what he was looking for.

The purple slug was not in her body.

He scanned the area with a black light filter on his torch and was quick to find a dark trail of blood hidden within the cracks of the cobblestones. The trail led back to a warehouse on the opposite side of the square.

He tried the door, but the lock wasn't one that he was familiar with, even with his lockpicking kit. He stepped back and looked at it.

Something didn't add up with it. It was cleaner than the rest of the building. Removing his portal from his inside pocket, he pointed it at the door and the readout told him exactly what he needed to know. It was light locked.

It took him a few attempts to find the correct frequency, but due to the lack of tech in this age, it wasn't too difficult to find. Soon the door dissolved into a million fragments of light.

Inside was huge, but sparse. There was a stink in the air that he recognised, instantly. 'Hello? Is there anyone here?' he half whispered; half shouted into the cavernous room.

There was no answer.

He knew there was someone here, his hunch was screaming at him, so he continued his search with caution.

The smell of sweat and faeces that he'd noticed earlier was cloying, almost to the point where it was making him baulk. As he entered further, he could just about make something out in the darkness. He had an inkling of what it was but couldn't be sure. A small beep from inside his cloak informed him of more out-of-time technology in his immediate vicinity. He sighed and turned his torch back on. What he saw in the beam shocked him at first. It was a naked woman, sitting, seemingly untethered, on a chair in the centre of the room.

He then noticed the spherical object in front of her.

*Binding beam*, he thought.

The woman looked asleep and not disturbed by his presence. He did another scan around the room with his black light and located more blood on the floor in front of the woman.

'I wonder...' he muttered as he inspected the blood.

He made his way back outside to the body in the square and ran a scan over her face for DNA. There were three different types present, her own and two other traces of saliva. Delicately, he selected small amounts of the DNA and returned into the warehouse. He ran both samples through the same scanner that he had used on the blood.

A few moments later, the portal beeped with a match. The first was Aaron Kosminski. *What the hell has that animal been doing with this woman?* He disregarded this result as the device beeped again. Abberline looked at the screen. The second result was a whole lot more interesting. He raised his eyebrows, nodded, and put the device away.

He deactivated the spherical device holding the woman, before slapping her lightly in the face.

She stirred.

'Emily Callaghan?' he asked, there was no sympathy in his voice. 'Where is the man who captured you?'

Her vacant eyes flicked around the room as if trying to decipher where she was. Eventually they rested on him. She stretched her eyes and her mouth, as if lack of use had stiffened them. When she eventually looked up, she had the air of someone who knew where she was but was afraid to be there.

'Who are you? Where is… the man?' she asked groggily.

'That's what I want to know. I'm assuming he was here not so long ago. Where did he go?'

Emily sat back in the chair—her body was responding to not being bound by the beam, and she was stretching her limbs. Her movements looked painful.

The stench of the room was coming, mostly, from her. He noticed a few discarded scraps of food lying around, but mostly he saw that the woman was sitting in her own faeces. 'How long have you been here?' he asked in a hushed tone.

'A while,' she replied, her body sagging. 'And yes, he was here earlier. The bastard killed Eddowes,' she spat, pointing at the spot where a quantum slug was lying covered in drying gore. She sat back again, sucking in a deep breath and rubbing her neck.

As he bent down to retrieve it, Emily made her move. She lashed out at him with her foot, knocking him off balance. Then she was up and out of the chair. Even though her body was emaciated from the lengthy captivity, and bare minimum food and water, she had the strength to pick her chair up and bring it down onto Abberline's head, hard.

He grunted once, then fell forward, face first onto the hard floor. She made a move for the door and was out into the cold September night.

~~~~

A short while later, Abberline roused, rubbing at the back of his head. The chair lay broken in pieces around him, but he had escaped serious injury. He looked over to the empty space where the chair had been. It took him a moment or two before he realised that Emily wasn't there. 'Damn,' he muttered as he got shakily to his feet and made his way out of the warehouse and into the square outside. There was no sign of the girl anywhere. He reached into his cape producing the small box again. Turning it on, he typed a command into it and a screen appeared showing all the incidences of technology that should not exist in this age. There were now only five, and of the five, only one was moving.

He gave chase.

The device told him that she was heading along Leadenhall Street, and she was moving at quite a pace for an emaciated, naked, woman in the centre of London.

He ran out of the square, heading in the direction his device indicated. According to it, she either didn't know where she was going, or she was trying to put him off her scent, as her course was heading erratically towards the river.

Abberline quickened his pace.

She was now moving along the Thames Embankment. It looked like she was bearing towards the New Scotland Yard buildings that were currently being constructed on Queen Victoria Street. He calculated a shortcut into the device that would allow him to head her off on Westminster Bridge. He turned onto Blackfriars Bridge and crossed the river at a fine pace. He was going to take the dog leg off the river and head up Westminster Bridge before her. He kept his pace while checking hers, estimating that he should make it there with time to catch his breath. It was getting onto four in the morning, and he was aware that London would soon be waking up. He quickened his pace, intending to meet with her at the corner of Embankment.

As he arrived, he checked her progress. She was a good two minutes behind him, giving him plenty of time to spring his trap.

He hid on the corner of Embankment and waited. He slowed his breathing back to normal, thankful that he had maintained his fitness, not an easy thing to do in Victorian London. He checked the portal again. She was less than a minute away, her quick pace had slowed somewhat. Running naked on a diet of scraps would do that to you over three miles. He took the spherical object out of his pocket and readied his cutter while he waited until her heavy breathing could be heard along the cobbled street.

When she was close enough, he stepped out on her, causing her to reel back. Before she could yell, he activated the binding beam. Instantly she was bathed in green light and completely immobilised. He dragged her into the darkness of the tunnel area beneath the bridge and laid her down on the floor. He noticed the flashing purple light that was residing in her chest. Her quantum slug. He would need to extract this to stop her from getting back to her own time.

He checked his watch before peering out of the darkness of the tunnel. There were precious few people in the vicinity, and he guessed he had maybe less than half an hour before the area would begin to fill up with passing trade and the like.

~~~~

Emily's eyes were open wide. This wasn't the man who had held her prisoner, but he had the same technology. Her neck muscles allowed her to look down towards the purple flashing light, then at the stranger who was pointing the cutting beam towards her. She watched helplessly as he activated the device, and the red beam burnt into her grimy flesh. There was nothing she could do but watch as the purple light danced around her body, evading the searing beam at every turn. Eventually, cold, raw agony overcame her, and her head rolled back; she was on the verge of fainting. A number of blood-curdling screams attempted to escape her, but she could emit no sound.

The man was obviously not in good practice with the beam. Reality was a vague concept to her as she witnessed her left arm detach from her body. He then flicked his hand, and the beam clipped and pierced the femoral artery in her leg.

Pain was shutting down the functions of her central nervous system. This had the unsettling effect of allowing her to watch thick jets of blood pumping out of what was left of her body. She noted that it was in perfect time with the slowing of her heartbeat. Finally, she felt one last tearing jolt of torture as the beam cut through the hip joint on her left side, severing her leg.

Then... merciful blackness overcame her.

~~~

Abberline was covered from head to toe in blood and gore, but still the quantum slug evaded his beam. He had severed both arms and a leg. The girl was obviously dead, but the bastard slug would not give up the game.

Finally, as the pulse of her blood began to diminish, he caught the damned thing. It was residing in her neck, and as he attempted to extract it, he inadvertently severed her head too.

Finally, he had it.

He watched in grim satisfaction as its purple glow dimmed on contact with the fresh air. Eventually, it blinked out altogether, and the slug became nothing more than a small metallic square. He turned off his locater, and the cutting beam, and surveyed the carnage before him.

He took a long look at the remains of Emily Callaghan and sighed. Yes, he had done a service to the future, but yes, he had also made a mess here in the present.

Her corpse was headless, armless, and at present, only had one leg still attached. There were also many deep cuts all over the trunk of her body. Rolling his eyes at the thought of what he was about to do, he took the cutting beam and lopped off her other leg before wrapping the trunk of her body in his cloak. He looked at the remaining limbs and decided it would be best to cut them up into smaller pieces and discarded them into the murky waters of the Thames below him. He kept the head and wrapped it into the same bundle as her body. He then proceeded to drag the grisly remains back up the embankment towards the New Scotland Yard building that was still under construction.

He had the idea that if he dumped the trunk of the body into one of the many vaults that had been built within the basement of the building, she might not be discovered for at least a few years or so. *It'll cause a great mystery.* He smiled. It was his first, and only smile, of the night.

On his way past another part of the site, he tossed her head into a pit marked for filling with concrete.

He had built up quite a sweat by the time the evidence of Emily Callaghan's existence, and death, had been discarded. The only thing left for him to do was to get home, as fast as he could, and wash the blood off his body and clothes. Tomorrow was going to be a busy day. There would be at least another two murders to investigate.

## 54.

Orbital Platform One. 2288

YOUSSEF WAS IN the control room as Vincent performed his final checks, ready for his test mission. 'Are you set?' he asked as Kevin did a further inspection on his kit.

'Probably about as ready for something I've never done before as I can be,' he replied with a smile, but Youssef could see the nervousness in his face.

'We've tried our best to prepare him for something we know nothing about,' Kevin offered as he tightened another strap on Vincent's back. 'But the truth is, we've not had nearly enough time to prepare for this.'

He nodded, acknowledging what Kevin had said. 'I know, but the fact of the matter is that we would never have enough time to prepare for any of this. Jacqueline, is everything in place?'

'I just have to inject him with the quantum slug, then programme our transponder codes, test the communications, and he's good to go.'

'How long?' Youssef asked.

'It'll take about ten minutes to do all of the above, then get the Collider up and running, maybe about half an hour.'

'Are you OK with this, Vincent? All set, mentally? It's going to be a little bit...'

'Oh, he'll have a bit of a problem with the mental part of it, sir,' she quipped.

They both laughed.

Satisfied with the reports and mental health of their test subject, Youssef made his way to the door. 'OK, I'll be back in half an hour, then we can progress this test,' he said prior to leaving the room.

'OK, now that he's gone, there's a few things you're going to need.' Kevin opened a small bag that was hidden underneath the table. 'You probably won't need them in Wales, not unless some of those Welsh lasses latch themselves onto you. But we're going to need to know if they work in the past,' he said handing Vincent a number of objects. 'Youssef knows you need them, but he also knows their destructive properties. He still has hopes of you getting those codes via coercion, and he also knows what you're going to have to do if they won't give them up.'

'A binding beam?' Vincent asked.

'Not just a binding beam, it's a quantum slug tracker too. Now you're going to need a steady hand using this,' Kevin said, handing him a small gun shaped object.

Vincent nodded as he received it. 'A retriever?'

'Yes. These two devices are linked, the tracker and the locator, but here's the rub: because the locator taps into the slug, it also knows it's being located, and it's a smart little bastard. It doesn't want to be found and extracted. You'll have a battle on your hands with it, a battle that the recipient won't survive.'

'There's no way we can nail down the slug without cutting the carrier?' Vincent asked.

Kevin shook his head. 'No way we can stop that from happening, I'm afraid. It's going to be dirty, wet work, my friend, unless you can get them to give up their codes.'

Vincent nodded in agreement.

'Have you used these before?' Jacqueline asked, trying to change the mood.

'Yeah, I've had training. Only, I haven't ever had to use one to try to remove a non-responsive slug before.' He flashed a smile at her; the meaning of it was not lost on Kevin. 'What's the battery life on them? I'm going to be gone for a week.'

'These ones are cellular. They should be good for, maybe a year, before the life will begin to degrade,' Jaqueline replied as she handed the devices over.

'Right, I think you're all set to go, kiddo. I'll just go and see Youssef to get the go ahead. You two can, erm, run through the mission logs, if you want.' He made a gesture for them to carry on as he hastily made his way out of the room.

When the door closed behind him, Jacqueline was in Vincent's arms like a shot. They kissed. 'Are you really ready for this? I mean, those devices are not toys.'

'They're lethal, Jacqs. I'm not going to need them for this part of the trial. I can't help thinking that there should be two people sent back on the main mission. I'm not a negotiator. I can't talk them into giving up the codes. I'm a grunt, someone to do the dangerous, or the dirty stuff. It should be someone like you, or Youssef, going back.'

'I'd do it. I'd love to come back with you.'

Vincent shook his head. 'I said someone *like* you. I don't want you in any danger, and anyway, you'd be rubbish with the extractor.'

She gave him a mock punch in the arm. 'I'd be just as good as you,' she replied with a laugh.

'I'm serious, though, I don't think you have the heart for this type of operation, and I don't mean that in a condescending way. There's a new order to things here on Earth. The EA could slip its hold on the planet, and chaos and anarchy would rule. We're going to need you and Youssef to keep order and to make a difference. Can you imagine Kevin trying to keep the peace?'

She tried to laugh as a small tear slipped down her face 'Are you ready?' she asked, not wanting to look at him.

He held her close and kissed her. It was a long, passionate kiss, filled with intensity, longing, and tinged with more than a little sorrow and fear. 'I am now!' he said, winking at her.

She turned away from him and pressed a few buttons on the portal behind her. A small syringe extended forth. Inside the syringe was a metallic looking liquid. 'This is going to hurt for a small while, probably about five minutes while the slug sets itself into your blood stream. I've built a mild sedative into it to take most of the sting away.'

He took his shirt off and sat down before her. She swabbed a localised area of his upper arm and injected the fluid.

'Ow!' he shouted as the needle penetrated his skin.

'Don't be such a baby,' she scolded.

After the needle receded, she turned back to her portal and linked the slug with a transponder code. Everything was working correctly.

'You need to test the communication device on your wrist,' she said. 'And then the two spare devices that you have.'

Vincent left the room while Jacqueline monitored the quantum link for the piggybacked communication signals.

'One, two, can you hear me?' came the voice over the portal speakers.

'Loud and clear. Try the next one.'

A few seconds later, 'Jacqs, this is device number two, can you hear me?'

'Again, loud and clear, now the third device.'

'Jacqs, will you marry me?'

'Loud and cle—' she stopped abruptly. 'What did you say?'

'I said, will you marry me? I'm going to need some serious motivation when I'm back there, and I want it to be you. I want you to be my wife when all this is over.'

'Get your ass back in here,' she shouted.

He walked back through the door with a sheepish look on his face.

Hers was like thunder. 'How could you do this to me? How could you ask me the most important thing in the world, right before you're off, back in time, for at least a week?'

'I need to know if we're both on the same page. I need to know that there's something special waiting for me. This is going to be the longest week, until I get back to you.'

Her anger relented after this little speech, and a shy smile broke through. 'Well, I'll let you know when you get back, but I am almost fifty-one percent that it'll be a yes.'

'YES!' Vincent shouted and punched the air.

'Calm down,' Jacqueline hissed, trying to shush him. 'I only said fifty-one percent'

At this point, Youssef and Kevin walked back into the room. They both eyed the youngsters with bemused looks.

'What's with all these happy faces?' Kevin asked, his look switching between the two of them.

'We're just eager to get this mission on track, that's all. Can we get this Hadron Collider started up, please? I've got a date one hundred years ago.'

She punched the commands into the portal, and the Collider began to spin into life. Vincent climbed onto the racetrack after he had shaken the hands of both his friends, and an exaggerated shake of

Jacqueline's, coupled with a sly wink and a smile. She, in turn, blushed a little and looked away. Youssef noticed a small tear in her eye. Vincent gave the three of them an exaggerated salute as the Collider began to spin around him.

'Injecting the Higgs-Boson gas now,' Jacqueline reported as purple gas obscured Vincent from their view. 'Injecting the modified hydrogen,' she continued.

The massive Hadron Collider kicked into another gear around Vincent. There was a bright purple flash, and the racetrack where he had been standing, only moments ago, filled with the dark purple Higgs Storm. The extractor fans kicked in and sucked it all into the containment bubble.

The lights on her portal flickered. 'I can confirm I'm receiving signals from Cardiff, from...' she paused as the telemetry came through, then she smiled and wiped the tear from her eye. '...from one-hundred years ago, exactly. It looks like he's made it safely. Thank God.'

## 55.

<u>London. 1888</u>

CARRIE MILLWOOD WAS in her lodging room with the remaining members of The Quest. They'd had confirmation of the murders of Liz Stride and Catherine Eddowes. Emily Callaghan was still missing. It left only four of them. 'This can't go on. I've sent a message to twenty-two-eighty-eight, to the castle, but on our own instructions, they'll not be able to retrieve it for at least another five weeks. The problem we have is, if there *is* someone here from the EA, or worse, then my communication back home may well allow them to locate our quantum signals. We'll have to watch out for each other at every stage until The Quest can retrieve us.'

Mary Kelly stood, her face grim, as she regarded her best friend. 'You know that you've compromised our situation?' She shook her head, there was more sorrow than anger in her face. 'All of this could be your doing.'

Carrie shook her head. 'No, it can't. I only sent the message two days ago. There's already been at least five murders, and God only knows where Emily can be.'

Mary closed her eyes and breathed through her nostrils. 'Did you not listen to anything I told you about temporal shifting?'

Carrie looked a little embarrassed—after all, this whole thing had been her idea. She had thought that they had covered every base of this operation, and now she had contravened everything.

'Time will carry on back in twenty-two-eighty-eight, but the temporal shift will allow for events to happen here that the people in the future will be able to use just by going backwards a little later.'

Everyone in the room looked baffled.

Mary sighed and continued. 'If the EA intercepted Carrie's signal, say they've compromised the castle, then they'll be able to decipher every move we've made since we got here. They could then send their operative back to the same time we arrived but armed with all the knowledge that they have obtained from the codes.'

'But what about the paradoxical law? I thought that nothing that we do here could affect the timeline back in twenty-two-eighty-eight,' Rose Mylett asked. 'So how can this affect what they'd know then?'

'That's a good question,' Mary replied, looking at the woman who had asked it. 'What you have to take into consideration is that we can do anything we want to each other while we're here, we just can't do anything to any key people from this time. So, when Carrie sent the signal, because she is from twenty-two-eighty-eight, all she did was change events *in* twenty-two-eighty-eight. It's a good bet that they're monitoring us right now.'

The room went very quiet.

'I think, from here on in, we need to stick together at all times, especially at night. We need to keep our eyes peeled and our ears on the street to find Emily. Other than that, we stay in each other's company at all times,' Carrie commanded, obviously shaken.

'Agreed,' Annabelle Farmer—one of the four left—commented. 'But what are we going to do about work and the like? Regardless if we're getting recalled in the next few weeks, we've still got to live. I'm not letting the filthy wretches of this time get their hands on me.'

'What are our cash reserves like?' Mary asked Carrie. 'Do we have enough for us all to live for the next few weeks together in one lodging?'

'Doubtful. We could find somewhere a little more ramshackle and ask the landlord nicely if he'd allow us all to live together, but the odds of that are slim. I'll make it my priority to start searching today. Does anyone else have any ideas?'

'I can get another one of us a job in the Princess Alice; they're always looking for more staff,' Annabelle suggested.

'That's a good idea,' Carrie replied. 'If two of us can work the same shift and make sure we always finish together, then the others can sit in the bar each night and we all walk home together.'

'What are we going to do about food?' Mary shouted. 'It's going to be tough living on two wages and eating at the same time.'

'Remember Martha's trick with the men?' Rose Mylett spoke up. 'You know, where she tricked them up into the alley and then knocked them out. I know how to do that. She was making a fortune from it.'

Carrie gave her a reproachful look. 'But that would mean you would be off, in secluded locations, with no backup.' She shook her head. 'I'm sorry, Rose; but it's out of the question.'

'Just a thought, but what if we offered two at a time? The dirty bastards would love that,' she continued with a playful smile, trying to make a little light of the dire situation.

'OK, listen, we'll keep it in mind, but we'll have to play it by ear for now. Let's all get to our jobs for today, and I'll begin looking for new lodgings.' She paused and looked around the room at the three scared and desperate faces looking back at her. 'Let's be careful out there, ladies.'

They all mumbled agreement and filed out of the room.

When Carrie was alone, she put her head in her hands and wept.

## 56.

'SIR, IT'S CONFIRMED. The *Dear Boss* letter was genuine.' Officer Bellis walked confidently into Abberline's office with the news.

Abberline looked up at him. 'What makes you so sure, officer?'

'The coroner has finished his preliminary reports on both the bodies found two night ago. It's his consideration that the women were killed with the same blade. He thinks he must have been disturbed with the Stride woman and didn't get the chance to finish his mutilations. The Eddowes woman *was* mutilated, sir, he had a right old go at her, but all evidence points to the fact that he cut off her ear lobe, as promised.'

Abberline cursed inwardly. *Kosminski, you bastard*, he thought.

'There was also writing on a wall, sir, a few yards from where she was found, along with her shawl covered in blood. We read it, and it looked like the same writing in the Dear Boss letter.'

Abberline stood up, suddenly angry. 'Take me to this writing,' he demanded.

'Can't,' was Bellis's one-word reply.

'What do you mean, can't?'

'I mean, the sergeant on duty wiped it off, sir. He reckoned what it said would have caused a major incident if he'd left it on there.'

'Do we at least know what it said?' Abberline snapped.

Bellis took out his notebook, licked his finger, and opened it. 'The Juwes, that bit was spelt wrong, sir, not that I'm a good speller or anything but even I know you don't spell Jews j – u – w – e – s-.'

'Please continue, Officer Bellis,' Abberline said, sitting back down at his desk and putting his hands to his head.

Bellis cleared his throat again. 'Anyways, it said, 'The Juwes are the men that will not be blamed for nothing.' That's all, sir. Although a few of the lads are saying that it actually read 'The Juwes are not the men who will be blamed for nothing.' And another officer said it read 'The Juwes are not the men To, with a capital T, sir, be blamed for nothing.' Although, there is still a differing of opinion that the word Juwes was spelled—'

'Enough,' Abberline cut him off. He rubbed at his temples with his hands. 'Does the press know anything about this?'

'Not yet, sir, but you know how leaky a police station is. It won't be long, by my reckoning.'

'Right, I want this played down as much as possible. I think it's a diversion, as I think the letter may well be. I have an individual in mind.'

'Kosminski, sir?' Bellis asked.

'Yes, him. I'll be seeing him this very afternoon.'

'Right-o, sir, I'll get myself attached to your investigation pronto.'

'That's very kind of you, Bellis, but I'll be going alone. I don't have enough evidence to arrest him yet, but I do want to let him know that we're watching him.'

'Agreed, sir, good plan.' The officer, looking a little disappointed, turned to leave.

'Erm, Bellis?'

'Yes, sir?'

'Were there any other murders reported last night?'

'Not that I know of, sir, and I've been on most of the morning. Do you want me to check?'

'No, no, it's fine. That'll be all, officer, you are doing a fine job.'

Bellis tried not to beam too much as he walked out of Abberline's office.

~~~~

Kosminski hadn't slept a wink in two nights. Every time he closed his eyes, the visions of the mutilated women flashed before him, with Abberline coming from the future to kill them; and that bitch, the one who had possessed him and made him think that she was some sort of relation, laughing at him, pointing at him, accusing him of murders that he hadn't committed. *As if someone like that could be related to me*, he thought. He was also torturing himself with his longing. He had come so tantalisingly close to 'ripping' one of them himself. So close that it frustrated the hell out of him that he hadn't been able to finish the job.

He was also thinking of the violence, and the chaos, that will be unleashed when the rubbish he wrote on the wall came into play.

He looked down at the small postcard he had on his desk before him. His first letter had been so well received and used, that he now just wanted to play.

> I was not codding dear old Boss when I gave you the tip, you'll hear about Saucy Jacky's work tomorrow double event this time number one squealed a bit couldn't finish straight off. Had not time to get ears off for police thanks for keeping last letter back till I got to work again.
>
> Jack the Ripper

As he read his words back, he couldn't help but stifle a laugh. *This will give that time traveller something to work on,* he thought.

He had been busy in the marketplace today. He'd purchased a cloak just like the mystery man had worn, and he had purchased himself a surgeon's bag and tools from a shady man on a market stall in Spitalfields. He was determined to 'rip' at least one of the witches, even if it killed him in the process.

He had also bought himself a large kidney. It was a pig's kidney, and he had two intentions with it. The first one, he was going to make himself a large pie from half of the organ; he did enjoy a bit of kidney pie, with ale. The other half he was going to package up and send to the Whitechapel Vigilance Committee, along with his letter. He wanted to see what mischief this would bring.

The game was becoming fun!

A long line of drool hung, unnoticed, from his bottom lip as he re-read the postcard, when a loud bang from downstairs in his barber shop snapped him back to reality; or what passed for it these days. It was closely followed by another bang, this one accompanied by the shattering of glass.

He jumped from the table and grabbed one of the knives from the surgeon's bag. His heart was thumping in his throat as he grasped the handle of the small, but sharp blade, ready to defend himself against whoever it was who had broken into his shop.

'Kosminski, are you in here, you bastard?' came the shout.

*Oh, shit!* he thought, *Abberline*. He realised that the small surgeon's knife he was holding was not going to do much against the weaponry that this man had in his arsenal.

'Up here, Inspector,' he called, his voice wavering. 'What can I do for you?'

As Abberline made his way up the stairs towards the living area, Kosminski could hear every boot stomp on every stair. He struggled to put the knife back into the bag and hide it underneath his table.

'What the fuck were you doing the other night? Why are you trying to mess with this operation?' the inspector shouted at him.

Kosminski backed away from the smaller man until he hit the corner of the room and could back off no more. 'I was observing, like you told me to, and I reported it all back, as promised.'

'I don't know how, or why, you're connected to what's going on here, but if you try to mess this up, you're doing something really stupid, something that will have huge repercussions hundreds of years from now.'

'Talk to me, will you?' Kosminski begged. 'I'm haunted here. My head is raging with manic thoughts.' He slid down the wall into a crouching position. He put his head into his hands and began to cry. 'I'm not a good person, this I know, but when I watched that bitch appear that night, I knew I was destined to do something about it. Then that other one touched me, it took me to another place, like she was a future version of me or something. I lost my mind on that one, like I'd been taking laudanum. Then you turn up with your fancy glowing paper, and the killer, whoever he is, with his fancy glowing...' he paused as if thinking of the words to use, or just to take in a shaky breath, '...I don't know, death rays. Nobody is listening to me; you're not listening to me. You may well be from the future where all this is commonplace, but I'm a simple-minded man from this time. I know I've gotten myself too deep into something I've no right being involved in.'

Abberline sat on the arm of a chair and looked at the snivelling man. 'Listen to me. Broken or not, you're my only link to what's going on here, and I need you. So, pull yourself together, man. I need whatever link you have to this case to find me the time and location of the next murder. There'll only be another four of them, of this I can assure you, but I can't see the other man's signal on my portal, in much the same way that I can't see my own. You have to get back out there and find me the person responsible for these killings; I have much to discuss with them.'

'You and me both, sir, you and me both,' he muttered underneath his breath as Abberline made his way out of the room.

'And don't forget to contact me with your wrist communicator. I'm always listening!' he shouted as he descended the stairs.

## 57.

'TWO MISSING SLUGS. I was disturbed in one extraction, and the other one was Emily. I had her in captivity. I was hoping to flip her into giving me the codes, but she's gone. Is there any way we can track her?'

The voice from the other end of the communication replied with a burst of static. 'We're receiving telemetry from…' the voice paused for a second, '…four signals. How many have been harvested?'

'Martha Tabram, Mary Nichols, Annie Chapman, Catherine Eddowes. Liz Stride was the one I was disturbed before extraction, and Emily Callaghan is the one who's missing.'

'So, the four we're reading must be Mary Kelly, Annie Farmer, Rose Mylett, and Carrie Millwood. Is everything all right back there? Are you having any settlement issues?'

'No, but I'm looking forward to coming home.'

'Roger that, we're looking forward to having you back too. OP-One, out.'

## 58.

THE TWO BUILDERS were easing themselves, lazily, into their working day. The hour was early, even for them. To combat the morning cold, they were both wearing long, woollen coats and leather boots. Neither looked like they had been washed since yesterday's shift had ended, in fact, one of them looked like he hadn't even been home.

'I can't be bothered with this today,' the larger of the two men mumbled as he opened the doors to the vault they'd been assigned to. He was feeling as bad as he looked, and that was bad. George, his partner, looked inside and squinted his eyes, trying to see down the steps. It was pitch-black inside. He sighed and reached into the inside pocket of his coat, pulling out a large hip flask. He took a long swig from it before passing it over to his colleague.

'Oh, Christ, George. You're a life saver, and no mistake,' he muttered, accepting the flask.

George took it back, had himself another nip of whatever rot was inside, then slipped it back into his inside pocket. 'Right,' he said with an Irish lilt. 'We need to start on this cement. I hope this frigging bunker kept all the tools dry. I'm not lumping a big heavy bag of ruined cement backwards and forwards again, that's for sure,' he said as he made his way down into the dark vault.

'Hold your horses there, George, I'll light the lamp. Don't want you going arse over tit down there.' He fumbled around for the matches in his pockets while bending into the doorway to fetch the lamp. 'Jesus, that's a funny smell. It stinks like something's died in here.'

'You're not wrong, Pat,' George said as he leaned into the bunker. He felt around in the darkness for the bags of dry cement they had left by the door in easy reach for today. 'Bastard rats down here are a nuisance. It feels like the frigging cement has gotten wet too, this bag's awfully queer,' he said as he gripped it and swung it over his shoulder.

Patrick swung the illuminated lamp down inside the vault. The first thing he saw was his friend's face; it was covered in something black and sticky. He jumped back, dropping the lamp. 'George, what the fuck have you got there? That's not cement, by the Lord Jesus Christ on the cross, that's *not* cement!'

George did a little dance, trying his best to drop the bag from his shoulder. Once satisfied that it was off, he turned around and took a long, hard look at what he had just picked up.

'Oh Lord! Oh, Sweet Jesus the Saviour,' he spat while crossing himself. 'In the name of the Father, the Son, and the Holy Ghost. Is that what I think it is?' he shouted as he clambered, shivering, out of the dark vault.

'If what you think it is, is a dead body, then yes, it's what you think it is,' Patrick shouted running off towards the main gate of the New Scotland Yard building site. He turned to see George running after him, still covered in gore.

George thought Patrick was screaming but he couldn't be sure.

Lying, just inside the doorway to the dark vault, was the headless, limbless torso of a naked woman.

~~~~

'Sir, everyone's talking about the latest body being the work of Jack the Ripper. A group of vigilantes calling themselves the Whitechapel Vigilant Committee are patrolling the streets. They're taking the law into their own hands, sir. Mostly they're taking this opportunity to settle personal grudges, all in the name of capturing this killer. What's your take on it?' Bellis was asking as he brought in Abberline's paperwork for the day.

The inspector sighed as he looked over the files. 'I'm just off to the scene, officer. I'll publish my findings after that and not one moment sooner,' he snapped at the nosey officer.

'Do you need a squad with you, Inspector?' Bellis asked, not taking any notice of the irritation in Abberline's voice.

Abberline sighed again. 'Yes, I expect so, Bellis,' he replied, his voice softening. *No reason to take this feeling out on Bellis, he wouldn't understand the sarcasm anyway.* 'Would you do me the favour of picking five of the most trustworthy officers you can for me?'

'At once, sir,' he replied, snapping a salute before making his way out of the office.

~~~~

An hour and a half later, Abberline was once again at the New Scotland Yard vaults. This time under different circumstances. A small crowd, all trying to gawp past the cordon of officers to get a good look at the grisly scene, had gathered. *Whitechapel Vigilant Committee, my arse,* he thought looking at them with contempt. 'Officer, I need three men to assist me in the vault. They must have strong stomachs, though. I believe this may be a bad scene,' he shouted towards Bellis. He smiled as he watched the officer pick three men out and send them down to assist him, noting that he never included himself in this detail. 'OK, I need to assess this corpse in-situ. Do *not* let anyone pass here. Do you understand?'

All three of them nodded their acknowledgement.

Abberline made his way into the vault where, three nights ago, he dumped Emily Callaghan's torso after amputating her limbs and head. The thought of going in here again was abhorrent, but he knew it was required. He removed a small, concentrated packet of powdered lye from his pocket and sprinkled it over the husk of the corpse. The concentration of the powder caused the body to begin decomposing immediately. He waited a few moments for the right conditions, holding his nose against the stink of the rotting flesh. He turned back to the three officers who had accompanied him. 'I've examined the scene and found no clues as to who this woman could be. The body is ready to be removed now,' he shouted up to the officers, one of whom called over the men who would take the body to the morgue to attempt to find the cause, and the time, of death. Abberline guessed that when they got her there, it would look like she had been dead for at least three weeks, therefore taking all the onus off the two recent murders. He would then, at least, have himself an alibi for his whereabouts on the night of the thirtieth of September.

As the body was hauled up and taken away in a large black carriage, the Whitechapel Vigilant Committee were straining to get a glimpse of what, or who, it was. Abberline walked past them with an air of disgust. Due to his aloofness, he never noticed Aaron Kosminski standing among the crowd of onlookers. There was a small, slightly unsettled, smile on his face.

## 59.

<u>Cardiff. 2188</u>

VINCENT CLARENCE SPENT his week in Cardiff living in a small barn on the outskirts of the town. The farm had been chosen prior to him leaving, as research had shown the farmer, and all his aides, would be away in London, attending a farmer's market for two full weeks. There would be no one around in all that time.

His time there was uneventful. He was allowed to send one message a day back to twenty-two-eighty-eight, just a brief five-minute dialogue. He was to leave the channel open for any emergencies that may arise on either side of the time rift.

He was to interact as much as he could with the natives of this time but not to make any spectacle of himself and not to draw any unwarranted attention either. He needed to be as inconspicuous as possible.

He had been there for two days, and already was bored to tears.

He decided to take a walk into the small, but affluent town of Pant-y-Ffynnon. While there, he made polite conversation with eight people before wandering into The Red Griffin pub. Once inside, he noticed that it was an authentic old pub and not one that had been decorated to make it look that way. He made it to the bar and looked to see what ales they might be brewing in this time. 'Are these all real ales?' he asked the older man behind the bar.

The bartender looked up at him from wiping down some of the glasses. 'Do I detect a London accent, boyo?' he asked with a smile.

Vincent smiled back. 'You do, sir. Why do you ask?'

'Well, it's just we don't get many visitors around here, mostly on account of the rain,' he laughed.

'Ah, well, I'm camping in a field not far from here, so I thought I'd spend some time with the locals.'

'Ah, yes. The great unwashed outside of our main cities, you mean?'

Vincent laughed. 'You got me there, sir. So, getting back to your real ales, what selection do you have?'

'Are you sure you're wanting a real ale, boyo? They're strong, you know.'

Vincent tipped the bartender a wink. 'I'm a big lad, you know. I think I can handle a few brews.'

The older man laughed again as he began to pour a pint of something called Sheep Dip. 'How old are you? If you don't mind me asking.'

'Twenty-five, sir. I'm just out of the EA academy. I wanted to stretch my legs a little before joining up completely.'

'Right then, Mr EA, this one's on the house, but you're paying for the rest of them. If you make it past five, I'll give you another free,' he winked.

'Deal,' Vincent agreed shaking the bartender's hand.

~~~~

Two hours later, Vincent staggered out of the Red Griffin pub after having made it to six pints of Sheep Dip. The bartender was helping him.

'Are you sure you don't want a lift? Do you remember where you left your tent?' he shouted as he watched the youngster stagger off towards a field.

Vincent waved him away while concentrating on trying to see the road ahead of him and trying to not succumb to the tilting cobbles of the road. 'I'll be fine,' he shouted back towards the locals who were all looking out of the door.

In reality, he shouted 'Aillsbe foon.'

## 60.

### London. 1888

ABBERLINE HAD BEEN a regular visitor to the morgue since the bodies of Stride and Eddowes had been brought in. However, there hadn't been an opportunity, that he could take advantage of, to retrieve the slug he knew was still residing within Stride. Even though it was inactive, he still wanted it out of her.

Today he had a chance of doing what needed to be done. Ever since the trunk of Callaghan's body had come in three days ago, there had been non-stop interest on whether or not it had been the work of Jack the Ripper. Most of the doctors, surgeons, and analysts were too busy trying to find out who this mystery woman was to be bothered with the body of a woman who had been dead for a few days.

Abberline was able to access the disposal room. The stink from inside was horrendous. There were no number of lilies, or bottles of perfume, in the whole of London that would be able to mask the smell.

Stride was tagged and wrapped in a muslin cloth. She was marked to be buried the next day in a sparse ceremony paid for by the parish of Plaistow. He had a window of about ten minutes to get in, locate the device, and extract it. The plus this time would be that the inactive slug would offer no resistance.

He removed her muslin and retched at the week old, untreated corpse. He could feel hot bile rising in his throat, but he had a job to do, and he couldn't allow any level of repugnance to hinder it. He set up his spherical locater and instantly her decomposing body was bathed in a green light. There was one dark area located just above her left breast. He quickly used the retriever to cut the body open. The gas that escaped from the wound was atrocious; and this time he did gag. He leaned over the small sink next to the body and retched up everything he had eaten today. *This is worse than killing that other poor woman*, he thought.

The extractor latched onto the device and pulled it out of the grey, putrefying flesh, easily. He snatched it out of the air and put it in his pocket just as Bob Droog, the chief mortician, walked into the room.

'Inspector Abberline, can I help you with anything?' he asked, with a look of suspicion on his face.

'Dr Droog! I was just doing a last-minute inspection of the body, sir. I heard she's to be buried tomorrow. Today would prove to be my last opportunity.'

The fat surgeon shook his head, his jowls jabbering as he did. 'I don't think you are going to get any more information from this one, Inspector. She's a ripe old bird now, sir, look...' he pointed towards the muslin cloth and the brown stain that had only just appeared. 'She's rotten! Any evidence she may have on her will be long gone now.'

Abberline smiled and wiped at his moist lips. 'No harm in trying, eh, Doctor? Is there any news regarding the other body yet?'

'Nothing yet, I'm afraid. The poor woman had been quite torn apart. We're thinking, because of the advanced decomposition, that she's been dead for at least six weeks. We're no longer entertaining the notion that this poor unfortunate is a victim of this Jack the Ripper character, but we still don't know who she is.'

'Well, we do know that if she's been dead for six weeks then she must have been moved. Those builders swear there was no body there last week when they dug out the vault. So, it looks like we still have a Whitechapel mystery on our hands, Doctor.'

'All I can say is good luck with that, sir. I must get back to it, she isn't going to identify herself, you know,' the doctor muttered, attempting to dismiss the inspector.

'Have you thought anything about that girl who's been reported missing? Gallagher, or something like that. The case fell on my desk a while back, but I had far too much on to take it. I gave it over to Inspector Peckham, Whitechapel.'

'Hmm, never even gave that a thought. Until her head and limbs turn up, I don't believe we'll ever know, eh?'

With that, the fat mortician slapped him on the back heartily and walked out of the room.

Abberline, with the reassuring weight of the quantum slug in his trouser pocket, followed him.

61.

THE WHOLE OF London was rife with talk of the killings. Even though the police and press had officially put out the word that the headless and limbless corpse was not involved in the Jack the Ripper investigation, the people did not believe it. Six murders were the talk in the taverns, six *savage* murders. The assailant there one minute, gone the next. Some people were saying he was a ghost, some were saying he was a demon from Hell. Others were saying he was an Angel from Heaven sent down to smite sinners, or that Spring Heeled Jack was back and was wreaking revenge on the people of London. Some people were likening him to the barber murders in Fleet Street all those years ago. But whatever he was, there were mixed feeling about him among the pub owners and breweries. During the day, their trade had risen by nearly one hundred percent, with gangs of people huddled around their booths and tables, passing drunken gossip about who he might be, what his motives were, and why what he was doing was being covered up by the police. However, as soon as it went dark, which it did early in late October, all the pubs and taverns in, and around, Whitechapel emptied quickly. Only the few die-hard drinkers, mostly the men, stayed on late.

This early trade was good news for Annabelle Farmer. She was no longer required to do evening shifts in the Princess Alice pub, and because of the influx of patronage during the day, the landlord had grudgingly agreed to allow her friend, Mary Kelly, to do a few shifts too. Annabelle had struck a deal with him to allow them to work the same hours so they could walk home together. Against her better judgement, and against her higher morals, she had reluctantly agreed to perform certain acts upon the landlord for this favour, although she stipulated that they would stop if any of his bodily fluids went anywhere near her.

'I don't care what the fuck happens to it,' the landlord growled with a dirty sneer. 'But I still want to be able to touch yer.'

She had no other choice than to allow this. It made her sick, but if it kept the four of them alive, then her reward, when they returned to twenty-two-eighty-eight, would be worth it.

So, each day, Annabelle and Mary would work behind the bar of the Princess Alice. The landlord would get a little something for the honour of him allowing them to work together, and Carrie and Rose could sit in the corner and drink a little. The extra money coming in from Mary's work, and from the 'extra' that the landlord would sometimes give Annabelle for his pleasure (although not all the time), allowed them to pay up on their rents for their individual lodgings and all move in to share a one room lodge that would benefit a small family on Millers Court, daubed *the worst street in London.*

This was how it went on for almost three weeks.

Tonight however, the landlord was in no mood for levity. His wife had voiced her suspicions earlier that he'd been dabbling with at least one of the girls in their employ and had taken it out on him the night before. All day he'd been stomping around the pub sporting a black eye and a thick lip. He was also in no mood for troublemakers either.

His wife was a large woman with big flabby arms. She always looked dirty and had a strange smell about her, like ingrained dirt that had been masked with inexpensive perfume. The landlord was no slouch either; he stood about six foot four, which made him huge in this time. He wore his hair long, curly, and dirty, and he sported a thick bushy moustache that was always filled with bits of food. No-one ever talked back to him as he'd been known to physically throw men out of his pub, either singlehandedly, or with the help of his large wife.

Today he was aware that there was not going to be any 'special favours' from Annabelle, therefore, there was not going to be any trouble-causers in his pub.

It was a simple equation.

He was out in the bar area collecting tankards when he heard a commotion from one of the booths in the corner. This heightened his spirits a little; he was in the mood for hurting someone. What he saw heightened his mood even further. Three drunken soldiers were slouching over the booth harassing two women.

He thought he recognised the women, but he couldn't be sure. Either way, it didn't matter to him, he was about to have some fun.

'Is everything all right here, ladies?' he asked, leaning his large frame into the booth.

One of the soldiers turned and looked at him as if he was dirt that had been brought in on someone's shoes. 'No, it's not, old man,' the soldier replied. 'Be a sir and kindly fill our tankards with your shit ale, will you? We're busy with these whores.' He then dropped his pewter tankard on the floor, where it broke into five pieces.

The landlord exploded in a rage. He was not so bothered about how he had been spoken to, but he was bothered about the tankards—they cost him money.

He grabbed the soldier by his hair and yanked his head back so hard that he was pulled away from the booth. He then held onto the soldier, dangling him in the air. His face was turning bright red as his feet struggled to gain purchase on the slippery floor.

The other two jumped from their seats and stood ready to fight. The landlord smiled and grabbed one of them in his meaty arm and put him in a headlock. The third one hesitated in his attack. He held his fists out towards the landlord, but his eyes kept switching between his friend in a headlock and his friend dangling by his hair.

'Don't just stand there, Smithers, hit the bastard,' shouted the first soldier as he dangled, trying to grab the landlord's arm. The second one was struggling too, but as his face was buried deep into the landlord's stinking arm pit, no one could understand what he was trying to say.

Smithers's defensive stance was wilting. He looked around the bar as if searching for someone, anyone who could help him. No one was stepping up to that mantle. The landlord nudged his head in the direction of the exit. Smithers took this as his cue to leave, and swiftly left.

Still in a rage, he dragged the other two soldiers through the pub and threw them both out into the street to the cheer and applause of his drunken patrons.

Outside, the three soldiers dusted themselves off, shouted some obscenities back through the door, and left the vicinity, scarpering off along Commercial Road.

# TimeRipper

As he turned back into the pub, all the patrons who had been cheering and whistling, abruptly stopped as he glared at them. He then stomped back over to the two grateful looking women in the booth.

Rose Mylett stood up and offered her hand out to him. 'Thank you, sir, those soldiers were taking liberties. Frankly they were scaring—'

'Get out! The pair of you,' he grunted. 'We run a clean pub, and we don't want whores like you coming in here, stinking the place out.'

'I can assure you sir, we were not—' Rose began.

'Well, what are you drinking then?' he gestured down to the table. There were two vessels half filled with ale. 'I can only see two tankards here, and one smashed one. I know the soldiers were drinking 'cause I served 'em, so what are you *ladies* drinking then?'

Rose looked at the empty table before glancing over to the bar. Mary Kelly, watching the proceedings, caught her eye and then began to pour two tankards of ale. 'I got their drinks right here, sir,' she shouted over.

He didn't even bother looking in her direction. 'Don't bother, these *ladies* are leaving,' he growled.

Carrie Millwood stood and brushed the creases out of her dress. 'Don't argue with the gentleman, Rose. If he wants us to take our business elsewhere, then that's what we'll do.'

'If there was any business to take from you besides the obvious, then maybe I'd care,' he replied.

The rest of the pub was silent while they hungrily watched this exchange. The audience included a certain Aaron Kosminski, who was sat in the opposite corner eating a bowl of broth. He hadn't noticed the two women in the corner, and when he had been served, both Annabelle and Mary had been on a break. He was astonished to see all four of them in the same pub with him. *Why does this keep happening to me?* He thought. *What connection do I have with these witches?* He watched as Carrie and Rose walked towards the door with their heads held high and proceeded out onto Commercial Street. He turned back towards the bar just as Mary Kelly and Annabelle Farmer exchanged glances.

*What's going to happen here?* He wondered. *Should I stay and watch these two, or follow the other two out there?* He lifted his wrist to contact Abberline but stopped. He hurriedly finished his soup, then exited the pub, following Carrie and Rose.

~~~

Kosminski was becoming paranoid regarding the witches. He knew that he wasn't a good man, not by a long shot. He was a wife beater, and given half the chance, he would have been a murderer. The night he had witnessed the first one arrive from whatever dimension witches came from; he had been there to kill the man he suspected his wife of having an affair with. After that, he had almost killed beaten her to death, and on more than one occasion, had been ready to kill all the witches, one by one, only something had stopped him.

That something had been the mystery man.

How had he not seen this man on any nights other than when he did his killings? Was it because he was a ghost? Maybe he kept going backwards and forwards through time, like something Abberline was talking about. Either way, he scared the Hell out of him.

He was mulling this over as he watched the two women enter their lodgings unmolested. *Maybe old Jacky isn't playing out tonight after all*, he thought. He turned away, back towards the Princess Alice pub. As he did, he lifted his wrist and spoke into it. 'Can you hear me, Inspector?'

'Hold on, just one minute,' the voice rasped through his communication device. It sounded like a hushed whisper.

He shrugged and walked on.

About five minutes later, his device spoke to him. 'Kosminski, are you there?'

'Loud and clear,' he hissed into the device. This form of communication never ceased to amaze him.

'I'm sorry I couldn't talk. I've had that bastard George Lusk in my office all day, riding me on about the stupid postcard and now the 'From Hell' letter, plus the half a kidney. If I find that this was you again, I'll have you behind bars so fast.'

'I assure you, sir, they weren't me,' he lied, stifling a laugh.

'Well, it looks like it's a pig's kidney anyways, and the handwriting's all different. So, what is it you want?'

'I suppose you already know that the four remaining witches—sorry, women—are all holed up together now, and that you know the address?'

'I do, but that's not going to help. This person isn't going to make a full-on attack and take on four of the women at once. At least one of them are trained in unarmed combat; it would be far too risky.'

'Well, did you know that two of them are hard at work in the Princess Alice pub? Both doing the afternoon shifts?'

There was a pause on the other end. 'No, I didn't know that. Thank you, Mr Kosminski. I'll look into it. Where are you now?'

'I'm heading to The Ten Bells, where I'm going to get myself rotten drunk. Care to join me?'

'Hardly,' was Abberline's one-word answer before the connection was severed.

The big man chuckled as he headed in the direction of his favourite drinking establishment.

## 62.

Orbital Platform One. 2288

VINCENT MADE IT back from twenty-one-eighty-eight without incident, although he now had a newfound liking for real ale. Youssef was happy with the successful communications and that the return journey was executed without a hitch. The Higgs Storm compensators had worked within their expected tolerance on the boy's return.

Jacqueline was exceptionally happy to have Vincent back in one piece, and they soon slipped back into their, not-so-secret, relationship. He gave her his grandmother's wedding ring in lieu of an engagement one. 'We'll make it official when I get back from the main mission, I promise,' he whispered into her ear when they had finished making love on his first night back.

Kevin was busy making tactical plans. They were still not sure how to track the women in such a heavily populated area.

The science team were worrying about how the Higgs Compensators would deal with the excessive amounts of Storm that would be produced on Vincent's return. They wanted to ensure they wouldn't overload when he brought the women back; to avoid catastrophe if he brought them all back in one trip. It was decided that the return would have to be undertaken in Inverness, where they had the facilities to store the Storm, before it naturally degraded over time.

Dr Hausen was finding co-ordinating EA work on Earth to be a tougher job than anticipated. The people were becoming more hostile towards the EA. Most of the countries still functioning were starving, while the rest were hoarding. It was a mess of riots and mass upheavals. The EA were struggling to keep peace wherever they could.

## 63.

London. 1888

ABBERLINE WAS WORRIED. He had picked up a signal sent from a portal somewhere within the Whitechapel area. The signal was masked and encrypted, but there was no mistaking that it had been from the women. He was concerned because since the night it had been sent, the only murders had been the Stride woman, the Eddowes woman, and the Callaghan woman that he did himself. Since then, there had been nothing; over a month and not one more murder.

He had been fed some interesting information by Kosminski regarding the movements of the women, but nothing of any real importance.

*What could the signal have been? Was it a cry for help? They probably didn't expect to be found this far back in time. Maybe it was a shout for reinforcements? Send more bodies in order for us to complete the mission?*

As these thoughts ran through his head, he consulted his portal. It only showed the four signals, nothing more. 'But that's not real proof that there's someone else here. Why can't I see the other damned signal?' he cursed.

~~~~

Less than a week later, the pubs were back in full swing. Annabelle Farmer had been keeping her distance from the landlord of the Princess Alice, and he had been keeping his distance from her, at least while his wife was around. Tonight however, she was out. She had travelled to Liverpool to visit some of her family who had arrived from Dublin. This left him in charge for a few days, and there was chaos concerning staffing levels for the late shifts. 'Farmer! Get over here, will yer?' he shouted to her as she turned up for her shift with Mary. 'I need someone to work a shift tonight. Since our little *arrangement* seems to have gone out of the window, it looks like it's going to have to be you, or your mate.'

Annabelle's heart sank. 'What do you mean? We only ever do the afternoons, you know that.'

'Not tonight, darlin'. Sort it out between yers. I don't rightly care either way which one of yer it is, but one of yers it will be.'

'Is there anything I can do to sort this out?' she asked, brushing herself into him and giving him a wink.

He looked down her low-cut top and licked his lips, then he shook his head. 'No, love, nothing doing. I need cover for tonight, and that's the end of it. If you want to do the cover and then, when we close up, we can have a, erm, conversation about the future, then that's fine by me.'

'What if I tell you that you can put it in my mouth?' she whispered into his ear.

His face changed suddenly, and he shoved her into the wall behind her, where she slid down onto the floor. 'What? Do you think I'm queer or somethin'? If I'm gonna put it into you then it's gonna be in your stinking quim,' he shouted, wiping a sheen of sweat from his brow.

She got up off the floor and straightened her dress. The huge man was towering above her with his fists clenched. 'Get out, slut! Get the fuck out of my pub, and don't you even think of coming back in here. I won't have the likes of you thinking that I'm a pufter with all that French shit. Tonight, I'm gonna fuck your mate over there after closing. I'm gonna fuck her raw, and all the time I'll be thinking of you, you whore. Out the back way, now.' He picked her up and carried her effortlessly to the back door.

Still dazed from her crash into the wall, she didn't have the energy in her to scream and fight her manhandling. He opened the door and tossed her, like a discarded toy, into the back yard. He then slammed the door hard enough to knock some of the cheap plaster off the frame.

Mary Kelly was busy working the outside of the bar when it had happened and was ignorant of the drama when the landlord stormed over to her. She noticed his face was red and his eyes looked angry

TimeRipper

and dangerous. *Maybe Annie's been paying our dues again*, she thought, sadness tinging her face at the thought of what her friend had to endure to help keep them safe.

'Kelly,' he roared. 'Farmer's gone home sick. You're working tonight until we close, you got that? If you tell me no, then you can leave right now and never come back.'

Mary's heart dropped into the pit of her stomach, and her eyes slowly widened at the news. 'Tonight? Till three?' she whimpered. It was not like her to whimper anything, but this change of events, put the fear of God into her. 'I...'

The landlord cocked his head. 'What was that? Were you just about to say, can't?'

Mary hung her head. She was stuck in a difficult situation. They needed the money, but she didn't want to have to walk home alone at three in the morning. She hoped that when one of the others found out that Annabelle was sick, they'd come in and walk home with her.

'No, I'm fine. I can do it.' She smiled before walking away to collect more tankards.

~~~~

Aaron Kosminski woke late in the afternoon. He hadn't opened his barber shop in over a week; he'd been far too agitated to trust himself to cut hair. Something was about to happen; he could feel it. He didn't know what, but he knew it was going to be huge. For some reason, the strangest urge to drink in the Princess Alice pub had come over him.

With his heart beating fast and butterflies fluttering around his stomach, he dressed in his new cape and hat and took off for the drinking establishment. He had a full purse of coins in his pocket, and he was determined to spend it.

*Tonight, may well be something spectacular*, he thought.

~~~~

'Mary, I want you in the back room after your shift, OK? It's not a fucking request,' the landlord grunted as she passed him with a tray full of drinks. The night had been busy indeed, as the fear regarding

Jack the Ripper, or Spring Heeled Jack, or even Leather Apron, was dying down around the East End.

'Erm, OK. Can I ask what's it about?' she shouted in reply as she passed him.

'Your future,' he replied with a sneer. 'Or lack of...' he mumbled under his breath, thinking she couldn't hear as he walked off into the bar.

She watched him push into some unsuspecting punters, spilling their drinks before turning towards them as if goading them into saying something, anything.

None of them did.

With her mind anywhere else, other than on the job at hand, she spilled a drink over the table she was serving. One of the men at the table jumped up, trying to wipe the wet, sticky mess from his trousers. With a sneer, he reached out and grabbed at her. Without thinking, acting purely on impulse, she turned and slapped him in the face.

~~~

Kosminski was surreptitiously hidden in the corner of the room. He'd been there most of the day, keeping a low profile and dodging the attention of the witches as best he could. He'd been drinking heavily, but it was having very little effect on him. In fact, he felt as sober as a judge. He watched as the one known as Rose slipped behind the back door with the landlord. He'd heard some shouting and then noticed that she had not returned all night. 'So, Mary Kelly. I think it may well be your turn tonight,' he mumbled as he sipped his warm ale.

He walked over to the bar, expertly avoiding Kelly. He waited until the landlord caught his glance and shuffled over to serve him. 'What's yours, then?' he grunted.

'I'll have a grog, please, barman, and maybe a little bit of information.' He slid a threepenny bit over the bar. The landlord looked at it, put his hand over it, and leaned in, listening to what he had to ask.

'What's happened to that little bit of quim who works behind here? You know, the small blonde one with the low-cut top?' He smiled at the landlord, tipping him a knowing wink. 'You know, she could blow the head off my ale all night long, that one.'

The big man looked at him as if he had a plague and snatched the threepenny bit off the bar. 'She's gone home sick, she has. Dunno if she'll even be coming back. That little whore has gotten me into a lot of trouble with the missus, if you get my meaning.'

Kosminski pouted and nodded as if he was pondering something. 'What about that one?' he asked, thumbing in the direction of Mary Kelly just as she managed to walk into a punter as he was coming in from the back yard fixing his fly. She narrowly managed to stop the empties she was carrying from falling and breaking everywhere.

'That useless bitch? I'll tell ya! She won't make it until tomorrow, that one.' He then winked at Kosminski and made a show of putting the coin in his pocket. He stood back to regard the gentleman before him, then leaned back in. 'Unless maybe she spreads them wide enough, that is.' With that, he rolled his head back and laughed riotously, slapping Kosminski on the shoulder so hard that the big man was pushed away from the bar, narrowly missing barging into the men drinking behind him.

He offered the landlord a conspiratorial grin before tipping his tankard towards him. The landlord looked at it for a few moments before grunting, grabbing it off him, and filling it full of ale.

Kosminski got back to his seat, then placed his ale onto the table and stared right at Mary Kelly. She was struggling to pour a drink for a tall, skinny man and avoid his lecherous advances at the same time.

'You definitely won't be making it 'til tomorrow,' he smiled. 'I'll be keeping an eye on you tonight, Mary Kelly. You best believe I will.'

~~~

'Carrie, that bastard has sacked me! He's gotten rid of me, and I think he's making Mary work the late shift tonight. She'll be alone with him,' Annabelle cried as she burst into the lodging room they shared, only there was no one there to greet her.

*Where is everyone?* she thought. Tendrils of panic began to sneak into her stomach. Then she remembered Carrie and Rose had gone to sit in The Ten Bells as they had been barred from the Princess Alice.

They wanted to stay in the company of others, so they had elected for that pub as it was closer to where they were living. She slammed the door on her way out and ran down the lane towards the busy and bustling Whitechapel.

Because of the trade passing through Commercial Street and because it was a Thursday night, traditionally a busy drinking night, they had large men working the doors. Primarily, they were there to stop trouble, but most times they managed to start it. As she tried to push her way into the pub the two burly men stood in her way.

'Whoa there beautiful, where do you think you're going?' one of them asked as he grabbed her by the arm.

'I've got to go in there and see my friends. They might be in trouble,' she spat, trying to shake off the man's strong grip.

'And what sort of trouble would that be?' the other asked, raising his eyebrows. 'I'm only askin' because we don't want any trouble on our shift, see!'

'They're not *causing* trouble, they're just *in* trouble,' Farmer replied, shouting in the men's faces. This seemed to gear them up.

'Well, hows about you tell me what they look like and I'll go and get them, bring them out to you, like.'

'Can't I just go in and see them?'

'Well that would be a little too easy, wouldn't it? You go in to *tell your friends they're in trouble*, then you get involved in a conversation, next thing we know, you're causing all sorts of havoc in there, and me, and my old mate Pete here, have to go and clean it all up, isn't that right, Pete?'

The second man grinned and nodded.

'All right, all right,' she succumbed to the bigger men's reasoning. 'There're two of them. One is tall with long, straight hair. It's going a little grey. The other is smaller and younger, with curly blonde hair. Their names are Carrie and Rose.'

'You keep her here, Burt. I'll go and see if I can see where these two tarts are.'

'They're not tarts, they're respectable women,' Annabelle argued. The moment it came out of her mouth, she regretted it.

Pete leaned in close to her, she could smell the stale ale on his breath, mixed with fried meat and sweat. One of his eyes was squinting as if it was made of glass. 'Two women, drinking alone in

# TimeRipper

The Ten Bells pub? Tarts, I calls 'em,' he whispered, his eyebrows raised. There was more than a threatening nature to his voice. 'What about you, Bert?'

'Aye, Pete, tarts, I say.'

Annie shook her head and shrugged out of Bert's grip again. 'OK, tarts then, just please go in and see them for me. Tell them Annabelle is waiting for them.'

Pete bowed theatrically low and removed the dirty cap off the top of his, even dirtier, head. 'Oh, my lady, why didn't you say it was yourself. Lady Annabelle! I am humbled to be in your service, and I'll perform your request, post haste,' he replied.

This performance cracked Bert up.

'Would you please just go and see if they're in there?' she shouted, her patience at these two buffoons was wearing thin.

She heard the slap across her face a few seconds before the sting of it caused her to wince. Reeling backwards, she saw Burt looking at her with a furious expression on his face. 'Don't you talk to us like that, you whore. Not after we've so graciously decided to help you out and go and see your friends.'

'You know what, Burt? I've decided that I'm not going to tend to Lady Muck's request here. I do believe that m'lady can go and right royally fuck herself,' Pete growled before pushing her hard in the direction of the road.

Annabelle went sprawling from the step of the busy pub, into a small, dirty puddle in the middle of the road. A gang of young boys who were stood by, smoking and watching this little commotion, almost fell over themselves laughing as she splashed onto the floor.

'And stay out, you slag. That'll teach you to bark orders at us,' Pete shouted, more playing up for the crowd's sake than for Annabelle's.

She pulled herself up, out of the muddy road, and brushed the dirt from her apron. She looked at the two men who were gawping back at her, then gritted her teeth before stomping in the puddle and storming off in the direction of Fournier Street. She could hear them laughing behind her back.

When she turned the corner, she looked through the dirty window of the other side of the pub. She had to cover her eyes to shield the glare from the streetlight overhead. She could just about make out the people inside through the grime of the windows and the smoke inside. Carrie and Rose were sat quietly in the corner. Neither of them was talking.

In frustration, she rapped on the window, attempting to get their attention, but they obviously couldn't hear her over the hubbub inside.

'Carrie!' she shouted and banged some more, 'Rose!'

All the noise and the shouting caught the attention of Burt and Pete, again, who rounded the corner to see what all the fuss was about. 'Oy, you,' Pete shouted as Burt grabbed her, holding her tightly around the waist, almost squeezing the breath out of her as he picked her up. 'I thought we told you to sling yer hook. This is yer last warning yer mad trollop, now... git!'

Burt dropped her onto the pavement and hocked a spit her way as she lay there. 'Don't let me catch you around here again. Next time, we'll not be as nice,' he growled.

As they walked back around to the front of the pub, Annabelle looked up at the clock tower on Christchurch. It read ten-forty-seven. She needed to get the attention of Carrie and Rose, and quickly. She took off, further down Fournier Street, desperation turning her stomach. *How can I get them to see me?*

As she continued down the street, her feet tripped on a large iron bar that must have fallen off a horse and cart. She picked it up and looked at it, then ran back towards the pub window she had been banging on not minutes before. Without thinking too much about it, she swung the bar crashing it into the large pane of glass.

It shattered everywhere, slivers covered her, slicing her skin, and covering many of the patrons of the pub too. They were jumping out of the way of the dangerous shards coming their way as she shouted through the open window.

'Carrie, Rose! Mary's in trouble. We need to go and help her. Come on.'

The two women inside the pub were already on their feet.

Everyone was gawping at the mad woman outside holding an iron bar who was staring wide eyed back into the pub. As she dropped the bar, the clang was deafening in the shocked silence, and it snapped her back into the dangerous reality she was in. Carrie and Rose had seen her and were making their way through the crowd, towards the open window. They both climbed out, careful not to cut themselves on the vicious slivers poking out of the frame.

'What the Hell are you doing?' Carrie shouted at her.

'I've been sacked from the Princess Alice. Mary's there alone. She's being forced to do the late shift. I couldn't hang around as the bastard landlord physically threw me out. We need to get back there as soon as possible.'

'Let's go,' Rose said.

Just then, Pete and Burt made it around the corner, both rubbernecking at the large, smashed window. Pete eyes the three women before looking at the floor where the iron bar was lying, surrounded by smashed glass. 'What the fucking hell have you done here, missus?' he asked slowly, ignoring the moaning and complaining of the patrons peering out into the street.

'You three, over here now!' Burt demanded stepping towards them.

'Leave them to me,' Rose whispered as she made a self-defence stance, raising her arms towards them and bending her legs to give herself a lower centre of gravity.

The two men saw this and stopped.

'What's she doing?' Pete asked, looking more than a little taken aback.

'I dunno, mate. Can we just hit her?' Burt replied.

'Yeah, she's only a little woman,' Pete said, as he made his way towards her. 'I won't hurt her too much, though,' he laughed.

Rose anticipated his advance and kicked her leg high, catching him square on the chin. He dropped, like a stone, onto the pavement. Burt, shocked by what had just happened to his friend, ran at her. Rose caught him by the arm and spun him back in the direction he came from. His arm was so far up his back, with his thumb twisted somehow, that he couldn't move a muscle.

'OK, *mate*,' Rose whispered in his ear. 'This is what's going to happen. Me and my friends here are just going to walk away from this little melee, and you are going to tell the pol—'

She didn't get the chance to finish her sentence as a heavy, wooden truncheon caught her around the back of the head. It was her turn to fall like a stone onto the pavement.

Carrie and Annabelle turned to see three policemen behind them. They had come from the direction of Fournier Street; no-one had seen them arrive.

'Right, you lot, don't any of you move a muscle,' one of the officers shouted. 'You're all coming with us.'

Another policeman grabbed Carrie and the third grabbed Annabelle. Before they knew it, they were all in shackles and forced onto their knees in the broken glass. The third policeman was on the floor next to Rose, checking her pulse. 'She's alive!' he announced. 'She'll have a head on her in the morning, though.' He shackled her and then slapped her across the face, hard enough to wake her up. Which she did with a groan.

'What happened here, Burt?' the policemen holding Rose asked the large man.

'These three are trouble, Phil. This one's been giving me and Pete here…' he gestured to his colleague who was still out cold on the floor, '…some grief at the door. She was saying these two are in some sort of trouble. Then the mad cow smashed the window, and the others climbed out of it. They're all crazy as shit-house rats if you ask me.'

'OK, ladies, you're all going to spend the night courtesy of Her Majesty, Queen Victoria, tonight, and no amount of wriggling or shouting is going to stop that,' the first policeman stated. 'Do you wanna press charges, Burt? You know, for him lying there on the floor?'

Burt looked at Pete, who was just starting to moan on the cold floor. He smiled. 'Nah, I think the stick he'll be getting from being beaten up by a cheap sort will be enough for him.'

'You weren't doing too good yourself there, Burt,' Rose spat as the policeman dragged her off in the direction of Brick Lane Police Station.

'Officer, can we talk about this?' Carrie spoke to her captor in a calm, placid voice. 'We have a friend who's in mortal danger. She'll be the next victim of Jack the Ripper if we're not there to save her.'

'Oh yeah, the next Jack the Ripper victim, eh? Oh, well remind me to give frigging Spring Heeled Jack the heads up, eh? Now, all of you shut your whore mouths and come quietly,' the policeman snarled.

## TimeRipper

Mary Kelly was having the worst night of her life. It was nearly midnight, and Annabelle had not come back for her with the others. The landlord wanted to see her in his office after the shift, and she had a good inkling what it was he wanted. If the looks and the rub ups that she had been receiving all night were anything to go by, she didn't think it would be a talk about a promotion. *Why did I take this shift?* she thought as she very nearly spilt another pint of ale over a customer.

'Watch what you are doing, you stupid cunt,' scolded the drunk customer. 'That's the third drink you've poured over me today. What is this? The public baths?' The men at the table all erupted into laughter as if it was the best joke they had ever heard. Then the man grabbed her arm and twisted it.

Kosminski watched as the man twisted the witch's arm. Although he was in a group of other men, he looked like could be in the pub alone. *Could this be our man?* he thought.

'Stupid bitch!' he shouted at her and pushed her to the ground. He then glared at her and walked off.

*No, that's not him. He wouldn't have made a show of himself like that*, he thought, a little disappointed. He ordered himself another ale and sat back on his table watching the night's pantomime continue.

Mary wandered through the tables, occasionally talking to the customers, but mostly avoiding the grabbing hands, and lecherous advances, that frequently came her way. Kosminski watched as she spent some time talking to another woman. He couldn't make out her face, but he knew that she wasn't one of the witches because they were all barred from this pub. She looked rather friendly with this woman, and it confused him quite a bit. He'd seldom seen them fraternize with anyone other than each other.

He watched, with interest, as they stood in conversation for almost five minutes. It looked like she might have stayed longer if the landlord hadn't seen her dallying and yelled at her to get on with her work. 'I'll catch you later,' he heard her say to the mystery woman. 'I've got to get this done.' The woman waved her hand to her in a familial, friendly dismissal. With a smile, Mary continued around the bar.

He walked over to where the mystery woman was sitting and made a point to pass her, making as if he was going to the latrines. He gave a cursory glance in her direction, but she turned away from him at the last moment, checking something in the large purse she had on the table next to her.

Fuming, he continued towards the back of the pub and outside to the privy. *I'll get a good look on the way back*, he thought as he relieved himself against a fence. He buttoned himself up and returned into the bar area. His eyes immediately darted to the mystery woman's location, but there was no one there. He scanned the room and found her standing at the bar, with her back to him, while Kelly poured her a drink. 'Bollocks,' he murmured under his breath and returned to his seat. He picked up his ale and took a long drink from the tankard.

All night long, she avoided his gaze as he tried, time and time again, to identify her. Inevitably, he was beginning to succumb to the effects of the ale, and his vision was becoming blurred. He checked his pocket watch and was surprised to see that it was getting on for two-forty-five in the morning.

'Come on folks, time for yers to get off home to yer loved ones, or to yer beds,' the landlord shouted as he was on his way to the bar to get one last ale. 'That means last orders, yer feckers, now git. I got a bed I want to get to too, you know.'

'Just one more for the road?' Kosminski slurred as he made it to the bar.

'Are you mutton, sir?' the landlord asked, giving him a look like he wanted to punch him in his face, just for the sake of it.

'Deaf? No, why?'

'Because I just told you to fuck off home, that's why.'

This caused raucous laughter from a group of drunk men who were standing at the bar finishing off their own drinks. As they laughed, Kosminski snapped into a kind of sobriety, realising that he might have given himself away. He was relieved when he saw Kelly stood in the far corner. She was once again talking to the mystery woman. *Who the hell could she be?* he thought. *She's ruining my plans.*

'Come on, fella, you're out on your heels you are,' he heard the landlord growl before he felt himself being lifted and dragged towards the door, an event that took some doing, considering his size.

As he was pulled, he looked around and saw the woman pass something to Kelly. *Was it a note?* That was the only thought to pass through his head before he was unceremoniously hauled outside into the cold, night, air.

'Go home, sir, and sleep it off, then you can come back tomorrow and do it all again.' The landlord was laughing as he turned back inside the emptying bar, wiping his hands on the dirty apron tied around his waist.

Kosminski lay, dazed, on the pavement. His head had cracked on the kerbstone, and once the dizziness had cleared, he rubbed at it, checking to see if there was blood. There wasn't, although he knew there would be a considerable lump there in the morning.

He sat up, and the world tilted around him, causing nausea to take a grip of him. He struggled uneasily to his feet and rested against a lamppost by the front door of the pub. All the good—or bad—intentions he had planned for tonight had gone down the drain.

He'd gotten himself far too drunk to do anything.

He eased himself off the pavement, wiping the mud from his trousers, before attempting to walk off in the direction of George's Yard. That was when the pain in his head flared up again, and he tripped over his own feet.

He hit the pavement again, this time on his chin, and he went out cold.

~~~~

He came around sometime later in a doorway of a shop a little way along from the pub. He had no idea how he had gotten there. As he tried to move his arms and legs, he found it difficult. For a moment, he panicked. *Am I in one of those holding beams?* he thought, before realising that it was only because he had been sitting in one position for far too long.

He opened his eyes and looked around. After a few moments of double vision, the street began to focus. It was mostly deserted, except for a few stragglers a way off down Commercial Road, all heading off somewhere to continue whatever party they had been part of. As he attempted to get up, another wave of dizziness hit him, and he decided it would be best to rest where he was for another few moments.

'...and don't think of coming back here again for work. You were rubbish. If it wasn't for your snatch of a mate, you'd never have worked here at all.'

The gruff voice sounded familiar. It was the landlord shouting at someone, someone who he couldn't make out from his position. Then Mary Kelly walked into his field of vision. She looked like she had been crying and was buttoning up her blouse.

'Fucking tart,' he heard the landlord shout into the night.

His heart began to pound. *I need to follow her. I can't pass up this opportunity.* He struggled one more time to get to his feet, but a cramp in his calf caused him to fall over again. Half in pain, but mostly just drunk, he pretended to be asleep as the woman passed him, almost as if he wasn't even there. Through one eye, he watched her hurry her way down Commercial Street towards Millers Court.

As she got a little further down the road, she stopped and looked around. Wrapping her shawl around herself as if she were cold, she just stood, waiting. He could tell that she was both nervous and scared. With a sly smile, he did his best to get up. He knew that he might not get another chance to get one of these women alone. *I'll call Abberline,* he thought.

'Abberline, are you there?' he slurred into his wrist.

'Kosminski, where are you?' came the curt reply.

'I'm sat in a doorway, outside the Princess Alice. I've been watching Mary Kelly all night.'

'Why didn't you let me know you were there? Is she still there? Is she alone?'

'Yes, and yes.' He hiccupped into the device. 'I'm watching her right now. It looks like she's waiting for her friends, who I don't think are coming. I'm going to go and get her. I'll rip this one for you, sir, make no mistake about that!'

# TimeRipper

'No! Do *not* do anything. Just follow her and let me know if she's going home. If she's alone, then this is the opportunity I need.'

'Righty-o, sir, oh... Oh ohh, it looks like you're too late. It looks like she's got herself some company.'

'What? Who is it?'

Kosminski squinted his blurring eyes to try to get a look at who the newcomer could be. 'To be honest, sir, I don't know. It's someone I've never seen before, but they seem to know each other, that's for sure.'

'Which way are they heading? I received word earlier that three women have been picked up, and detained for drunk and disorderly and criminal damage, at The Ten Bells pub. I'm looking at the map, and they all seem to be ours. All the signals are in one place, all of them except one. That'll be Mary.'

'Well, I don't know who this person is, but I can assure you that she's not alone.'

'Can you follow them? Also, let me know if this person leaves.'

'That will be a little harder than it sounds. I'm a bit...' as if on cue, he hiccupped and giggled, '...inebriated at the moment, and I seem to be in some considerable pain after a few falls onto the pavement. I wouldn't be able to keep up with them, and even if I did, I'd hardly be inconspicuous looking like this. I fear my face is a little bit bloody.'

'Kosminski, you're fucking useless,' Abberline hissed through the wrist device, and the connection broke.

Aaron Kosminski blew air out of his mouth and promptly fell back asleep in the doorway.

64.

'Oh, Murder!' The scream rose over Miller's Court. Abberline was counting on the fact that, even though cries of this nature were very common in this area, possibly the worst in London, because of what had been happening recently, people might come running to investigate.

After he'd finished communicating with Kosminski, he had left his home and made his way, on foot, through the night, to Miller's Court, where the women were currently living. Tonight, he knew that Mary Kelly would be there on her own, or maybe with the other person Kosminski had been babbling about. He took a long, mostly indirect route towards their lodgings. This way he would be able to throw anyone who may be following him, off his scent. It was nearly four-thirty in the morning when he reached the dwelling.

His intel had informed him that the women were living on the ground floor, in number thirteen. It was a larger dwelling, intended for a small family who could all live within the same room.

Miller's Court was, quite rightly, daubed as the 'worst street in London' with reference to the gangs and thugs that operated from it. Even the police wouldn't walk down it if there were less than three of them. Tonight, it was dark, quiet, and uninviting. As his purpose for being there was also dark and uninviting, it seemed fitting.

He kept his hand on the trigger of the laser cutter in his pocket, ready for any unexpected, and unwanted, company on the street. Luckily for him, he made it to the dwelling unmolested.

He crept up to the window of the small apartment and peered inside. The tenement was gloomy and silent; the only sound he could decipher was a dog barking somewhere in the distance. Inside, the room was dim. He could only make out vague shapes, but nothing that he could identify as his target.

From the shadows, he noticed, that a group of people were investigating his 'murder' cry from the other side of the road. He knew that no one would be looking his way for a small while, giving him ample time to do what he need to do.

Something in the corner of his eye caught his attention.

A small movement.

It was just a shadow, really, but he thought it might be a dangerous one. It was only then that he noticed something that rang alarm bells in his mind. The window was quartered, four small sections of glass separated by a thin frame of wood. The bottom, right hand corner window had been broken, the glass had been fitted with some kind of rag, obviously to keep the chill of the night out. Silently, he tried the door, it was locked from the inside. He held his breath, slid his hand through the broken windowpane, and without straining, found that he could reach through and unlock the door. As he entered the room, there was a movement from the corner and something black rushed at him from the shadows. Abberline had just enough time to dodge the attacker, and whoever it was, was out through the door in no time. He thought about running after them, giving chase, but when he saw what was over the other side of the room, he forgot all about the assailant.

The thing on the bed wasn't moving.

In the dark, it looked only remotely human.

Abberline took a moment to study the carnage.

He felt the gorge rising in his throat, and he knew he had to get out of this little room.

*She's not going anywhere,* he thought as he burst out of the dwelling to chase the shadow who had nearly knocked him over. Whoever it was, was making their way towards Bell Lane.

Abberline began his pursuit.

The shadow was almost at Wentworth Street and was still moving fast, but Abberline, although he had reached the age of fifty nearly two years ago, was in perfect health, the peak of physical fitness.

The shadow was fast, but Abberline was faster.

Wentworth Street quickly turned into Old Castle Street, heading towards his familiar haunt of Whitechapel High Street. *Jesus, this guy can run*, Abberline thought as, finally, the ravages of his age began to overtake his fitness. By a stroke of good luck, the shadow turned onto Whitechapel High Street and ran right into a set of bins that had been left out on the pavement outside the workhouse. The assailant hit the obstacles and went reeling to one side, attempting to keep his balance. This mistake gave Abberline all the time he needed to catch up. He dived onto the struggling figure and a tussle ensued.

Of the two men, Abberline was the larger, and it didn't take long for him to get the upper hand in the fight.

'Stop, will you, just stop,' he shouted, holding the struggling figure beneath him in a headlock grip.

The smaller man, the shadow, was bucking, trying his best to wriggle away from his grip as opposed to fighting. Abberline squeezed his arms tighter, closing the headlock, until the fight left his captive. 'Will you just stop for a second,' he panted, badly out of breath from the chase and the tussle. 'Will you just stop and talk to me?'

Eventually, the figure stopped struggling and turned to look at him.

'You?' the shadow whispered, slightly out of breath. 'But... but how?'

## 65.

Orbital Platform One. 2288

VINCENT, KEVIN, YOUSSEF, and Jacqueline were gathered in the large Hadron Collider room. Vincent was ready and prepared, dressed in the style of the day as a gentleman, but not one who would be affluent enough to stand out in the crowd. His quantum slug had been updated with a new transponder code for the new time zone. He looked fit and healthy and raring to go.

'You're going to need this,' Youssef said, handing him a bundle of paper. 'What is all that?'

'It's roughly three thousand pounds in old cash, relative to the date. It's a fortune back then. You'll need it to survive. Secure yourself somewhere large enough and secluded enough to hold the women until we can safely bring them back. You're also going to need to buy clothes and find somewhere to live. This amount of cash should allow you to do all that and still live nicely for the time. Don't go extravagant, whatever you do. Remember your week in Cardiff; you cannot make a splash or make any of the headlines.'

'You know the drill,' Kevin continued. 'You get in, get your targets, and get out. I'll be coordinating your moves from here and communicating them through Jacqueline. She'll be your sole point of contact. If you have any problems, you contact her and get an emergency extraction. You hear me? You're not to take any chances. This mission is a priority, and you're our best hope of fulfilling it.'

'Got it,' Vincent replied, nodding. He turned his attention to Jacqueline, who was busying herself monitoring the communications board, perhaps a little too intently. 'I'm counting on you, rookie. You give me the best communications ever and get me the hell out of there when I need it. Agreed?'

'Agreed,' she replied, her eyes lingering a little too long on his. It was all she could say as tears were choking up her words.

She picked up a large backpack, the zipper was open, and she was rummaging through the contents. Vincent knew exactly what was in it. It was the tools of his trade. 'Because you'll be going back longer this time, we realised that the cellular powered devices you took to Cardiff might not have the charge needed for them to function correctly. So, we set these ones up with nuclear power charges. Basically, they will run forever,' she smiled, handing the backpack to him.

Vincent winked at her and accepted the gift. There was a moment where she didn't want to release the bag to him. After a couple of awkward seconds, she did. He removed his cape, slid the pack on, and replaced it. To the casual observer, the pack would not be visible. He looked at her and swallowed. It was his turn for his eyes to linger a little too long. 'Start her up, sweetheart,' he directed at the whole room.

'Good luck, Vincent. We know this is going to be tough, but if anyone can do it, I know it's you and this team,' Youssef said, shaking him by the hand.

'Good luck, kiddo. Don't you dare go letting me down now.' Kevin smiled, nearly breaking his bones with his over enthusiastic hug.

One of the monitors chirped, and an image of Dr Hausen appeared on it. 'I haven't missed him, have I?' he shouted into the screen.

'No, doctor, you haven't missed me,' Vincent smiled.

'Good, I just wanted to tell you good luck, son, we're all behind you. I'm sorry I couldn't be there, but I couldn't let you go without a wave.'

'Thanks, doc,' Vincent nodded, smiling. He turned back towards the room and was surprised to see Jacqueline standing behind him. She wrapped her arms around him and gave him a big kiss. 'I don't care if they know,' she whispered. 'I just had to give you that.' Vincent kissed her back and everyone in the room turned away, allowing them their moment.

After a small while, she cleared her throat and backed off, a little red in the face, as was Vincent. 'Right then, good luck, Mr Clarence.' She straightened her tunic and returned to her station.

# TimeRipper

'Would I have gotten one of them if it was me going?' Kevin asked, breaking the tension of the room.

'I wouldn't count on it,' she smiled, sitting back at her monitor.

'OK, well that's that then. Let's get this show on the road. Vincent, are you ready for this mission?' Kevin asked, clapping his hands together.

He snapped to attention. 'I am, sir.'

'And you understand the risks?'

'I do, sir.'

'Then go forward and complete your mission. The retrieval of the fugitive terrorists of The Quest, or at the very least their slugs, to stop them from returning to twenty-two-eighty-eight.'

'I'll perform this to the best of my abilities, sir.'

'I know you will, son. Then, God Speed, and may Allah guide your hand,' Youssef said.

'Thank you, sir.'

Vincent turned to everyone in the room and saluted; everyone saluted back. He then blew a kiss to Jacqueline and stepped into the Hadron Collider racetrack. As the glass doors closed, Jacqueline fired up the collider. The lights began to twist and turn and race along the track. She activated the hydrogen injectors, and a purple light shone from inside the glass room.

'All systems working within normal parameters,' she reported.

'Set the Higgs-Boson particle now,' Youssef instructed over the noise of the Collider.

'Injecting, sir,' she reported, trying to sound professional, although her voice sounded thicker than normal, possibly due to the tears streaming down her face. She pressed the buttons on her portal, and instantly, there was a flash of bright white light in the room.

They were expecting a purple light.

An alarm sounded in the room that resonated around the complex.

'What's happening?' Youssef shouted rushing to the adjoining portal to Jacqueline's.

'I, I don't know sir. It looks like a power surge. It's coming from the collider itself.'

He frantically typed commands into the collider's main console, but the white light prevailed, and the alarms did not turn off.

'It's a malfunction in the primary straight of the collider. The hydrogen is spinning too fast. What date did you send him back to?' Youssef shouted, still looking at his screen.

'July twenty-second, eighteen-eighty-eight, as we discussed. The day after the women arrived.'

'Maybe the residue from their trips are interfering with ours. That's not reading eighteen-eighty-eight.' He turned towards Jacqueline. Her face had lost all colour, and tears were streaming down her face faster and fatter than before. 'I don't know when it's sending him. Can you compensate for the primary straight by injecting more modified hydrogen?'

'If we use more hydrogen, that'll kill him?' she shouted, horrified.

'It's a risk, but it might be enough to stabilise his signal and either bring it back here or strengthen it into eighteen-eighty-eight. At this moment, it's fluctuating wildly. If we don't do anything, we'll lose him completely.'

'Modified hydrogen going in now, sir,' she reported.

'Youssef, what will happen to Vincent if this doesn't work?' Kevin asked, his face a mask of concern.

Youssef looked at him before gesturing towards Jacqueline with his eyes.

'It's OK, sir. I know what'll happen,' she shouted to the two men after witnessing the look.

Youssef turned away from her, back to Kevin. He exhaled a large breath. 'At present, he's spinning. The worst-case scenario is that he could be torn apart by the eddies of time and different parts of him would arrive at the same location, but at different times. Or, he'll materialize in another time fully intact.' He shrugged, shaking his head slowly. 'We just don't know.'

Kevin turned to Jacqueline. She was dutifully punching buttons on her portal. He could see tears running down her face as she did, and he knew exactly how she felt. Vincent had become more than just a trainee to him, he had also become a friend.

Suddenly, the light abated, and the klaxon stopped. The Hadron Collider began to slow. The silence was almost complete, as everyone strained to see into the glass room. Smoke that had been building up from the Collider's fail-safe engines began to clear, and

Jacqueline ran to the glass door. It was fogged over with condensation. She wiped at the mist on the glass and saw the Higgs Storm bubble inside. The containment field was working. The extractor fans kicked in and removed the Storm. The very fact that there had been Storm at all told her everything she needed to know.

It told her what would be within the Collider's racetrack.

Nothing!

Vincent had been successfully displaced.

'Nooooooo!' she screamed, running back to the portal. She mashed at the keys and stared intently at the screen. 'No, no, no…' she repeated, 'Why? Why?'

'What's happening?' Kevin shouted over to her—although the noise had abated, it was still ringing in his head.

'I don't know, sir. All I can confirm is… he's gone.' She looked up from her console screen, a faint but sad smile on her lips. 'I can also confirm that he's reached his destination, but…' she paused then to swallow the grief that had lumped in her throat. '…I can't confirm *when* he is. He could be anytime. I also can't confirm that he survived the trip.'

'What? What do you mean he could be anytime?' Kevin shouted.

'I mean that we're not getting any quantum signal or magnetic tag signal from him. He's fallen into time, and we've absolutely no way of tracking him. The portal is telling me that he has reached his destination, but the power spike, or whatever it was, has erased all information regarding when he is. All I can confirm is that he has been sent to the correct location: latitude and longitude 51.315.99, 0.10418.60. Spitalfields, London, sir.'

'Is there no redundancy backup on the portal? No OS backup?' Kevin asked, surprising himself on the knowledge that he had picked up.

'Normally, yes, sir; right now, no. There's nothing! Our secondary system is fried. I'll check to see if it's sent any information to the cloud, but at this point, I would seriously doubt it. She tapped keys at an expediential rate on the portal, trying her utmost to find anything relating to the last transmission.'

Her calm veneer was slipping as she looked at Youssef, her eyes were raw and sore. 'There's nothing here. When could he be? How far back could this thing have thrown him?'

Youssef walked over and wrapped his arms around her, pulling her tight into his embrace. 'I don't know. I really don't. I won't try to hide the truth from you. He could be absolutely anytime. The only thing we can do is hope he's fine, and that he may go on to live as productive a life as possible, or as much as the paradoxical laws will allow.'

Jacqueline sank into the hug. Eventually, she looked up into his face. Youssef's heart broke as he stared into her eyes. She was a child asking if her puppy was going to be OK.

'Do you think he might find a way to get back here, back to me?' She already knew the answer, and when Youssef's only response was to hug her tighter, it confirmed it to her.

She buried her head into his chest and wept.

Kevin watched with the unfolding realization that Vincent was gone. The realist in him knew that this part of the mission was now a failure. He knew they would need to find another way of stopping the women. *I fucking hate being a pragmatist*, he thought. He turned away from the unfolding melodrama, mainly to avert his eyes and allow Jacqueline to continue her grief in semi-privacy. As he did, he looked at the board with the ten signals coming from eighteen-eighty-eight. It was how they knew where the women were in time and in some vague way, where they were geographically. The lights were all still on, but most of them were now flashing, erratically. It was as if the computer couldn't tell if it was receiving data from the slugs, or not. Dates flashed up. There one moment, then gone the next, only to come back again moments later. Locations began to change, accompanied by map grids, GPS locations, latitude, and longitude references.

Kevin was shaking his head. 'Youssef get over here and look at this. I think Vincent's doing something. Something good.'

'What?' both Youssef and Jacqueline asked as they walked over to where Kevin was gawping at the board.

'Look.' He pointed at the signals on the wall.

'What is all that information?' she asked as he looked at the readouts.

'I'm not sure, but it looks like dates and locations of slugs,' Youssef replied.

# TimeRipper

'But they're not moving, they're showing the same date and time, the same location every time they flash up.'

Kevin moved closer to study the signals. 'Do you know what? I'd bet good money that this monitor is showing us the times, dates, and locations that the slugs broadcast *last*.'

'But they're still broadcasting, look.' Youssef pointed to the wall; the signals were still functioning within the normal parameters while the lights were on but stopped when the information flashed up.

'How can that be?'

The room was silent. No one could figure out what was happening.

'Maybe it's something to do with Vincent. Maybe he's located the women and eliminated them already,' Jacqueline burst with an enthusiasm that she didn't think she had left in her. There was also something else in her voice, Youssef thought it might have been hope.

He hated to contradict her, especially at this junction, but he thought she was wrong. 'If he'd have eliminated them, then the lights would be dead, not bouncing between sending signals and then dying. It must be something to do with the timeline. Maybe Vincent has altered it or influenced an alteration in it. If he's gone back to before we intended to send him, then maybe we're seeing two timelines, one where he hasn't met them yet, and one where he has.'

'Youssef, you're banging my head in here,' Kevin burst out, clearly interested in the theory but unable to grasp it.

'Look at it like a fork in the road. The lights are still reporting on one prong, but they've been eliminated on the other. I think we still have a mission on our hands here, people. Somehow, in one timeline they have been eliminated, we need to make sure that we finish the job. We don't know where they are, but we know where and when they terminate. Now, the way I see it is, in all the timelines, these fugitives will be at these locations. It must be a constant! All we need to do is be there to retrieve them.' He was pointing at Martha Tabram's dead-then-alive signal to emphasise his point. 'We capture her here and get the transponder codes from her. Then the rest of them don't need to die. We can take them one by one and bring them all back.'

'Of course, that is if they're willing. They might not come peacefully. In that case, we'll need to terminate them in situ,' Kevin pointed out.

'Agreed,' Youssef replied.

'Do you think Vincent has had a hand in all of this?' Jacqueline asked wistfully.

'I don't think it was a coincidence that after he disappeared, this started to happen,' Kevin replied.

'If we continue the mission then, do you think we might be able to rescue him, maybe bring him back?' she asked, the hope in her voice was not lost on Youssef.

'I don't see any reason why not. We'd have to take a spare slug with us to inject him with, for the portal to be able to locate him. But I believe it's possible,' he replied with a widening grin on his face. 'It just looks like a matter of finding a new Vincent,' he continued, looking at Kevin.

# TimeRipper

## 66.

London. 1863

WHEN VINCENT MATERIALISED, he was instantly disorientated. The dark room he had appeared in was spinning, and he could feel his legs wanting to buckle beneath him. It hadn't been like this the last time in Cardiff. That time, there had been a bright purple light and a small physical bump, and that was that, he was there. This time, he had been bathed in a stark, white light and he had the sensation of falling. He was supposed to have arrived in a large unused warehouse, the same warehouse that he was to rent, and use as a base of operations. Instead, he'd materialised in what he could only describe as a building site. There was hay, bricks, and wood everywhere. There were also some rudimentary saws and chisels, and a lot of cement.

As he took in his surroundings, something dawned on him. This *was* the warehouse he was due to materialise in, only it hadn't been built yet. *Something must have gone wrong in the transport*, he thought.

With his head still whirling, he lifted his wrist to his mouth and whispered into it. 'OP-One this is Clarence, are you receiving me?'

There was nothing.

'OP-One, can you hear me? Please acknowledge. This is Vincent Clarence reporting in.'

Once again, nothing. Not even static.

He reached into his pack and retrieved his backup communication device and tried that.

It was the same result.

He set the two devices to contact each other as a test, and instantly they reported each other's presence. *There's nothing wrong with the technology then*, he thought, taking in a deep breath through his teeth. He opened his portable portal and spread it out on the ground to its full extent. He called up a map of the city and did a scan for any out-of-time technology. There was none, including his own. *Why can't it see any tech? It should at least read itself as a device*, he pondered, getting rather worried at the predicament he found himself in.

A noise alerted him. It sounded like someone snooping around. Instinct kicked in, and he removed his extractor, just in case he needed it, and crept towards the source of the noise.

The night was dark, cloudy, and cold. Vincent crouched behind a sawhorse and waited for the noise to come again. As his eyes became accustomed, he scanned the area for movement. Eventually, he saw it: something, or someone, dressed head to toe in black was making their way across the yard. He could only just make out their silhouette as whoever it was got closer. The oversized helmet he was wearing made it obvious that it was a policeman. He was holding a tilley lamp but had not yet lit it.

'Hello, is anyone there?' the man shouted in a thick London accent. 'Look, I saw the fireworks, you best get out of there right now. You're breaking the law. If you want me to take you in, just stay where you are, and I'll get you.'

Vincent watched as he fiddled with the lamp, trying to light it with a flint. He knew he couldn't allow the policeman to arrest him. He couldn't risk being thrown into an eighteen-hundred's prison. He needed to make his escape.

'I can see you back there,' the policeman shouted as Vincent attempted to make his way out of the area using the shadows as camouflage. He raised the illuminated tilley lamp before jerking backwards. Vincent was closer to him than he'd expected. 'What the...' was all he managed to utter as he lost his footing and fell, dropping the lamp.

Vincent tried to catch him but was a second too late. He missed, and the policeman fell into a puddle with a splash. A distressed moan escaped him as he landed hard. Vincent assumed it was the wet and the cold that had made him complain; he hadn't assumed it might have been a pickaxe that had been left on the ground, unattended by the builders, in their haste to leave that afternoon.

## TimeRipper

In the distorted light of the fallen lamp, Vincent watched as a dark stream leaked into the muddy water around the policeman's head.

'Fuck!' he whispered falling on his knees next to him. Reaching into the pool of bloody water, he reached around the fallen man's head, and felt the head of the pickaxe buried within the poor man's neck.

Blood was frothing from his mouth as he stuttered, attempting to speak. 'W... Who, who are you?' Vincent recognised the ugly sound coming from him as a death rattle.

'My name is Vincent Clarence. I'm not the bad guy. This was an accident. I'm so sorry. What's your name?' He couldn't think of anything else to ask him. 'What is your name? I'll need to contact an ambulance or whatever you have in this age. Come on, tell me your name?'

'Frederick, my name's Frederick. Officer Frederick Abberline, warrant number 43519.'

He tried to lift his hand to touch Vincent's face, but it fell short as his eyes glazed over. His hand dropped limply into the puddle. Vincent stared into the lifeless eyes of the young police officer.

He felt like crying, but he knew that he had no time to mourn this young man. He needed to disappear, but not before he got rid of this body. He also needed to configure his tools for this timeframe, if he was ever going to get back home. But, in order to do all of this, he needed to know what year it was. He had a sneaking suspicion he was going to be stuck here for a while.

He lifted the body of the policeman, wincing as the pickaxe dislodged from his neck. He noticed that the man was roughly the same size, build, and age as him. He wondered how easy it would be to integrate himself into the police force of this time. He reasoned that his training and insights would be far superior to the whole force put together.

He began to strip the corpse of his uniform.

It wasn't exact, but it was at least a half decent fit.

~~~~

## D E McCluskey

In the year eighteen-sixty-three, Frederick Abberline joined the Metropolitan Police force with the rank of Officer. Later that year, the same Frederick Abberline was killed in the line of duty while investigating a possible break-in at a building site in Spitalfields.

Undeterred by his untimely death, in eighteen-sixty-five, due to exemplary service, he was promoted to Sergeant and moved from Whitechapel to Highgate. He settled there and worked hard, eventually earning himself the position of Inspector in eighteen-seventy-three.

In eighteen-seventy-eight, he moved back to Whitechapel and was promoted once again to Local Inspector.

Then, in eighteen-eighty-seven, for his exemplary work on several high-profile cases, he was moved to Scotland Yard.

In February eighteen-eighty-eight, he was promoted again to Inspector First Class, mainly due to his undercover duties and uncanny knack and hunches as to how the criminal mind worked.

All of this was not bad for a deceased policeman whose true calling finally came to him in the summer and autumn of eighteen-eighty-eight.

## 67.

### Orbital Platform One. 2288

'SHOULDN'T WE GO through the same process as we did with Vincent? A week's training in another time?' Youssef asked.

Kevin shook his head. 'It won't be necessary. We were all involved with that week's training and were all privy to the information as it happened.'

'That's as maybe, but we weren't there. We were here, safe and sound,' Youssef replied hesitantly.

'You worry too much. It's basic training; we've all done it.'

'But what if the women won't give up the transponder codes and an extraction has to be made? That's not basic training.'

'Well, I hate to be insensitive, but it's a case of get on with it. It has to be done, and it's not like I haven't done wet-work before.'

Youssef shook his head. 'OK then, agreed. Are you ready to go?'

'All set. Injections done, supplies ready, backpack filled. I'm ready to go, sir,' Kevin replied with a salute.

Jacqueline handed a similar backpack to Kevin to the one she had handed to Vincent, a couple of days earlier. 'Do we have any further idea of what could have caused the malfunction?' Kevin asked as her accepted the pack.

She shook her head. 'We have a theory, but that's all it is. We think the nuclear power packs on the tools we equipped him with become unstable in the displacement. We're still looking into it, so, for now, we're issuing you with cellular ones. Just in case.'

Kevin could see the sadness in her eyes as he slipped the backpack on, concealing it beneath his cape. He nodded. 'OK then, let's do this.'

'Start up the Hadron Collider,' Youssef shouted.

## 68.

<u>London. 1888</u>

'VINCENT, IS THAT you?'

Abberline was shaking as he held the mystery man in his arms. He had never felt like crying as much as he did right now. He removed the hat from the shadow's head before reaching behind and untying the hair that had been bunched up in the back. He then removed the false moustache. Even though he knew who he had in his arms, he still couldn't believe what he was seeing. It *was* her, she looked exactly the same as she had the last time he'd seen her. Twenty-six years ago.

'Jacqueline?'

'Vincent? Vincent, I, I don't know what to say,' she stuttered as the dawning reality that it was an aged Vincent Clarence holding her. 'How could you have aged so quickly?'

Abberline laughed. 'Maybe it's been quick for you, Jacqs, but I've been here twenty-six years.'

As he smiled at her; she could see, beneath his aged face, that it was the same smile he flashed at her prior to stepping into the pod.

'What happened?' she asked.

'I was going to ask you the same thing. I was in the Collider. It was a bumpy ride, and then I turned up in eighteen-sixty-three. There was an accident, and a young policeman died. It turned out that he was about my age and build. I realised that there had been an accident in sending me back. None of my tech would connect to twenty-two-eighty-eight. I concluded that I was alone. I decided, in honour of the dead policeman, I would become Officer Frederick Abberline, warrant number 43509!'

She was shaking her head. There was disbelief in her eyes, but also relief that Vincent was still alive. 'You've been here for twenty-six years?' She reached her hand to touched him, her fingertips tracing the lines of his face. 'So, you're what now? Fifty?'

'Fifty-two,' he nodded, the sadness in his smile almost broke her heart.

'There was a power surge,' she continued, trying to take her mind off the tears that were welling in her eyes. 'It was the nuclear cores of your tools. They're still in the process of dismantling Hadron One. We think that the nuclear power packs in the tools is not convivial to time travel. You'd been gone for three days before we made the decision to continue the mission.'

'Why did they send you? Why didn't Kevin take my place?'

Jacqueline laughed. 'Youssef didn't want anyone at first, but then we saw all the women's quantum signals begin to flux until there were only three left. Whatever you'd done allowed us to know the locations, and times, of the women's demises, so we made sure we were there for all of them. He said there was a chance that you had continued your mission, and we wanted to see if we could contact you. Initially, we did send Kevin. He got Martha's slug, did a fine job too, but on the Nichols job, he was attacked by Callaghan and she almost killed him. We had to bring him back in an emergency transport.'

Abberline laughed, rocking back on his heels as he did. 'You're telling me that Kevin got taken out on his second job?'

Jacqueline laughed too. 'Yeah, he was ribbed pretty hard about it once we got him back. After that, the decision was made. It was decided that I was to come back to search for you. I jumped at the chance, I was hoping you were still alive and well. But when I got here, I couldn't connect to your tech, so I had to undertake the mission myself. I was hoping that you would turn up at one of the times and locations.'

Abberline shook his head. 'I didn't do anything! What happened after I left?'

'All the women's quantum signals began to fluctuate. They began to report times and locations of termination. It was strange as they were all still showing as live too. So, we thought that you were responsible for the extractions. I was sent back to get you. That never went to plan.'

'I've had to jury rig my tech quite a few times, and the biographies of the women got lost somewhere amongst time. It became less of a memory, more like a dream. It wasn't until I went undercover to try to locate a rogue reporter, to oust him for unscrupulous work practices, when I witnessed Tabram come back. The purple smoke, the strange light, the woman appearing from nowhere. It brought everything back to me, the reason I was here. I dusted off my portal and my other tools and attempted to locate them. I was getting new reports coming in all the time, but due to my elevated position in the force, I couldn't just go and get them. I've employed the services of a local I know. He's a bit deranged, and on edge, but for some reason, he's tied to the women. He was also there when they arrived and has been there at most of your extractions.'

'Am I being investigated?' she asked.

Abberline chuffed at the question. 'You're the biggest news that has happened around here for a long time. A sensation! They call you Jack the Ripper; my acquaintance gave you the name. He heard you talking one time after an extraction, and he overheard Jack, ripper, so he thought that was your name.'

'That would have been after I got the Nichols slug,' she laughed. 'Jacqueline here! I've extracted the slug. I had to rip it out of her. That would have been one of my logs.'

Abberline laughed again. 'You've been the cause of mass hysteria here in the East End. No one has felt safe, not even the men. People have been blaming the aristocracy, the Jews, the freemasons.'

She shook her head. 'I still haven't finished. I've lost one woman; Emily Callaghan. I had her in my warehouse, but she got away, her signal went with it, even though I never took it. I don't have Liz Stride's slug either. I was disturbed in the process of extracting that one.'

'I've got them both,' he smiled. 'I took Stride's just before she was buried, and I took the other one from the woman in your warehouse. I extracted that one myself.'

She rolled her eyes. 'That's a relief. I was worrying about that one, as the date had passed regarding the signal terminating, but I knew that I hadn't gotten to her. I'd given up faith on meeting you and was worrying that the paradoxical laws were not true and someone from this time had gotten to her.'

'Well, someone kind of from this time, did get to her,' he laughed.

'What do we do now? If I'm big news, then surely there's a large section of the populace and the police force looking for me.'

Abberline smiled. 'There is a large section of the police looking for you, but I'm the lead inspector on the case.' He stood up and smoothed out his jacket, putting his shoulders back and standing to attention. 'Inspector Abberline, First Class, at your service, ma'am.' He offered out his hand to shake, and she accepted it.

He noticed there was something different about this young woman. There was something distant in her eyes, something hard. The killing of the fugitives had changed her from the sweet, innocent girl he remembered all those years ago, into something, or someone, else. He remembered her soft eyes, her mouth quick to laugh, and quick to kiss. She could always see the good in everyone. Maybe it was the years playing tricks with him, or maybe it was the fact that she was now a stone-cold killer.

'Was Mary Kelly in the room with you, then?' he asked.

She flipped the little flat metallic slug out of her pocket and threw it to him. 'Yes,' she replied.

He caught it and looked it over. It was still warm from the extraction.

'That one was a bugger to get out as well. I'm telling you; you don't want to see the state that I left her in back there.'

Abberline shuddered at the memory, and then shuddered at the thought of his Jacqueline saying something like that, with a smile on her face.

'So, that one was the last of the ones we knew about. It looks like we're on our own for the last three. What were you saying about this man who's connected to the crimes?'

'Kosminski is his name, Aaron Kosminski. I've got him set up to be the patsy when all this is finished. His wires are more than a little loose anyway. I'm sure you must have noticed him at some of the extractions.'

She shook her head. 'I can't say I did.'

'Well, I think we should keep our eye on him. He might be our link to their movements. Is your tech working correctly?'

'Yeah. Doesn't yours show where they are?'

'It does, but I thought you might have had a better handle on where they were going to be.'

'No, all we had was the times when the signals were terminated. I can see where they are now, they're all huddled together in a room on...' she took a moment to reach for her portal.

'Brick Lane,' he finished for her. 'It's a small bridewell, an overnight one, but at least we've now got an idea of where they'll be tonight.' Abberline then leaned in. He had an idea. He lifted his wrist up to his mouth and spoke into it.

'Kosminski, this is Abberline, can you hear me?' he looked into her eyes as he was speaking. They were just as deep and brown as he had remembered them twenty-six years ago.

'Hoo, Abberline, wadda you want?' came the voice from the communications device.

'Shit, I forgot, he's rotten drunk. Probably still asleep outside the Princess Alice pub.'

'That's where I was earlier. I figured that the women would be expecting a man, so I took off my disguise and befriended Mary, as I'd noticed she was on her own.'

'Yeah, well I told you he's connected to the extractions in some form or other, so he was there for the same reason, only he got drunk. He won't be any good to us now. Unless...'

~~~~

Kosminski was asleep. He was strangely comfortable in his little doorway, and he was dreaming. In his dream, he was sitting in his barbershop, his wife was sweeping up all the hair he'd cut that day, and he was taking a well-earned break. There was a knock on the window, a man was stood outside. He was wearing a cape and a tall, top hat; he was demanding to come inside.

His wife was ignoring him, but there was something about the man that he just could not put his finger on. He opened the door, allowing him to enter. As he did, his cape swished in the wind and out from underneath it strode six women. He recognised them all. Tabram came in first, then Nichols. Next was the witch who had possessed him, Annie Chapman. She strode in, walked up to him, and touched his face. 'Grandfather,' she whispered, 'great, great, great,

# TimeRipper

great, great, great, grandfather.' Then Elizabeth Stride and Catherine Eddowes and finally another woman, one who he thought he knew but he couldn't quite make out.

The shadow of the man then sat in his chair, resting his cane against his sideboard. Kosminski noticed the handle on the top of it was a fine silver spherical shape, but there was a nozzle sticking out of it. He'd seen it before but didn't know where.

'Cut it all off,' the man demanded as he removed his top hat. The long hair beneath unfurled and flowed down his back. The girl, who he thought he knew, then took the hat and put it on her head, tucking her hair beneath the rim.

'All of it?' he asked.

'Yes, all of it. And get rid of her,' he demanded, pointing to Kosminski's wife, who was still sweeping, showing no interest in what was happening.

'Right away, sir,' he said and walked over to his wife. As he got closer, she began to crouch onto the floor, large bruises appeared over her eyes and her nose began to gush with blood. He then watched as her nose snapped and another bruise appeared over her temple. Then she was gone.

He returned to his mysterious customer. 'Was that to your satisfaction, sir?'

'Yes' came the curt reply.

He stood in front of the man; he was still only a shadow. He removed his cutthroat razor, relishing the fine ivory handle and the weight of it in his grasp, before sharpening it on a leather strap.

'Have you been in London long?' he asked conversationally.

'Twenty-six years, sir. And only a few months too.' Although this answer didn't make any sense, Kosminski understood exactly what he was saying.

He began to work.

He walked behind him, reached over, and took hold of his chin. With a stroke of the razor, he removed a thin swathe of shadow, and a feminine chin came into view. It was full of colour. He took another swipe and then another. It was like pulling paper from a wall, revealing the older paper beneath.

All the time he swiped at the man, the woman sitting in the shop window, wearing his top hat, became covered in shadow. It then occurred to him: the man in the shadow *was* the woman who he couldn't quite see. Then the penny dropped: the man in shadow was the woman in the bar who Mary Kelly had been talking too.

He woke with a start, to two silhouettes looming over him.

~~~~

The larger of the two figures kicked out at him and caught him in the ribs. 'Aaron Kosminski, you are a disgrace! Wake up, man.'

He opened his eyes and tried to shield himself from another attack. 'What do you want? Leave me alone!' he shouted.

'Kosminski, it's me, Abberline. I've got another job for you. Get up now, man.'

It took him a moment to recognise who his attackers were. He knew Abberline straight away, but it took further scrutiny before he could place the second one. It was the woman from his dream, who was also from the pub tonight, who was also the killer. 'Jack?' he uttered.

'Nearly,' she replied, holding out her hand towards him. 'Pleased to meet you. I understand that you're a fan of my, erm, handiwork.'

He recoiled from the hand and tried to scurry further back into the doorway where he'd been sleeping. 'Get away from me, the pair of you, get away.'

Jacqueline looked at him and smiled.

Abberline took his cue and kneeled, offering him his hand. 'Come now, Kosminski, we're about to make history here. We need your help to complete the job.'

Reluctantly, like a small child reacting to kind words from an abusive parent, but the only real authority they had ever known, Kosminski took Abberline's hand.

'Good lad! Thank you, Aaron.'

As soon as he was up, he watched as Abberline turned towards the woman, he apologised to her, then hit her with all his rather considerable force, full in the face. He wasn't quite sure what he had just witnessed. He looked from the woman on the floor with the bleeding face to Abberline standing next to her, smiling. The policeman from the future put a steel whistle in his mouth, winked at him, and then blew it.

# TimeRipper

A high-pitched, shrill filled the air. Kosminski covered his ears as he thought the sound might pierce his skull. Abberline put something into his hands and then something into his coat pocket. He was trying to see what they were when the strange policeman punched him full in the face too. His vision blurred, and he had a sensation of falling. There was another blow to his head to add to the ones he had already suffered tonight, and everything went black, although he could still hear through the darkness and pain.

Another man appeared at their location, followed by another and then another

'You there,' one of the newcomers shouted. 'Halt in the name of the law.'

'I'm Inspector Frederick Abberline of the Metropolitan Police, Inspector First Class. Here's my warrant. I believe I've captured Jack the Ripper.'

'Bloody-hell, sir, it looks like you have too. He certainly fits the description.'

'And just look at that knife he's holding,' came another voice.

'My word, sir, this is gonna make you famous all over London, and no mistake. Jack the Ripper, as I live and breathe.'

'I'm not interested in fame; I just want you to get this wretch to Brick Lane. I'll follow shortly. I need to make sure this poor woman is OK.'

'Is she still alive, sir? I can see quite a bit of blood.'

'I think she is. I'll see to her. Get him into a cell as soon as you can. I'll be there shortly to interrogate him myself.'

Kosminski felt himself lifted from the floor as the world around him turned fuzzy.

~~~~

Abberline and Jacqueline entered Brick Lane station to a herald of applause from the coppers who were working the late shift.

'Three cheers for Inspector Abberline!'

'We knew you'd get 'im, sir'

'We got the bastard, eh?'

'Men, I think the time to celebrate is not too far into the future, but, before all that, we need to determine the man's guilt. We cannot render him guilty just because he held a surgeon's knife.'

'Sir, we found this in his pocket too.'

The policeman handed Abberline a small, folded razorblade. He flipped it open and it revealed a clean, sharp swathe of steel.

'This is good work, officer. Now, I'd like to speak to the prisoner, alone. Could you please look after this lady, officer? Take care of her wounds. I think she's going to be vital to this case. See if she wants a cup of tea, or a gin, or something.'

'Righty-o, sir. She can sit in the mess room, there's no one in there right now.'

'Good man! Oh, officer, can you tell me how many men are in this station right now?'

'About twelve, sir. May I ask why?'

'Good, I just don't trust this fella. There's something about him, you know. I wanted to make sure that if he starts anything then we'll be able to detain him.'

'I understand, sir,' the officer replied tipping his hat. 'You won't have anything to worry about anything on that score. I'll personally keep an eye on him for you, if you like.'

'That would be excellent, but first I want ten minutes with him, alone, in a room.'

Abberline grabbed the stunned Kosminski and pulled him into an interrogation room, slamming the door shut behind him.

'Abberline, what is going on?' he hissed.

'You, sir, are about to make history. You may become more famous than anyone has ever imagined. Maybe even bigger than The Beatles.'

'The what?'

'Never mind, just sit down and shut up.'

Kosminski did as he was told. Abberline opened the door and leaned out into the office. 'Officer, where is the woman I brought in with me?'

'She is in the mess, sir, drinking sweet tea laced with gin, just as you ordered.'

'Right, listen to me. Be very careful with her, from the information I've just been given, she may well be an accomplice to these murders. He's just confessed as much. I want you to put her in the cell.'

'Sir, the cell's full tonight, we've got three women on drunk and disorderly and criminal damage to The Ten Bells pub.'

'I don't care, officer. Put her in with them. Do it now, not a moment to waste. Oh, and I want you to send another two patrols out as well. If what this man is telling me is true, we're going to have trouble in the Jewish quarter tonight.'

'Another two patrols will leave only six officers in here, sir, to guard the prisoners.'

'Officer, we have a cell full of drunk women and one male prisoner. What do you think is going to happen?'

The officer bit the inside of his cheek as he looked at his commanding officer. He rolled his eyes and walked past the door, towards the mess. 'Righty-o,' he sighed. 'I'll get the woman in the cell, and then sort out the patrols straight away, sir.'

'Good man,' Abberline said as he closed the door on the policeman.

~~~~

'Officer! Get in here right now! I require assistance,' Abberline shouted from inside the room. 'Help me now.' The two officers on the front desk looked at each other, and the third who was at the paperwork desk stood up, straightened his tunic, and looked at his colleagues.

'What is going on in there?' one of them asked.

As if in answer, a crash rang out from the room, as something was smashed inside, and Abberline gave a shout of pain.

'Get in there,' the desk officer shouted to his two colleagues. 'See what's going on.'

Two of the officers raced into the interrogation room, truncheons drawn, ready for trouble.

When they entered, Abberline was hiding behind the door. It closed behind the second officer and Abberline shot him with the stun setting on his extractor. The officer fell silently to the ground in an instant. Just as the first one was about to turn around, Abberline grabbed him from behind, wrapping his arms around his neck and cutting off the circulation to his brain just long enough to render him unconscious.

He reached into the officer's top pocket and removed his whistle. 'Grab this,' he whispered as he thrust it into Kosminski's hand. 'Take it and run out of this station, hit the desk officer if you must, but be quick.' Abberline grabbed him by the face and stared into his eyes. 'If you value your life, you'll run, fast. When you get out, you blow that whistle, and you just keep going.'

'But, what if—' he stuttered.

'But what if, nothing,' Abberline replied curtly. 'Do it now.' He pushed the big man through the door and retreated into the room.

The officer behind the desk watched, his jaw slacking. He stood up as Jack the Ripper came bounding out of the interrogation room. His eyes were as wild as his manic grin, but not as wild as his thick, black hair.

'What the...' was all he had time to utter before Kosminski was upon him. He grabbed him by the front of his tunic, looked him right in the eye, and then punched him in the face. The officer was on the floor nursing a bleeding mouth, before he even knew what had happened, and Kosminski was out of the door.

The stricken officer quickly regained his composure and brushed himself down. He rubbed his chin and looked towards the room where the inspector was. He sighed, shook his head, and then shouted. 'Escaped prisoner, escaped prisoner, in pursuit, need assistance.'

Another officer came from the direction of the mess, holding a mug of tea, 'What's going on?' he shouted.

'Jack the Ripper's escaped, we need to pursue.'

The newcomer slammed his mug down on the front desk, spilling most of the contents over the various papers that were there. 'If we go now, who's left in the station?' he asked, drawing his truncheon.

'Griff's in the back with Driscoll, they're guarding the prisoners, and Inspector Abberline is in the office.' he replied, absentmindedly forgetting that Jack the Ripper had just burst out of that office.

'Come on, then,' he shouted enthusiastically. 'Let's go.'

As they made their way outside, they heard the report of a police whistle, the shrill sound was coming from the direction of Commercial Street, and, automatically, they both followed the sound.

TimeRipper

Kosminski was sweating and tired, but he was having fun. He was running, hiding, and blowing his whistle as if there was no tomorrow. He was enjoying sending the flatfoots on a merry goose chase.

~~~~

Jacqueline was in the cell with the three other women. They were all huddled together on one end of the small room, and none of them would even look at her, never mind talk.

*I know more about every one of you than you probably know about yourselves,* she thought. She observed the tall woman with the straight hair, hair that was now mostly grey. On the footage of her she'd seen, back in OP-One, her hair had been a deep dark brown, like milk chocolate. Her eyes were twitching this way and that, and Jacqueline noticed that she had very little left in the way of fingernails. *Getting a little anxious are we, Carrie Millwood? You're looking a little rough these days. Is it too much burden on you, the mass murder of nearly three billion people, and then the killing of seven of your closest friends?*

A commotion began outside the cell. She could hear shouting and running; she took this as her cue. 'Help me, help me,' she screamed. 'They're attacking me, get them off me, help please...'

That was Abberline's cue!

She began shouting at the top of her voice. The three women turned to look at her at once.

She smiled inwardly.

Jacqueline heard the door to the cell room open, and she jumped in the middle of the three startled women and began thrashing about.

Two officers piled in. 'Oy, you lot, stop what you're doing at once. Don't make me come in there with you whores and start with this,' the first officer shouted drawing out his truncheon.

She kept on thrashing. It was clear that the other women were not at all comfortable with the mad woman.

'OK, you were warned!' the officer shouted and turned the key in the lock to the cell.

As he did, Abberline burst through from the other room. He took out the officer closest to the door in the same manner that he had dispatched the other in the office. The policeman in the cell turned to see what was happening, and Jacqueline struck him from behind, pushing his head against the thick iron bars of the cell. The officer's eyes glazed over as he fell to the floor.

'Drag him out of the cell, and I'll get the other one,' she shouted to Abberline as she exited the cell. As soon as he was clear of the door, she closed it again, locking the three dumbfounded women inside.

'Perfect,' she said as she looked at them. They were all filthy, all wearing dishevelled clothing, and all looking like they didn't have the slightest idea what was happening to them. *As if butter wouldn't melt.* 'Now I've got you just where I want you. These officers will be out of action for quite some time.' She looked at the women, gazing into the faces of each one individually. 'Speaking of time…'

Realisation, mixed with horror, dawned on all their faces.

## 69.

THEY WERE TRAPPED, the remaining three women responsible for the near destruction of humanity.

'How could you do it? How could you kill billions of people on a whim? What makes you so hell bent on destruction?' Jacqueline asked through the bars of the cell.

Carrie Millwood stood up. As she did, Jacqueline could see why this woman was the leader. If you removed the anxiety that had obviously built up during her time here, she could see the leader in her. 'Destruction? Is that what you think it was all about?' she asked.

'It looks that way to me.'

Carrie moved closer to the rusty bars and peered through them. 'You know nothing about the Higgs Storm, do you? How could you? You're a grunt, a foot soldier, tied to the Earth Alliance, giving unwavering loyalty to a fascist state.'

Jacqueline moved closer to the bars, her face millimetres away from Carrie's. She smiled a cold smile. 'I'm not a soldier. I'm a scientist. I was brought into this because the Earth has run short of resources, and that includes personnel. That is due to you! The EA is not a fascist state! We're there to allow the planet to run in union, hence the word alliance. There's no racial hatred, religious intolerance, homophobic, or sexist behaviour, everyone is equal.'

'It's an illusion of equality! Do you not call your superiors sir?'

'Yes, but it's a mark of respect. People in the EA have gotten to elevated positions due to their abilities. Gone are the days of reaching the heights by birth right or who you knew in the system giving you an opening. That is no longer tolerated.'

'But you still have an academy, yes?'

'Yes, we do. It's a fine institution for the youth to enhance themselves through the ranks.'

Carrie laughed; it was a cold sound. 'That, too, is an illusion! The wheels are greased like they always have been. We saw a need to change everything, to start again from grass roots. To build a world solely dependent on science, not religion.'

'Excuse me, but you said to *build* a world? The way I see it, you tried to *destroy* a world. There is a big, big difference.'

Carrie laughed. 'Once again, you assume that bringing everything back to its base elements is destroying. Did you study the Higgs Storm completely, as an entity, not just its destructive properties? No, I bet you didn't. Well, I did!' Carrie smiled as she let go of the bars, wiping the rust residue from her palms onto her already dirty dress. 'Let me tell you, it has the most fantastic properties of any element I've ever seen. Yes, it destroys, but what it leaves behind is the most fertile ground you will ever see on the planet.' She grabbed hold of the bars again and pressed her face closer to Jacqueline's. Her eyes were wide and animated, in complete contrast to how they looked just a few moments ago. 'We have a cave beneath an island in Fiji,' she whispered. 'It's vast, and it's where we conducted our experiments. The Higgs Storm doesn't just destroy, it creates too. We have an unlimited source of natural growing abilities. It literally terraforms. It destroys life in order to create life, it re-creates the whole essence of the big bang.'

'And to reach this utopia, you didn't mind killing billions of people?'

'Don't you see? We weren't killing them; we were liberating them.'

'Did you ask the people, the ones who suffered, who *are* suffering for your megalomania, if they wanted liberating? No, you didn't. Do you know why? Because you're nothing but a crazed lunatic, fulfilling your psychopathic urges and passing them off as an ideal. You, my crazy friend, are the biggest mass murderer history has ever seen. I'm not going to give you the option of going back to twenty-two-eighty-eight peacefully. You're going to join your friends in the eighteen-eighty-eight morgue.'

Abberline stepped in and held Jacqueline's shoulders. 'Jacqs, come on, don't let her get to you. It's what she wants. We only have a small amount of time left; we need to get these women back home as soon as we can.'

## TimeRipper

Jacqueline reluctantly moved away from the bars. As she did, she saw a small commodity of amusement in Carrie's eyes, and a faint smile.

'I'll go back to twenty-two-eighty-eight with you,' Annabelle Farmer said, standing up from her seat. Carrie Millwood turned and looked at her with very little emotion in her face. 'Will you?' she asked very slowly.

'Yeah.' she replied, her head dropping. 'Our mission here is done. We failed. It was a good idea at the time, the best idea; but that time has passed. We don't have the right to liberate people from their lives, even if it is to facilitate a better world to live in. No, I'll accompany you back to twenty-two-eighty-eight. I'll go home and face the charges. Anything has to be better than living here, in this squalor!'

'You can count me in too,' Rose Mylett said standing up. Carrie closed her eyes as she did. 'I think what we did was extreme, but believe me, I'd do it again. We failed in our mission to finish the job we started, and I now believe that by standing trial in twenty-two-eighty-eight, we can bring an understanding of The Event and why we did it. We can still relish in our ideals and watch as the terraforming takes place in the already affected areas.'

'Give me your transponder codes, and we'll make the preparations to get you home,' Jacqueline spoke, calmly.

Annabelle Farmer stepped closer to the bars. 'My code is, AF-3465-JB—'

As quick as a flash, Carrie Millwood produced a short, thin knife from her stockings and flashed it across Annabelle's throat. For a moment, the poor woman didn't understand what had happened. All she knew was that all sound had stopped coming from her mouth.

She brought her hands up to her throat as if to feel why her voice had simply disappeared. As she did, slivers of blood began to drip down her neck. They were slow at first, and then, as if directed by the movement of her fingers, the drips became a flow, which soon became a gush.

Annabelle Farmer fell onto the floor, choking on her own blood.

'Youssef, this is Jacqueline, if I was to give you a partial transponder code, with what we know of their signals, could you do an emergency extraction?'

'I think so,' came the raspy voice from her communicator. 'All we need are the first five digits, and with the quantum signal we already have, I think we'd have them. Why? What's happened?'

'No time to explain!'

Abberline was looking at her communicator with awe. *How many years has it been since I heard that voice?* he thought. Then he watched as Millwood turned towards Rose, threatening her with the same blade that had struck Annabelle.

Rose shrank back into the cell.

The sight of one of her sister's, killing another, was obviously too much for her to take. Abberline knew from her records that Mylett was a formidable woman, a trained killer, but to see her cowering in the cell as she was threatened by the woman who was supposed to be their leader, shocked him. He entered the cell before anyone realised. He grabbed Millwood's arm, forcing it around her back. She dropped the knife with little resistance.

'Youssef, try this: AF-3465-JB. That's all we have. She's been wounded, her neck has been slashed, get her immediate hospital care. We may be too late.'

'Got her! Prepare for extraction.'

A small bright purple light shone from the centre of Annabelle's stomach. The light turned into a small hurricane as purple smoke enveloped her body. The whole thing lasted roughly thirty seconds; and then she was gone.

Carrie Millwood, while still being held by Abberline, watched impassively as her colleague disappeared.

'My code is RM-8437-JK-000-RFT. Get me out of this stinking time,' Rose Mylett shouted from the corner of the room.

'Did you copy that code?'

'No, can you repeat it?'

As Rose repeated the code, Abberline dragged Millwood out of the cell, in restraint.

'Wait...' Rose Mylett said. 'She'll never give you her code, she'd rather die. I'd like her to stand trial with me.'

Carrie flashed a dangerous look towards Rose. 'Don't,' she said.

'I will. You deserve the recognition you'll receive as being a visionary, and revolutionary.'

TimeRipper

'A madwoman, you mean,' she snarled. 'We'll be reviled when we get back. The populous will hate us for what we've done.'

'No, they won't. We had six million followers when we left. I bet that that has tripled by now. They'll understand what you wanted to do for them.'

Abberline interjected. 'I think they, what's left of them, will see what you tried to do *to* them, rather than for them. I think you might be surprised by your lack of followers when you get back.'

Mylett glared at him, then dropped her head. 'Her code is, CM-1115-JC-2121-RFT.'

The moment she finished relaying this information, the small bright purple light lit up her stomach and she was engulfed the thick purple smoke.

Rose Mylett was gone, four hundred years into the future.

Abberline, Jacqueline, and Carrie Millwood were the only three people left, conscious, in the police station.

'Are you ready to come home, Inspector Abberline?' Jacqueline asked, smiling.

Vincent, or was he Frederick now? He could no longer tell. He looked at her. There was sadness in his weathered, and wizened, face. He half smiled at her.

Jacqueline could see something in his eyes and knew he was seeing her as the same girl he'd left behind twenty-six years ago, but she was also aware that he knew she was looking at him as the boy who had left her less than a few months ago but had aged a lifetime.

'I don't know,' he replied, shaking his head. 'I'm not sure I've got anything to go back to. I've built a life for myself here. How would I get back anyway? You can't track me.'

'I brought a spare slug,' Jacqueline replied, holding out a syringe with metallic fluid within it. 'Whatever an extraction target is holding onto during the procedure will be extracted with them. All you have to do is hold on tight.'

He looked at the syringe. 'I'll restrain Carrie for the extraction. She may well have another surprise up her sleeve.' He proceeded to frisk her for any other devices or weapons. 'She does appear to be clean, though.'

'Right then, I'll go first and get your extraction ready. We'll have to double the Higgs Storm Compensators and the power to the colliders, then we'll call you. It should take about five minutes. Are you OK with that?'

'Yeah,' he nodded. 'No worries. Get a move on, though, as I don't know how long Kosminski will be able to stave off those policemen.'

'I will.' Jacqueline looked at him. 'It's really good to see you again, you know.' She smiled, but he could see that the smile was for an old friend, not a lover. Not anymore.

'Yeah, you too, kid.' He flashed her a smile that was every inch the Vincent of old.

She lifted her wrist to her mouth, and without taking her eyes off him, spoke into it. 'Youssef, this is Jacqueline. I'm ready for extraction.'

'Bringing you in now.'

The now-familiar purple light shone from her stomach as she became embroiled in the purple tornado. Then she was gone, leaving just Abberline and the detained Millwood alone in the cell.

## 70.

Orbital Platform One. 2288

ANNABELLE FARMER MATERIALISED in the racetrack at the same time a medical team arrived, having been teleported in from OP-Seven. A thick, arterial spray was pulsing from out of the deep gash in her neck, and she was gasping for air. They covered her in a stasis beam and then teleported a full stasis pod over from the other OP.

'Will she live?' Youssef asked, concerned with the amount of blood loss she had sustained in the extraction.

'It'll be touch and go. She's lost a lot of blood, and she looks malnourished, weak. We'll do the best we can. What in the world happened to her, anyways?' one of the medics asked as Farmer was carefully placed inside the stasis pod.

'You don't need to know just yet,' he replied. 'But you do need to know that her whole body will have sustained trauma in the past few seconds. You will also find a metallic slug that is giving out magnetic signals in her body, among other things. Do not try to remove it, it'll kill her outright. She may need to be de-loused and cleaned too.'

The medic looked at him like he was pulling his leg, but the grim expression on his face told him he was doing anything but.

'Got it! Is there anything else we need to know?'

'Not right now, only that we'd really like to keep her alive.'

'On it!'

With that, the medical team, along with the stasis pod carrying Annabelle Farmer, left the room.

'We're bringing in Rose Mylett now. Jacqueline's just let us know that she's still a hostile. She's not dangerous or armed, but she still believes in the cause.'

'OK, then. Let's get a security detail in here,' Youssef instructed the room.

After the huge amounts of Higgs Storm from Annabelle's return had been extracted, the Hadron Collider started up again. Within a minute, Rose Mylett appeared within the racetrack.

'Get her out of there and into a holding cell straight away. If she's still a believer in the cause, then she's still a danger to us,' Kevin instructed over the sound of the Collider still rotating.

The extraction of Rose Mylett's Higgs Storm began.

'Who's next?' Kevin shouted.

'Jacqueline's coming in next. She says that Vincent's coming back with her too. He's currently detaining Millwood. We're going to have to boost power to the extraction process for this one.'

'Vincent?' he asked, his face barely able to contain his smile.

The Collider began again, and less than a minute later, Jacqueline appeared inside the racetrack. Immediately, the Higgs Storm extraction began.

'Jacqueline! It's so good to see you. I'm glad you're OK.' Youssef rushed into the glass room and gave her a hug. '*Are* you OK?' he asked. 'I hate that you had to do that mission, but with what happened to Kevin, we had no other choice.'

She shook her head and hugged him back. 'I understand, honestly, I do.'

He noticed more than a little hardness in her persona that had not been there prior to her deployment. *She's going to need a full psych assessment after this ordeal*, he thought, *I'll need to look into that.*

'Come here, you,' Kevin shouted as he made his way into the Collider room. He grabbed her, and squeezed her, lifting her clear off the floor. 'You found Vincent too? That's sterling work, soldier.'

She began to remove the filthy clothing she was wearing. 'Yeah, he's coming in now with Millwood. Have we compensated for the Higgs Storm? And the power?'

Kevin winked at her. 'It's all set, Jacqs, just let him know we're bringing him home.'

Now in a latex under suit, she was looking at the monitor next to the Collider. 'You're going to have to reassess the quantum compensation,' she said as she addressed the controls on the station.

# TimeRipper

'Vincent went back further than we did. Add another twenty-six years onto your calculations.'

'Twenty-six years?' Youssef repeated, his brow ruffling as he looked at her.

'Yes! The malfunction sent him to the correct location but to the wrong time. He now goes under the mantle of Frederick Abberline, Inspector First Class of the Metropolitan Police Force.'

Kevin was looking at Jacqueline, almost beaming with pride for his student. 'First Class, eh? This guy's got delusions of grandeur. Well, let's not keep the Inspector waiting, eh?' he said as Youssef added the compensation calculations into the portal.

'I think we're going to need extra security with this one too. It's my belief that Carrie Millwood is psychotic.'

'Yeah, we had an idea she might be. Let's bring them back in now,' Kevin shouted as Youssef started up the Hadron Collider one more time.

## 71.

London. 1888

'ARE YOU READY for the extraction?' Jacqueline's voice over the wrist communicator was crisp, not at all like she was talking four hundred years in the future.

'All set back here. Whenever you're ready,' Abberline replied.

'Do you have any of your tools on you?' Jaqueline asked.

'Yeah,' he replied. I've got my extractor.'

'Ditch it. It's got a nuclear power signature. That's what caused you accident in the first place.'

With his free hand, the other one was still holding Carrie Millwood, he removed his extractor took from his pocket and placed it on the table next to him. He then removed his communicator too. 'All done,' he reported.

The purple light shone in the centre of Carrie's body, and Abberline waited for the purple hurricane.

Carrie, however, had other ideas. At the last moment, she shifted to her left, taking Abberline off guard. She broke away from his hold and she swivelled around. She reached over to the communicator, and the extractor on the table, and activated it. The extraction light shifted. She turned the beam onto herself, and cut into her left leg, she then turned it into her stomach, and cut herself again. The glow shifted again as the displacement struggled with the nuclear power signal coming from the tools she held.

Abberline watched in sickened disgust as his extractor beam mutilated his prisoner It took him a few moments for him to realise that she was attempting to cut the quantum slug out herself, to avoid going back to twenty-two-eighty-eight.

~~~~

TimeRipper

Orbital Platform One. 2288

'There's something wrong with the extraction. I'm struggling to keep contact with her quantum slug. It looks like a problem with the signal. It looks like the same issue we had with Vincent last time,' Youssef shouted across the room towards Kevin and Jacqueline.
'It there any way you can compensate for the loss of signal?' Kevin replied, 'Maybe boost the hydrogen levels?'
He looked at his friend for a moment before frantically pressing buttons on his portal. 'I'm losing them. Millwood's slug has entered into the time-stream, but I don't know where they are.'

London. 1888

Abberline watched, helpless, as Carrie viciously attacked herself with the beam. He could see the slug evading it with ease, but one stroke got lucky. She must have nicked the corner of it, and Abberline noticed the purple glow dim. 'What's happening at your end?' he shouted, hoping his communicator was still working.
'We're trying to boost the signal, what's going on there?' asked the male voice from the other end. Vincent thought it must have been Kevin.
'She's attempting to remove her own slug. I can't move to stop her. I feel like I'm glued to the floor or something.'
'You're caught in a temporal flux similar to the one you experienced at the start of your mission.'
'Brilliant...' Abberline replied.

Orbital Platform One. 2288

'I'm losing Carrie's signal completely,' Youssef shouted over the noise of the collider. 'It's going, going...' He sighed and banged his head against the portal screen. He turned, shaking his head. 'It's gone.' he said, stepping away from the console. His hair was plastered to his face as tears of sweat trickled down his cheeks. 'I don't have them on my portal anymore. Wherever they've gone, they're stuck there.'

Jacqueline and Kevin were silent as they watched their leader's misery.

She turned and punched in a few commands on her own portal, trying some backdoors that she knew about, some she had even programmed in herself, but it was all to no avail. She could see nothing from either Carrie or Vincent in any of the records.

The silence hung in the room like a physical presence.

After a few moments, Youssef broke it. 'The mission was a success, relatively speaking,' he said in a heavy voice with his head hanging low. 'We got most of the devices back, thanks to you and to Vincent.' The last words were directed towards Jacqueline.

She picked up her backpack and opened it. She removed seven flattened metallic pieces and threw them to the floor. 'Seven there, plus the two within the prisoners. That gives us nine out of ten.'

'Well, that's good news, isn't it?' Kevin asked a little unsure, his gaze flicking between Youssef and Jacqueline.

'It means that, theoretically, she has the means to return to our time, and if she does, she could still produce Higgs Storm. She still has the potential to target an EA facility or a densely populated area. I guess we'll just all have to monitor for temporal activity for the rest of our lives.' Youssef walked over to Jacqueline and wrapped his arms around her, giving her a fatherly kiss on her forehead. She nodded, accepting the show of emotion. He then clapped Kevin on the back before slowly walking out of the room.

72.

London. 1888

Three-thirty a.m., on the morning of February 25th, eighteen-eighty-eight, the doors of the Whitechapel Workhouse Infirmary were barged open and three men blustered inside, shouting and hollering. All three of them were covered in blood. They were carrying a bundle of clothing between them; the bundle was leaving behind a dripping trail of thick red liquid.
'Someone come quickly, somebody help,' one of the men shouted as the bloodied arm of a woman lolled out of the sheets she was being carried in.
'I think she's dying,' another man shouted.
Two doctors made their way, lazily, out of the rest room where they had been drinking and playing cards.
'Get her onto this table,' one of them shouted as he directed the men towards a long table in the centre of the room.
The other doctor began removing all the objects from the table and placing them onto the floor. Rolling his eyes, he turned towards the room they had just come from and bellowed. 'We've got another casualty. It looks like I'm going to need some bandages and some alcohol for the wounds.'
The woman was unceremoniously dumped onto the table as the second doctor, now armed with the supplies, arrived. He put the bandages to one side and took a long swig from the alcohol bottle. 'They look like knife wounds,' he said, stating the obvious. He then looked towards the three bloodied men who were standing to one side, not really knowing what to do. 'Where did you find this woman?' he asked.
'White's Row, sir,' the first man answered—he had removed his cap and was now wringing it in his hands. 'I swear, we were working

away on some of the windows, on account of them falling out, you see, and then there was a blinding light and a load of wind.'

'Then this purple smoke appeared leaving this gal lying there, all covered in blood like. I swear on me daughter's life, she was not there one moment and then was the next. We wasted no time getting her here, I can tell yer,' he continued.

'Did you see who made the wounds?' the second doctor asked while examining the woman.

All three men shook their heads, none of them wanting to be any more involved than they already were.

The second doctor was sniffing the men who had brought her in. 'What's her name? Does anyone know?' he asked, his voice sounding a little blurry.

'We think her name might be Millwood. At least I think that's what she said. It sounded like Annie or Carrie or something like that,' the third man answered, as he continued wringing his cloth cap before him.

'Right, I'll need to clean these wounds,' the doctor shouted, dismissing the men and directing his shout at the woman on the table. 'Miss Millwood, you'll feel a sting, but that's a good thing. It'll be the alcohol cleansing your wounds.' He looked up at the other doctor, who was taking another drink from the bottle. 'Do you think she might be able to get some of that?'

The second doctor poured some of the brown liquid onto the woman's lower abdomen, and to everyone's surprise, she screamed, sitting up, aggravating her existing wounds, causing them to bleed harder.

Eventually, the two doctors were able to pacify her. They managed to get the stricken woman to lie back down on the table and were able to stem her bleeding while simultaneously feeding her laudanum to ease the pain.

Eventually, Carrie Millwood slept.

## 73.

A FEW WEEKS after the appearance of the mysterious woman in White's Row, another bright light and purple wind heralded the arrival of a confused and disorientated Abberline. When the wind died, taking the white light with it, he fell onto his knees and vomited. The maelstrom he had just traversed made him sick to his stomach. He tried to stand, but was unsuccessful, his head was reeling from the ordeal. His eyesight was blurred and all he could hear was a loud whining noise drilling in his head.

The cramps in the pit of his stomach felt like they were tearing him apart. As he continued to retch, nothing came out.

Two men wearing work clothes ran to his aid. 'Mister, are you all right? Can you hear me?'

He tried to talk but couldn't form any words.

'He's hot, so bleeding hot,' a voice said as rough hands grabbed him.

Sweat was dripping from his brow. He lifted his hand to his face, but it looked distorted and grotesque in his blurred vision.

'You're coming with us, mate,' came another voice from God only knew where. 'We're gonna get you to the hospital sharpish, I can tell ya that for nuthin'.'

He felt hands underneath his armpits. As they lifted him off the floor, searing pain coursed through his flesh where he was manhandled. There was a strange sensation of being dragged. For how long, or how far, he couldn't tell. He couldn't even tell in what direction he was being taken. He felt himself hoisted onto a cart and driven away.

He could make out a blue sky. The heat of the day felt like it was cracking his skin. He could feel his flesh blistering and peeling from his face.

'We found this fella on the floor in Whites Row. He doesn't look in a good way,' a voice above him spoke.

'We're gonna leave him here with you, as we don't want any of what he's got, that's for sure,' another voice, from somewhere he couldn't see, filtered in through the whining in his head.

There was more agonising pain as the rough hands grabbed him again, then stars in his eyes as he was dumped onto a hard-stone floor.

'Get this man into a bed, straight away,' someone shouted as he was dragged again somewhere else. His protests of torture were ignored as his clothes were cut from him. Everywhere anything touched his skin, it felt like it was sinking through his flesh and wrapping itself around his bones.

'Laudanum... get me laudanum, now! Make it a big shot.'

A bottle was shoved into his face.

'Here, have yourself some of this,' a male voice growled. 'It'll stop you from feeling anything, for at least the next few hours.'

The contents of the bottle stank, and as the bitter tasting liquid was forced down his burning throat, he thought he was going to vomit it all back up again.

Thankfully, it somehow managed to stay down. After that, he felt nothing.

~~~~

Orbital Platform One. 2288

'We've got him! I can't believe it. Vincent Clarence's quantum signal has just flashed up on the portal,' Kevin said looking at his screen in disbelief.

'Where is he?' Jacqueline asked anxiously.

'You'll never believe this, but he's back where he should have gone originally. Whites Row, London. March twenty-first, eighteen-eighty-eight. How could that be?' Kevin shook his head in wonder.

'Maybe he's gone back in time and is now his same younger self,' she hoped.

'No, I don't think the paradoxical laws would allow that. Time continues on.' Youssef stopped dead after speaking his sentence.

'Oh, shit...' both Kevin and Youssef cursed at the same time.

'What?' Jacqueline asked, her eyes switching between the two men.

'The paradoxical law! If he's gone back in time to March twenty-first, eighteen-eighty-eight, that means he already exists in that time.' Youssef shook his head as he looked at her. 'That law won't allow it to happen. It'll kill him, and soon.'

'Get him back, now,' she ordered.

'Hold on, we never got around to my 'Oh Shit' statement.' Kevin continued. 'Carrie Millwood's there too. I'm tracing his signal, and I've inadvertently picked up hers. Its weak, and it looks damaged, but it's her. For some reason, I can't lock onto it. It's disrupting Vincent's too.' He was punching commands into his portal keyboard. 'I can't lock onto either of them. One of us is going to have to go back and retrieve them.'

'Inject me now, I'm going back for him,' Jacqueline demanded offering up her arm. Youssef nodded his agreement. 'I can take out Millwood at the same time.'

'I've got something for you to take back. You can't just waltz in there and slice her open; you'd be arrested before you even touched the slug. You'll need to take this.' He handed her a long shaft with a trigger on one end and a nozzle on the other.

'What is it?' she asked.

'All you need to do is press it against her skin and pull the trigger. It'll release a tracker that will eventually get to the slug. It might take a few days, as they're evasive bastards, but it'll get it in the end, and it will kill it. With any luck, it'll kill her too. Oh, and there's a special feature added.'

Jacqueline looked at the weapon in her hands. She weighed it and gripped it before looking at Kevin with more than a hint of a smile on her face.

'Press this ... here!' he pointed to a small button on one side, a little further away from the min trigger. 'It releases a bunch of enzymes into her blood stream that are attracted to her cerebral cortex. Once they reach her brain, the bitch will be flooded with the memories of everything that's happened, or in her time *will* happen. I wouldn't want her living, thinking she's gotten away with anything.'

Jacqueline smiled as she holstered the weapon. 'Thanks.'

'Don't thank me, it was your team who've been working on it. They thought it was a little more humane than our trusty extractor here. Not that she deserves humane, understand. That's why I got them to add the memory shot.'

Youssef injected her with a slug and located her on the portal.

'OK, we're all set to go. Get back there, do whatever you need to do with that thing to Carrie, get hold of Vincent, and we'll bring you both right back. You got that?'

'Let's go,' she replied as she climbed into the racetrack.

'Firing up the Hadron Collider now,' Kevin shouted.

~~~

London. 1888

'Well, we've patched up your wounds,' the doctor in charge of the infirmary said, checking Carrie's pulse and looking at his pocket watch. 'Are you sure you want to leave us? You're a very lucky woman, Annie. I would like you to stay a little longer, until your wounds have completely healed, but we have no reason to keep you in. Are you sure that you don't know who did this to you? He might still be at large, waiting for you.'

'No doctor,' she whispered; the wounds in her neck had damaged her vocal cords and it was still painful for her to talk. 'He was a complete stranger, drunk I presume. I didn't even get a good look at him.'

Somehow, she had survived the lacerations to her body, and all she wanted now was to get out of this hospital and somehow get back to twenty-two-eighty-eight. She needed to start everything all over again.

'Nurse, can you arrange for the dismissal of Ms Millwood, please? Get her clothes and any belongings. Thank you so much,' the doctor called as he took his leave of his patient.

Carrie smiled at him calling her Annie. The men bringing her in must have misheard her when they asked her name, and she was liking the anonymity her new name gave her.

She eased herself out of bed and began to shuffle around the room, stretching her legs before she was set free.

# TimeRipper

A commotion within the corridor outside her room caught her interest. There were shouts and screams, and she poked her head out of the room to see what was happening.

What she saw made her heart beat faster.

A hospital porter was wheeling a man on a gurney along the corridor. The man looked in a bad way as he lay on his back. His arms were wrapped around himself, and he was shaking uncontrollably.

But this wasn't what was causing the commotion.

Something else was happening at the far end of the corridor. Something a lot more interesting, not only to her.

A bright light was forming, seemingly from out of nowhere, a bright, purple, light that she recognised.

'Nurse,' she croaked. 'Nurse, can you get my clothes now, please.' She wanted to shout as she watched the familiar light grow, but her throat was too tight. 'Nurse, nurse!' She turned away from the light and back into the ward, but everyone inside was agog at the phenomenon.

A small wind whipped around the corridor as a cloud of purple smoke appeared around the light.

Everyone who could run, did.

Chaos ensued.

A young woman stepped out of the smoke. Carrie's face fell as she recognised her; it was the same one who had hunted down and killed her colleagues.

She could do nothing but watch as Jacqueline turned towards the man on the gurney. She frowned as the newcomer recognised him; she leaned in and touched his arm...

*That must be Abberline*, Carrie thought, as she stepped through the door into the corridor.

It was moslty deserted now, everyone who could, had left the scene, screaming holy murder and crossing themselves against the unholy spirits that had just arrived from another dimension.

Carrie stepped into the corridor and Jacqueline turned to face her.

~~~~

Abberline sat slowly up on his gurney. His breathing was laboured, and Jacqueline could see that he was in considerable pain. He was clawing at his own skin, ripping strips of it with his fingernails, causing deep, bloody welts to his face.

'Help me,' he half whispered, half cried to anyone. 'Help me, I'm burning,' he croaked.

'Vincent,' Jacqueline whispered to him as she put her hand on his shoulder. He winced at the touch. The wet gurgle from his mouth echoed through the almost deserted corridor. His eyes opened wide, and she could see that they were clouded with a strange, milky substance.

'Jacqs, is that you?' he replied, his voice several octaves higher than it should have been for a man of his age.

'Yes, Vincent, it is. I'll be back for you in a moment, there's something I need to do first,' she whispered into his ear. Then, she turned towards the end of the corridor, only to see that Carrie was gone. A door further down the corridor was swinging, and she surmised that she had headed off that way.

Jacqueline reached the door and looked through it. There was no sign of anyone in the adjacent corridor. *Shit*, she thought as she realised that Carrie had not gone this way. *Bitch double crossed me.* She then realised what had just happened. 'Vincent,' she whispered sprinting back towards the corridor.

Carrie was standing next to Vincent's gurney. She had one hand on his chest and was pushing down on it, all the time not taking her eyes from Jacqueline.

Vincent was whimpering in agony.

She had never heard such a horrific, pathetic sound, not even when she was ripping the women to retrieve their slugs. She watched as his body spasmed, as the pain of being touched tore through him.

'You see how much it hurts when it's someone you care about?' Carrie asked in a low voice.

'Step away from him now, or I swear...'

Carrie was shaking her head. 'I'm afraid I can't do that. You see, I don't have any tech here with me, and I think I'm going to need some of yours.'

Jacqueline shook her head. 'There's no way I'm going to give a mad bitch like you a way back to twenty-two-eighty-eight. Believe me, I'd sacrifice him and me to stop that. You know I would.' There was a small quiver in her voice.

Carrie noticed it straight away.

'Was that doubt in your voice then, little girl? Your tells have given you away. You care for this man, don't you?' With the question, Carrie grabbed one of his arms and raked her fingers down his sodden flesh. The scream from Vincent was loud, unmerciful, and wet. 'I believe that this poor man has only a few precious moments left before the paradoxical law tears him apart. Give me your tech, and I'll let him go. I'll take him to a time where he doesn't already exist. If you don't, he dies, right here, and his last few moments will be filled with unbearable pain.'

She raised the wand that Kevin had given her. 'Do you want this?'

Carrie nodded. 'Yes, give it to me,' she demanded, holding her hand out.

She switched the first trigger, the one that sent the enzymes into the frontal lobe of the brain, the ones that brought the memories of the murders, still yet to happen in this time, to the fore, and give the recipient reoccurring nightmares. She nodded towards the madwoman. 'OK, if you want it, you can have it.' She pressed the trigger and was about to point it towards Carrie when the noise of a door opening startled her. She turned, pressing the button on the wand as she did. A luminescent, blue beam emanated from the nozzle and arched overhead, it hit a man who was walking through the door.

It hit him between the eyes, and he screamed in shock as he fell back through the door.

He raised a bandaged hand to block the beam from hurting him, but when he realised that there was no pain, he dropped it.

Jacqueline got the surprise of her life.

Standing before her was Aaron Kosminski. His other bandaged hand, the one not protecting his face, was around a timid looking blonde woman who had many injuries to her face. Mostly bruises and cuts.

'Get that thing out of my face, you whore,' he screamed.

He dropped his arm and looked around the corridor, sheepish, due to his unmanly scream. He quickly noticed that he was the only one on the ward apart from the two strange women and a man on a bed, who was shaking and moaning. Without looking back, he pushed his timid, beaten, wife back through the door they had just appeared from and scurried away, behind her.

Vincent screamed again. The wetness of this scream sounded thicker than before. She guessed that his blood was now congealing in his throat. She knew that she had to get him back to twenty-two-eighty-eight as soon as possible.

'Tick tock, young lady,' Carrie sang. '*We* may have all the time in the world, but your lover here has precious little. Give me your tech, and I'll leave him alone.'

Jacqueline dropped her head and her shoulders fell. She sighed, a slow release of breath. 'You win,' she whispered. 'Let him go and you can have my tech.'

'That's the spirit, now hand it over and you can take…' she turned to look at Vincent. He looked to be visibly shrinking on the gurney. She was sneering as she looked back at Jacqueline. '…*this* with you.'

Jacqueline stepped forward, and reaching into her cape, took out the orb that produced the holding beam. Carrie laughed as she held out her hand, accepting it. 'That's it, it's not that hard, now is it? Give me what I want and maybe you get to keep your…'

Jacqueline took hold of the outstretched arm and lifted the wand. Carrie tried to pull away, but the younger woman had the element of surprise, and pulled her towards her, knocking the taller woman off balance. Carrie flinched as the wand touched her skin. Expecting something more painful than the small pinch she felt as the trigger was released, she laughed again and pulled away.

'Whatever it was that you wanted to do there, failed,' she laughed, grabbing the orb. With it concealed on her person, she turned, and ran out of the corridor. Jacqueline considered giving chase, but there was no point. What she had wanted to do, was done. 'We'll see,' she whispered as the door at the other end of the corridor swung closed.

'That's it, you did it,' Kevin's voice spoke from her wrist. 'We can trace the locator in her bloodstream, she'll be dead in a few days anyway. Either from the slug, or when the paradoxical laws catch up to her. Now, get Vincent and get out of there.'

# TimeRipper

Jacqueline turned to where Vincent was lying on the gurney. His face was a single contortion of agony. His skin was covered in large, unsightly, red and yellow blisters, and his eyes were almost completely white. Thick saliva was trickling from his mouth, turning pink where it mixed with the blood from his nose and tear ducts.

'I have him, he's in a bad way. Can we get a medical team to meet us as soon as we material...'

Vincent's hand grabbed hers and pulled it away from her mouth, effectively severing the communication between her and Kevin. She looked down at him. His skin had peeled away from his face where he had been raking it, and his cheeks were hollow.

'Did we do it?' he whispered to her. 'Did we get them all?'

She couldn't bear to look at him, but she couldn't bear not to either. She wanted to see him as the twenty-five-year-old she'd fallen in love with, what felt like five minutes ago, but she also needed to see him as the distinguished, older man who had been so heroic, helping her complete her mission. Tears filled her eyes as she held his emaciated hand. His claw-like fingers attempted to grasp hers, and a ghost of a smile shadowed across his torn lips.

'Yes, we did it! We got every last one of them.'

'Earth is... safe?' he whispered.

A single tear dripped down her cheek, landing on the off-white bed linen, momentarily making it darker than it had been. 'Thanks to you.'

'And you too, kiddo.' The small smile made it all the way this time, cutting into his paper-thin skin, causing his lips to bleed.

'Vincent,' she whispered, moving her face closer to his. 'I love you, and I always will.'

'Hey, I know...' he replied, wincing, but she could see he was determined to finish what he started to say. 'Twenty-six years... I never thought... I would see you again. Jacqs, in my head... I, I married you every... single... day!'

She held her brave man in her arms as he succumbed to the struggle of one of nature's fundamental laws.

After a few moments, the familiar purple light began to shine from her stomach, and she disappeared, leaving the body of the bravest man she would ever know, four hundred years behind her.

74.

London. 1888

TEN DAYS LATER, Annie Millwood, as she was now known, was taking a break in the back yard of the factory where she had managed to gain employment, mainly washing dishes, and pots, after the men had eaten. The factory manufactured small parts for agricultural machinery.

She had taken the orb that powered the holding beam and had been attempting to bastardize it, to send a signal back home to Inverness, twenty-two-eighty-eight. It was very nearly complete. Power had been her biggest problem. As this orb had been cellular, the power was almost depleted, but she'd managed to retain enough to send a message back, just one, so she knew that she had to make it count.

It had to be today that the message was sent.

She had kept meticulous records of how time was moving in twenty-two-eighty-eight, and she had a good idea that someone would be monitoring all lines of communication. Maybe not from the castle in Inverness, but from the cave in Fiji.

'This is Carrie Millwood, this message is for anyone from The Quest, can you hear me?'

A small cackle of static ensued, then a voice from the future, a voice she knew and trusted, spoke to her. Her heart almost missed a beat.

'Carrie, this is Brian Malone. We can hear you loud and clear. The EA stated you were dead.'

'Not dead,' she cried into the small orb. 'They thought I would be by now. Are you able to lock onto my signal and perform an emergency extraction?'

'I don't see why not. I'm locking on right now. Is it possible to boost your signal?'

At that exact moment, the seeker that had been placed in her bloodstream by Jacqueline's wand located its prey. It enveloped itself around the quantum slug and expelled an electro-magnetic pulse, rendering the slug expired.

The shock rippled through Carrie Millwood's central nervous system, killing her instantly.

As some of her newfound work colleagues watched, Carrie, or Annie as they had come to know her, dropped like a stone, in the back yard of the factory.

'Carrie, we've lost your signal! Can you hear us, your signal has degra—'

One of her friends, in a rush to help her, accidentally trampled on the device she had dropped, crushing it underfoot, into the dirt and dust of eighteen-eighty-eight.

Carrie Millwood was dead.

As was The Quest, and their mission.

75.

Earth. 2288

ACTING UPON INTELLIGENCE received from their two prisoners, and from information recovered from the castle in Inverness, an EA expedition led by Youssef Haseem made its way to Fiji. Within the exact co-ordinates given, they found a hidden cave beneath a volcano. Inside the cave was a vast underground farm that stretched out as far as the eye could see. There were multiple forms of sustainable crops growing from a seemingly source less energy.

'The Higgs Storm is the most destructive force known to man, but it's also a powerful terraforming tool,' Youssef whispered to Jacqueline as they, and their team, entered the cave.

TimeRipper

## EPILOGUE

London. 1888

Aaron Kosminski began having nightmares about witches and people travelling to and from the future, the same night he took his wife home from the hospital, after beating her severely. The next night he took up hiding outside the Ten Bells pub, waiting for the bastard who was fucking his wife.
This started the strangest chain of events, that would forever shape his destiny.

~~~~

After the events were over, and Abberline and the witches were out of his life, forever, he managed to make his escape from London, handing ownership of his barber shop to his cousin Antonowicz Kłosowski.
He found that the witch, the one who had gotten into his head, still resided there. She was *always* there, in his dreams, haunting him. For some reason, when the time inevitably came for him to change his name, he felt himself compelled to take hers.
He continued his life, illegitimately, as George Chapman.
Aaron Kosminski became one of the most wanted men in England. He was the number one suspect for the Whitechapel atrocities and was subsequently blamed for hundreds, maybe even thousands, of other murders in and around the Whitechapel area of the East End of London.
None of them were ever proven.
Due to the notoriety, and the infamy, of Whitechapel for its violence and immorality, plus the international scrutiny that came with the crimes Kosminski was wanted for, the East End of London found itself in the spotlight, on a world stage. Parliament, grudgingly,

passed a motion to plough money into the area as the depravity and squalor had become something of an embarrassment to the city, and the country at large.

George acted upon his murderous impulses twice.

He finally got to 'rip' his women. Using the same motives as the time travelling woman, who had been pretending to be a man, he took the two bodies he needed to balance everything out in his head, and to quell the nightmares that afflicted him.

He killed the first woman on November $20^{th}$, and the second, one month later, on December $20^{th}$. Both women were prostitutes, both were alcoholics, and he did enough damage to both their bodies to make identification almost impossible.

He was careful to leave evidence pointing to the identities of his victims. His first murder was identified as Annabelle, or 'Annie' Farmer, and his second as Rose Mylett. In the course of these killings, he found that he didn't quite have the stomach for murder that he thought he might, but the hideous dreams he had been suffering began to abate after the second.

He took the cash that Abberline had left him, a princely sum, and relocated to The New World, taking passage on a steamship travelling to America.

Aaron Kosminski was dead, and George Chapman was never again to visit the shores of England.

He might have been gone, but in his wake, he left a legend, a legacy, and the eternal mystery that would forever be known as:

Jack the Ripper.

TimeRipper

D E McCluskey

**Author's Notes**

Picture, if you will, a dark, wet night in London's East End. The fog is lying thick in the air. The streets are deserted, as the party revellers and heavy drinkers have finally staggered home, after enjoying themselves, in some cases too much, for most of the day and all of the night.

A lonesome figure cuts a shadow through the mist, illuminated by a single gas-powered streetlamp.

It's a woman.

She's cold, and she's terrified as she runs along a narrow lane, pulling her shawl around her shoulders, staving off the chill of the night. Her frantic eyes search the night as she stumbles onwards, attempting to evade the menacing figure who is following her.

It is a man.

She can only see him in silhouette. He is wearing a tall, top hat and a cape. He is carrying a cane in one hand and a large black bag, the kind a doctor might carry while out on his rounds, in the other.

He is relentless in his pursuit of the woman through the dirty, close streets of London's notorious East End.

\*\*\**Insert sound effect of a needle being dragged along a vinyl record*\*\*\*

This is all fiction… a narrative that the media have enforced to sell us the legend of Jack the Ripper. And I know, before you all start shouting at me, I've used quite a bit of this imagery in this tale, but it's all for dramatic licence.

On the nights of the killings, be it of the 'canonical five' or the extended eight, that many others chalk up to his hand, there was no fog, or smog. The nights were apparently both crisp and clear.

Another reason this imagery couldn't be correct is because of the location.

Imagine Whitechapel, the worst, most depraved, run down area of the already deprived East End of London. There are street gangs,

TimeRipper

truncheon happy police, drunken revellers falling out of the many pubs in the area, at all times of the night. There are prostitutes on every corner, enticing the many drunken sailors from the dock yards, or the soldiers out for a good time. Now, can you imagine a well-to-do man, dressed in a cape and a top hat, carrying a surgeons bag and a cane? This man wouldn't have lasted two minutes in those streets before being rolled and robbed, and possibly even murdered himself, for whatever money he held within his expensive pockets, or for the contents of his bag; or even for just the warmth of his cloak, maybe even his boots.

Life in the East End of London, in those days was cheap.

He would have been easy pickings as he strolled the back streets of dirty, filthy, London, standing out from the crowd, possibly still covered in the spatter of blood from his five (or eight, or even more) victims.

Also, when you think about how the murderer 'disappeared' into the night without even a trace. This implies a thorough knowledge of the area he stalked, including the multiple rat-runs and back alleyways of the time. A gentleman in a cape and top hat would never have been able to get away from the scene using these escape routes.

In my opinion, all these factors point to a local of the region. Someone with a comprehensive knowledge of the area, and a hatred of women, or prostitutes. Also, I would wager, someone unhinged and possibly even marginalised from the community. Of all the theories, of which there are probably thousands of, my best guess (and I stress that it is a *GUESS*, this goes out to any 'ripperologists,' amateur or professional, who may read this and want to argue my theory) was that it was a local barber, a man called Aaron Kosminski.

But, don't take my word for it… go and study it for yourself!

~~~~

I have been in love with the legend of Jack the Ripper for many years. I love the fact that it will *probably* never be solved. As soon as one theory is produced to disclose the identity of the killer, then another emerges to counter that discovery! There is far too much money to be made in the mystery for it to ever be solved.

D E McCluskey

In the research of this book, I undertook the 'ripper tours' around London maybe fifteen times—I think the people running them might have gotten bored of seeing me there, asking questions and generally being a smart-arse.

I also read many books on the subject. Some of them stated just the facts of the case, and others offered up their own theories.

I have to give a huge shout out to the one book that started this journey for me, and that was '...*From Hell!*' The graphic novel by Alan Moore, illustrated by Eddie Campbell. The way the story weaves the thrill and the romance of this mystery with the history of London just blew me away! If you're that way inclined, go find yourself a copy of it and read it. (disclaimer- stay as FAR AWAY from the movie that was made of the book with Johnny Depp, as possible- it's atrocious!)

One of the most outstanding books I read as part of my research was *The Five: The Untold Lives of the Women Killed by Jack the Ripper* by Hallie Rubenhold. This is a fantastic, and well researched, investigation into the five victims of this murderer and how they found themselves to be destitute in London during eighteen-eighty-eight. It's a fascinating read, and well recommended by my good self.

Another good book I read was *Naming Jack the Ripper* by Russel Edwards. This is the guy who is in possession of Catherine Eddowes's shawl, and how he managed (or claimed, depending on the multiple theories disclaiming it) to find DNA evidence of Jack the Ripper on the shawl. This guy also conducts Ripper Tours around the sights of the East End, and of all the ones I attended, I think I took the most information in during his.

All these books are great reads and very highly recommended.

Now, I'm aware that this novel is very different from other Jack the Ripper books, and I hope that the science contained in it didn't put you off. I must confess that it is *all* made up—there's hardly one shred of any credible science in this tale. That is, of course, with the exception of the hadron colliders and the Higgs-Boson particle; they are real, but everything else about quantum slugs, piggybacking magnetic signals, and all that other malarkey, that's all straight out of my brain, Flash Gordon, Star Trek, and other science-fiction (that I love) mumbo jumbo!

TimeRipper

Please don't try any of the experiments, that are in this novel, at home... that's my disclaimer, kids!

~~~

So, this is the part where I offer thanks to the people who have helped me along the way with the writing of this novel.

First and foremost, I have to thank Tony Higginson, a long-term collaborator in my novels. He takes my words, reads them, points out mistakes, and then does it all over again. He has the patience of a saint!

My editor, Lisa Lee... once again taking my final drafts and putting them into something that looks like a finished article... without her, it would just be pages of jumble that looks like a book. Peter Folklore is the artist who produced the most excellent, and striking, cover art for this novel. He has produced the art on a few of my books, and I can see the relationship carrying on well into the future (forgive the pun). He has a unique eye and is a top bloke too. Check out his work on Instagram and Twitter via @forsakenfolklore.

I need to thank my army of proof-readers too, Annmarie Barrell, Christina Rangel Eleanor (www.thevoraciousgnome.wordpress.com), Rita Goodall, Charley Moor, Natalie Anne Webb, Melanie Bingle Marsh, and Tara Lane!

If I didn't mention my final proof-reader in her own paragraph, then my life wouldn't be worth living... Lauren Davies! She not only does my final proof-read, but she has to live, every single day, of these books with me. She has a lot to put up with!

I want to thank my family, Ann, Grace, Sian, Helen, Annmarie, Ashley, Emily, Joanne, Christopher, Myles, Gary, Steve, Liam, Kirsty, Darren, Stacey, Felicity, Olivia, Jacob... the list could go on and on!

But mostly, I need to thank you guys, the readers. Once again, and I say this with my hand on my heart, as I always do, there is no point in writing these books if no one reads them.

So, thank you, thank you, thank you!

Dave McCluskey

D E McCluskey

Liverpool
January 2020

Printed in Great Britain
by Amazon